Bridget's
WAR

Shirley Mann is a Derbyshire-based journalist who spent most of her career at the BBC before going on to make films for organisations such as the Heritage Lottery Fund. Her first novel, *Lily's War*, was inspired by Shirley's mother, who was a WAAF and her father who was in the Eighth Army. Her second book, *Bobby's War* is about a young ATA pilot. *Hannah's War*, her third novel, is about a Land Girl. *Bridget's War* is the fourth novel in the series.

Bridget's WAR

Shirley Mann

ZAFFRE

First published in the UK In ebook in 2023 by
ZAFFRE
An imprint of Bonnier Books UK
4th Floor, Victoria House, Bloomsbury Square, London, England, WC1B 4DA
Owned by Bonnier Books
Sveavägen 56, Stockholm, Sweden

A CIP catalogue record for this book is
available from the British Library.

ISBN: 978-1-83877-447-9
Ebook ISBN: 978-1-83877-446-2

Also available as an audiobook

1 3 5 7 9 10 8 6 4 2
Typeset by IDSUK (Data Connection) Ltd
Printed and bound in Great Britain by Clays Ltd, Elcograf S.p.A.

Zaffre is an imprint of Bonnier Books UK
www.bonnierbooks.co.uk

*For my sister, Hilary, who shares
my love of the Isle of Man.*

Chapter One

Port Erin, Isle of Man, January 1943

Bridget's heavy policewoman's shoes resounded in the streets of Port Erin as she ran towards the beach below. She put all her concentration into getting to the angry shouting she could hear at the bottom of the hill, ignoring the familiar shop frontages. At the piercing sound of a scream, she quickened her pace.

Bridget looked behind her to see if there was any sign of backup, but the streets were depressingly empty.

'Bugger,' she hissed. Swearing was a new skill she had learned during her police officer training in London, but she was not sure the satisfying expletive was going to be enough to help her deal with this situation.

Ahead of her she saw a group of people, crowded into the narrow path by Christian's Cottage, silhouetted in the last rays of winter sunlight. As usual, it was a mix of arrogant Nazis, German Jews hanging back trying to vanish into the background and some fascist followers of Oswald

Mosely who looked as if they were on their way to a cocktail party. As Bridget neared the commotion, the crowd stepped back, looking at her with relief and anticipation.

Feeling anything but the saviour they were all expecting, Bridget stepped forward.

'All right, all right, what's going on here?' she asked in the same commanding voice she had used as Lady Bracknell in one of her school plays ... but then she breathed in sharply. Glistening in the weak January light was a serrated kitchen knife. It was being held by a tall woman in her thirties, with faded peroxide blonde hair and wearing a floral pinny. Bridget identified her at once as Helga Fischer, one of the fierce Nazi supporters at Rushen Internment Camp. At her feet was the curled figure of a girl with hands clasped protectively over her head. The outline of her assailant cast a dark shadow, just like a blood-stain, over the tarmac all around.

Bridget edged slowly forwards, recognising the pale face of a timid Jewish girl, Ursula Apler, panting with terror at Helga's feet. The next few seconds could mean the difference between life and death for her. Bridget's mind was racing. How was she going to deal with this?

'Now, Helga, hand me that knife,' Bridget said slowly, reaching out her hand towards the German woman and inwardly cursing whichever landlady had failed to lock it away. 'You don't want to end up prison, now, do you? What you do in the next minute will make that decision for you.'

Helga's eyes darted around her, as if trying to work out where the voice was coming from. They finally focused on Bridget.

'You do not understand . . . she took my soap . . .' she said in broken English, 'and . . .' she added, looking at the Nazi supporters in the crowd for approval, 'she is a. . . . Jüdin.' There was a shuffling amongst the different factions in the group, with some gasping at the bitterness of the accusation, while the Nazis murmured that Jews deserved everything they got.

For women in the internment camp on the Isle of Man, soap was a commodity as valuable as gold, but the severity of the crime suddenly took on a completely different perspective. To some, Hitler was a leader whose hatred of the Jews was to be applauded, but to others, the young girl's religion made her plight even more pitiable.

'I know,' Bridget said in a voice calculated to calm the tension, 'but it's not worth risking a long gaol sentence for. You've never been to prison, Helga, but I can tell you, you won't like it and . . . what about your little girl?'

Seeing the woman hesitate gave Bridget confidence. With more twists and turns to her life than anyone on the Island suspected, Helga exuded a ferocity that terrified those weaker than her. But Bridget was not going to be cowed. She didn't know much about this woman, but she did know that her Achilles heel was her little girl, Karin, and Bridget felt if she was ever going to capitalise

3

on that knowledge, now was the time. She could see her warnings being weighed up, but without any idea of how the German would react to them, Bridget had to be poised for any eventuality.

'I want you to think about this,' Bridget went on, 'threatening someone with a knife is very, very serious. You want to get out of here and have a new life with that little girl of yours when all this is over, don't you? So, don't throw everything away by doing something you'll regret.'

Helga held the knife out in front of her, as if it were a match burning down towards her fingers. Her eyes flicked from its gleaming blade to Bridget and then back to the blade again. With limited English, she didn't understand all the policewoman's words but knew the implications of the implement in her hand. There was an edgy silence that echoed eerily around the crowd and the little group witnessing the drama collectively held their breath.

For a brief second, Helga looked as if she was about to lunge forwards, and Bridget tensed like a cat waiting to pounce on a mouse. Her whole body was taut, and, in her head, she was already assessing how she would get round to the back of the attacker to disarm her. 'Your daughter,' she whispered urgently to the woman. '*Think of her.*'

The purple haze of rage suddenly faded and Helga dropped the knife onto the ground, prompting a sigh of relief from the non-Nazis in the crowd. The curled-up Ursula peered through her fingers but once she heard the clatter of the weapon hitting the pathway, she warily started to stand up, anxious to melt back into the crowd.

'Good,' Bridget said, trying not to sound as thankful as she felt. She looked at the huge, solid frame in front of her, aware she would have had little chance of preventing a violent attack if she'd failed to divert Helga's attention. Playing out the different outcomes was something she would agonise over later that night, trying to learn from it, to prepare herself for the next altercation.

'Now, Helga, I'm going to have to take you in, you know that. But the fact that you've given up the knife will help.' She bent down to pick it up, cross with herself that she hadn't done that straight away. Under pressure, it was so hard to remember each step in a situation like this.

Bridget got out her brown, leather-bound notebook and flicked it open, licking her pencil in readiness to record the essential details of the event. Scribbling quickly, she automatically recited a caution to Helga who seemed to shrink in size. Bridget took a mental note of the scene and the witnesses, committing it all to memory for her report and then marched Helga off towards the police station. In her head, she silently cursed Winston Churchill, the British Prime Minister, who, when faced with the dilemma of what to do with thousands of people from alien countries living in Britain at the beginning of the war, decided they were all a threat to security and issued the order to 'collar the lot'.

The little group stared after her. They included Germans, Austrians and Italians; some were supporters of Hitler and others, many of them Jews, were most definitely not. Peering from the back were some fascists but the Island also housed prostitutes and conscientious objectors – those people, the newspapers claimed – who represented every possible extreme view that abounded in Britain in the late 1930s.

Four thousand women had been sent to Rushen Camp in the south of the Island over the past three years. There were also men's camps dotted from the north of the Island to Peel but the one thing all the camps had in common was that they were encircled by barbed wire, creating cauldrons that simmered until they bubbled over, fuelled by something as simple as who was next to use the bathroom. Resentment, indignation, boredom, and fights like this one were an inevitable result.

As the sun went down, Bridget marched Helga past the rows of guesthouses and hotels that housed all the bored, lonely women and thought how her homeland had been changed by the Island's 'guests'. On either side of the street, making the most of their last moments of being outside before curfew, little groups of women stared with interest at the policewoman and her prisoner, desperate for some gossip to take back to supper to break the monotony of the day. They may have been free to roam the areas within the camp during daylight, but their spirits were confined by the barbed wire that marked the limit of their world for the duration of their detention.

Bridget glanced at her watch. Booking this woman was going to take time and poor old Greeba, her black Labrador, was going to have to wait, once again, for her walk.

*　*　*

It was dark by the time Bridget and Greeba finally got onto Bradda Head above Port Erin. The dog bounded ahead, wagging her tail furiously, while Bridget peered to see if she could spot the incongruous barbed wire that had been put up almost overnight three years earlier.

The views around Bridget were completely recognisable but it was as if she was watching an edited film of her childhood home, seen through a distorting lens. The village below offered no help in guiding her route, thanks to the blackout that protected it from German aircraft above, but Bridget had been walking these paths since she was little and knew every rock and twist and turn and so did Greeba. Pulling up the collar of her old tweed coat against the icy blasts which took her breath away, Bridget rounded Milner's Tower. The bay inlet surrounding Port Erin below was calmer, as always, protected by the huge presence of Bradda Head but beyond that, white horses were being stirred up to dance like an empty carousel at a washed-out fairground.

She'd spent so many years careering across these paths, trying to keep up with the little gang which included her brothers, Aedan and Brendan, and the two Moore boys, Fynn and Kieran. Her brothers had gone to fly Lancasters for the RAF, the last she'd heard of Kieran was that he'd become a hero in the Battle of Britain. The three of them were in the thick of the war, fighting the enemy, while she was back home, babysitting a load of women, as she dismissively called it.

Fynn, however, was another matter. Not long after she stepped foot back on the Island, the three newly-appointed policewomen had attended a dance to raise money for spitfires and Fynn had been there. As a child, she'd been a little in awe of the boy who always seemed so much older than her, but when he strode across the room to ask her to dance, prompting jealous looks from all the rest of the girls, Bridget found herself torn between wanting to find out more about this enigmatic man, and believing that the last thing an ambitious policewoman needed was to be trapped by a romance with a Manxman.

Being one of the female recruits into the Metropolitan Police Force had given her and her colleagues almost celebrity status. Even the Blitz had failed to quell her enthusiasm for a job that she loved with every fibre of her being and, amidst the grey of the destruction of war, she'd searched out colour and excitement. It was the prospect of living her life in black and white in the backwaters of the Isle of Man that distressed her. London might still be a major target for the enemy but to WPC Harrison, it was the only place she wanted to be.

Bridget let out an exasperated sigh. She loved this island; it was her home, but she shouldn't be here – not now, not during the war, and she scuffed her wellington boots against the gravel path as if to wipe out her footsteps and erase her presence from the Island.

'Come on, Greeba, I'm frozen,' she called to the dog, who ran back to her, enticed by the prospect of a cosy bed. Turning one more time towards the sea, Bridget shouted into the wind,

'Bugger, damn and blast!'

Chapter Two

Bridget made her way past Christian's Cottage where the incident had taken place earlier that day and shivered at how close she'd come to dealing with a murder case. Along the path was the little fisherman's house that she shared with the other two policewomen at the camp where, she hoped, a welcome cup of tea would be waiting. It had been painted white in a more prosperous age, but its stones were showing signs of being exposed to the elements and every time Bridget went past, she couldn't resist peeling a little of the flaking paint off. She flicked the bits into the wind and opened the front door.

'Hello, I'm back,' Bridget called into the gloom of the hallway. A voice called back.

'I'm in the snug, come through.'

She took off her coat and hung it on the wooden stand in the hall. It was crammed with old coats, sou'wester rain hats and woolly cardigans that each of the girls could grab on their way out. They hardly ever took their uniforms off so would just add another layer on top. Each of them wore a band around their sleeve cuffs to indicate they were on duty – an identifying system that had worked well in London but on the Isle of Man was a waste of time, as everyone knew who they were, so as a result, they'd all given up ever taking the armbands off.

Bridget closed the blackout curtain behind her to make her way to the narrow room at the back of the house, mockingly called 'The Snug' by the girls, where a small paraffin heater gave out precious little heat. The cluttered room showed no sign that the girls had only been there for a few months, sent to help with the 'moral welfare' of the women in the camp. On either side were wooden cupboards surrounding a large white ceramic sink traced with dark veins of age. Clothes were hanging up to dry from every cupboard door and Bridget had to duck to avoid thick lisle stockings and brassieres that were dangling down. Greeba immediately headed for her blanket under the wooden table that served as the girls' dining area and curled up, grunting with pleasure. Forced to leave her precious pet with her parents when she set off for London, Bridget had delightedly reclaimed her dog as soon as she arrived home and while there was an understanding among the three young women that the dog could be walked or fed by any of them, Bridget was the one she looked adoringly at from her position under the table.

In front of the fire, her feet up on a pine stool to catch the warmth, was a tall girl in her late twenties with a powerful physique developed from years of riding a motorbike. Born near London docklands Molly Smith had jumped at the chance of being stationed on the TT Mecca for all motorbike riders, the Isle of Man, and sometimes, claiming petrol on police business, she was seen careering off up towards the top of Snaefell, a plume of smoke behind her. She was sitting with her shoulders bent over her body to preserve every bit of heat and her knees were pulled up towards her with both arms circling them. No hostage to fashion, she pushed a blonde fringe out of her green eyes, merging it into her unruly hair while her cheeks shone with a natural attractiveness that came from spending hours in the fresh air.

'I heard about Helga,' Molly said, with a frown. 'That sounds like a nasty moment, were you OK?'

'Oh, you know Helga. She was fine, all I had to do was mention that daughter of hers and she crumpled. I did feel sorry for her victim, though, she looked terrified.'

'Yes,' Molly said, 'I heard it was young Ursula Apler, she wouldn't say boo to a goose.'

Bridget remembered the frightened face that had faded back into the crowd at the first opportunity.

'Well, she's a German Jew, no wonder she was so terrified. Helga's a pretty fierce Nazi. There'll be consequences for Helga though, you can't just threaten someone with a knife and get away with it. But I think the Camp Commandant will deal with her fairly – if he's allowed – you know the constant battle that goes on between the Chief Inspector and the commandant for control of the internees.'

'Hmm, I think this might be one for the police to be honest,' Molly said.

At that moment, the front door banged and the blackout curtain in the windows fluttered in the draught. A voice called through the corridor: 'Anyone in?'

'Yes, we're in here,' Molly shouted back.

'Well, put that kettle on, I'm dying for a brew,' the voice went on, as through the door came a girl with freckles, chestnut-coloured curly hair and sparkling brown eyes.

'Long shift?' Molly asked.

'Endless!' Betty said. 'I took three on a walk out towards Port St Mary, dealt with a fight between two dogs and Harry Kelly had made some potcheen and was as drunk as a skunk. I had to get the lifeboat lads to help me get him home.' She collapsed into one of the pine chairs around the table and put her feet up on a spare one opposite, leaned back and sighed.

'Make me that cuppa, Bridg, I can't move.' Then she sat up straight, casting her eyes suspiciously over the kitchen worktop. 'Please tell me the milkman's been, I can't bear Carnation again.'

'It's OK, we have fresh,' Bridget told her, grabbing the whistling kettle off the gas to add the water to the teapot. 'We had a delivery this morning.'

'Oh, thank heaven for that,' Betty said, leaning back again. A girl from the East End of London who'd married her beloved Joe Perkins just before war broke out, she was only nineteen when he was conscripted and, intending to make her new husband proud of her, had joined the police force. The posting to the Isle of Man had, at first, made her feel even more distant from Joe who was in the Eighth Army but then she'd felt its welcoming arms embrace her and she now asserted to anyone who would listen that the Island was the best place on earth. However, that didn't stop her from spending her nights listening intently to the radio for news of the Eighth Army in Africa, her fist crammed in her mouth.

Betty glanced at the white china jug of milk that Bridget placed on the table and gave thanks for the fresh produce the Island was able to miraculously conjure up. All of them had been subjected to increasing rationing in London during their training and even Bridget had to admit, there were some advantages to living on the Isle of Man where local farms kept the islanders supplied with fresh produce.

There was silence for a moment as the tea was reverently poured into three chipped cups, the precious milk added and then Betty reached forward for the honey to sweeten hers.

'I suppose you want one of my mum's special biscuits with that, do you?' Bridget asked, laughing and reaching for the battered tin with a picture of thatched cottages on the front that looked like the old houses at Cregneash. She peered inside.

'Only a few bits left,' she said, looking accusingly at Molly, who was gazing innocently up at the cornice above the doorway and whistling to herself. Bridget chuckled and handed the tin over to a crestfallen Betty who scooped her fingers around the corners to extricate the oaty crumbs.

Bridget let out a deep sigh while Greeba snored beneath her feet.

There were some moments of contentment that she knew she should savour, but they were overwhelmed by the feelings of dissatisfaction, anger and frustration that were threatening to engulf her.

* * *

At RAF Cranwell in Lincolnshire, her childhood friend, Squadron Leader Kieran Moore was also feeling on edge, perched on a green leather-backed chair in the Medical Officer's consulting room.

'It's just my right hand, that's not a reason for me to be grounded. Is it ...?' he tailed off, looking up at the bespectacled man standing in front of him.

'I can't help you,' the kindly man in the white coat said. 'It's more than just burn damage; your nerves aren't working. You can't operate the controls. You've no grip in your right hand.'

The doctor moved towards the door, giving Kieran no alternative but to do the same. As his legs started to wobble, he reached out to grasp the wall at the side of him with his good hand.

'Is there really nothing you can do?' he asked plaintively.

'Nope, I'm really sorry, lad, I know what flying means to you.'

And with that Kieran walked out into the corridor in a daze. Surgeons had fought to save his right hand after his Spitfire's control panel caught fire during the Battle of Britain. Despite being surrounded by flames, he'd managed to shoot down two of the enemy before bailing out from his plummeting aircraft over Dover and had been decorated for it with the Distinguished Flying Cross. Saline baths had helped to improve many of the burns on his body, but his hand was so badly damaged, it was hardly any use at all, a blatant fact this determined young pilot had been ignoring. The last few months had been spent teaching theory to young pilots in a classroom at Cranwell, but some final physiotherapy tests were going to be his passport back to active duty. It had never occurred to him that the results of those tests would be so cruel.

A couple of pilots came down the corridor and they braced up to greet a senior officer. Squadron Leader Moore's exploits during the Battle of Britain were legendary but he looked blankly at them. One nudged his friend, pointing to the MO's office as a clue and the other nodded, realising last night's speculation about Squadron Leader Moore in the mess had been proved correct. They looked sympathetically at the retreating figure, recognising that stricken look; it was the one they all dreaded, even more so than the terrors they faced during combat.

Kieran stumbled to the front of the building, under the colourful standards of abandoned RAF squadrons that dominated the Rotunda above and made his way out to the grass outside. He wanted to get out of sight as quickly as possible, so he propelled his weak legs across to the brick huts opposite. Once there, he looked all around to make sure no one was watching and sank to his knees, his head bowed. He looked in disgust at his damaged hand and cursed it to Kingdom Come.

A pilot who'd survived the battles to secure British airspace when so many of his colleagues had not, he had felt the only way to pay homage to their memory was to keep fighting and defeat the enemy once and for all and he'd been defiantly proud to wear the blue uniform with the gold wings on. Fingering those wings on his tunic now, he desperately tried to think of a way that he could get around the MO's decision, but those thoughts just prompted a rising panic. Tears were threatening to fall, so he got to his feet quickly and cleared his throat. A pragmatic young man of twenty-four, he'd decided years before that whatever fate had in store for him, he wouldn't fight it, but his thoughts had been of facing death or losing a limb or an eye, not of something so prosaic as a burned hand. It was almost laughable, he thought . . . almost.

Kieran made his way back towards one of the brick huts and stomped noisily down the centre aisle towards his bunk, cordoned off with a thin partition wall at the end of the room, in deference to those of a higher rank.

'Shhh, for God's sake man, I'm on again at two and I've only had twenty winks,' a voice groaned from behind the dividing curtain between their bunks.

'Well, it's gone one and you've been in bed since eight,' Kieran replied, his voice flat.

The face of a young man with brown, ruffled hair peeped out blearily around the curtain. Bob Chapman, a fellow squadron leader.

'It's all right for you, you're safe and sound in a classroom, teaching theory. My lot are likely to pancake on the tarmac if I don't watch them.'

Kieran sat down with a thump on his three mattresses, known as 'biscuits'. They were useful for pressing trousers if the uniform was spread under them at night, but they were also renowned for edging apart during the night to reveal metal springs underneath. None of that mattered to the distraught airman who exhaled with a groan and leaned back, his head resting on his hands.

'What's up with you?' Bob, asked, rubbing his eyes and frowning at the uncharacteristic misery etched on Kieran's face.

'Results are in; I'm grounded.'

At this, Bob gasped and sat up.

'What? How long for?'

'Forever,' Kieran muttered through clenched teeth.

Bob looked closely at the miserable man opposite him. 'It can't be. *Why?*'

He simply held up his twisted hand which was disfigured with white scarring and dark burn marks.

Bob took a moment to take in the significance of the bent fingers being held up to the light.

After a long pause, he spoke. 'So . . . it's nerve damage, is it? To be honest, I thought it might be. I'm so sorry, mate. I don't know what to say.'

'Say you'll meet me in the mess after your duty finishes. You should just get a last drink in. I'll probably have had several by then and you can help me back to bed.'

'Of course,' Bob nodded, 'least I can do. But, oh hell, Kieran, what are they going to do with you now?'

Kieran shrugged.

'Probably put me on a permanent desk job.' The thought of it made him shudder.

At that moment, a figure appeared by the partition and stood to attention in front of the two senior officers.

'Evening, Sergeant Major Wilkes,' Bob said.

'Evening, sirs. Squadron Leader Moore, please follow me, the CO wants to see you,' and he turned sharply on his heels and marched out, leaving Kieran no option but to follow him, knowing his future was now out of his hands for good.

Chapter Three

It was still dark the following morning when Bridget made her way to the police station at Port Erin. She could still taste the porridge she'd rushed down for breakfast. As usual, Sergeant Alister Cubbon was leaning his large frame on the front desk, his helmet hung up on the peg behind him. He was tilting his head from one side to the other as he tried to decipher Bridget's notes on the fracas of the day before.

'Hello, young Bridget,' he said, standing up to his full six-foot height and smiling at her. He'd known her since she was seven years old when he'd told her off for racing her bike down Station Road and had always admired the young tomboy who kept up with the boys, showing a determination that belied her small frame and young age. He had never known her to cry or complain – until she had been sent back to the Island. On that first day, he had been treated to a barrage of protests and a fierce indignation at the injustice of being plucked out of her job in London to act as referee to the internees and, as he assessed her dark expression, he thought with a sigh, that today did not bode well either.

'You off to get statements?' he asked her, trying to fend off the catalogue of grievancess she might have stored up overnight.

She grunted in reply.

'And what about interviewing Helga Fischer, do you want me to do that?' Alister persevered.

'Nope, thanks Alister, I'll do it, it's more exciting than trying to find Mrs Perkins's cat,' and she placed her own cap on the peg next to Alister's, before delving under the front counter for a new pad and pencil.

'I might need a tea first, though,' she told him, giving him a begrudging smile. 'Suppose you want one too, do you?'

'Always, Bridget, always,' Alister laughed.

Bridget went into the back room to see if the urn was hot and searched in the cupboard for two cups that weren't stained with tannin from the endless cups of tea demanded by her superiors and got out the brown, earthenware teapot.

'Ah, you're making a brew,' a commanding voice came from behind her. Bridget grimaced and added another tea-spoon of leaves to the pot. There was a rumour that tea was about to be rationed so they were all making the most of the chance to indulge, but it was uncanny how Sergeant Maureen Robinson always managed to time her arrival.

'And make it strong this time will you, dear. The last cup wasn't weak – it was fortnight.'

The older woman tittered at her own wit and went back in to check that Alister was making out his forms correctly. She was the sergeant to the women police officers for the camp while Alister Cubbon was in charge of the locals, but they saw each other not as colleagues, but as rivals.

At that moment, the back door opened and Molly sneaked through.

'She here yet?' she whispered, hanging her coat up in the small alleyway.

Bridget nodded and held up a teacup questioningly.

Molly gave her a thumbs up and a wink before going noisily into the front counter, as if she'd just nipped out to the privy at the back and had been in for ages.

Sergeant Robinson looked up suspiciously, but both Molly and Alister smiled innocently.

A woman in her fifties, Maureen Robinson had given her life to firstly the Red Cross and then the police force. Her manner commanded respect and many a pulled face behind her back, as she issued order after order to those she felt she could boss around. And that certainly included easy-going fellow sergeants like Alister Cubbon.

He bent his head to avoid the inevitable criticism that was heading his way. A man, who, in his youth had been something of a wrestling hero on the Island with trophies lining his mantlepiece at home, Alister Cubbon had been enjoying living a more leisurely life until his pleasant existence had been shattered by the arrival of Sergeant Robinson, who'd marched into the office like a cold wind from the east. The backlog of paperwork and his cheerfully disordered filing system was a special target for her scrutiny – an unforgiveable error on her part and a step too far for the easy-going Alister. The two had been sworn enemies ever since.

Alister frequently threatened to retire and buy a thatched cottage at Cregneash where he could tend a few Loaghtan sheep and his wife, Mary, could hand spin their fleece but, despite his bad knees, he was fitter than he pretended and occasionally could be seen using weights or doing press-ups in one of the interview rooms. With the war putting an end to any ideas of retiring, he just wished this officious woman in front of him would leave him in peace.

'Molly, are you doing roll call this morning?' Sergeant Robinson asked brusquely, purposefully rearranging some of the papers on the counter. 'I think you'd better get off or you're going to be late.' As soon as she turned to face Molly, Alister leaned over and determinedly replaced the documents to their original position.

Molly peered through the door to a grinning Bridget, who was ostentatiously putting the fourth cup back in the cupboard.

Molly gave a low moan of capitulation and turned back to her superior.

'Yes, Sarge, I'm on my way,' and she reluctantly went back to gather up her coat and make her way to do the morning roll call at the large Golf Links Hotel. The insistence on all the internees gathering for roll call every day was the source of jokes in both the police station and the camp. After all, everyone agreed, where was there to flee to? There was barbed wire all around and even more forbidding, a huge, often angry sea, that would only invite the most desperate of would-be escapees.

Bridget was glad she was down to interview Helga; it was the most exciting thing to have happened in the camp for ages and at least it could be done in the relative warmth of the back of the holding cell at Douglas. She quickly drank down her tea and then, checking her watch, ran out to get the bus.

With her elbow leaning against the window, Bridget looked out at the sea on her right. She had been brought up at Castletown, in a house along the front overlooking the Langness peninsula and had spent an idyllic childhood wandering the shorelines that formed her playground. There were no rules, no boundaries and she was left to her own devices by her mother, more interested in painting dramatic landscapes than marshalling three self-sufficient children on an island where danger was limited to sea or rocks. A child who wore shorts all year round, the only time Bridget gave in to her father's pleadings was on a Sunday, when she would sulkily wear a dress for the service at Malew Church but, even then, she would spend her time staring through the stained-glass windows or tying her dress ribbons into nautical rope knots.

The woman clutching a wicker shopping basket turned hopefully to her fellow passenger, hoping to chat but Bridget was miles away, thinking of how often she had mithered her brothers to take her with them on their adventures. Neither of them had made any dispensation for age, height or sex and Bridget had to climb every tree, scramble up every hill and meet every dangerous challenge with equanimity or be told, bluntly, to go home. Bridget made sure she was never told to go home.

Then there were the Moore brothers. A blush spread over Bridget's face at the embarrassing memory of her agonising schoolgirl crush on Kieran Moore but, now as an adult, she was pleased to find it was his older brother's lopsided grin that came immediately to mind and their occasional recent dates had piqued her interest more than she wanted to admit.

Every corner the bus went round held its own memory and as it trundled past Ronaldsway Airport, then Ballasalla and on past the Fairy Bridge where, in the traditional nod to fairy folklore, she automatically greeted the 'Little People,' Bridget felt it was as if this journey was full of signposts of her life.

She'd cycled these roads or travelled them in the back of her father's Riley, his pride and joy, feeling sick as he took the corners too fast. Squashed between her two brothers, she'd hardly been able to see out and had always preferred travelling this route by bicycle when she had imagined herself on a motorbike, just like the ones who came over for the TT races. The wind in her hair, she would race as fast as she could down the hills, her legs outstretched in pure joy.

Bridget had begun to think of herself as a cosmopolitan from the city of London rather than a girl from a small island, but coming back, she was surprised how those childhood memories seemed as much a part of her as the scars she'd suffered from those tumbles off her bike.

The ding of the bell made her jump as they approached Victoria Road in Douglas and the conductor was surprised to see such a fierce frown on the face of the lovely young policewoman who stepped off the bus.

* * *

The interview with Helga didn't start off well and Bridget tried to insist that the furious prisoner stopped pacing the cell to come and sit on the cold slab next to her while she made her notes.

Many of the internees spoke English well, helped by regular lessons, but when Helga was angry, her words became a jumble of English and German and it was almost impossible to follow her.

'Would you like an interpreter?' Bridget asked her in despair, looking at the disjointed notes on the pad in front of her.

'*Nein, nein, ich kann* good English speak,' the woman said, 'even if it is the language of my enemy.'

'Very well,' Bridget agreed, 'but you have to talk slowly and do, for heaven's sake, come and sit down.'

Helga's large body finally moved towards the stone seat, her face showing no remorse or willingness to compromise. She folded her arms and turned to look defiantly at Bridget.

'So, tell me what happened ... slowly,' Bridget said quietly.

The confused, disjointed tale that followed was a familiar tirade of hatred, anger and constant assertions that she was loyal to the Nazi cause. Ursula, the young Jewish girl, was, Bridget knew, terrified of Helga, identifying her as one of a group of women who would use any opportunity to intimidate the Jewish internees.

The woman's body on the plinth next to her was taut with belligerence so Bridget quickly brought the conversation round to her daughter, hoping that at the mention of Karin's name, Helga's fierceness would melt away, leaving only a doting mother who would die to save her child.

'So,' Bridget explained in a very slow, patient voice, 'Karin is being looked after by the women at The Imperial, but you have to stay here until you stand trial. If you plead not guilty, that is, that you say you didn't do it, then we'll have to bring all those people who saw you – they're called witnesses – before the court and the case will take a long time. But, I warn you, there are so many witnesses, the outcome is undoubtedly going to be the same – you will be found guilty and you will go to prison.' Bridget paused to make sure the woman next to her was understanding. Helga nodded, she understood all too well.

Bridget continued. 'But, if you plead guilty, then there is a chance you may not have to spend too long in prison.'

She saw Helga process the words, then start to waver. The young policewoman pushed her advantage.

'I'm not saying you won't have to pay for threatening Ursula with a knife, but the sentence may be shorter if you admit your crime . . .'

She stopped, waiting to see if Helga's body language changed at all. When it did, and her shoulders suddenly drooped, Bridget breathed a sigh of relief. Helga was two different women, she thought – one a belligerent Nazi and the other a protective mother.

'So, to be with my child, I have no choice, I must, as you say, plead the guilty?' Helga asked, hesitatingly.

'Well, it's up to you,' Bridget told her, sensing victory. She stood up. 'I'm just going to leave that with you while you think about it.'

Bridget smiled to herself. A few nights in a cold cell should prompt the result she needed.

Chapter Four

Bridget made her way round the back of Douglas's promenade, only to be barraged by a torrent of shouts from behind the wire of Hutchinson men's camp. A few were raucous comments but many of them pleaded with her for information about the women internees at Rushen. The desperate, grey faces were like the gaunt pictures in her family's *Children's Bible* of the 'lost souls'. One man reached out his hand to the wire and she took a step nearer to it to clasp it. His knuckles stood out as if they belonged to a white skeleton.

'My children, my wife,' he said, his eyes wide with fear. 'I hear nothing, can you help me? Are they in the women's camp?'

Bridget was not supposed to talk to these men, however she couldn't help but whisper, 'Give me your name and I'll see what I can find out.' She leaned towards him to hear him say: '*Ich heisse Otto Kruger*, I come from Berlin but I had escaped to London with my family; I thought we were safe at last, but then . . . how could your government do this to us? We are Jews, we hate the Nazis.' His despair deserved an answer, but Bridget didn't have one. She thought how cruel these round-ups had been and was about to reply to the man when four others came up to the wire behind him. They said something to him in German and he shook his head.

'They want to know if you can help them too,' he told Bridget. She looked at the increasing crowd that was gathering around Otto and immediately regretted her rash offer. Stepping back, she made Otto release her hand and the words that came out of her mouth sounded more officious than she intended.

'I suggest you talk to the commander of your camp,' and then more gently, she added, 'I'm sure he'll help if he can.' And with that, she gave them a weak smile and moved off down the pavement.

Bridget raised her head to feel the pale, winter sunlight on her face, wishing she was older, wiser and certainly more powerful to be able to help these poor internees.

A married camp had been set up in Port St Mary but there were still so many families forced to live apart because of the mountain of paperwork that had to be tracked down, checked and verified. To Bridget, it seemed ridiculous that couples were on the same island, only to be separated by the barbed wire that seemed to be strangling the humanity of the Isle of Man.

She quickened her pace towards the red-brick archway to the railway station at the corner of Athol Street. It was

Thursday, the day the policewomen took internees to the pictures. A train had just arrived and the platform was full so Bridget stood to one side and delved into her pocket to find one of her mother's delicious oaty biscuits she kept in a paper bag for when she didn't have time for meals. She munched on it gratefully, savouring the welcome flavour of butter from the local farm that gave it a lovely taste.

A voice behind her made her jump. 'It's Bridget Harrison, isn't it?'

An elderly man stepped out of the crowd to greet her. He was dressed in a tweed suit with a cap and a muffler to keep out the chill and was leaning on a walnut walking stick, every bit the country squire.

'Hello, Mr Moore,' she said, recognising Kieran and Fynn's father. Bridget felt a moment of squirming discomfiture, wondering how much he knew of her unbearable childhood crush on Kieran and the recent dates with Fynn. Unnerved by the inquisitive stare of the father of these two men in her life, she started to stutter.

'How . . . are . . . you?' and then gushed, 'I haven't seen you for ages. And Mrs Moore?'

'Yes, yes, we're both fine,' he said, nodding and preening his grey moustache. He gave a knowing smile. 'Fynn mentioned you were back; Margaret's been telling him to bring you over for tea. It's lovely to see you. You're in the police now, I've heard,' he added.

Bridget blushed, realising Fynn must have discussed her with his parents. 'Yes,' she said, fingering her dark navy King's uniform lapel. 'I'm a member of His Majesty's police force now.'

'Hmm,' Mr Moore said, with a slightly disapproving air. 'Well, I suppose all you young women have to do something now all the men are away. Talking of which, did you hear Kieran's coming back?'

Bridget was taken aback. Fynn hadn't said anything about his brother returning home.

'I thought he was doing something terribly important in the RAF', she said. 'What's he doing coming back here?'

'We're not really sure,' his father replied. 'He has a problem with his hand – the one that was damaged in the Battle of Britain.' He stopped and added proudly and unnecessarily, 'You know he got the DFC for his bravery in that, don't you?'

Bridget nodded. A local boy being awarded the Distinguished Flying Cross had been the talk of the Island. She'd heard nothing else for months.

'Well, he's being posted back here and, from what we gather, he's not too happy about it.'

Bridget squirmed, remembering the daredevil young man who was always getting her brothers into trouble. Her childish devotion to the boy with the dazzling smile had led to brave but ineffectual confrontations with her own father when he accused Kieran of being the ringleader in a series of escapades. Despite spelling out his attributes through the gaps in her front teeth, she had been unable to save Kieran from either her own father's admonishments or a school ruler administered by his own parent when he got home. She recalled the time he'd led Aedan and Brendan across The Chasms to the Sugarloaf, looking for guillemot eggs, leaving a furious Fynn at the top who quickly raised the alarm to initiate a dramatic rescue by the local lifeboatmen. It had been three very scared young boys who were finally helped down a rope from the top and onto the boat to safety. She remembered how proud she'd been when Kieran lived up to every hero in her adventure books, taking the blame, but then realised with shame that she had been oblivious to the bravery of Fynn who had run all the way from the cliffs to sound the alarm.

It was only as a truculent adolescent that she had finally become weary of raising Kieran Moore to the status of a god on a pedestal that no mere mortal could ever hope to emulate. Once she began to have adventures of her own, she consigned this mythical creature to the pages of her tear-smeared diaries and with the superiority of a girl cured of a disorder, developed a burning desire to kick that pedestal from under his feet. However, it was unsettling how the thought of him returning to the Island sent a shiver up her spine.

'When's he coming back?' she asked as casually as she could. The train she was waiting for was due in at any moment.

'A couple of weeks,' Mr Moore replied, and tipped his hat at her to make his way out of the railway station. She smiled at his gentlemanly farewell and then craned her neck as she heard the familiar toot from down the line, heralded by a plume of steam billowing into the sky in the distance and found herself wondering whether she'd feel quite as dispassionate when her childhood hero was standing in front of her.

Bridget cursed the strange twist of fate that seemed intent on putting both Moore brothers in her path until it suddenly occurred to her that Kieran's fury at being sent back to the Island might just mirror her own.

* * *

Bridget had to run to get to the cinema in time for the start of the programme and arrived to pant her apology to Betty and Molly, who were just making their way in alongside a long line of internees. They grinned and pushed her towards the front of the queue to deal with the unruly clamour for tickets, telling her it was her punishment for being late.

Near the front of the queue was a woman in her sixties with grey hair. Her arm was tucked nervously into that of a younger girl who was beaming at the rare treat of being able to go to the pictures.

Bridget turned to the pair to hand them their tickets. She was trying hard to remember the names of all these women.

'Hello, Frau Schneider, isn't it . . . and Greta too? Are you both well?' Greta smiled and answered for them both in good English.

'Yes, thank you, we are both fine. My mother . . .'

She looked at the vacant expression on her mother's face and confided, 'She is finding it all very hard. You know, she misses my brothers and, you know, my mother, she is a healer . . . she needs her herbs and plants, without them, she loses interest in everything.'

'I didn't know she was interested in healing,' Bridget said, pricking up her ears, but then music struck up for the start of the afternoon's programme and she hurriedly ushered them in.

Babes on Broadway was a welcome contrast after the depressing Pathé News which bemoaned the appalling conditions in the battle for Stalingrad but rather than settle in the stepped seats at the Strand Cinema, the girls had to patrol the aisles to enforce separation of the different groups. The two factions of locals and internees were getting used to living next to each other but the rules against fraternising were very strict and fines to both sides were not uncommon. That didn't stop some of the local men glancing curiously across the aisle at the good-looking foreign women and, in the dark, the WPCs had to keep a sharp eye out for any crouched figures making their way along the rows before they could relax and enjoy the antics of Mickey Rooney and Judy Garland.

The feature film always finished with the National Anthem and, as usual, there was a moment of tension as the small group of Nazis in the audience either raced to the toilets or sat solidly in their seats with their arms folded while the rest of the group and the locals jeered and hurled abuse at them. The three policewomen determinedly kept their charges back as everyone else filed out to avoid the jostling and pushing that would inevitably take place on the way. Finally signalling those on the ends of the rows to start moving, Bridget caught sight of the timid face of Helga's victim, Ursula Apler. The girl hated the open aggression of the ritual of leaving the cinema, and since Helga's attack on her, had become even more fearful. Bridget noticed her eyes were darting from side to side in panic.

'Don't worry, Ursula, we won't go into the foyer until they've all gone.'

Ursula smiled weakly but still hung back.

To take her mind off the tension, Bridget continued.

'So, anyway, how *are* you?'

'Mmmm, *ich denke* . . . yes, I think I am, but, Helga, she is a big woman, no?'

'Yes, she is,' Bridget agreed, 'but the law is bigger than she is and you'll be safe from now on.' Ursula gave her a doubtful look and then turned to walk slowly to follow the crowd along Church Road. Her hunched shoulders were a familiar symbol worn by all the Jews on the Island, just as identifiable as the yellow badges they had to wear in Germany.

Betty came up from behind. 'You're almost off duty, aren't you, Bridget? We can get this lot back to their digs, so why don't you scoot off? We'll walk Greeba. Aren't you going to meet Fynn this afternoon?'

'Well, if you're sure . . .' Bridget said gratefully and ran off towards the Darragh.

Her heart was pounding and she wasn't sure whether it was the exertion of running to their arranged meeting place or the anticipation of seeing Fynn. Grateful that on this occasion they were simply going for a walk, she hoped there would be none of the usual awkwardness between them as they tentatively moved from being childhood friends to being an adult couple.

* * *

'I believe Kieran's coming back,' she said as they made their way along the lane, trying to keep her voice casual.

Fynn froze. He had been dreading this moment since he had first spotted Bridget at the dance. Years before, as a young lad with pimples, he had watched in agony as Bridget's adoring eyes followed his younger brother's every move. With Kieran miles away on the east side of England, he'd garnered enough courage to ask her to dance that night but now ... now, he could see all his hopes crumbling.

'Uh huh,' he said quietly.

'It's a while since you've seen him, though, isn't it?'

'Uh huh.'

Bridget couldn't help but smile. Sometimes Fynn's tendency to be the taciturn farmer was taken to extremes.

'How do you feel about that?' she asked.

Fynn tensed at Bridget's interest in his brother's home-coming, but then he turned to face her, warily searching for answers to the questions that were plaguing his nights.

'I feel fine about it,' he lied, 'he's my brother. But how do *you* feel about it?'

Bridget tossed her hair out of her eyes and started to move forward again, saying as casually as she could, 'Oh, I'll be glad to see him too, it's been such a long time since we've been together; it's such a shame Aedan and Brendan can't be here though.'

Fynn suddenly didn't want to hear any more and abruptly changed the subject.

'So, how's work?' Fynn started, as they made their way up the lane. He had no sooner finished speaking than Bridget launched into a tirade about how she had been given no option but to take this posting and how her job involved nothing but cases of petty theft, jealousy and disputes over who was in the right – Hitler or Church-ill. Fynn noted that her pace had quickened to keep time with the constant barrage of complaints that were now pouring out of her mouth and even with his long legs, he had to stride out to keep up. The indignation on her face was almost comical and he tried his best to keep a straight face but eventually burst out laughing, making her stop in her tracks.

She looked across furiously at him.

'What? What?'

'I'm sorry, Bridget, but you look just like you did when Aedan said you were too young to climb that oak tree. Do you remember?'

Bridget frowned and then broke into a broad smile.

'Oh dear, was I ranting?'

'Maybe just a little,' Fynn laughed and then reached for her hand. His large, calloused palm seemed to fit perfectly in hers and Bridget felt a warmth that calmed her and gave her the same security she'd felt when he'd helped her across rocky streams.

She looked shyly up at him. It was so long since anyone had teased her, she'd forgotten what it was like. Determined to always be a competent policewoman, she knew she took herself too seriously and found an unexpected relief in being able to be herself.

'OK,' she told him, with a laugh, 'I'll stop now and anyway, I do have a really exciting crime I'm dealing with at the moment.'

Everyone had heard about the knife confrontation outside Christian's Cottage and Fynn didn't want to confess that when it had been discussed in the Falcon's Nest bar, his only thought had been for Bridget's safety.

'Yes, it's the talk of the south of the Island. I'm so proud of you, Bridg,' he told her, his face reddening, 'you're a real policewoman dealing with real crime while I only have an awkward bull to deal with.'

'I'd rather face an angry German woman than a huge bull any day,' she said and then grinned. 'Although, one day, you might need to outrun him so come on, I'll race you to the fence at the top.' And she set off at a pace that had won her many prizes at sports days at school.

He watched Bridget go for a moment, as his face softened with the love he'd felt for so many years and then he started after her. When he caught her, he gathered her in his arms and kissed her. She felt every muscle in her body go weak and almost fell back against the fence in shock.

'Are you all right?' he said, suddenly concerned.

'Y-yes, fine ...' she stammered. She hadn't expected such a strong reaction to a kiss from a boy she'd grown up with. 'I'm just out of condition. Come on, let's go to the front and we can make a sandcastle.'

Fynn chuckled. 'You'll be lucky. It's so cold the sand's almost frozen.'

'Oh, not strong enough to cope with a bit of cold sand, huh?' she giggled, wondering what it was about this man that could turn her to jelly one minute and be her familiar playmate the next.

'That sounds like a challenge to me,' Fynn said, and took off down the road, leaving her to follow in his wake.

Chapter Five

At the Imperial Hotel in Port Erin, one of the hotels where prostitutes were housed, a group of ladies of the night were huddled around a little girl who was standing tearfully in the middle of the circle. Six-year-old Karin Fischer looked around from one to another of the women who were surrounding her, searching for her mother. She'd been spending fitful nights sharing a bed with two of the internees who would tuck her in, saying simply that her mama 'would be back soon'.

'Soho Suzy', who had appointed herself as the leader of the group, strode in through the large doors at the end of the ballroom.

'So, who is going to look after this child, then?' she barked in a deep, cigarette-catarrhal voice.

The women looked from one to another, waiting to see if anyone spoke. Karin bit her lip and her chin quivered as one single tear slowly rolled down her cheek. One weak voice was heard from the back of the group.

'I will.' A passage cleared like the Red Sea from the child in the middle to the small, young girl at the back. Her hair was tucked back behind her ears and her complexion was pallid.

'*You*?' Suzy said incredulously. 'But you can hardly look after yourself.'

Ursula Apler may have been a diminutive five foot and look younger than her seventeen years, but at that moment, she raised her chin and looked challengingly at the suspicious faces around her to speak in German with a trace of a Liverpudlian accent; the city she had lived in since arriving in England four years earlier.

'*Ja, ich kann,*' she replied. For a reason she could not understand, Ursula felt she was responsible for this child's mother being in gaol. As well as this, Ursula ached for a human touch to ease the homesickness and the thought that someone might need her had made her heart leap with the first glimmer of hope in three long years.

She moved nervously forward to the front of the group and knelt down in front of the little girl's tear-smeared face.

'I'll look after yous,' she said gently, lapsing into the dialect of her adopted English city. Recognising a kind face, Karin reached out her arms to be picked up.

Ursula hugged the child to her, clinging on so tightly that the girl started to wriggle.

'Sorry,' Ursula said, loosening her grip, but then she felt the child's arms tighten around her in a desperate hug and the two clung together like two drowning passengers on the *Titanic*.

Suzy was a prostitute in her fifties who had worked the Soho streets for so long she'd almost forgotten her native German. She said loudly, 'Right, that's that sorted then. OK, back to work. Who's going to help me with the patchwork?'

A woman with grey roots peeping out from her jet-black hair murmured in German, 'I'd prefer to be humping a couple of those nice guards who patrol the wire out towards Spaldrick.'

The two on her left started to giggle nervously. They'd actually been enjoying doing the creative sessions on the Island rather than being at the whim of some randy soldier or sailor.

In the early days, with so many bored, displaced internees to keep entertained, a system of keeping the women occupied had been set up. Called the Service Exchange, it had had a dual benefit: firstly, they were kept busy making everything from toys to cakes to furnishings and then those goods could be sold off to fellow prisoners using cut-out pieces of Cornflake packets as tokens. With a wide range of skills such as baking, dressmaking, laundry work, gardening and hairdressing, the internees, many of whom had no money, found a way to improve both their standards of living and their wardrobes.

Once interest in the Service Exchange began to wane, Suzy was desperate to keep this potent mix of prostitutes of all political persuasions alongside Jews and fascists from becoming a hotbed of arguments, fights and disagreements and had come up with the idea of making colourful bed covers from the lovely Loaghtan sheep wool bartered from the haberdashery shop in the village. To her relief, it had inspired a new enthusiasm for crocheting and knitting that was keeping the women busy as they vied with each other to think up the most innovative design. Heating was not allowed in their bedrooms so a cosy blanket was a popular addition to their beds and there were even rumours that they might eventually be able to sell their wares to local people. With a five-shilling withdrawal limit a week for any internees who actually had any funds of their own, to be able to once again earn some cash was a tempting prospect.

Ursula left them to the sudden flurry of activity and took Karin up to her room that she shared with the terrifying Ira. Ira reminded her of the huge statue of Queen Victoria in Derby Square in Liverpool which, with its black coating, had always blocked out the sun when she had scurried past it. Ira's solid frame always seemed to dominate the room and in the double bed they were forced to share, the woman's backside would frequently push Ursula onto the edge of the mattress, so much so that the young girl occasionally tumbled out onto the bare floor, waking up with a thud. Ursula was examining her surroundings to see how she could make it cosy for little Karin, thinking wistfully of the warm patchwork covers that the women were making downstairs when there was a knock on the door.

'You all right in there?' Ursula went to open it to see the kindly face of Ruth, the Quaker woman who helped with the women's practical needs. As a member of the Quaker German Emergency Committee, it was her job to check on the welfare situation of the women in Rushen Camp and her days were filled with dealing with situations like the one that faced her now.

Ursula's face blossomed into a weak smile, making her brown eyes stand out against her pale complexion. Ruth smiled indulgently at the young girl she'd first seen clasping her battered case on the ferry coming over a year ago and knew she'd been correct in her assessment of the gentle and open-hearted personality that was hidden behind a strained, anxious face.

'I heard you're going to look after little Karin.'

'*Ja*, I think she needs a friend.'

Ruth looked at the child who was perched nervously on the edge of the bed, waiting to see what sort of future these two women had in mind for her.

'We all need a friend,' Ruth said, and went to sit on the bed next to Karin. Out of her dress pocket, she brought a peg doll which she handed to Karin, who fingered it in disbelief. She gently smoothed out the gingham skirt and spread her fingers through the rope hair.

'Is this for me?' she whispered.

Ruth, with eight grandchildren of her own, smiled indulgently as the little girl immediately put the doll behind her, covering it with her skirt in case the nice lady changed her mind.

Ruth put out her hand to stroke her hair, but Karin jumped back as if she had been burned. Ursula vowed there and then to do everything she could to protect this child.

*　*　*

By the time Kieran Moore arrived back in Douglas, his mood was as dark as the seas he had just travelled across on. The journey had been tense with everyone on board the *Ben-my-Chree* scanning the choppy waters for any sign of the U-boats that stalked the area but Kieran hardly registered their fear. He sat on the deck, ignoring the spray from the high waves that tossed the boat from side to side. In his misery, he failed to notice that people were having to step over his stretched-out feet in front of him and simply pulled his greatcoat around him. The only time he looked up was when he heard aircraft engines in the distance. There was a moment's sharp intake of breath by the passengers around him as they checked to see if the familiar RAF insignia could be seen on the underside of the wings, and once they saw the reassuring paint marks, they went back to their anxious search for signs of the next danger – a periscope. No one, except Kieran who was absorbed in his own world, relaxed for the entire, fraught journey. The only time he looked remotely interested in what was going on around him was when he glanced up at those planes above him with envy, almost expecting them to at least acknowledge there was an ex-pilot below and he banged his feet as if he could shake off the wooden deck beneath him and take off into the air to join them.

Once in Douglas, he hurled his kitbag over his shoulder and made his way out of the ferry terminal into the night air. *Nothing's changed*, he thought bitterly, looking out at Castle Refuge guarding the harbour. But then he looked over to the promenade and took a sharp intake of breath. All along the frontages of the hotels and guest houses, there was barbed wire, glistening in the early evening twilight. Behind it, he could see men in drab clothing wandering listlessly up and down with bored soldiers watching them at regular distances. He'd heard about the wire, but to see it on his own island, providing such a stark contrast to the cheerful holidaymakers and ice cream stands of pre-war days, shook him to the core and he stood transfixed.

'Hello, I know that ugly face,' a voice said from the quayside behind him.

He turned round to see his older brother, Fynn. He hardly recognised him. It had been a few years since they'd met face-to-face, communicating by short, perfunctory letters swapping essential details about both their lives and the state of the farm. As boys, they'd been close, with Fynn spending most of his time protecting his young brother from escapades, defending his wild behaviour to the authorities and making excuses to a succession of discarded girlfriends. Once war broke out, the two boys had talked excitedly about joining up – Fynn wanted to join the navy and Kieran had always wanted to be a pilot but their plans were put in jeopardy when an angry bull charged at their father, badly injuring his leg. Fynn, as the older son, immediately volunteered to stay and look after the farm but Kieran had always blamed himself for giving in so easily to the plan. Now, with a damaged hand and a shattered career, he felt fate had got its revenge.

Looking closely at the familiar face with the weatherbeaten complexion in front of him, Kieran experienced the same inadequacy that his elder brother always instilled in him. It was as if Fynn somehow managed to make him feel inferior simply by doing the right thing. Kieran's initial intention had been to search for a way to make everyone feel proud of him but somehow, even the DFC made him feel hollow; too many other men had died to allow him to achieve it and now his hand was a constant reminder of his failure to die alongside them. Fynn was dressed in a yellow sou'wester and was carrying a Mae West lifejacket with the letters RNLI which crinkled as Kieran reached forward to give his brother a warm hug, realising how much he'd missed him.

'Fynn, it's so good to see you. Glad to see you're still on the lifeboats.'

Fynn nodded and although he tried not to sound bitter, he knew his voice had a sharp edge to it. 'Yes . . . I try to fit it around the farm; some of us need to keep this country fed, you know, while you chaps get all the glory. But,' he admitted, 'you know how I've always loved the lifeboat. I've just been to a training session.'

Fynn saw his younger brother wince guiltily and softened his tone. 'I knew you were coming but wasn't expecting you until the end of the week. Mum and dad'll be thrilled. So, how come you're early?'

'Managed to get a few days leave before my posting.' Kieran waved an arm to encompass the scene in front of him. 'I can't believe all this, Fynn,' he said. 'What's happened to this island? I know you told me about the wire, but I didn't believe it could all look so . . . so brutal. So, it's true then, we've been taken over by foreigners?'

'Just about; you know they only gave islanders twenty-four hours to leave their homes to make way for them, don't you? Only the landladies were pleased, it gave them some paying guests at least. But how long do you think you'll be staying this time? Dad said you weren't sure about your future'

Kieran groaned. 'This looks like it . . . for ever . . . and ever . . . and ever. No one else wants me.'

Fynn took one look at the dejected expression on his brother's face and took his arm.

'Sounds like you need a drink, Kier, before I take you home. Come on, I know just the place. I haven't got long before milking but we can fit in a pint before we go back and Mum gets out the fatted calf.' And he marched him off to The Albert on Chapel Row to promptly order two beers. Fynn carried them to the table in the corner where they'd last sat in 1939.

'To be honest, Kieran, you look terrible. What happened?' Fynn said in his usual, straight way.

'The burns I got haven't healed and I can't fly anymore,' was the bland reply.

After the telegram had arrived telling the family that Kieran was missing, Fynn had spent a month waiting with his anxious parents and his sister, Kathleen, for news. The initial fear that the youngest member of the family had been killed was replaced by relief when the postman finally brought some post, but an impersonal letter dictated from Kieran's hospital bed did little to provide the family with any details of his injuries. As far as they knew he had a 'bit of a burn' on his hand and they hardly heard any more until another telegram arrived, simply telling them he was being transferred to the Isle of Man. There had been no mention of not being able to fly, so Fynn sidestepped the temptation to sound shocked and said evenly, 'OK, what now?'

There was a sourness to Kieran's voice. 'I'm being sent to RAF Jurby.'

Fynn sat back and assessed his brother's furious expression with a frown, then he leaned forward.

'You've done your bit, Kier, let some of the younger lads take over.'

'I'm only twenty-four,' his brother protested. 'But you're right, I feel as if I'm on the scrapheap.'

'Hmm, what you need is a good night out. Listen, I'm taking ...' He paused for a moment, aware he had been preparing this speech for days in readiness for his brother's return ... 'Bridget out on Saturday. Why don't you join us?' Fynn's cheeks suddenly developed a red tinge and he hurried on. 'You remember Bridget Harrison, don't you? She's back here too and now you mention it, she's as bad-tempered about it as you are.'

For a moment, Kieran forgot his own unhappiness and smiled at his elder brother with delight.

'You've got a girlfriend? And Bridget Harrison? Well, that's lovely news, Fynn, she's a great girl. What's she doing back here?' Kieran asked, surprised. 'I heard she went to be a policewoman and knowing how she couldn't wait to get off the Island, I didn't think she'd come back. Not for a while anyway. So,' he smiled, 'she found the streets of London aren't paved with gold, huh? 'Praps she's not as brave as she thought she was? Maybe Hitler's changed all that for her?'

'No, she's as feisty as ever and a fully qualified police-woman,' Fynn replied, with a tinge of pride. 'She's been sent back to look after the women in Rushen Camp but isn't too pleased about it.'

He looked curiously at his brother opposite him and felt a slight quiver of fear. The vision of Bridget following Kieran around like an adoring puppy had been replaying in his head for days, torturing him.

When he'd spotted her at the dance to raise money for a Spitfire, all grown up with her beautiful, shining eyes, he'd felt his throat constricting just as it had as a shy twelve-year-old. Since then, he had been trying very hard not to let anyone – least of all a young woman who seemed to hate everything about the Island he loved – know how his hopes had been raised. Fynn assessed his good-looking brother across the table from him and wondered whether this homecoming could put an end to those hopes.

'Oh yeah,' Kieran was saying, oblivious of the turbulent thoughts racing through his brother's head, 'she always thought she could do everything a boy could do; she got into nearly as many scrapes as I did.

'So, you're going out with her, are you?' he went on. 'Well, if she's half as cross as I am, she won't be much fun. Good for you, but she'll be hard work.'

'Enjoying the challenge, Kier,' Fynn retorted, feeling his face flush. 'Another pint?'

'I thought you'd never ask.'

Chapter Six

The three girls were cramped in the little kitchen at the back of Port Erin police station, the only place they could talk without being overheard and were discussing ways to help little Karin who had been making progress under Ursula's tender care, but still woke during the night calling for her mother. At a complete loss, Bridget finally changed the subject.

'Are either of you two free on Saturday? Fynn's asked me out and he's bringing along his brother; you know, the one with the DFC.' She uttered the words as casually as she could but was disturbed to feel a slight shiver.

Betty looked doubtful. 'You know, I'd love a night out, but I don't want anyone getting the wrong idea.'

"It'll do you good to come,' Bridget insisted, then added, 'Heard from Joe?"

'No, nothing.' Betty's expression darkened and she fingered the wedding band on her left hand.

"I'm sure he's fine," Bridget said, as reassuringly as she could, but Betty had seen the headlines warning of the fierce battle for Tripoli and with letters taking weeks to reach England, she was spending hours tossing and turning at night in the little room that the girls shared, imagining all kinds of disasters, finding loneliness almost as unbearable as the worry.

'What's he like, this brother then?' Molly asked curiously. A girl with a fearsome reputation for going out with men and then ditching them for no reason, she was always happy to move onto the next.

Bridget felt immediately nervous. Firstly, she wasn't convinced she should really be organising a date between the two of them, remembering Kieran's reputation at school for flirting and secondly, she wasn't sure how she felt about her housemate getting together with her childhood fantasy. It then occurred to her that Molly might treat him badly and she experienced a quiver of guilty delight.

'He's all right, I haven't seen him for years, but I suspect he's a bit full of himself now he's a war hero. He could be good fun, though, when we were children,' she added reluctantly. She really hoped she wouldn't live to regret this selfless act of handing Kieran Moore over to her friend. 'They're meeting us at eight o'clock at the Falcon's Nest.'

Betty gulped. 'What? You're going to a pub?

In London, it was a common occurrence for women to frequent public houses but Bridget knew that many of the people from the Island were definitely not ready to embrace such brazen behaviour.

'It's all right,' Bridget said, trying to reassure Betty, as well as herself, 'we'll have the men with us and, honestly, Bet, so many of the WAAFs stationed here are doing it that the locals are just going to have to get used to it.'

'I think you should ask Sarge,' Betty said, looking worried, 'after all, we'll be in uniform.'

Molly had no such qualms and was too busy weighing up Bridget's invitation. She suddenly looked across the room suspiciously and then threw a tea towel at Bridget, which landed firmly on her face.

'You've already said I'll join you on this date, haven't you? Well, just beware, if he's ugly, you'll be doing roll call all week!'

Betty turned towards the tea urn; she felt so left out when the other two talked like this. She'd only been married to Joe for three months when he'd been sent overseas with the army and sometimes, she had difficulty remembering what he looked like. His face, last glimpsed on a departing train from Waterloo Station, was fading like a dream on waking and she frequently had to check the dog-eared photograph she kept in her purse to remind herself of his smile. She looked at her wedding ring, wondering, not for the first time, whether she had done the right thing by getting married at nineteen.

Sergeant Robinson's face around the door dispelled any more chatter and all three girls suddenly busied themselves with what might, or might not have been, very important tasks.

Betty nudged Bridget to prompt her to ask about the pub with a meaningful look.

Bridget gave in. 'Sarge, would it be all right if we went into a public house? With male escorts, of course.' Molly glared at her for raising the issue, fearing their strict boss would say no, but Maureen Robinson thought for a moment.

'I think so, Bridget, I'm sure you girls know how to behave and to be honest, I think it's been too much of a man's world up to now.'

All three of the girls were stunned. They hadn't expected such an answer and Bridget had all her arguments ready, but the sergeant had moved onto another subject. 'Oh and Bridget, we've found Otto Kruger's wife's file. I think things will be in place for them to be moved to the married camp next week, so well done for bringing him to my attention.'

Bridget glowed at the unexpected praise but then the sergeant reverted to her usual officious tone.

'I'll need you at court next week, Bridget, Helga's up for remand.'

With no admission of guilt by Helga, the appearances in court were a formality that would be repeated until the trial, which could be months. There was little chance of bail with a not guilty plea and the only issue would be Karin's welfare and whether she was being looked after properly.

'In that case, I might go and check up on Karin,' Bridget said. 'At least then, the court'll have up-to-date information about that little mite.'

Sergeant Robinson looked at the young girl with approval. She'd been about to suggest just that, and she was pleased to note that, once again, Bridget Harrison had pre-empted her. This WPC was turning out to be quite a useful addition to the force, she thought. She just wished Bridget would be a little more grateful for being in what could only be described as a 'cushy number'. Sergeant Robinson had been delighted to escape from the rough area of Charing Cross in London where she'd been brought up. As a woman who had always defied conventionality, she'd joined the Red Cross and then, inspired by a woman police officer who helped her own mother fend off her violent father, had joined the police force. Her mentor, a gorgeous woman in her forties, gently helped Maureen realise she was not like other women and their relationship led to a double life that would have scandalised her family, friends and colleagues. It was only when a bomb near Trafalgar Square obliterated the love of her life that Maureen Robinson plunged into the depths of despair and began to look further afield to flee the narrow streets and the narrow minds that were threatening her professional career – and her sanity.

The posting to the Isle of Man had offered her the escape she craved and, desperate to reinvent herself, she worked on losing her strong Cockney accent, spending hours in front of her bedroom mirror trying out different voices until she found the peremptory tone she was now famous for. No one would have thought for a moment that this terrifying woman sobbed uncontrollably into a cushion every night. It was that deception that gave her the power to keep all those around her at a safe distance and she guarded it zealously.

* * *

Bridget arrived at the Imperial Hotel just before supper time to look for Karin and Ursula. There were groups of women gathered in the dining room, huddling against the cold draught emanating from the windows, but Bridget was too busy looking enviously at the plates of Spam fritters and potato, wondering why she wasn't as thin as a stick insect; she certainly never got time to eat.

One of the women who came in from the village to help with mealtimes signalled to Bridget.

'Want a plateful, love?' Mrs Corkhill asked. She had known the Harrison family since the children were little, occasionally babysitting for them. 'You look half-starved.'

'I am hungry,' Bridget admitted, 'but I can't be seen to be taking their food, so, thanks, Mrs Corkhill, but no.'

Rations were eked out to the internees at a rate that was the envy of the islanders and the full menus often prompted resentment, but Bridget only felt pity for the lonely, bored women in front of her. However, the fritters did smell good.

Trying to ignore the pangs of hunger, she told Mrs Corkhill she would just sit at the back until the women had finished.

As the women filed out slowly, not sure how to fill the hours between teatime and bed, Bridget craned her neck to spot Ursula standing in the queue, biting her lip nervously. Hanging onto Ursula's faded dress was little Karin, looking equally uneasy.

Bridget made her way towards them both.

'Hello, you two, have you got a minute?' and she ushered them into the far side of the foyer where there were a few chairs, left from the days when tourists would order their afternoon tea while gazing out at the peaceful bay beyond.

Ursula looked hesitant. She was always fearful when she saw a uniform, even on someone as approachable as Bridget.

'It's all right, Ursula, there's no problem, I just wanted to see how you were both getting on.' And with that, she smiled reassuringly at Karin who was sucking the woollen hair of her peg doll.

'Is that your dolly?' Bridget asked her kindly, and then immediately regretted her casual interest because Karin thrust the doll behind her back.

'She's lovely and don't worry, pet, I'm not going to take her off you.'

Karin looked at Ursula for reassurance, but her doll remained firmly behind her back.

The conversation was brief and perfunctory but the whole time the young police officer was watching Karin out of the corner of her eye, noting how Karin shrank into Ursula's side for safety and that the little girl was clean, well-dressed and her hair was braided. Ursula was obviously an expert at looking after young children.

The eldest of three, Ursula had been brought up in a back street of Berlin as the daughter of a prostitute, until, just before war broke out, hearing there were better pickings in Liverpool where Jews were better tolerated, her mother had smuggled the family onto a cargo ship across the Channel.

To Ursula, the clean bedroom at The Imperial Hotel was a vast improvement on the cellar room near the railway arches in Bentinck Street in Liverpool. There, dripping walls and a dank atmosphere had provided a bleak place of refuge for Ursula, her sister and their mother with a lumpy mattress for a bed and a wooden drawer next to them for her baby brother. A bomb on the 28th of November 1940 had shattered the house above them, and all their lives. At only fifteen, Ursula emerged from the damp cellar through the smoking rubble, dragging her sister and the baby in her arms to find a stiletto shoe belonging to her mother. That was all that was left of the grimly determined woman who had tried so hard to keep her children from the workhouse. After that, terrified that her siblings would be taken off her, the young Ursula had avoided all contact with the authorities by hiding in an outbuilding where she'd tried to make a home for them all. They would have starved had it not been for the prostitutes around the docks who would pass scraps of food and clothing on to the little family. But all that ended when a police van arrived to pick up all German prostitutes and Ursula had been scooped up with the rest of them. Her last sight of her brother and sister was of them being taken off down the street by a thin woman in a brown suit with a clipboard and she now spent dark hours through the night wondering what had happened to the beloved siblings she'd been forced to abandon.

Snuggling Karin's little warm body next to her at night was the only thing saving her from walking into the sea.

* * *

Helga Fischer pummelled the thin, straw pillow but it remained stubbornly inflexible. She thought of her little girl searching the faces at The Imperial Hotel for her mother's familiar features in vain and gave a little sob. Wrapping her arms around herself in an attempt to bring some heat into the freezing cold cell, she hoped that it might also recall the warmth of her little daughter's body, but it was hopeless. Since she'd been told that that Jewish girl was going to take care of her, she had felt sick. The thought of her beautiful little girl being cuddled by a woman of that race made her tremble.

Maybe this is my punishment, she thought, pacing up and down the cell, *I deserve this.* Helga Fischer had far more secrets to hide than most of the internees in the camp and, unable to share them with anyone, all she wanted to do was hide away. Her eventful journey to England had been a risk but now it seemed the shame that had made her flee might have followed her here and she wasn't safe on the Isle of Man either.

Sitting down heavily on the hard bunk, its springs beneath barely yielding to her large frame, she looked around. The cell was bare apart from a small table and chair, a little window above with a grille to keep the world out and prisoners in, and a bucket in the corner that she knew would stink within a day. But then, two things occurred to her. Firstly, that deprivation was a small price to pay to keep Karin safe and secondly, that these walls might protect her from the penetrating eyes of one Nazi in particular. All she had to do was survive.

Chapter Seven

Bridget went away from the hotel thoughtfully at the end of her shift. There were too many troubled faces in this camp and she was feeling out of her depth. Her work in London had been so straightforward with a discernible division between the innocent and the guilty but here, the lines were blurred.

'*Guten tag*, officer,' a woman stopped in front of her.

And here's another one, Bridget thought, smiling in recognition at the German woman who loved her herbs.

'Hello, Frau Schneider. How are you?'

In her late sixties, the German woman looked older than her years and the constant worried frown suggested a life of hardship and mistrust. Erika Schneider had so far found English a difficult language to learn and even though she had been attending lessons at Collinson's Café, still didn't have confidence in her ability.

Her daughter, Greta, tutted.

'Come on, *Mutter*, you know how to answer this.'

Frau Schneider turned back to Bridget and said, slowly, 'Thank you, I am well.'

Then she paused, looking at the world-weary face of the police officer in front of her.

'But you, I think, are not.'

Bridget smiled. She was in awe of Erika Schneider. Like her own grandmother, Frau Schneider could see into your soul, something Bridget had recognised from the first moment when she helped the German woman off the ferry. Her physical features suggested exhaustion and defeat, but her eyes told a different story.

'It's just . . . hard,' Bridget muttered.

'*Ja,* we know. We have so many . . . what you call them . . . problems here and there are not so many of you.'

Bridget felt tears pricking behind her eyes. Sympathy from this older, wise woman was something she could not cope with right now. She was a professional who certainly couldn't cry, so she coughed loudly and pushed her shoulders back.

'No, I'm fine, thank you. Umm,' she looked from Erika Schneider to Greta, 'do you both have everything you need?'

Greta smiled. 'Everything except our families, our homes and our freedom.'

Bridget could deal with their squabbles, provide them with blankets or point them towards a hairdresser but she could not solve the main problem for all of them, which was separation, exemplified every day by the sight of so many internees who would stand and stare at the horizon as if it could miraculously conjure up a husband, a child, a lover.

'I am sorry, have you heard from anyone . . . your baker, Greta?

Greta had moved to East Anglia in 1938, to learn how to make English white bread with a baker in Kings Lynn. Her eyes misted as she remembered Albert Taylor, the large, kind man with two enormous dimples in his pink cheeks and a mischievous sense of humour. In the warm atmosphere of the tiny kitchen at the back of the shop, she had fallen in love with him before the loaves had cooled. Greta touched her empty ring finger; he'd been about to ask her to marry him, she was sure of that. If only he had, she furiously thought every night, staring at the faded wallpaper in their tiny bedroom, then she would have had the protection of being his wife and would not have been arrested.

Bridget waited expectantly for Greta's answer, knowing that a brutal decision not to allow letters to and from internees, had finally been overturned.

'Yes, thank you, at last I hear from my dear Albert, but not from my brothers.'

Bridget saw the girl's mother suddenly tense up.

'Have you heard anything from anyone at home, Frau Schneider?' she asked, struggling to recall anything but the barest details about this woman's past. Her file, like so many, was woefully thin, mentioning only two sons in the German army and another one who was missing. There was only the barest information about how she had arrived in England, apart from the fact she'd been found hiding in the back of the bakery when the police van arrived to arrest her daughter and that the accelerating vehicle had been pursued down the street by a distraught Albert Taylor.

A sad shake of Erika's head was accompanied by a biting of her lip. This was a woman who'd had to learn how to disappear into the shadows.

Her daughter glanced thoughtfully at the pale face next to her. All she knew of her mother's journey to England was that just days before the police arrived to arrest aliens, she had found her on the bakery doorstep, slumped against the Open sign. Every time Greta broached the subject of her escape, her mother would start to shake and Greta quickly backed off, hoping that time would heal whatever trauma was haunting her.

'At least we two are together,' Greta said, linking her mother's arm and giving it a squeeze. 'And maybe we can hunt out some of the Island's herbs, Mother. That would cheer you up.'

Erika gave a wan smile.

Bridget's face suddenly cleared and she said, 'Excuse me, I think it's time I paid my grandmother a visit.'

* * *

Bridget's grandmother lived on the road to Scarlett Point and was what was known as a wise woman; previous generations had called them Fairy Doctors. As an expert on herbs, potions and even charms, she was constantly consulted by Manx people about their ailments, anxiety or lovesick misery and there was nothing Bridget liked more than pottering around her aroma-filled outhouse where all the herbs were stored. But tonight, she had a special request to ask her.

'Is that you, Breesha?'

'Yes, Granny,' Bridget replied, smiling at how her grandmother always preferred the Manx version of her name. She pushed the blackout curtain back in place to allow her to hang her coat on the wooden peg in the freezing cold hallway and, for a moment, hovered with her arms half in and half out of the warm sleeves but then crossed her fingers that the fire might be lit in the back room.

'Did you remember the thyme?' the elderly woman, sitting on a rocking chair in the corner of the room, asked her.

Bridget walked over to the weak fire in the inglenook and warmed her hands, before she delved in her pocket to fish out a few sprigs of the herb that she'd collected the previous weekend.

'Here you go, Granny, is that enough?'

'Yes, me darlin' that'll be grand.'

Her grandmother's gnarled fingers reached out to take the faded stalks and then she stood up to enfold Bridget in a warm hug that made up for the paltry fire that was flickering in the grate.

Bridget found her shoulders relaxing as they always did when she arrived in this tiny cottage. From childhood, she'd thought of it as a treasure trove worthy of her Aladdin storybook; it was so full of flowers, medicinal herbs and clinking containers of strange-smelling liquids. Every wooden shelf was crammed with different-coloured bottles and jars; above her hung strings of plants that were drying out ready for use and in one corner was a pine table full of saucers, some filled with small amounts of liquids, others with squashed leaves or bark, twigs or shells. To one side, was a notebook with scribblings, drawings and bits of paper stuck to its yellowed pages. This was Mona's 'bible'. It held every remedy, every recipe for spells and every charm known to the few women who still practised on the Island. Mona Quayle was originally a Teare, the family on the Island who were known for their special knowledge. In her late seventies, she had white, wispy hair that would never stay in the bun she tied carelessly every morning. She wore a long, brown skirt and a shawl that she crossed over a faded cream blouse to tuck into her waistband. No one could ever remember her wearing anything else. A Christian woman who believed strongly that Providence had given her skills to heal, she would never countenance any suggestion that they should be besmirched with anything other than a desire to do good.

After her own daughter had retreated from the old ways, too intent on her paintings, Mona had been delighted to find young Breesha had a natural aptitude and a keen interest.

'Are you staying for supper, Caillin?' she asked, using the old Manx word for girl.

Bridget sniffed the air, there was an appealing aroma of neck-end stew emanating from the pot on a metal stand to one side of the fireplace. She went and lifted the heavy black lid and stirred the wooden spoon around the meat and vegetables. The smell made her realise how hungry she was.

'Is there enough?' she asked her granny, knowing the answer would be yes. Mona had loved cooking for her large family and could never quite get the hang of cooking for one.

Mona gave a chuckle and got down a second, cracked white bowl and spoon to put on the old gingham table-cloth on the table.

'You sit yourself, down, girl and we'll talk until the black cats go out. You could bed down if you want and get off early in the morning.'

Bridget glanced over at the settle in the corner with its cosy plaid blanket.

She nodded gratefully; she didn't feel like walking in the pitch-black back to Port Erin and sat down on the wooden chair next to the table. All the cares of the day seemed to slip off like a silk shawl from her shoulders.

'So, you want to ask me something, do you?' her grandmother said.

Bridget didn't need to ask how the old woman knew; she was used to this ability to pre-empt people's wishes.

'I do, Granny. I've got a woman in the camp who seems to know a lot about natural remedies, would you come and meet her?'

Mona looked sharply at her granddaughter.

'Kraut, is she?'

'Well, yes,' Bridget admitted. 'But she's not a Nazi and she's . . . well, really . . . nice . . . I think you'd like her.'

'Hah!' her grandmother replied. 'Never met a German I liked yet so why would I need to meet her?'

Bridget groaned inwardly. She loved this woman, but she did have some very definite ideas about the universe and everyone's place in it. She had prepared a speech but when those watery eyes looked past Bridget's green ones into her very soul, the words faded. Her grandmother's views had been set in stone in 1918 when her beloved husband, Thomas, returned from Passchendaele with trench fever. It had taken him another ten years to die, beset with fevers and rashes that even her most efficacious treatments and charms could not dispel, and she'd never forgiven herself for not being able to save him.

She had railed at Germany, its entire populace and anyone with blond hair and blue eyes ever since.

'I think she's from a farm in Germany,' Bridget pleaded, 'and has got three . . . yes, three sons who've been forced to fight.' The face in front of her remained impassive.

She took a deep breath and carried on, aware she was starting to babble. 'Her daughter was learning to be a baker in England and I suspect this woman had a terrible time escaping the Nazis to get over to join her. Then, just think, Granny, this woman thought she'd got to safety only to be scooped up and sent over here. Please, give her a chance. She's really nice . . .' She tailed off, realising she had already made that point.

Mona Quayle thought for a moment, the spoon of stew suspended between her bowl and her mouth. Then she firmly clasped the metal spoon in her faded teeth.

'No. No, I won't. Now eat your supper and then we can go through those charms you wanted to know about.'

Bridget resigned herself to a long campaign to change this stubborn woman's mind and reluctantly ate her stew.

* * *

That night, Bridget tossed and turned in the tiny cot bed, first dreaming of being chased out of the cinema by Nazis, then of the 'Little People,' as real in the minds of the Manx as the enemy across the Channel, chasing those same Nazis down the street and in each dream, her grandmother was sitting, calmly watching the proceedings while smoking her white clay pipe.

Bridget woke with her hair all over her face and to her grandmother peering over her, looking as innocent as a child and offering her a cup of herbal tea.

'Here you are, my Breesha, get this tea down you. You look as if you need it.'

Bridget pushed her hair back crossly.

'Ah well, my "veen", you look as fretted as when you were told you couldn't play with my potions as a "babban". Come on now, and get your breakfast, you'll need it before you go out into that big, bad world.'

And with that, she chuckled and went over to the fire in the corner to mix the porridge.

Bridget still had some time before her shift so she gave in, edged her long legs out of the coloured squared rug that had covered her and made her way in her bare feet to the table as if she were treading over spikes, the tiled floor was so cold. Her granny handed her some thick woollen socks and she gratefully put them on. The porridge aroma wafted in the air and by the time she had spooned some honey from the bees at the bottom of her grandmother's garden into it and stirred it round, she felt a familiar calmness start to seep through her body.

'What did you put in this porridge?' she asked.

'Never you mind,' Mona Quayle said with a wicked grin. 'You won't be chased by any more gremlins today, that's all.'

Bridget blew out a sigh and shook her head. Getting cross with this woman was a waste of time; she knew before you did how you were going to feel that day.

'I heard Kieran Moore's coming back to the Island,' Bridget said between mouthfuls.

'Uh huh,' came the enigmatic reply.

'He's got some problem with his hand so, if he can't fly, he won't be happy about that, you know how he thinks he's an ace pilot,' Bridget ventured, waiting for a reaction.

'How's that elder brother of his?' Mona asked pointedly. Her grandmother had a soft spot for Fynn, the boy who would offer to bring in some wood from the store while Kieran and her two grandsons tried to mess with her herbs. She'd always saved a lollipop for Fynn while dispatching the other three out of her workshop with a broomstick and had greeted Bridget's shy admission that she had been on a few dates with him with a satisfied smile.

'He's fine,' Bridget said defensively, 'but we're both really busy, you know.' She felt her cheeks reddening at the memory of his passionate kiss and hoped her grandmother could not read her mind.

'Hmm,' her grandmother replied with a knowing smirk and then said, 'Do you want to see my latest charm? It's really good for people who think they can outwit fate.'

'Oh, who's that for?' Bridget asked, putting her bowl and spoon in the sink.

'Just anyone who needs it,' and with that, her grand-mother went out into the back lean-to where she kept more of her herbs and potions, knowing that Bridget would follow her.

While she sorted the large pile of herbs on the side, working in companiable silence with her grandmother, the memories of Kieran Moore flooded in. The last time she had seen him had been at the leavers' event at King William's School. Her eldest brother, Aedan, was going to university in Edinburgh and Kieran was heading for Durham and there had been a brief meeting in the school refectory where very small glasses of sherry were distributed to the families. She, with her plaits and long white socks, had been automatically passed over by a prefect with a silver tray but Kieran had surreptitiously sneaked one to pass over for her to sip. It had been a moment that had justified all those years of adoration from afar and she'd had trouble stopping her knees from buckling. But then Kieran wandered over to a blonde girl and put his arm around her waist, confident his irresistible smile would have its desired effect on his quarry, leaving Bridget to die a little inside.

Bridget sighed; all those young men's education had been cut short by the war and within a very short space of time, Kieran and her brothers had been sent to Cranwell to train. It seemed such a long time since she had seen any of them and she wondered what sort of man Kieran had grown into and whether the fame had gone to his head. Although her brothers were now posted to somewhere in Lincolnshire, flying huge bombers on impossibly dangerous missions, their rushed letters were sparse in detail, so there was one reason she'd be pleased to see him; it would make her feel her closer to them.

I bet he's still rubbish at fishing though, she thought with a certain amount of satisfaction, doing an unnecessarily tight knot in the rosemary bunches she was sorting.

Chapter Eight

Work gave little time for reflection and Bridget's morning was first taken up with a case of fraternising between a lonely middle-aged Italian woman and the local greengrocer. Bridget felt some sympathy towards them but it was her job to make sure the rules were adhered to. She sent the would-be lovers on their way with a fine notice and tried not to notice their wistful expressions.

Then there was a fight to deal with. In the foyer were two women sitting with a chair between them. Both had blood on their faces and a sulky expression.

Alister grinned when he saw Bridget.

'Yours, I think,' he said cheerfully.

She grimaced at him and sat between the pair, her notebook in hand.

As she listened to their broken English complaints, she didn't dare look towards Alister, who was enjoying every minute of this and it was only when she had sent them on their way with Germolene and a strict warning, that she was able to turn towards Alister,

'You are a horrible man,' she burst out with a chortle. 'Here I am trying to be a proper policewoman and deal with these problems and all I can hear is you guffawing in the background.'

Alister took on a penitent look.

'No, it's no good, Sergeant Cubbon,' Bridget admonished with a smile. 'If you do that again, I'll tell Mary and she'll put you on a diet.'

Alister clasped his hand to his head in a melodramatic stance.

'Anything but that, Officer Harrison, please . . .'

'Well, you can take over the petty thefts in penance,' she told him and, grabbing her hat from the counter with a triumphant twirl, she announced, 'I've finished for the day now, so . . .'

His voice trailed after her as she shut the door.

'You owe me, Bridget Harrison, you owe me,' Alister called after her.

With the other two still on duty, the cottage was blissfully quiet and Bridget took the opportunity to do some washing. Looking down at the limited suds formed by the remains of the soap they had left, she swished them around, wishing she could pop her own worries as easily as her finger could pop the bubbles.

From the moment she'd left on the ferry for her training, Bridget had been determined to be the best policewoman in the force. Always a resolute child, she'd made sure she was the most conscientious trainee and got the highest marks in her examinations. Somehow, she always felt under pressure to prove herself and her confidence was as fragile as the tiny piece of soap in her hand. The needs of the internees were complex and the blank stares suggested background stories she was only beginning to understand. All efforts to help them seemed to be thwarted by rules and regulations and Bridget was struggling to juggle her professionalism with the compassion that tore at her heart.

Helga's case could drag on for months if she continued to refuse to plead guilty and with Sergeant Robinson watching her every move, Bridget was under pressure to find a way to shake the German woman's intransigence.

Then there were those Moore brothers.

She took out her frustration on the precious silk knickers she had saved up her rations for three months to buy and rubbed them fiercely between her fingers. Fynn had an unnerving ability to make her laugh at herself and then there was that kiss. When he pulled her towards him on their walk, she had felt a passion that had done more than surprise her, it had made her reel in shock.

And now, she thought, rubbing her lingerie against the side of the sink, *now, Kieran is back.*

A vision of Kieran Moore's boyish cheeks dimpling with mischief came into her mind, making her insides turn and forcing her to stop for a moment to grab the sides of the cold tub.

'Don't be ridiculous, Bridget Harrison,' she said crossly to herself and moved across to pass the clothes through the wooden mangle, 'you're no longer a child.'

Hmm, but neither's Kieran, she thought. The good-looking boy had hardly noticed she was a female when they were youngsters but, catching sight of herself in a small mirror on the wall, she couldn't help but wonder whether the grown-up Bridget might have more allure. It occurred to her that if Kieran Moore was attracted to her, it might provide a satisfying moment of revenge for all those nights when she had sobbed into her pillow.

She strung the washing out on the clothes horse next to the back door and turned round, almost tripping up on Greeba, who had emerged from under the table to look pathetically at her.

'No, Greeb, I've still got my shirts to do,' Bridget said, but the dog had already gone over to sit next to the lead.

'You're very demanding,' she told her pet, who looked crestfallen at her tone until a conciliatory tickle behind the ears prompted her to wag her tail with anticipation.

'Come on, then, I give in,' Bridget said, and putting the rest of the washing back in the basket, she headed out into the freezing cold February night, gasping as the cold air hit her. This was nothing like the stale air of London and she had to admit, was a welcome change from the taste of dust from burned-out houses that had pervaded the capital. For a brief moment she saw the Island as others did – as an oasis in the midst of a desert of chaos. Still, she couldn't dispel the suspicion she was hiding away from the war, while, as a policewoman, she should be in the thick of it all.

'You don't feel any guilt, do you, Greeb?' she called after the dog who was racing ahead of her, yelping with eagerness.

Once on Bradda Head, Greeba sniffed every smell as if she had never walked this way before and Bridget smiled at the way this dog embraced life with joy, in complete oblivion of the turmoil in her mistress's head. She sometimes wished she were a dog.

* * *

The cattle at the Moore farm at Glendown were shuffling in the cowshed, sensing the feeling of unsettled tension in the air. Fynn was noisily shovelling up the muck to put in the wheelbarrow in front of him. He was making a variety of exasperated noises that had nothing to do with the task in hand.

'What's up with you?' his sister, Kathleen, said from the doorway. She was leaning against the wooden doorframe with her arms folded. Older than Fynn by one year, she loved the Island with every fibre of her being and had never married, happy to live in the farmhouse with her parents. She was close to her brother but the continued sharp thumping of the metal on the flagstones suggested this taciturn man might not yet be ready to talk.

'Nothing,' Fynn replied, chucking the dirty-smelling fork load onto the wheelbarrow.

'Uh huh,' Kathleen said, smiling. 'Whatever you say.' And she turned to go but then Fynn called to her.

'I don't understand women,' he blurted out.

'No man does,' she agreed, and she slowed her pace out of the barn to see if he was going to say any more.

Fynn put down the fork, a sure sign that he was actually prepared to share his thoughts.

Kathleen turned around and waited.

'It's just that now Kieran's back . . .' he said simply, sitting down on a bale of hay with a thump.

Kathleen nodded. She understood the significance of that remark. Everyone had known about Bridget Harrison's crush on their younger brother who always jumped the highest, ran the fastest and got into the most trouble. Kieran was the only one who was unaware of her obsession, hardly acknowledging the little girl who trailed everywhere after him and his friends, but Kathleen had known for years how Fynn spent his time dreaming of the day Bridget would notice him instead. A loyal sister who had watched Fynn sacrifice his own happiness time and time again for the rest of the family, she'd been delighted when he'd practically skipped into their kitchen a couple of months ago to announce he was, finally, taking Bridget out on a date.

'But,' Kathleen protested, 'she's going out with you now.'

'Hmm,' he said, unconvinced. 'With the work here and all her duties, we hardly seem to have time to even meet and, in any case, how do I compete? You know Kieran and how he swans around looking like a film star . . . AND he's got the DFC for heaven's sake.'

Kathleen eyes took in the unglamorous barn floor covered in muck and she went and sat down glumly next to Fynn. He flicked some mud off his boots with his pitchfork and she put her arms around him. They barely managed to encompass his strong body, but to her, he was still the little brother who had cried himself to sleep because the girl he loved didn't love him back.

Fynn extricated himself from her grasp and gave her a rueful smile.

'And do you know what, Kath? I'm my own worst enemy. I've actually asked him to join us tonight for a drink.'

She couldn't help it, she burst out laughing.

'Oh Fynn,' she said, 'what am I going to do with you?'

He looked so forlorn, she regretted her levity and tried to think of something positive to say. She'd been watching Kieran since his return and had been troubled by the deep sadness in his eyes. She decided to concentrate on one brother at a time.

'Well, you know what Kieran's like, he loves 'em and leaves 'em and you'll at least see how she reacts when she sees him . . .' she tailed off.

'Exactly,' Fynn said and picked up the fork to pierce it meaningfully into the dirty mass on the floor.

She turned away, leaving Fynn shovelling muck into the wheelbarrow with far more force than the task warranted.

It had been Bridget's outburst on their walk that had made Fynn acknowledge his own resentment about having to take over the farm. Watching her eyes flash like an animal who'd escaped only to be recaptured, he'd recognised the feelings he'd experienced but suppressed. Bridget was too busy venting her indignation to notice that Fynn was nodding in understanding. He, too, sometimes felt a prison didn't need walls; a sea on all sides was enough.

Since then, he'd spent every day trying to rationalise the logic behind the fact that the war was going on without him and that while his brother and all his friends were off fighting for their country, his battles involved mud, muck and feed shortages but, like his love for Bridget, any confessions were buried deep beneath the brown overalls he wore for work every day.

Exhausted by his anger, he pushed the wheelbarrow towards the door.

* * *

It was past eight o'clock when Kieran arrived at the Falcon's Nest. Fynn had taken the old Land Rover, picking up some feed on the way but Kieran insisted on walking, saying he needed the exercise. His brother resisted the temptation to suggest that if he'd spent the day on the farm helping him, he wouldn't need it.

Kieran's progress had been delayed by the number of people who wanted to shake the hand of this famous man. But too many of them recoiled when they saw the misshapen fingers and Kieran now shuffled into the bar, feeling defeated, once again, by his deformity. He stood by the entrance, peering over the crowd of locals until he spotted Fynn's imposing figure at the end of the bar. For so many years, Kieran had looked up to his older brother, wondering how on earth Fynn managed to always do everything right when danger, disaster and disobedience beckoned Kieran like a siren. The moment that the DFC had been pinned on him, Kieran's first thought had been that, finally, his brother would be proud of him but when he saw the tall figure towering over the heads of the crowd in the room, he felt that familiar feeling of failure and almost turned and walked out of the bar. It was too late, however; Fynn had spotted him and called him over. Sitting in the corner behind his brother were three women, all in police uniform. One was a tall girl with blonde, short hair who was holding out her hand to take the half pint of beer offered by Fynn. She was laughing with her friend, a pretty girl, who looked as if she would prefer to be anywhere except in a bar surrounded by disapproving men. The third, sitting quietly to one side was Bridget Harrison. He hadn't seen her for years and almost didn't recognise her. Her pigtails had turned into long, wavy, dark brown curls that reflected in the light of the lamp above the bar and she had a neat figure that was certainly nothing like the scrawny kid with knobbly knees he remembered. He made his way over to them. The girl with short hair looked him up and down critically.

'Hmm, a bit weedy, but not bad I suppose,' she said.

Kieran looked shocked for a moment but then burst out laughing. It was the first time he'd remembered his sense of humour since he stepped foot off the gangway at Douglas.

'I'm glad I meet the lady's approval, well almost,' he said with a weak chuckle, pulling up a stool. 'Hello, Bridget, how are you? It's good to see you.'

Bridget muttered something into her drink. She was suddenly nervous. Fynn glanced suspiciously at her; he'd been on edge all day and as he watched her twiddle her glass of port and lemon in her hand, he felt a sinking feeling in the pit of his stomach.

While Fynn introduced Kieran to Molly and Betty, Bridget looked out of the corner of her eye at the boy who had turned into a man. She tried to remind herself that she'd painfully and determinedly got over her crush on Kieran Moore, but it was hard to be dispassionate when his fringe tipped over one side of his face covering his deep brown eyes. She shook herself and turned to Fynn to find he was watching her with similar intensity and she smiled, almost apologetically, at him.

Molly was taking over the conversation and was busy grilling Kieran about his flying, his reasons for coming back and then, suddenly, she broached the subject that everyone else was trying to avoid.

'So, let's see your hand then,' she said, grabbing his wrist. He recoiled for a second and then shrugged. He needed to get this over with, so he jerkily pulled his right hand out of his pocket and laid it on the table in front of them all. He looked up, challenging them all to react. Bridget took a sharp intake of breath; the skin was partially shrivelled and it was a dark purple colour, two of Kieran's fingers were bent over and the white patches where the skin grafts had been inserted were ghostly against the deep colours of the rest of the hand. Betty looked embarrassed, a reaction Kieran had seen so often in his peers, but Molly grabbed hold of it and examined it with an expert eye.

'Hmm, saline should have worked better than this. Bit of a rubbish job, I'd say. Did you go to Sir Archibald McIndoe? Are you in his "guinea pig" club?' She didn't stop for his answers, but the others looked impressed.

'How do you know about all that?' Betty asked in awe.

'Oh, my cousin, Alan, was on the *Dundee*. He was burned when it was torpedoed. Lucky to be alive to be honest but badly burned. He went to McIndoe for some of those new cosmetic surgery techniques. You were lucky it was just your hand, Kieran, at least your good looks are still intact,' she laughed.

And with that, she turned to Fynn and said, 'I think we need another round here.' Kieran pushed forward his glass far too quickly.

Molly's matter-of-fact attitude dispelled the tense atmosphere and after that, the little group started to relax. Kieran, in particular, was drinking more and faster than the others and it didn't take long for the barman to have to ask them to quieten down as they were disturbing Arthur, who was trying to have a peaceful pint in the corner. Bridget was surprised at how easy it was to slip back into an easy banter with Kieran and failed to notice how Fynn slid his arm around her in a proprietary fashion. He wanted to make sure there was no mistake about their relationship but, looking glumly at the heads bent in together in front of him, he was disappointed to realise no one was watching.

Molly was certainly too busy leaning forward, demanding Kieran's full attention.

'So what heroic acts are you going to carry out here, then?' she asked him. 'You know we don't get much war action here as Bridget will tell you – every flaming minute of the day if you let her,' she added, making a face at her friend. 'To be honest, the last excitement we had was when a German bomb was dropped near Eary Cushlin.

That killed a frog,' she added gravely and crossed herself dramatically.

'I heard about that,' Kieran said, feeling more light-hearted with two pints in him. 'I also heard that none of the Manx people are frightened now, but that all the frogs are!'

'What are you going to do, though, Kieran?' Bridget asked more seriously.

'I'm to be stationed at Jurby,' he said vaguely, unable to breach the secrecy surrounding the pilots' training centre, 'but I won't be allowed up in a plane.' To still be in uniform and not allowed to fly was something he was dreading.

Bridget couldn't help it, she reached over and placed her hand over his damaged one. Fynn tensed and drew back, a move that only Molly spotted.

* * *

It was on their way home that Molly challenged Bridget.

'OK, spill the beans, what's the history with you and the good-looking Kieran?'

'There isn't one,' Bridget replied with a hint of regret in her voice.

'Ah, but you wanted one, didn't you, Bridg?'

She shrugged her shoulders.

'He was just a schoolgirl crush, that's all. I was a child to him. He only saw me as the pesky little sister of my brothers.'

Then she slowed down and in the anonymity of the darkness of the blackout, added, 'Still, you are right, Moll, I was obsessed with him.' She paused, took a breath and went on, 'But, now we're adults and it's a very different situation these days.'

'Hmm,' Molly replied.

Chapter Nine

Kieran Moore reported for duty at RAF Jurby, arriving at the entrance with his kitbag on his shoulder. A guard with a clipboard saluted and asked his name.

He coughed and said loudly, 'Squadron Leader Kieran Moore.'

The guard checked his list.

'Ah, yes, Sir, welcome to Jurby, we've been expecting you. Follow me if you would.' And with that, he marched off towards some buildings in the distance. The camp to train pilots was spread out across a large flat piece of land in the north of the Island and the regular sight of planes dipping and diving left little doubt of its true purpose. The guard showed him into a low, Nissen hut and led him to a bed at the end, partitioned off by a curtain.

'Your quarters, Sir. Supper is at six o'clock in the dining room over there.' And he pointed through the window at a building on the other side of the accommodation huts.

Kieran automatically unpacked his kit, putting everything in the right order at the end of the bunk. He then leaned down to put his shoes neatly under the bed when he heard footsteps behind him.

'You Moore?' a voice said.

He stood up to see an airman in an impeccable uniform of equal rank peering down at him. Kieran Moore was almost six foot tall but the man in front of him stood a head and shoulders above him. Kieran looked up like a schoolboy at a prefect.

'Heard you're a DFC,' the man said dismissively, 'well, it won't do you any favours here. We've got far too many recruits here all thinking they're flying aces. Listening to tales by fellows like you only leads them to try stunts they won't come out of. Anyway, get yourself over to the Briefing Room in ten and you'll meet the rest of the chaps.'

And with that, he marched smartly back down the hut between the neat beds.

'Hmm, welcome to Jurby,' Kieran muttered. 'Nice to meet you too.'

The session was already in progress when Kieran found the right room, so he crept into the back and quietly listened while the officer in charge outlined a timetable of lessons that made Kieran inwardly groan. How to get in and out of the aircraft was going to take the sprogs more time than learning how to kill the enemy, he thought, lowering his head to make notes with his left hand and cursing the scrawl that was the result of his efforts. The rest of the men were older than he was, many were veteran flyers who, he suspected, welcomed the chance to stay safely on the ground in a classroom but they all peered back curiously at the new arrival. The talk in the Officers' Mess that week had been of this flying ace coming into their midst and most of them weren't sure whether he was going to be an asset or a hindrance.

Kieran was unaware of all the hidden tensions in the room; his only goal was to hide his damaged hand so that no one would see it.

At the end of the briefing, he stood by the doorway, uncertain what to do next, when two instructors came up to him. They were only a few years older than him and greeted him with a smile.

'Believe you're a friend of Aedan Harrison' one said. Kieran nodded, relieved to see a couple of friendly faces.

'He told us to look out for you. Said you'd be coming. Time for a drink?'

'Oh yes,' Kieran said with relief. A drink was exactly what he needed.

*　　*　　*

Bridget's regular trips to Douglas always left her irritated and with more questions than answers. Helga seemed resigned to her fate and made no effort to talk to either the advocate dealing with her case or Bridget. The propaganda leaflets provided by the British Government were left in the corner, untouched, and Helga constantly repeated that she supported Hitler and that was all anyone needed to know.

At the end of her tether, it was a frustrated Bridget who voiced her feelings on the girls back at the police station.

'It's enough to make you give up trying,' she told them. 'Even telling her how much Karin's missing her doesn't seem to work. I've checked her file and that tells me so little, I don't know where to begin to get through to her but there's just something that doesn't seem quite right. I can't put my finger on it.'

She pursed her mouth in frustration.

'Maybe I'll start with some of these Nazis. There's one called Lena Braun, who seems to be having a lot to say and she and Helga were thick as thieves when Helga first arrived but then, just before the attempted stabbing, Ruth said she'd heard them arguing. Lena's well-known for intimidating some of the Jewish women in particular, and I suspect she's behind the goose-stepping outside Jewish accommodation we've been hearing about.'

'Are you going to mention your suspicions to the sergeant?' Betty asked.

Bridget paused, spooning the tea leaves into the pot. 'No, I don't think so; after all, I've nothing to tell ... yet ... but I might go and have a little chat with Lena Braun. Now, shall we have some of my mum's biscuits? She baked them specially for us. You know she thinks we never have time to eat?'

'She's right,' Molly replied, looking at her watch. She was due to pick some women up from the farm The Howe in half an hour, where internees with a rural background had been welcomed with open arms. 'I'll have to eat mine on the way, but good old Mrs Harrison,' she laughed, grabbing a piece of cake out of Bridget's hand and heading for the door. 'See you later. By the way, when are we going out again with those men, Bridg? That Kieran was quite good fun.'

Bridget yelled after her, 'No idea, he's off to Jurby soon. You'll have to be patient.'

She automatically stirred the teapot, watching the leaves swirl like the thoughts in her head. Since the boy from her childhood fantasies had reappeared, she'd found herself questioning her burgeoning relationship with Fynn but when she tried to concentrate on his kiss, she was horrified to find it was Kieran's lips she was imagining. It took her back to when, as a young girl, she'd pressed her own lips against the bedroom mirror or kissed the back of her hand to try to conjure up the moment when Kieran would be hers. She poured the tea roughly into the cream china cups, spilling it all over the wooden work surface.

* * *

'Post's here!' Molly called from the front door. Betty raced down the hallway as always, desperate for a letter but

Molly sadly shook her head, hanging onto one envelope and passing the other to Bridget, leaving a dejected Betty to walk slowly back to the kitchen.

Molly followed her and said, as reassuringly as she could, 'There'll be something soon, I'm sure there will. I know it's been ages but, Bet, you know how slow the post is from Africa. After all,' Molly told her, trying to lighten the tone, 'first they have to find a passing camel, then they have to send it back across the desert . . .' She tailed off; Betty had already gone out of the back door towards the privy where both girls knew she would cry for at least ten minutes.

'I could shake Joe,' Molly said fiercely. 'Doesn't he know what this is doing to her?'

'I don't hear from my brothers and they're only in Lincolnshire,' Bridget replied flatly.

'Yes, but your brothers aren't in love with you,' Molly said thoughtfully, then added, 'Actually, maybe I should meet them.' She waved her letter in the air. 'My sister, Gloria keeps telling me I'm too picky. I can't seem to find a man who sets me on fire.' She smiled and shrugged: 'And here we are with so much choice . . . I mean with pin-ups like Alister Cubbon, you'd think a girl would be spoilt for choice.'

Bridget threw a cushion at her and they both giggled but then stopped abruptly when they heard the back door open.

'Well, that's it, I'm not going to pine away,' Betty said from the doorway, wiping her eyes fiercely with her sleeve. 'Joe's doing what he can over there and the least I can do is be strong for him. He'll write when he gets the chance, I know he will.'

She looked at them both for confirmation.

'Of course he will, Betty,' Bridget said 'I'm sure he's told all his mates about his gorgeous wife back home and how proud he is of her becoming a policewoman.'

'Well, yes, he did say in his last letter that they were all impressed,' Betty said brightly, perking up a little. 'Most of their wives work in munitions. Anyway, who's your letter from Bridget?'

Distracted by Betty's plight, Bridget realised she hadn't looked. She curled up in the tapestry armchair and glanced down at the writing on the envelope.

'Oh, it's from Nancy! Nancy Gorry! You know, the Ramsey girl I became friends with when we moved to London? Oh, that's lovely; it's been ages since I heard from her. I was beginning to worry something had happened.'

The other two girls were looking up with understanding. No one was safe in this war.

'Oh, well, that's great. You two'd love her, she's such good fun. I saw lots of her when I was there and she just gobbles life up like it's a huge ice cream.'

Betty leaned forward. She loved hearing about Bridget's exciting life in London. Molly looked sceptical.

'How did you meet her?' Betty asked, settling down for a detailed story.

'On the ferry to Liverpool. She went to Roedean boarding school and I was at Douglas High so we'd never met. She was far too posh for me and anyway, I know Molly won't believe me, but we don't all know each other on this Island!'

Molly gave a casual wave of her hand and went back to reading her newspaper.

'Anyway, there I was, heading over for my training,' Bridget went on. 'I was having a wonderful time breathing in all that freedom when an old couple, who must have been at least fifty, decided, as a girl alone, I needed to be invited to join them for their picnic tea. They had a lace cloth and silver teapot and everything – all laid out on a lifeboat and I just saw my life being folded up in that cloth,' she laughed.

'Go on,' Betty prompted.

'Yes, well, then this stranger dressed in a fabulous red suit with a scarf over her dark curls just came up and tapped me on the shoulder,' she told Betty – noting that Molly didn't seem interested. 'She must have seen the panic on my face so pretended to know me and whisked me away. That saved me. I was unbelievably grateful. Then we found out we were both going to be in London; she worked for the BBC as something important in telephony,' she finished proudly.

Betty's face lit up. She was an avid listener to the Home Service and anyone who had touched the hallowed halls of the BBC was akin to royalty as far as she was concerned.

There was a pause and then Bridget said, 'It's been months. She went to join the WAAFs and then I was transferred over here, but she hasn't replied to my letters in ages.

'It's so unfair,' Bridget said with a pout 'I was having a great time in London before I was clapped in irons over here.'

'What do you mean?' Molly put in, glad for an excuse to change the subject from the glamorous Nancy 'This place is paradise. I mean, look at this kitchen.' And with that she dramatically waved a pair of wet stockings about her face.

Bridget and Betty reluctantly started to laugh.

'That's better,' Molly said with a triumphant grin. 'I'm going to make the most of every minute over here and I don't want two wet weeks spoiling my fun. Now where's that Spam? I'm starving.'

Molly had been an independent child who scampered around the boatyards near Limehouse Basin in London with her sister, Gloria and a little gang of lads who lived on the boats nearby. The boys saw the girls not as females, but as fellow gang members and Molly certainly never needed any of the fripperies that seemed to absorb the other girls. Their parents, far too busy delivering goods around the canals of London, hardly noticed what time their wayward daughters came in, which gave the girls almost total freedom. As soon as she met Bridget, Molly had been excited to meet another free spirit, but every time she sat next to the girl with sparkling eyes, she was left with an unnerving feeling that she didn't want to understand and a sharp pain had hit her in the stomach when she heard Bridget enthuse about Nancy. She banged open the cupboard door to search for the Spam.

Bridget was fingering the envelope in her pocket as if the touch could bring her closer to her previous life in the capital. Nancy's glamorous life had always left her feeling inadequate and now she was back on the Island, that feeling was even more acute. Any hopes of reading it were dispelled by Molly's insistence that it was her turn to peel the potatoes, so she jumped up, leaving all thoughts of Nancy until after tea.

* * *

Settling herself onto her bed, Bridget ripped open the envelope, eager for news from her dear friend. Two Manx girls far from home, they'd immediately set about exploring the capital's nightlife, meeting up regularly to swap their experiences of their new jobs. Bridget would recount stories about the rigours of her training while Nancy listed the well-known names she had spotted in the foyer of Broadcasting House. They'd felt on top of the world and even the outbreak of war and the subsequent devastation of the Blitz had failed to quell their enthusiasm for life in the big city. It seemed like another world and Bridget let out a deep sigh of frustration at having been forced to leave it – and Nancy – behind but then she read the letter.

Dear Bridget,

I'm sorry I haven't been in touch but oh, I have so much to tell you. Bridget, my flat was bombed! I thought they'd finished with us after the Blitz but I was on a three-day pass back to the flat in London in the middle of my training when there was an air raid and the whole street was hit! Eight people were killed, including the lovely elderly couple next door – you remember them? It was just so horrible, I couldn't stop shaking for days. There was hardly anything left of any of the houses and, I still can't believe it – I'd only left the house ten minutes before the air raid sounded! I'd just popped to what's left of Selfridges to pick up some elastic for my bloomers and managed to get to the underground when the sirens went off. I heard the explosion – which was so loud and terrifying – but it never occurred to me it was my street that was being hit. I got back to nothing but rubble and was just so shocked but also, just think, Bridg, I could have been there. I've never been more grateful to those dreadful WAAF bloomers!

After that your letters never reached me and now we know why. They must have been sitting in a pigeon-hole somewhere until some poor clerk managed to track me down to send them on. I finally got a pile of them yesterday and was so pleased to hear all your news. I really envy you being back on the Island. I so wish I was there. You know my father lost far more money than we ever knew during The Great Depression and they're having to sell our lovely family home in Ramsey to move to a much smaller house in Castletown but his health is poor and Mother could really do with my help. I'm in Compton Bassett at the moment, finishing off my training and although I've put in a request for compassionate leave to come home, I've got no idea where they'll send me next. I certainly don't want to go back to London, it's so awful there. Mother was moaning about you all having to queue to show passes to get through the barbed wire of the camps but it seems like heaven to me. In London, when I left, the queues were so long to get even a bit of scrag-end and everyone's so dispirited. I keep dreaming about the Island where at least there's some fresh farm stuff! I bet you're not appreciating it though, you were so bad-tempered about being sent back!

Oh, must go, more aircraft insignia to learn about. I'll write soon. I've really missed you,
Lots of love
Nancy. Xxx

Bridget's eyes scanned the letter in disbelief. So much had happened to her friend and she'd known nothing about it. Reading it over again, Bridget sat back on her pillow. Nancy had always been like a film star to her with far more money and a house in Ramsey that sounded like a mansion but now there was a wistful tone to the letter that was totally unlike the lively Nancy she knew.

Bridget folded up the letter carefully and headed down the stairs. She experienced a pang of guilt about Londoners having so few supplies, knowing there were fresh kippers for tea, but it was Nancy's longing to be back on the Isle of Man that concerned her the most.

Chapter Ten

Twice a week there was an option for the women to be escorted between the two coastlines of the camp and, on a day when Lena Braun put her name down to go to Port St Mary, Bridget seized the opportunity and volunteered to lead the group in an effort to find out more about Helga's former Nazi ally. Once there, she followed her to Cowley's Corner Café, a favourite meeting place for Nazis, where there was already a little group at the table in the corner. They stopped talking as she walked in to stare aggressively at her.

'I want to talk to Lena,' Bridget said, feeling her skin prickle. These women really did strike fear into anyone who opposed their views and Bridget suddenly had a huge sympathy for young Jews like Ursula. She coughed and pulled her shoulders back – after all, she was the authority around here, not these women.

Lena looked up, her head held high.

'*Ja?*' she said.

'I said I want to talk to you,' Bridget said in a voice that sounded very loud, even to her. 'Outside.'

'*Ich verstehe nicht.*'

Bridget drew a sharp breath. Of course this woman understood her. She was just being as difficult as she could be but without an interpreter, there was nothing the policewoman could do.

'I will come back, with an interpreter, and you will talk to me,' and with that, Bridget turned on her heel and walked out of the café with as much dignity as she could muster, hearing muffled laughter behind her.

'Where have you been, Bridget?' Sergeant Robinson fired at her as she walked in the door of the police station.

'I was on the Port St Mary run and just popped into Cowley's to check on the Nazis, Sarge,' Bridget said.

'Were they there?' the sergeant asked her.

'Yes, just a group of them, you know, the usual suspects. Just wanted to check up on them and make sure they weren't causing any trouble.'

'Well, you know you'll need an interpreter to get any sense out of any of them. They won't admit they speak English,' Maureen Robinson told her, not seeing Bridget raise her eyes to heaven. She hated hearing the obvious and especially from her superior.

'Yes, well, it was just as I was passing but I'll remember that for future, thanks.'

'Well, make sure you do, we haven't got time for you to be making social visits and you were supposed to be staying on the front to watch for anyone not obeying the rules.

We've had far too much fraternising going on between the locals and the internees,' the sergeant went on. She was aware of Bridget's frustration at the mundane tasks but with so much day-to-day work to be accomplished at Rushen Camp, the sergeant did not need an aspiring Sherlock Holmes on her staff, so she added crushingly, 'But now you're back, you may as well make a brew. I'm parched. This paperwork is never-ending.'

All the bubbling excitement of being on the trail of something vaguely interesting evaporated with the steam that came out of the urn and Bridget resignedly got out the tea caddy and the pot. She had been in the police force for nearly four years and there was no doubt about it, her skills as a teamaker were second to none.

Despite her irritation, a tingling in Bridget's body reminded her of a conversation she'd had with Alister in her first few weeks back on the Island. He had explained that being a real police officer started as a wriggling worm in the pit of the stomach that would rise into the throat to make you short of breath.

'It's called intuition, and it's what makes the best police officers,' he had said with a satisfied smile.

Bridget felt that worm squirming around inside her, prompting niggling doubts. For some reason, she felt Helga was hiding something and then wondered whether Lena Braun knew what it was, but without any evidence that something strange was going on, the sergeant was not going to give her any time to dig deeper. So, with some resignation, when she took the tray out to the front desk, she asked, 'Would it be all right if I went to Douglas soon, Sarge? I think I need to check in on Helga.'

Helga's case was at a standstill as she wasn't co-operating with her defence advocate at all, stubbornly refusing to say what she was going to plead, but Helga didn't seem to care.

'Well, yes, if you think you can get her to admit,' Sergeant Robinson said. 'But go on your half-day next week and then if you're late back, it won't matter.'

Time off was a debatable privilege in any case, so Bridget agreed without argument.

In the meantime, she had a petty theft of a hairbrush, an argument between two landladies who felt the other was being paid more and a distraught Austrian mother of a poorly child to deal with. Her intuition was going to have to wait.

* * *

'Hello, you,' she said, shyly, bumping into Fynn one day near the lifeboat station. It had been a couple of weeks since she had seen him, and their last date had hardly been a huge success. The film, *Her Cardboard Lover* had featured a plot about a couple and an old boyfriend and although she had been unaware that Fynn was squirming in his seat at the storyline which was too close to the thoughts that were going through his head, as they had emerged into the cold night, he'd used the excuse of having to go and see to a sick cow, but Bridget feared he simply needed to escape her company and was left feeling bewildered and hurt. The more time she spent with Fynn, the more intrigued she was becoming and to a police-woman, mystery was irresistible.

Now, Fynn recoiled at her greeting, and Bridget looked into his eyes with a frown. It was as if a wall had come up between them, leaving her at a complete loss as to what to say next.

Fynn's face might have given nothing away, but his mind and body were taut with tension; he was obsessed with this girl, but he'd seen how she had longed for his brother's touch in the pub when she reached for his hand, leading him to conclude that a farmhand had no chance against a glamorous flying hero. Fynn's shoulders slumped and the proximity of her lovely face made him step back from her more abruptly than he had intended.

There was an embarrassed silence and then Fynn finally spoke.

'It's been really busy on the farm. We're under pressure to do twice as much work in half the time, you know.'

Bridget had no choice but to nod.

'Apparently,' he went on, sarcasm creeping into his voice, '. . . we're supposed to be meeting up, aren't we?

On Kieran's next weekend pass. As you know, when my brother calls, we all jump.'

'That would be lovely, Fynn,' she replied with a genuine smile, ignoring the barbed comment. 'I'd really like that. It's been a while since you and I have been out.'

Fynn couldn't stop himself before he retorted, 'Yes, well, that's if Kieran lets any of us get a word in ... or,' he added quietly, 'if you listen to anything anyone else says.'

Bridget would spend the next three days wishing she had thought of something reassuring to say at that moment but, in fact, she was so taken aback at the accusation that all she did was mutter a non-committal 'Hmmmm.'

'Anyway, got to go, milking awaits,' Fynn said with a false breeziness. 'See you soon, Bridget.'

She watched him go with a sinking feeling in her stomach and quietly cursed the long-lost brother, Squadron Leader Kieran Moore, to hell.

* * *

The meeting with Sergeant Robinson didn't improve Bridget's mood. The relentless questioning about when she was going to get Helga to admit her guilt had used up all her excuses and she headed off with a determined pout to The Imperial Hotel to find Karin. She knew Ursula was struggling to get Karin to engage in any of the activities that Ruth suggested and, instead, was sitting for hours on end playing with her peg doll but, today, Bridget had an idea that might soften Helga's resolve.

'Ursula,' Bridget called across when she spotted her, 'do you think Karin would like to make a drawing for her mother? Do you think it would help?'

The girl's eyes lit up. 'Yes, of course, that's a good idea. But I have no paper. . . .'

Bridget handed over some card and crayons she had brought with her in her handbag.

'Here, use this and she can keep the crayons.'

Ursula almost skipped off back into the dining room to find Karin who was sitting on her own in a corner, clutching her doll to her chest. Struggling to remember the warm cuddles her mother used to give her, Karin was blaming herself, believing that her own dislike of that Hitler man meant her *Mütti* didn't want to be with her, but at Ursula's suggestion, her eyes brightened. This might be her chance to let her mother know she still loved her, so she grabbed the crayons and paper, went over to the table and started to draw a picture of a house with a large sun in the corner. The house had two windows and a door to one side. Karin drew a fence and to one side she started to sketch out a tree. But then her entire body language changed and her face screwed up into a fierce frown. Karin took hold of the black crayon and scribbled furiously at the tree, obliterating it from the picture. Bridget was on her way to the kitchens but stopped and looked over the child's shoulder, intending to praise her.

'That's a lovely house, Karin . . . but why have you got rid of the tree?'

Karin looked up in terror and said simply, 'The man . . .'

Bridget sat down next to her and gently asked, 'What man?'

'His feet, they were in the air . . . that was when we had to leave.'

She couldn't say any more and Bridget looked into the child's wide eyes. They should have been bright but today they seemed like a deep, black pool where indescribable horrors lurked. Bridget felt completely out of her depth and looked around the room for Ruth, who was talking to Ursula next to the kitchen. A woman who had worked with desperate refugees in Manchester before volunteering to help on the Isle of Man, she exuded calm experience, which was exactly what Bridget needed now.

'Ruth, have you got a minute?' she called over, her voice quivering. Both she and Ursula came over to look at the scribbled-out drawing. Ruth widened her eyes but sat down to smile reassuringly at the child before she began to speak.

'Officer Harrison, pass me that spare piece of paper, I think Karin needs a new piece,' and she sat next to Karin to encourage her to draw a new picture. With that, Bridget casually picked up the first drawing and slipped it in her pocket, jerking her head meaningfully to Ursula.

Once out of earshot, she whispered, 'Do you know what that's all about?'

There was a slow nod of Ursula's head. 'The little one has had nightmares about this. I think someone was hung on that tree.'

'Do you know any more?' Bridget asked.

'Not really, but in the middle of the night she talks about her neighbour, I think. He was kind to her apparently and gave her cherries off his tree. But something happened and Karin said they had to suddenly leave and travel to England. She was only tiny but I think she's haunted by whatever she saw – I think it was that man, that neighbour.'

They all glanced back at the hunched figure of the little girl who was now drawing a picture of a flower, encouraged by Ruth.

'I'll look into this,' Bridget said, 'but let me know if she says anything else.'

'I've got an idea,' Ruth said, coming over to join them, 'one of the kitchen cats had kittens, that'll cheer her up.'

But when the little black kitten was presented to Karin, she screamed and ran to hide behind an old armchair.

'I want *meine Mutti*, I want *meine Mutti*,' Karin kept repeating in a muffled voice. 'This place is very bad, I don't like it, there are . . .' she sometimes struggled between the native language her mother spoke to her and the

English that she had heard from everyone around her, 'monsters . . .' she finished triumphantly.

Ruth peered around the chair and held out her hand.

'There are no monsters here, poppet, what makes you think that?'

Karin slowly emerged from the chair and looked up, wiping her tear-stained face with the back of her sleeve. A look of terror shadowed her face.

'There are . . . there are all those "Little People", who hide at the side of the road waiting to attack you if you don't say hello to them,' she said, 'and now, there are . . . animals like this . . . that . . .'

And with that, she pointed at the kitten and started to cry again.

Bridget and Ruth were perplexed until Ursula pointed to the animal's rear end.

'There is no tail,' she said, surprised.

Laughing, Bridget explained that Manx cats did not have tails and that they were very special to the Island.

'*Nein, nein,* it is a *Dämon*, yes?' Karin spluttered. 'And it will come and get me in the middle of the night.'

'Not at all, why would you think that?'

'Mama said that if I told people I did not like Herr Hitler then bad things would happen to me.'

In a quiet, reassuring voice, Ruth said, 'It's not a demon, it's a little pussy cat and see, it wants to be friends with you.'

Still not convinced, Karin stood back as Ruth put the animal on the floor but then suddenly giggled in delight.

'It has no tail, look, it has no tail!' And with that, she skipped around to examine the kitten that was spreading itself out on and floor and rolling over, waiting to have its tummy tickled.

She giggled again.

'I will call it Hitler,' Karin announced, 'and then, if I have his cat, he won't let anyone hurt me.'

Her words chilled both Bridget and Ruth who were beginning to wonder how they were ever going to chase away this child's own demons.

'How about the name of a powerful fairy from here instead? After all, you are on her island and she will most certainly protect you. What about Dana?' Bridget suggested kindly.

'Dana,' the child said slowly. 'Yes, that is a good name!' And she skipped off with the little kitten in her arms while Ursula hovered nearby, ready to fight off anything or anybody that might hurt the child in her care.

*   *   *

That night, hugging the little girl to her, Ursula quietly hummed *Schlaf, Kindlein, schlaf*, the lullaby her mother had sung to her. She had no idea what time of the night it was, but the whimpering noises from the little body next to her had woken her up. Looking anxiously across at Ira, their snoring room mate, she gathered the child quietly into her arms. She couldn't remember all the words to the song, but the tune was there, somewhere in the depths of her memory. It made her think of her own brother and sister and she felt her throat start to constrict with that familiar, overwhelming sense of loss.

It was only once she felt the calmer breathing of Karin next to her that she allowed hot tears to fall on the rough pillow under both their heads. The promises by the authorities that families would one day be reunited did nothing to reassure her as, without any news, she had no means of finding her brother and sister or even knowing if they were alive. The hopelessness of it all made her bury her face in the curls of the sleeping Karin and gently sob until exhaustion finally allowed her to sleep.

Chapter Eleven

On her next visit to Helga, her head cleared by a cold March wind, Bridget decided to tackle the subject head on. 'When did you come to England, Helga?'

'At the beginning of the war.'

'And what happened with the tree in front of your house, Helga, to make you leave?'

Helga stiffened and her mouth set in a thin line then she shrugged casually.

'Nothing, why?'

'Because something is haunting your little girl.'

Bridget scanned the woman's face but there was an inscrutability about it that was well-practised, and it was hard to see beyond the bland expression.

Bridget delved into her bag.

'She made you this card,' she said, handing over the drawing of the flower.

Immediately, Helga's face softened and she stroked the card gently, seeing the scrawl that was supposed to be her daughter's signature.

'But she also drew this,' Bridget said, handing over the picture of the house and the blackened-out tree and watching for Helga's reaction. 'What's it all about?'

There was a sharp intake of breath.

'That is not for you to know,' Helga said aggressively. 'It is not, how you say, your business.'

'Anything that affects the welfare of that child is my business.' Bridget could feel herself getting cross. 'For God's sake, Helga, she's a little girl and she's having nightmares. How can we help her if you don't help us?'

But Helga folded her arms and turned her head away.

In exasperation, Bridget stood up to leave but as she was going out of the door, Helga said quietly from behind her:

'I will plead the guilty.'

* * *

Bridget couldn't help the triumphant tone in her voice when she casually mentioned to Sergeant Robinson that Helga had finally agreed to admit her crime and grinned as Alister put his thumbs up to her behind the sergeant's back.

'Oh, at last,' Sergeant Robinson said, reaching down under the high desk for a pen. 'About time too. Right, Bridget, you'd better let the advocate know.' And with that she marched out of the office.

'Oh, your face,' Alister Cubbon laughed, 'it's a picture. But come on, Bridget, what did you expect? That she'd run over and give you a hug?'

Bridget looked crestfallen. 'Nope, but a "well done" would have gone down nicely; it's taken weeks to get that woman to drop her defence. And I had to involve a little child to achieve it.'

Bridget had been feeling increasingly uncomfortable about what memories she had stirred in Karin to get her result, and she leaned on the counter to explain to the kindly sergeant why she felt the admission of guilt may have come at a high price.

Alister listened intently. His large frame was perched on the high wooden stool that he kept behind the desk to ease his aching legs and he tilted his head to one side, considering her words.

'Hmm, well, I think the earlier that child faces her fears the better. It'll not do her any good to bottle them up and there's plenty of people here who'll be able to help her. Starting with you, young Bridget Harrison.'

'*Me*? What can I do?'

'Well, you told me you've got two theories. One is that Helga may be hiding something and the second is that Lena might know what it is, so why don't you go and be a policewoman and find out? Then maybe you'll be able to help little Karin deal with it. As soon as you can, go and find that Braun woman again; I think she's your clue.

Didn't you hear something about her drawing threatening messages on mirrors in the bathroom? That could be your starting point.'

Bridget pondered for a minute.

'Yes,' she said, 'you're right. One of the Jewish women told me that when the mirror steamed up, there was a swastika that appeared on it and that Lena had just come out. That's brilliant, Alister. I can start off by challenging her with that. It'll have to be on my day off though; the sarge won't allow me to take time off from everything else just on a hunch.'

Alister agreed and then said with a grin, 'Anyway, onto more important things in life, are there any of your mum's biscuits with tea today?'

* * *

When Bridget arrived home, a letter was waiting for her; it was from Nancy.

Dear Bridget,

How are you? And that beautiful island of ours? I must have sounded really glum in my last letter but it really has been a bad time, what with the bombing and then you know Father's heart isn't good? I'm not sure the move from Ramsey helped. Although they love being near Castletown, he shouldn't have lifted all those boxes himself, I think he's done more damage. Mother's really struggling to cope with him and you can imagine how guilty I feel being over here.

Anyway, how's the job going? I'm sure you're not telling me the whole of it because you're not moaning nearly as much as I expected. I think the petty squabbles are a front for a thriving underground that's keeping that little brain of yours fully occupied – I know what you're like, you'll find a major crime network at Collinson's Café! I really long to have a good gossip with you, I've missed you so much.

The training's been great but I've found it hard to concentrate after all that happened in London. I can't believe I'm going to be a fully qualified WAAF telephone operator though! And I love my uniform, I finally feel I can hold my head up high and prove I'm doing my bit for the war. It's going on too long though, isn't it? Those poor people in the Far East and also Malta are still really suffering, aren't they? My cousin's a nurse in Malta and oh, Bridg, we're so frightened for her, It sounds horrendous. I think the whole island is almost at starvation point. My aunt is beside herself with worry. I'm so fed up with it. I just want our lives back! But every time you moan, all everyone says is 'Don't you know there's a war on?' No sympathy there then!

Oh, got to go, it's Domestic Night; I've got to find some of those free sanitary towels to polish the floor! I never

knew such mundane items would become so valuable
and you should see the shine they put on my shoes!
Do write back quickly. I long for your letters.
Love
Nancy. Xx

Bridget could almost hear Nancy's voice in the words but the line about 'all that had happened in London' made her frown. There was so much unsaid between them.

Oh, how I long to see that girl, she thought, but then she read the rest of the letter again, noting Nancy's casual joke about a crime network. What if there was a network operating between the camps somehow and there was a bigger plan afoot? So, distracted by her anger at being sidelined to the Isle of Man, it occurred to her that she might actually be missing something. Helga obviously had something to hide and Lena was never going to be satisfied with just sitting the war out.

Bridget Harrison decided it was about time she became a real policewoman again. But first she had to get through a date she wasn't looking forward to.

*   *   *

The Falcon's Nest lounge bar was crowded when Bridget and Molly went to meet Kieran and Fynn. They'd dragged a despondent Betty out with them. It had been ages since she had heard from Joe and she had convinced herself he was dead and she was now a widow.

'Over here, girls,' Kieran called. His cheeks looked flushed and his tie was at an angle. Molly waved breezily, but Bridget frowned. She had seen her brothers look like this after a night out in Peel before the war.

Fynn stood up from the round table in the corner to give her a perfunctory kiss on the cheek and she looked up at him warily. She had no idea whether they were still in a relationship or not.

'Mick, get these girls a drink,' Kieran was calling to the barman who grinned in recognition of Bridget and went over to the cider. There were so few women who frequented bars and the increasing visits by these girls was giving him hope that a new age was dawning and that might mean increased income. The rest of the men in the bar gave their usual glares, glad their wives and daughters didn't make an exhibition of themselves like these three.

'We made Betty come out,' Bridget whispered to Fynn, looking nervously at the stern faces around her. 'She needs cheering up.'

He nodded and turned towards Betty.

'I hear you've been doing great things with helping the women to learn English,' he said kindly.

She perked up and looked at him gratefully.

'Yes, they have classes but lots of them still struggle so I thought I'd give them a bit of extra tuition. It isn't easy though; they range from being quite good at learning to having no education at all.'

Bridget butted in. 'You've already got them able to ask for things they need though, and that makes Ruth's life so much easier.' Turning to Fynn, she added: 'You know, she's the Quaker woman who helps with the women's welfare. She's a real brick and at least she doesn't have to second-guess what they need as much now.'

Bridget glanced over at Molly and Kieran who were throwing their heads back in laughter at something Kieran had said.

'You seem very jolly, Kieran,' Bridget called over. 'Jurby suiting you?'

His face immediately fell.

'Hell, no, I hate it. I just miss flying so much. I just want to be of some use.'

'It's not all your responsibility,' Bridget said. 'There must be others there too. I'm sure you're all doing your bit.'

Kieran looked unconvinced. The pilots being trained were so young and there'd been two near misses that week making him fearful that a 'gung-ho' attitude was becoming too prevalent. He recognised, all too well, the bravado that left rookies convinced of their invulnerability. Being unable to get into the cockpit with them was leaving him feeling frustrated and powerless. He took a long slurp of his beer hoping it would help him sleep.

Bridget was busy watching both Kieran and Fynn out of the corner of her eye and what she saw left her feeling uneasy. Molly, however, was having a wonderful time. Even Fynn was paying particular attention to her – which Bridget took as a direct slight aimed at her – and Kieran was responding to the light banter that Molly specialised in. Betty was just so grateful to be out, she absorbed the distraction of the men's company like a dry sponge.

After a while and another couple of pints, Fynn watched Kieran swaying on his stool and stood up.

'Sorry, girls, but I'm going to have to call this evening to a close. Come on, old chap, I'd better get you back. You've only got tomorrow to sleep this off before you go back to Jurby.'

Betty stood up too. She felt uncomfortable, even in a lounge area of a bar, and couldn't stomach the gossip that would fly around the south of the Island if the girls remained without their escorts.

'Come on, Moll, time to go,' she said, but Molly was engrossed with talking to Kieran who was trying to ignore his brother.

Fynn was about to steer Kieran out of the bar when Bridget put her hand on his sleeve.

'Fynn, before you go, can we have a word?'

'Yes, yes, you take him off for a mo, Bridget,' Molly said, 'I haven't heard the punchline of this joke yet.'

Fynn had no choice but to follow Bridget to the end of the bar where she turned round to face him.

'What's going on, Fynn? Are we, or are we not, going out anymore? You're being so odd with me, I don't know whether I'm coming or going.'

Fynn's eyes softened for a brief moment but then he heard Kieran's laughter behind him.

'I don't think your heart's in it, Bridget, to be honest. And I can't be bothered with playing second fiddle. So, you just get on with your life and . . . I'll get on with mine.'

And with that, he pivoted on his heel to hide the hurt in his face and went to get Kieran, propelling his brother out towards the fresh air. Kieran looked wistfully over his shoulder to grin at the girls but then he stumbled into the doorway with Fynn steadying him. The girls gathered their things and left too.

'Well, that's a shame, we were just getting going,' Molly grumbled when the two men had vanished into the night. 'Your boyfriend didn't look too happy, Bridg. Is everything all right?'

'No idea, but I don't think he's my boyfriend anymore.'

The three of them turned for home while Molly and Betty kept mithering Bridget with questions. Eventually, she said, 'I think I'll give men a rest for a while, they're far too complicated.'

As they approached the cottage, they nearly bumped into a lad on a bicycle. It was dark but when Bridget saw he was a telegraph boy, she froze and looked into Betty's face that had gone as pale as the moonlight.

He was holding out a telegram and looked from one to the other but Betty bravely thrust her hand out.

'It's for Bridget Harrison,' the boy said. 'Is that you?'

'No,' Betty said quietly, feeling her legs go weak with relief.

Knowing that telegrams rarely brought good news during a war, Bridget felt a chill in her neck and reached out a shaking hand to grab the envelope. With her other hand, she took Betty's arm to steady her. Molly opened the front door and as the three of them went through to the hallway, Bridget was ripping open the telegram.

Her face cleared. 'It's from Nancy,' she said with relief, steering an unsteady Betty towards The Snug. Scanning the words, she let out a gasp.

'She's coming over! Got compassionate leave to help with her dad. Be here when her training finishes in a few weeks.'

Molly interrupted Bridget's reading. 'I'll put the kettle on, I think we all need a cup of tea after that. Poor old Betty's gone quite wobbly.'

Betty, at that moment, was sinking into the armchair in the corner. The telegram had come too close to a possibility she really did not want to face.

'Don't worry, Bet, he's fine, I'm sure he is,' Bridget said, with as much reassurance as she could muster.

Betty's reply was faint and unconvincing.

Chapter Twelve

Bridget marched the twenty-minute journey over the back road to Cowley's Café in record time, feeling in just the right mood to deal with Lena. Between Fynn being so obtuse and Betty's sobs keeping her awake all night, the young police officer was feeling as belligerent as the woman she was about to see. She needed information so had sent a young interpreter, Isabella, ahead of her. The plan was that the German-speaking young girl would listen in on Lena's conversation and meet her outside the café to report back.

Bridget peered from across the street to see the little group of Nazis at their usual table. At exactly three o'clock, Isabella came out of the café and ran across towards Bridget, who grabbed her arm to pull her out of sight.

Feeling like Madeleine Carroll in her favourite film, *Secret Agent*, Isabella had insisted on wearing a scarf and a pair of glasses as a disguise. She glanced around her before whispering.

'They didn't see me; they were too engrossed in their conversation.'

'Well done, Isabella,' Bridget said, smiling at the girl's enthusiasm. 'Now, tell me what you heard.'

The girl reported that they were talking excitedly about 'there were now a lot less people to worry about' in somewhere called Katyn. Bridget's mind was working fast: there had been nothing in the papers or on the radio so to be in possession of such up-to-date news must surely mean that information was somehow getting through the strict checks that were made. Radios were all locked up safely in landladies' cupboards, along with torches in case anyone used them to signal ships, but, she supposed, it was just possible that the protective measures were being breached and a communication network had already been established among the Nazis on the Island.

'They also talked about the fact they were getting some help soon,' she added with a flourish.

Bridget patted Isabella's arm, making the young girl flush with pleasure and then Bridget said, 'OK, let's go in and see what else we can find out.'

Followed by Isabella who scuttled behind her, minus the scarf and glasses, Bridget strode in and marched over to the women's table, making them jerk their heads back in astonishment.

'Lena, come outside for a moment,' and without waiting for Isabella to finish translating the instruction, she walked back out to the front of the café, giving Lena no time to argue.

Lena stood on the pavement with her arms folded, looking away from both the translator and Bridget.

'I need you to look at me, Lena. Right, let's start with how you've been intimidating the Jewish women.'

The policewoman made the German nervous. She knew the power of such a uniform in her own country and there was a huge amount at stake if she said anything incriminating.

'We know about your goose-stepping and now, apparently, you've been using detergent to make swastikas appear on the bathroom mirrors to terrify the Jewish women,' Bridget said brusquely, needing to put this woman on the wrong foot from the start. 'You are in a dangerous position, Lena. You understand that we have laws here that I can bring to bear if I need to.'

It wasn't a question.

Before Lena had time to react to Isabella's translation, Bridget moved on.

'Why did you become a Nazi?'

Lena pulled her shoulders back and in a belligerent tone, ignored Bridget and addressed her answer to the interpreter.

'I have always believed the Aryan people are superior and I am proud that Germany will win this war.'

'And now you've got a network over here that's working to help that happen, have you?' Bridget asked, pressing her advantage. It was time to test out her hunch.

Before the translation was made, a flash of panic crossed the German's face which revealed two things: one, that Lena did actually speak English and secondly, that the fears about a network being formed were justified.

'How is your network here communicating?'

The hairs on Lena's arms were standing on end. This policewoman was cleverer than she thought. She clamped her mouth shut.

Bridget had to keep the satisfied smile from her lips. She changed tack.

'Are you and Helga still friends?'

Lena nodded unconvincingly.

'But you argued, didn't you? Just before the knife incident?'

Lena decided to bluff her way out of any more confrontation with the policewoman.

'We are friends, sometimes friends disagree,' she told Isabella.

Lena cursed the close quarters in the camp. It was hard to maintain the subterfuge she was used to.

'I don't remember why,' she added, shrugging her shoulders.

Bridget didn't need to pursue this conversation any further. For now.

'You may go, for the time being. But we will be watching you, Lena, you and all your fellow Nazis. Just remember that.'

* * *

When Bridget got back to the police station at Port Erin, she found Sergeant Robinson waiting for her by the front desk.

'Come into my office.'

'How did you get on? she asked, going to sit behind her desk.

Bridget took a deep breath and filled her in on the details of the meeting, including her suspicions that there might be a network being established somewhere on the Island.

'I think we'll start with Peel,' the sergeant said, 'that camp is full of Nazis. Leave that with me; I'll start some investigations.'

Bridget opened her mouth to speak and then paused.

'Yes?' the sergeant said.

'Well, about Helga; it's just I've been thinking. She said she arrived as the war started whereas most of the other internees, including Lena, had been in Britain for ages. So why would she leave her country at a time when ardent Nazis would be needed there and then . . .' she hesitated . . . her thoughts clearing as she spoke . . . 'if that German man who was hung on the tree outside her house was lynched without trial, it can only mean two things: either he was a collaborator or he was a Jew. If she really is loyal to Hitler, neither of those explanations would have been a reason for a loyal Nazi like Helga to flee.

'Hmm, it certainly is strange,' Maureen Robinson agreed. 'OK, Bridget, you find out more; in the meantime, I'm snowed under with organising the start of these repatriations.

I've got all these files to go through. It's a huge responsibility to work out who's safe to send back. If I get these wrong, then the Nazis won't need a network over here, we'll have done their job for them.'

She fingered the long list of candidates to be assessed for the long-awaited repatriations on her desk and sighed.

Then she finally added, 'But well done, Officer Harrison, that's excellent police work. Now go and make a cup of tea.'

* * *

Molly and Bridget arrived home to hear the cheerful tones of 'Chattanooga Choo Choo' emanating from the back of the house. They glanced at each other and hurried down the corridor to be nearly bowled over by the emerging Greeba, her tail wagging like a metronome to greet the homecomers. Behind them came Betty, grinning broadly.

'He's alive, he's alive! I've finally had a letter.'

Betty took hold of their hands and tried to swing both girls around in the narrow hallway, her head flung back in pure joy. Molly stopped halfway round and asked, 'Is he OK?'

'Yes, well, I think so, he says he's having trouble with his eyes after a shell went off in front of him and he was blinded by it which is why he hasn't been able to write. His writing's gone worse,' she laughed and held out the letter.

Bridget took hold of it and scanned the scrawl. She clasped Betty into a hug and Molly said, 'Oh, I think that definitely deserves a celebratory garibaldi biscuit,' and reached for the tin.

Betty munched on the biscuit happily and immediately sat down to write back to Joe, while Bridget settled herself down at the table to confide in Molly about the events of her own afternoon.

As she recounted the stilted conversation outside Cowley's Café, Molly looked more and more puzzled.

'None of it makes sense. I mean, how on earth are they getting information from off the Island?' she asked, 'and what could be the possible reason for Helga fleeing Germany so quickly? And if Lena knows and it's something incriminating, then why hasn't she exposed her?'

Bridget shook her head. 'I don't know but what I do know is that it's strange that Helga wanted to come to a country that was already being seen as the enemy at a time when ardent Nazis were needed.'

'Well, I can't see scary Helga as a collaborator,' Molly said, reaching for the biscuit tin, 'and she certainly can't be a Jew so good luck with your inquiries, that's all I can say.'

'I wish we knew more about these women,' Bridget added.

Both girls sat back for a moment, remembering a time when subterfuge and deception were not part of everyday life.

Suddenly, Molly's tone changed. 'I need to tell you something, Bridg. Fynn asked me out.'

Bridget was taken aback but before she had chance to say anything, Molly went on quickly, 'I said no, obviously, but I needed you to know. I'm not sure what he's playing at.'

Bridget agreed. She had no idea either.

'You can go if you want to, Moll, I don't care. After all, we've finished . . . I think.'

'Nope, definitely not.' Molly's face darkened. She couldn't reveal the disturbing thoughts that were going through her head every time she thought of Bridget with her arms around a man. Going out with Fynn was the last thing on her mind.

Bridget gave a small laugh. 'You can have Kieran too, as far as I'm concerned. I think I'm done with men for now. The only one I've got any time for is Alister. He's nice and harmless and . . . happily married.'

'Well, that won't do,' Molly said, her spirits rising. 'A girl needs some fun in her life and I'm not sure Alister's conversation about sheep at Cregneash is going to give you the goosebumps!'

The recent weeks had revived feelings in Bridget that she thought she had buried. The obsession with Kieran had carried her through adolescence, blind to the other boys who seemed spotty and childish. There had been a stream of dates in London, usually when she was dragged along on a foursome with Nancy, but they had been with servicemen passing through the city, anxious to live every moment and she had been immune to their pleadings for more than a fumble in the dark shadows of Piccadilly, too intent on her career.

Once back on the Island, she'd convinced herself that Fynn had only asked her out as an old friend but she was far too aware that his passionate embrace was anything but a kiss from a childhood playmate. After that, she had started to look forward to their dates with an excitement that made her tremble but then Kieran had arrived on the scene and it had all gone terribly wrong.

German Nazi women were beginning to look less complicated, she thought, pushing her fingers through her hair.

Chapter Thirteen

Kieran was struggling to focus on the notes on the desk in front of him while the young airmen were beginning to twitch in their chairs. From hanging onto every word this legend of the Battle of Britain said during his first few weeks at No 5 Observers' School, they were becoming impatient with him. His bleary eyes bore testament to another night's drinking.

'Sir?' one of them said. 'Are you all right, Sir?'

Kieran looked up to see a lad on the front row looking concerned. He was a fresh-faced young man with an innocent expression and Kieran took a second look, astonished to see someone so young in uniform. He looked no older than the boys he saw waiting for the bus to school in the mornings.

'What's your name, lad?' he asked, making himself concentrate.

The boy sat up straight and grinned. 'Ashcroft, Sir.'

'Right, Ashcroft, pay attention, the next hour is important, more important that you will ever know.'

Kieran looked with concern around the room, they were all so young and so inexperienced. There were also bemused faces near the back of the classroom that belonged to the 307 Polish Squadron and 312 Czech Squadron and many of them were still struggling with English, never mind wind speeds, navigation and tactics.

He tried to pull himself together; these boys deserved better.

He turned to the blackboard and started to sketch out tactics in combat, in readiness for that evening's practical training. On familiar ground, he started to feel better and spent the rest of the morning trying to prepare them for every eventuality.

They were due to go on night manoeuvres and he felt more nervous for them than if he were doing them himself. He thought the Polish and Czech pilots should be OK; they at least had combat experience, but these British lads were too eager, too cocky.

As soon as the day ended, Kieran took himself off to the Officers' Mess near the Parade Ground. Weekly dances were held in the mess but he hadn't been able to face going to any of them, preferring to go back to his bunk where he flicked through training manuals that gave no hint of the crowded skies above Dover with gunfire and smoke everywhere. However, he did like to go first to the mess for a beer . . . or two. He told himself he didn't need one tonight but, forcing feet to move past the doorway, he was saluted by one of the Flight Lieutenants and, eager to make a good impression with this DFC, the young man offered to buy the officer a pint. Three drinks later, Kieran remembered the night manoeuvres; he wasn't on duty but had wanted to watch the young pilots from the control tower to make sure there were no mistakes.

As the April evening air caught him, he wobbled. *Probably just as well I'm not flying,* he thought with a giggle.

The atmosphere in the tower was tense, the wind conditions were stronger than had been forecast and the men were on mock attack training which involved them flying towards each other at high speed and then, hopefully, taking avoiding action. It was risky and Kieran stood at the back of the control room, straining his ears to hear what was being said through the crackly radios. As always, these days, he felt like a spare part and of no use to anyone.

The five aircraft involved in the training were all Blenheims, newly-modified twin-engined bombers. They housed a crew of three in each plane and flying next to them at a safe distance was their instructor who spoke to the young pilots in calm tones, giving them commands. But it was the responding high-pitched voices that gave away the tension his young pupils were feeling. The aircraft were flying down the west coast and so out of sight but every man in that control room had a visual image of the planes hurtling towards each other and there was a communal holding of breath.

The first few practice manoeuvres went well and Kieran, like everyone else, heaved a sigh of relief.

'I did it, I really did it!' they heard one triumphant voice saying over the speakers.

'Told you it wasn't that hard,' another one said, laughing. 'Just let us at the Hun now, we've got it.'

'Not so fast,' qualified Flying Instructor Blake said from his cockpit radio. 'We've got close contact to do now.' He was carefully co-ordinating, changing positions and instructions as necessary, reducing the men in the Control Tower to mere bystanders.

Kieran perched back on the desk in the corner; hearing the live action over the radios took him back to the English Channel on 31st August in 1940, when so many of his fellow fighter pilots had been killed. He closed his eyes but that just conjured up images of burning aircraft, determined Luftwaffe opponents and huge sprays of gunfire on all sides of him, so he opened them again quickly to concentrate on the commentary coming across the speakers.

'Cummings, take the starboard position and then change to port at the exact second when I say,' the calm instructor was saying. 'Ashcroft, you start with port and switch on my command.'

The only sound for the next couple of minutes was the drone of engines as the two planes accelerated and weaved. They were following a set pattern that had been drummed into them that morning by Kieran. He could see the diagram on the board in his head and he could also see an image of the insides of the cockpits as the pilots pulled and pushed the controls. Blake was calmly relaying instructions until he suddenly shouted, 'Now, Cummings, switch to starboard! Ashcroft to port, man. NOW, for God's sake!'

Then Kieran heard words that sobered him up in an instant. 'He's too close ... he's too close, I can't ... I'm going to hit him, I'm going to hit him,' came the screaming voice of a pilot over the airwaves.

'Bank, bank ... quicker. For Christ's sake man, not that way!' flight Instructor Blake yelled from his aircraft, knowing the young man behind the controls had frozen in terror. The first plane veered violently upwards out of harm's way but the second aircraft was, they all knew, heading for the dark, murky water that would be those young men's graves.

'Get out of there, NOW!' he shouted. But then there was a dreadful stillness, when only the clock on the wall in the Control Tower could be heard ticking. It was as if time had stopped. No one spoke or even breathed, willing the scene they could see in their heads to be different. Then, there was a huge bang that reverberated around the room and ... silence.

* * *

The following morning, the class was subdued when Kieran walked in. He scanned the room. There were three empty chairs – one of them was on the front row where that young lad had sat. Kieran swayed.

"Would you excuse me for a moment?' he said quietly and stumbled out of class, leaving gasps of disbelief behind him. The trainees were all in shock and needed their superior to show them how to behave in the wake of such a tragedy. They really expected someone like Squadron Leader Moore to have some answers.

Kieran leaned against the wall in the corridor. He felt physically sick at the waste of life he was being forced to watch over and over again. He had thought the Isle of Man would be a refuge from it all and a place where he could battle with his own demons, but yet again, he was supposed to be able to have reasons as to why all this death and destruction was necessary. He felt disgusted with the man he had become. Hearing footsteps, he looked up to see the same tall squadron leader who had been so dismissive of him when he first arrived. Kieran groaned quietly.

The man, whose name was Wilfred Fielding, stopped in front of him and looked him up and down. From his great height, he peered down, making Kieran, as always, feel inferior next to him.

'Abandoned your class, have you, Moore?' the man said with a sneer. 'You do know the men look to us to show an example when . . . well, when something like this happens, don't you? You can't become a snivelling wreck, particularly not one with a hangover. Not good show, old man.'

A voice came from behind.

They both jumped to attention. It was the Commanding Officer, Alan Pickering, and his face was grey, testament to the night he had just spent composing three letters to the families of the dead men.

'Follow me, Moore. I want to see you in my office. Fielding, take over his class.'

Kieran scuttled off behind him like a naughty schoolboy. It was as if his life was passing before his eyes and he saw his distinguished career being obliterated in a moment.

'Close the door behind you,' the CO said sharply, and Kieran stood up straight. After a moment considering his next move, his commander perched on the edge of his huge walnut desk and leaned towards the man in front of him, looking concerned. His voice softened.

'At ease, Squadron Leader. Now, tell me what's going on?'

'Sorry, Sir, I just needed a moment.' His CO waited, expectantly, he wanted more.

Kieran was about to protest that there wasn't any problem at all but faced with the piercing scrutiny of his commanding officer, he blurted out the truth.

'Drinking too much, Sir.'

'I know that,' Pickering said dismissively. 'Now tell me why. And I know it isn't just yesterday's tragedy. This has been going on for a while now.'

Kieran automatically hid his hand behind his back.

'The hand is it?' the CO said.

'No, well, yes, Sir, it is.' He looked down at it with a sneer.

'I'm no use, Sir. I can't fly and I can't teach. I don't know what to tell them, how to explain . . .' he waved his hands at the sky outside the window . . . 'all this.'

Wing Commander Pickering went over to the window Kieran was waving towards and stared out.

'You know, Moore, we've both lost a great many friends and I suspect, like me, you've run out of answers and actually just want to stop asking the questions. But I believe the real problem is that you almost envy those dead men because you're still here and are expected to carry on. And once the medics told you that you can't fly, you think your life is worthless.'

Kieran nodded, surprised at the understanding in the CO's voice, but Pickering was still gazing out at the parade ground in the distance. A veteran flyer, he had his own past to deal with. He turned to face Kieran.

'But that's enough now, airman. You sort yourself out. You stop drinking. As of this minute, no arguments, no excuses. This is your last warning.'

Kieran stood up straight again and focused his eyes forward. There was no discussion to be had.

'Prove to me you can do it, give those young men your undivided . . . and sober . . . attention and I'll see you again in a month. I need a man like you, but I can't let you near the project I've got in mind until I know I can trust you.'

And with that, he sat down at his desk and opened a file.

'Dismissed.'

Chapter Fourteen

In a small lounge area of her accommodation at the top of Port Erin, Lena Braun was pacing up and down, furious with herself for underestimating that policewoman. An experienced operative, she knew she would have to be more on her guard but in the meantime, she needed to get a message to Peel to inform them that the police were getting suspicious. If she was being watched, they would have to change their plans, starting with the use of the usual 'drop-off'/ point.

Lena had worked for many years for the emerging Nazi party, delivering messages as a schoolgirl in Germany and was finally despatched to England to set up an underground network there to prepare for the glorious German invasion. She fed information back to Nazi headquarters until the police van arrived with an arrest warrant for all aliens. Now, she was doing everything she could to continue that work but being stuck in a 'brown' boarding house – named after the Nazi uniforms – she was feeling frustrated that her investigations kept being impeded because she couldn't get past the wire.

The women, forbidden from using their bedrooms during the day, were crowded into the unwelcoming room at the front as their only refuge against the driving rain that was pounding the windows, when the landlady peered around the door to beckon to Lena who was nearest to her.

'You, take this up to the fourth floor,' she said to her, handing over a cup of tea. 'There's a handyman up there. And bring it back as soon as he's finished with it.'

The house had been without water for three days and the regular trips up the four flights of stairs with the endless cups of tea demanded by the handyman was playing havoc with the landlady's varicose veins.

Lena begrudgingly took the cup and saucer from the woman's hands and made her way up the stairs. At the top, there was a bathroom that was shared by more than a dozen women and sticking out from the sink cupboard were a pair of legs in brown overalls.

'Here,' Lena said ungraciously.

The man emerged backwards and assessed the woman in front of him.

'Hmm, a great deal better than the old bag who normally brings it,' he said, his mouth twisting into a lopsided smile.

Lena caught sight of herself in the mirror, almost surprised to see an attractive young blonde woman looking back at her.

With only boredom waiting for her below, she looked squarely at the man who was leaning casually back on the sink.

He was about forty-five and had a mop of deep auburn hair. He'd once been quite good-looking, she decided, but had a resentful look about him that she recognised from the image she'd just seen in the mirror.

'So . . . what's your name?' he asked her.

Lena was about to pretend she didn't understand but was intrigued by his accent.

She ignored his question but asked, in perfect English, 'Where are you from?'

'Ireland originally,' he said, slurping his tea noisily. 'Been here for years. You a Nazi?'

She nodded.

'Good, another one who hates the Brits then?' the man said. 'Well, I reckon you don't hate 'em as much as me.'

Lena's ears pricked up.

'Why?' she asked, but the man turned back to the sink to test out the taps.

'Never you mind,' he said. 'Thanks for the tea.'

She took the cup and saucer from him, looking keenly into his eyes.

'My name's Lena Braun,' she said, and he stretched out his hand to clasp hers.

'Damian O'Callaghan.'

* * *

Mona Kneale had gone to Port Erin to deliver some herbs to Bridget to cheer her up. Mona looked suspiciously at the wire that surrounded the camp in the town and skirted round the edges until she came to a guard post.

She marched up to the two men on duty.

'I need to see my granddaughter,' she said imperiously, daring them to refuse her entry but refuse her they did. All the locals needed a pass to get in and out of the camp and this woman did not have the necessary paperwork.

Mona tried another tack: 'She's a policewoman, for heaven's sake. Surely, I can be allowed in to see her?'

But the men would not be moved.

At that moment a line of women was being led along the road on the other side of the wire. Mona peered over to see if she could see Bridget, but they were being led by another woman in a police uniform with blonde hair.

Mona looked with curiosity at the internees; it was the first time she had seen them and she peered with disdain and suspicion. They might look like ordinary women but these were jabbering in that dreadful language, she thought. While she craned her neck, holding the herbs she had brought at arm's length, one woman in the line, about her age and pulling her thin, grey coat around her, halted in front of her and reached out to finger the leaves.

'What are you doing . . .?' Mona started but then she looked into the woman's eyes and stopped. There was a depth there she recognised and it was as if they both had been jettisoned from the same shipwreck in a storm.

'*Der Lavendel*,' the woman started and for a second both their fingers touched on the edge of the wire.

'Yes, lavender,' Mona replied, surprised.

The guards were distracted by Molly, who was arguing with them about which side of the road she was supposed to be walking her little group of internees on, and Mona heard the woman say, 'Ah the herbs, I miss my herbs.'

Mona found herself nodding in understanding. She'd only once before recognised a woman with the same soul as her and that was when she was a child in Ballawhane. It was a moment of connection that left her confused and yet at peace.

At that moment, the guards ushered the little line of internees on their way but then the woman turned round and over her shoulder called to Mona, 'I am Erika . . . Erika Schneider.'

Mona watched her walk away but then spotted Molly at the back of the group and motioned her over.

'Excuse me, officer, can you give something to my granddaughter for me? Bridget,' she explained. Molly smiled and went towards the wire, checking to make sure the guard wasn't looking and took the proffered package from Mona, looking curiously at this woman she had heard so much about.

As she handed it over, Mona whispered, 'You need to find yourself. You are looking for the wrong thing.'

Molly felt a chill creep up her neck. It was such a strange comment but it was like hearing a language she understood. Her sister, Gloria, had once said the same thing, just before she signed up to work the canals between London and Birmingham. Molly thought hard to remember them: 'Stop trying to be the person everyone expects you to be, Mol, you need to find yourself and it won't be easy.'

Now, hearing similar words from Bridget's grandmother, Molly realised she had always felt as if she was living the wrong person's life but had no idea why. She wanted to ask more but Mona had already moved away, straining her neck to follow the line of internees as they made their way along the road. Erika Schneider turned and smiled. Mona couldn't help it, her mouth turned upwards into a friendly smile in return.

* * *

There was a loud and rapid knock on the door of the girls' cottage. Bridget squealed with delight when she saw Nancy standing on the doorstep in the pouring rain.

'I'd forgotten about the bloody so-called "spring weather" on this island!' Nancy said, brushing herself on the step to form a puddle beneath her. She was being assailed by an excited dog who was rushing around her feet in glee at the unexpected visitor.

'Hello, you, you're a lovely animal, aren't you?' And Greeba immediately rolled over onto her back to allow her new admirer to tickle her tummy.

Nancy laughed.

'Come in, come in!' Bridget said, 'I wasn't expecting you until tomorrow.'

Nancy took off her WAAF hat and looked for somewhere to hang it. Bridget took it from her and plonked it on the hall stand, waiting for her to pass over her coat too.

'There now, *now* I can give you a hug,' Nancy said, with a grin. 'Oh, Bridget, it's so good to see you, and believe it or not, even with this terrible rain, to be here, to be home.'

'When did you arrive?'

'A few days ago,' Nancy told her, shaking her wet hair, 'but this is the first time mother's let me out of her sight. She's so relieved to have someone to share the load with.'

'How is your father?'

Nancy simply shrugged so Bridget pushed her along the corridor.

'Come through and see our glorious abode,' and she pushed open the kitchen door where Molly and Betty had both turned around to see who their guest was.

'This is my friend, Nancy,' Bridget said, with a certain pride in her voice. Nancy's chestnut-coloured hair was hanging round her face in wet tendrils, but she had on her WAAF uniform which looked much smarter than the policewomen's outfit. Betty looked enviously at the blue uniform and tucked her own badly-fitting skirt under her bottom.

There was a London look about this newcomer that Molly recognised from the posh areas of Mayfair. She somehow looked incredibly fashionable even in uniform and Molly suspected she'd had it tailored specially for her. She'd heard of some of the better-off girls spurning the air force issue tunic and skirt which were known for their itchy material and she looked with disdain at this vision in front of her. Noticing how excited Bridget was to see this newcomer, she decided she was not going to like her at all and turned back to her book with a cursory nod of hello.

Betty however, was deeply impressed. There was no-one who looked like this in the East End of London and this girl had a style that certainly could never have come from anywhere Betty was familiar with. It seemed the magazines weren't lying and women somewhere were still managing to look elegant, despite them being in uniform. She even had lipstick on, for heaven's sake. She stood up, reverently giving Nancy her chair while offering to make a cup of tea.

'Oh, I don't suppose you have any biscuits?' Nancy pleaded, looking round at the stocked shelves in disbelief. 'It's been impossible to get any sugar for weeks now in London and although it's been doing my figure good,' she patted her flat stomach, 'I'm dying for something sweet.'

Molly glanced up. So this girl was now going to eat all their supplies, was she?

'I don't think there are any left,' she said bluntly.

'Yes, there are,' Betty protested, reaching up for the tin and peering inside. 'Bridget's mother keeps us with a constant supply. See, there are some.' And with that, she passed over the tin to Nancy, who gleefully took one.

'Don't mind if I have two, do you?' she said, pulling out another.

'Oh, you just help yourself,' Molly muttered quietly to herself.

Bridget pulled out another chair and sat opposite Nancy.

'Now, you have to tell me everything. I want the whole story. Are you here for good? How's your father? What made you join up and leave the BBC?'

Betty bit her lip at the mention of the British Broadcasting Corporation, holding back the excitement. She listened avidly to all the programmes on the wireless and had previously begged Bridget for more information about her friend who actually worked there. She felt she was welcoming a film star to their little kitchen.

'I was just fed up of being in civvies,' Nancy said, waving her arm towards their police uniforms in vague explanation, 'so, no sooner had I signed on the dotted line than I was off to Blackpool for training followed by Compton Bassett. I've no idea what they've got in mind for me yet, but they're giving me compassionate leave for a bit, so, et voilà, here I am!'

Molly stood up; she'd had enough.

'Well, if no one else is going to take this dog out, then I will.' And with that she stomped across the kitchen towards the door, which led to Greeba skidding across the floor towards her in anticipation of her favourite time of the day. Molly noisily shut the door behind her, making a disgruntled noise as she went.

'What's up with her?' Nancy asked, munching her biscuit.

'Oh, she probably hasn't been out on her motorbike for a couple of days,' Bridget said with a concerned frown. 'She's always bad tempered when she hasn't got out for a ride.' But she was surprised by Molly's reaction; it wasn't like her to be rude.

She turned back to Nancy and leaned forward. 'Anyway, tell me all your news, I want every tiny little morsel of information and gossip.'

Nancy paused for one brief moment. There was so much more she wanted to tell her friend but instead, she launched into a safe anecdote of how she'd bumped into the famous bandleader, Henry Hall, in the foyer of Broadcasting House.

Betty sat quietly in the corner taking in this little bit of glamour that was sitting surrounded by wet bloomers and stockings. She was just happy to bask in the reflected glory of this vision from the capital until she started yawning and had to reluctantly drag herself off to bed.

Bridget and Nancy talked on, catching up on people they had known together in London and recalling some of the antics they got up to there, like the time they'd climbed the lions in Trafalgar Square and put lace doilies around the wild beasts' heads like scarves or when they'd walked all night along the whole of the Embankment singing 'Doing the Lambeth Walk' with a group of lads from the navy. At last Bridget sat back and sighed.

'Oh, we had such fun, Nancy, it's not like that here. I have to be so sensible and well-behaved.'

'What, no men?' Nancy exclaimed in disbelief. 'That's not like you.'

'There's no one left,' Bridget told her, ignoring the visions of Fynn and Kieran that came into her head. 'You forget, Nancy, I'm surrounded by hundreds of women in this camp; that's women, Nancy, you know, people with bosoms and long hair.'

The two of them collapsed into giggles, falling into one another and at that moment, the door opened and Molly came in.

'Seems like you two have found enough to talk about. I'm off to bed.' And with that, she turned on her heel and went back out towards the stairs.

* * *

Nancy left the girls' cottage and made her way in the dark, back towards the perimeter fence. Like all the locals, she had to show her new, un-creased permit before being allowed to pass through the checkpoint to go back to Castletown. But the wait at the gate gave her time to reflect on how the brutal changes to the Island had caused an uneasiness. It was as if the camps had brought the war directly onto Manx shores and even the barrier of the sea was no longer able to protect it. Handing over the pass, Nancy realised she'd been expecting the Island to obliterate the memory that haunted her of being hurled against the kitchen wall by a man stinking of whisky, but, after only a few days, it was clear the Isle of Man was certainly not the safe haven she had been hoping for. There were too many sad little trails of women languishing on the seafront, desperately searching for a purpose to their day. As she walked, she heard the loud noise of engines above and Nancy looked up, terror striking her heart. Her recent training had taught her how to identify every type of plane but with low cloud, she could only see the dark shapes of bombers rumbling overhead and she automatically backed up against the wall, still plagued by the sight of dismembered limbs outside her flat. Without a warning siren, locals passing by hardly glanced up, too used to training sessions that thundered regularly overhead, but the bravado that Nancy had shown in that little kitchen with Bridget that night was paper-thin, and she knew it would only take a tiny spark to ignite that paper into an inferno.

Chapter Fifteen

'Girls,' the sergeant called from her office, 'come in, please.'

'Sit down,' she said when Betty and Bridget appeared around the door. Molly came in behind, keeping her distance from Bridget.

'Right, we need to be extra vigilant. I've been in touch with the police at Peel. They weren't at all surprised to find out information's being disseminated around the camps but they've no idea how it's happening; they just know the Nazis who are at Peveril are a pretty violent lot. We need to do a check with all landladies to make sure their cupboards are locked and make a list of what radios and torches there are in Rushen so we can keep a tally if any go missing. OK?'

Betty and Bridget looked aghast at each other. This was a huge amount of work and would prompt resentment from the landladies, who hated being checked up on as if they were being negligent of their duties.

'Wouldn't it be better to ask each landlady to make that check?' Betty tentatively suggested.

'No,' the sergeant replied, 'I don't trust them to do it properly.'

'And that's exactly why many of them don't like us,' Molly muttered as the girls went out of the room. 'They know we don't trust them.'

* * *

Betty immediately went to her desk to start a list. She was feeling irrepressibly cheerful today having received another letter from Joe, this one written more carefully and in more detail. He said little about his injuries but seeing his improved handwriting was enough to help her deal with the difficult task the sergeant had given them.

Betty's hand flew across the page, indulging her obsession with bureaucracy, and after a few moments, she handed over part of the divided list to each of the other two.

Molly reached out to take hers and said casually, 'We've been asked to a dance at Jurby. There are a few of us going and we thought we'd get the bus up after work tonight. You up for that, Betty?'

Betty gave a pleased nod but Bridget looked up in surprise, she hadn't heard anything about a dance – or an invitation.

'Who's asked us?' she said.

Molly turned towards her as if noticing her for the first time.

'Oh, Kieran,' she said, tossing her hair out of her eyes. 'And Fynn for that matter.'

Bridget frowned but she felt hurt. It was as if both men – and Molly – were excluding her.

Suspecting Molly's change in attitude had something to do with Nancy, Bridget turned to face her.

'Have I done something to upset you, Molly?'

'Nope, you just have your new friend now so don't need us.'

Bridget burst out laughing but then stopped when she saw Molly's face.

'Don't look at me like that, Moll, you're my friend too.' She leaned over and put her arm on Molly's but it was immediately shrugged off.

'Hmm, well, I suppose you could come too,' Molly conceded, 'and if you must, ask that girl as well. I think they need as many women as possible.'

She went to walk out of the room and then turned. 'I'm off to start my checks, so I'll see you at the bus stop at six.'

* * *

The bus journey to Jurby was subdued, with Molly determinedly sitting in the seat in front of Bridget. The only person who seemed oblivious of the tension between the two of them was Betty. She had rollered her hair, done her nails and her cheeks were rosy with excitement. The reassurance that Joe was alive had made her almost giddy and she was really looking forward to a night out rather than sitting in the cottage hugging a cushion and sniffling. They met Nancy at the bus stop and then walked on to the mess at Jurby to find Kieran waiting for them by the door, a lemonade in hand. Bridget looked surprised.

'Not drinking, Kieran?'

A shadow crossed the young man's face. He didn't want to be reminded of the uncomfortable conversation with his CO, neither did he want the girls to know just how much alcohol he had been consuming on a regular basis.

'No, giving it a bit of a rest,' Kieran said cheerily, but Bridget looked at him keenly. Having watched him slyly out of the corner of her eye ever since she was a little girl, she knew every expression of his face and also, when he was lying.

Behind him came the tall figure of Fynn. He made a huge fuss of Molly and Betty and practically ignored Bridget until she introduced Nancy, who'd taken the opportunity of being on compassionate leave to dress in a red dress with a black leather belt. The vision of the beautiful girl with glistening, bobbing curls prompted both men's faces to light up and caused Bridget's shoulders to droop. She felt invisible.

Molly took charge.

'Drinks, I think. You may not be drinking, Kieran, but we certainly are!'

Fynn pushed his way to the front. 'I'll get them.' And with that, taking Molly on one arm and Betty on the other, led them both to the bar, making a particular point of telling Betty how pretty she looked, which caused her face to glow with delight.

Kieran ostentatiously offered his hand to Nancy who took it with a broad grin and Bridget was left to trail behind like a forgotten chaperone.

The band started up and Fynn immediately claimed Betty for the first dance – a foxtrot. Kieran turned to Nancy and took her onto the dance floor.

Molly shuffled her feet; she looked sideways at Bridget, noticing her embarrassment with satisfaction.

'Not reeling them in tonight, are you?' she said, with a bitter tone to her voice.

At that moment, two airmen came over and asked them both to dance and Bridget allowed herself to be led into the throng. Molly, however, hung back for a moment, watching Bridget disappear before taking the airman's proffered arm with a shrug.

Fynn was talking loudly and throwing his head back, letting out a laugh calculated to be heard by Bridget, who was negotiating a rather fast quickstep. She kept trying to avoid him but that only meant she was almost opposite Kieran, who was having an equally delightful conversation with Nancy.

'Oh, I'm sorry,' Bridget said to the young man whose toes she had just trod on.

'You maybe need to concentrate,' he said, looking meaningfully at the Squadron Leader, who was obviously more interesting than a mere Flight Lieutenant.

'Yes, of course,' Bridget said, glancing down at her feet which looked so ugly in the heavy policewomen's shoes. Nearly everyone in the room was in uniform, except Nancy, who stood out like a shining beacon in a dull sea of dark colours. Bridget had certainly never worried about her appearance, far too intent on making sure her clothes were practical enough to allow her to pursue her wide range of adventurous activities rather than impress anyone, but at that moment, she looked over at the striking figure of Nancy and felt a moment's envy.

After a succession of dances, Fynn saw Bridget heading over towards the entrance, obviously needing some fresh air. He wasn't sleeping and at three o'clock in the morning, his imagination about Kieran and Bridget was running wild. His sister had told him in no uncertain terms to stop tormenting himself and tackle Bridget head-on so when she pushed past the blackout curtain to go outside, he followed. But before he could speak, he heard Kieran's voice come out of the darkness.

'You too, huh, Bridget?'

Fynn saw the red light at the end of a cigarette glowing in the dark and immediately stumbled back behind the curtain as Kieran moved out of the trees, holding out an open cigarette case. Bridget took one and Kieran checked the dark skies above before leaning over to flick his lighter on for her.

'We have to be careful,' he said, 'don't want to give the enemy any clues about what goes on here, do we?'

She smiled wanly.

'Hmm, you're a bit fed up aren't you?' he said, twiddling his lighter in his left hand. He was dying for a drink, and had come out to fight off the compulsion that kept leading him towards the bar. He thought people would think him mad, the way he kept veering off suddenly to avoid getting too near to the smell of the beer.

'No, I'm fine,' Bridget cheerily lied. Just yards away, Fynn was clutching his chest as if in pain.

She sighed deeply.

'Well, that's obviously a lie,' Kieran said.

Bridget narrowed her eyes at him and said, 'I suspect that makes two of us then.'

Kieran nodded. He had known this girl all his life and at that moment, her familiarity gave him the confidence to speak openly.

'To be honest, Bridg, I've been drinking too much ever since, well ... you know ... the crash. I've been given one month to prove I can stop. Otherwise – well, I don't know. But I don't think there's any choice.' He stubbed out the cigarette on the floor. 'It's just much harder than I thought.'

Bridget felt a little quiver of excitement at the way he was confiding in her. He may have been sober, but she certainly wasn't.

Reaching out, she touched his lapel, looking up at him. He turned to her in surprise, noticing for the first time that there was a grown woman in front of him, not the little sister of his friend.

Bridget reached her face up and closing her eyes, she kissed him.

At that moment, Fynn, peering from behind the doorway, was sure everyone could hear his heart break.

*   *   *

All the way back on the bus, Bridget was uncharacteristically quiet. The chilly spring air had sobered her up and she was dissecting every moment of the rest of the evening, inwardly squirming. Kieran's face when she pressed her lips on his had shown a deep shock, as if the kiss had been delivered by his own cousin. She had immediately stepped away and muttering something about 'too much cider', had fled back indoors to ostentatiously dance with as many men as she could.

She tried to ignore how much her stomach had turned over when the moment she'd dreamed about all her life finally came true and for a few small seconds, tried to convince herself that she felt a warmth between them. But then, as the hours went on, she despondently told herself she'd imagined it.

'That was a fabulous evening,' Betty was saying with a gush. 'I'd forgotten how much I've missed going out and dancing.

'And you, Nancy,' she went on, 'you certainly were the belle of the ball, they were queuing up to dance with you. It was just a shame no one could get near you for that Fynn. He certainly wasn't going to let you out of his sight, was he?'

As a newcomer, Nancy failed to spot the look Molly gave Bridget but Bridget was too busy examining her shoes in misery to notice.

*   *   *

It was only a small piece of paper but it fitted perfectly behind the U-bend of the sink in the upstairs bathroom. Only someone examining the system thoroughly would see it, Damian O'Callaghan thought with a smile, tucking it carefully behind a wrench in his back pocket.

'Five o'clock by St Catherine's Church,' was all the note said, but the handyman knew who it was from.

At one minute past five, the camp handyman walked casually past the church until he heard a hissed 'Psst' from inside the stone porch.

As he expected, the German woman was waiting for him.

'Ah now, that's grand; are we going to be friends?' he said with a leer.

Lena looked doubtfully at him. 'I don't think so, but just tell me quickly why you do not like the British.'

All pretence at flirtation vanished in a second and Damian recalled the list of grievances that had plagued him for more than twenty years.

'Where do you want me to start? The murder of my 'da' or the torture of me brothers? That Churchill's got a lot to answer for. The men he sent over, the so-called "Black and Tans" in the War of Independence, they were ruthless.'

'So, are you a republican?' Lena asked.

Damian thought for a moment. He wasn't prepared to share that much with her just yet.

'That's for me to know,' he replied. 'But, while the Irish Government sits on the fence on this war, it's possible there might be a few of us who are happy to nudge things our way if we can.'

Lena's English was much better than she'd let on to Bridget but some of what Damian was saying was beyond her vocabulary. However, she knew enough about Irish politics to know that the IRA had said it would welcome Hitler's troops if they landed in Ireland.

'We will keep talking,' she said, 'and, now you have finished the work in our lodgings, if there are any messages, we need to put them in this wall here, you see it?'

Damian peered into the gloom to where she was prodding one of the stones. It was loose.

He nodded.

'All right, me darlin', we'll keep in touch; who knows, we might be useful to each other.' And with that he put his finger on the side of his nose and winked, before disappearing into the street.

Lena watched his receding back and wondered whether, in addition to fulfilling the demands of her superiors, this man could help her with her own agenda involving a certain German woman in a Douglas gaol.

Chapter Sixteen

'Can I borrow your motorbike?' Bridget asked Molly, who looked at her in surprise. 'I've got to go to Douglas and could do with feeling the wind in my hair.'

'Can you ride one?' she asked sharply. She wasn't going to lend her motorbike to anyone who was not an expert, even Bridget.

'Yes, I used to ride my brother's,' Bridget replied. 'And I used to race the lads on the TT course.'

Molly was still skirting around her friendship with Bridget, unsure as to why she was feeling so angry but, even so, she wasn't prepared to accept Bridget's assurances at face value when it came to her precious motorbike.

'Well, let's see about that. Get changed into some trousers and I'll meet you outside in ten minutes.'

Bridget felt a surge of excitement. She'd volunteered to pick up the latest release papers from Douglas and with petrol rationing not as strict as it was on the mainland, it had occurred to her she could take Molly's bike – if she'd let her. It had been so long since she had felt the freedom of racing around the lanes on a motorbike and it would assuage her desperate need to escape the confines of the camp. Bridget hated unanswered questions and as far as the camp and the gaol were concerned, there were too many of them.

Bridget swung her leg easily over the black leather seat and reached to turn the motor on.

'Hold on, not so fast,' Molly said, 'I'm going to put some tin cans on the road and let's see if you can go round them.' And with that, she marched off to place the tins at strategic points, making sure they were not too far apart to really test this girl out.

Bridget put on the goggles and attacked the course with gusto. She negotiated the obstacle course without any difficulty and revved up back at Molly's feet with a triumphant flourish of her hand.

'See, I haven't forgotten how.'

'No,' Molly said slowly. 'Oh, all right then, off you go, but just be careful, for God's sake, if not of yourself, then of my bike. If you damage it, you'll have to pay to get it fixed.'

'Thanks, Moll, you're a brick,' Bridget said with a warm smile. She so wanted to re-establish their friendship.

Molly gave a grimace, unable to remain cross with her irrepressible friend for long and as Bridget roared off, she gave a reluctant grin at Bridget's enthusiasm.

* * *

It was a bright day, and a bike ride was exactly what Bridget needed. Having no intention of rushing it, she passed through the checkpoint and out over The Sloc, racing up the moorland straights, leaning into the bends, her knee pushed out to give her balance. It was the first time in months she had felt like herself. Without the constraints of the uniform skirt, she felt free, free of responsibility, niggling questions, the war and gloriously free of men.

It was as if she had taken a pair of cutters to the barbed wire that had penned her and everyone else in, and she felt almost guilty that she was able to escape while so many others were not. It was at the Round Table that she pulled over, stopped and removed her goggles to take in the lovely coastline. Shaking her curls, she gazed out at the horizon looking for answers. Coming back to the Island, everything seemed to collide like the rough seas against the rocks. To her astonishment, her police work with Helga, and now Lena, was proving so much more challenging than anything she'd experienced in London. She was determined to uncover the truth of what was happening in the camps but wasn't sure where to start. She needed to concentrate, but the Moore brothers were proving to be more of a distraction than she'd ever anticipated. For years, she'd consigned Kieran Moore to a childhood crush. But a tipsy kiss had unleashed all her old feelings while Fynn had burst into her life, unleashing an excitement she had not been expecting.

'Fynn hates me,' she told the wind with a pout, 'and I don't know why. Surely he can't know how much of a muddle I am in over his brother?'

She fell silent. *And as for Kieran,* she thought, *he feels nothing, I'm sure. I'm just the boys' sister who's so stupid she messes up a friendship with a kiss.* Remembering his face as her lips had sought his brought on a deep, purple flush to her cheeks.

'So much for being in control, WPC Harrison.'

And she angrily swung her leg back over the bike and took off, leaving a trail of dust behind her.

Bridget rode slowly into Douglas, anxious to avoid attracting attention to herself and being accused of wasting resources. There was very little traffic on the roads after a local paper photograph had shown a line of parked cars in Victoria Street, condemning their claims that they were all making 'essential journeys'. Bridget felt justified that this trip was part of her police duties, but guiltily made a promise to herself that she would go everywhere by bus or bicycle in future, if she could just be allowed this very small rebellion. She picked up the documents ready for the eagerly awaited five o'clock announcement of which internees were going to be released that month, and tucked them in her satchel, before slinging it over her left shoulder. It was starting to be a constant flow of old, familiar faces leaving while younger, angrier or bemused ones were still continuing to arrive.

She took the eastern road back to Port Erin and as she approached Castletown, wondered whether she could pop in to see her grandmother – she needed her soothing influence. Pulling into the side of the road, she checked her watch. It was still quite early, so she gleefully put the bike into gear and veered off towards Scarlett Point, ignoring the fact that she practically passed the end of her own parents' road. She didn't have time for both, she thought, making a silent apology to her mother and father.

Before she had taken her goggles off, her grandmother appeared behind her on the track next to her cottage. She looked as if she were expecting her.

'Just for once, Granny, can't you pretend to be surprised?' Bridget said, laughing as she gave her a hug.

'Well, when you do surprise me, maybe I will, Breesha, maybe I will.' And she led the way into the house.

'I've been meaning to talk to you,' Mona Quayle said, straight to the point as usual.

'That woman you told me about, you didn't tell me she was interested in herbs . . . you know, like me.'

Now it was Bridget's turn to be surprised.

'How . . . when . . .?'

'I met her. Did you get those herbs I sent you, by the way? I gave them to that other policewoman. I presume that's her bike?'

Bridget nodded. 'Is that when you met Erika Schneider?'

'Never you mind,' her grandmother replied. 'Seriously, though, Breesha, how can I get to know her? I think we might have a lot to say to each other.'

After weeks of trying to work out how to get her grandmother to meet the German woman, here was her granny again taking control of the situation. Bridget gave up.

'Well, I can get you a permit and once that comes through, you can go and meet her at Collinson's Café.'

'Excellent,' Mona Quayle said. 'Have you got time for some camomile tea now? Seems to me you need it, it'll stop you being in such a fret.'

Bridget sat down in the wooden rocking chair and closed her eyes, feeling a wave of peace waft over her. There was never any need for words with this grandmother of hers.

* * *

Kieran Moore had kissed many girls, but Bridget's mouth on his had left him feeling bewildered, and making his way towards the teaching block at Jurby, he felt distinctly unsettled. The initial shock had quickly changed to a tingling feeling as he watched her walk away, so obviously mortified, her long, athletic legs and dark hair bouncing in the moonlight. Much of his childhood had involved memories of this girl with her pigtails, trailing behind, determined to do everything the three boys did and she'd never been anything other than Aedan and Brendan's sister. But, seeing that lovely face reach up towards him had been like watching a negative in a photographer's dark room transition into a bright, stunningly beautiful picture. Nobody was more surprised than Kieran Moore.

Kieran paused in the doorway of the classroom.

'Sir? Sir?' a Czech pilot was saying. Kieran shook himself out of his daydream and marched determinedly towards the blackboard.

'Yes, of course,' Kieran said. He was beginning to realise just how much alcohol had dulled his brain and as the concentration returned, so did his need to do a better job in this classroom.

For the rest of the lesson, he drilled them in pre-flight checks and safety, knowing that an automatic reaction could save their lives in an emergency if their brains seized up like poor Ashcroft's, leaving them incapable of rational decisions.

He was deeply troubled by the three young men who had died so needlessly and it was their faces he would see every time his feet veered towards the bar. The memory of that night in the control tower was hazy and he felt incredibly guilty that while they were facing death, he had been giggling on his journey from the mess. He was completely disgusted with himself and determined than no such accidents would happen again on his watch, resolving that if he couldn't be in the cockpit with them, it would be his words they would hear in their heads, leading them back to safety. Keeping those young men in mind was the only thing that was stopping Kieran from having just one more drink. It occurred to him that he'd become dependent on alcohol to block out the mental pain of watching too many aircraft going down in flames, and he wondered what had happened to the young man who had first set off from the Isle of Man, determined to change the world.

Walking resolutely past the mess that night back to his digs, Kieran took a moment to take in the dark skies above him. The stars were twinkling and he heard the distant drone of fighters being sent up from RAF Andreas down the road to protect both Belfast and Liverpool, so vulnerable on clear nights like this. He had to accept *he* wouldn't be able to fly again but his job here was to make sure other young men could. First, he had to beat this desperate need for a drink that arose at this time every evening. Kieran knew this was a battle that he had to win and thought it might just be harder than the Battle of Britain.

* * *

On her next visit, Bridget found Helga sitting bolt upright on the cold plinth, seemingly oblivious of the warm blanket that was on the bunk next to her. At the sound of the door opening, she raised her eyes slowly and almost without interest.

'It's only me,' Bridget said, and went to sit next to her, folding her skirt underneath her backside to give some protection from the cement slab. She shivered, looking up at the open, grilled little window that was high up on the opposite wall. It really was a miserable little cell and she suddenly felt sorry for the woman at her side, who was, she noticed, starting to look shrunken and even frail.

'You know,' she started, 'the hearing's been set for July and now you're pleading guilty, there is a chance they might give you bail. It's only a small chance but a chance nonetheless.'

Helga's face lit up for a moment, but then it darkened again.

'No, I don't want it. I will stay here until the court day, if, as you say, my little Karin is *gut* with that Jewish girl,' – she almost spat the word out – 'then here I will stay.'

'But why, Helga?'

'I am not the good mother, I am not who you think I am,' she said in a flat voice, tucking her hands under her thighs and swinging her feet angrily.

Bridget felt the hairs on the back of her neck rising. For days she had been mulling over all the possible reasons why Helga was acting so strangely and glancing at the stricken face next to her, she decided this might be her chance to push for some answers.

'What is it, Helga? Tell me.'

Helga's shoulders started to shake and she rocked backwards and forwards.

'*Ich kann nicht. Ich kann nicht.*'

She could not reveal the horrors that came to her during the night; the visions of a man's legs dangling in the wind; Karin's stricken face; the moment she had realised her whole life had been a lie. Left alone for hours in her cell, her thoughts seemed to bounce backwards and forwards between the white walls on either side. She would sit in the middle with her hands in her ears, trying to block them out.

'What is it, Helga?'

'It is nothing . . . nothing.'

And with that, it was as if a screen had come down over the woman's face. But Bridget persevered.

'Why did you leave Germany, Helga?'

There was no response.

'Was someone threatening you?'

The woman's face went as grey as the stone on the wall behind her.

'Was your neighbour a collaborator? A Jew?'

Helga gasped and started to her feet. She began to pace up and down, then seemed to compose herself enough to turn to face Bridget, her eyes wide with fear.

'I will say nothing, you hear me? *Nichts.*'

And with that, she turned to the wall with her arms crossed. Her reaction was enough to confirm Bridget's suspicions that the hanged man was the key to the mystery.

'Karin needs you, Helga. She really needs you,' she said, and knocked for the guard to let her out, knowing this interview was at an end. As the door closed, Bridget heard a sob that sounded as if it were being wrung from the very heart of the prisoner she was leaving behind.

Chapter Seventeen

Helga was distraught, overwhelmed by the secret she was carrying, but with no idea how she would cope with the shame if the truth was ever brought to light.

She had been brought up in the town of Kirchentellinsfurt by parents who, as soon as Hitler started to rise to power, suddenly went out of their way to proclaim the superiority of the Aryan race. Once her husband was conscripted, Helga and her little daughter, Karin, moved back in with them. It never occurred to her to question their enthusiasm for the new wave of optimism that was sweeping Germany.

On the night Helga received news that her soldier husband had been killed dealing with Jews in Polish ghettos, her life was turned upside down. It was only then that she found out why her parents had needed to express their loyalty to the new, emerging Third Reich regime so vehemently. While she was absorbing the words of the telegram in her trembling hands, their neighbour, Herr Müller, fuelled with brandy, staggered across to Helga's parents' house to rail at the events that were unfolding throughout Germany. He was distraught, thinking of his own Jewish relatives and condemned Helga's tears at the death of her soldier husband. When her mother had told him in no uncertain terms to get his 'dirty Jewish body off their land', he had retaliated with a jibe that would stay with Helga forever.

'How dare you,' he had shouted at Helga's mother, 'we all know your father was a Jew.' And with that he had fallen against the gatepost, leaving Helga standing dumbstruck on the front porch.

That night, her father, a local bookseller who prided himself on his reputation in the area, was desperate to prove his loyalty and protect his business. He visited the local Gestapo and an hour later, some figures in black balaclavas slunk along the street towards the Müller household. Helga's mother firmly closed the curtains and put the radio on full volume, her hands shaking, but little Karin heard the commotion and got up from her bed to totter to the window to pull back the drapes. She let out a piercing scream. The man who had always given her sweets was being hoisted, struggling, with a bag over his head, onto a rope on the tree outside both their houses. As his feet danced in the breeze before becoming chillingly still, Helga rushed to her daughter's side and in that instant, made up her mind. She went to pack, abandoning her parents, her home and her country.

It was a journey fraught with danger and a woman without money, travelling with a small child was an easy target. After a soldier found the pair huddled up in a goods yard, he told Helga to choose: either she gave him what he wanted – or the child would do instead. There was no choice.

Desperate to get to Britain and with them both on the edge of starvation, Helga gave into the inevitable; she would wait until Karin was asleep before offering herself to soldiers loitering on the stations, where the two of them would hide out under archways and in goods wagons. Proclaiming her ardent loyalty to Hitler and reluctantly offering sexual favours, her clients were only too willing to help her board trains, get food and travel across Europe until one of those clients, a cargo loader, smuggled her on board a ship to England to meet up with a subversive group of Nazi supporters.

Since she had been arrested with them and shipped over to the Isle of Man, she had felt she was being watched. One slip, one word out of place would reveal her dangerous secret. Lena Braun had already subjected her to unnerving intense questioning and Helga was living in fear.

* * *

While Bridget was waiting for the bus back to Port Erin, she heard a cough behind her. It was Fynn. He had spent the last ten minutes on the other side of the street watching her, unsure whether to cross over to talk to her, watching her bite her lip and frown as if mulling over some dilemma. Consumed with jealousy after what he had seen at the dance, his immediate thought was that she was thinking about Kieran, and he was about to walk away when he saw her stamp her feet in frustration. It raised a hope in him that all was not going as he feared it might be with his brother and he finally picked up the courage to walk over to find out.

'Hello, Bridget.'

He was taken aback to see the genuine delight in her face as she looked up at him.

'Fynn,' she exclaimed. 'How wonderful to see you.'

He shuffled his feet, unsure how to reply.

'How are you?' she went on.

'All right, s'pose,' Fynn said, 'just here to pick up supplies. Harvest looks OK for this year . . .'

She sighed at his reticence. If only this man would say what was really going through his head, she thought, completely ignoring the fact that honesty was something she too, had been failing at recently.

'That's good, Fynn. I'm pleased . . . but I could do with your advice, do you have time for a cup of tea somewhere?'

Fynn's astonishment was genuine but then his fear that she might be about to mention something to do with her relationship with Kieran made him shiver.

'I'm not an expert on affairs of the heart,' he muttered, adding, under his breath, 'especially where you're concerned.'

Bridget suddenly felt irritated. For once, more pressing police matters had overshadowed her emotions and she really needed his common sense and gentle understanding.

'It's about Helga, you know, the German woman who attacked young Ursula, the Jewish girl,' she said, taking a moment's satisfaction at the astonishment on his face.

His reply was immediate and ridiculously enthusiastic, to compensate for how petty his assumptions had been.

'Yes, yes, of course, I'd be delighted. Anything I can do to help.' And with that he pointed over at the Rendezvous Café across the street.

'I can't work it out,' she explained over a weak cup of tea with Carnation Milk, wincing at the taste. 'She was so full of bluster at the beginning but now she's got all this time to think, she seems to have shrunk somehow. Now she's insisting she will stay in gaol rather than come back to be with Karin. I have my own suspicions but as a total outsider, what possible reason do you think she could have?'

Fynn puzzled over her question, giving it his full attention.

'Maybe she feels safer in gaol. Maybe she's hiding from something . . . or someone?'

Bridget stirred her tea, longing for a bit of sugar to put in it, pondering his words which echoed her own thoughts.

She leaned forward and put her hand over his. 'It's so nice to talk to you, Fynn. I've missed you. '

His brief moment of triumph was suddenly shaded by the memory of her face lifting up towards Kieran's in the moonlight and he felt an anger bubbling up inside him.

'But you and Kieran ...' he started, pushing his chair back.

'Me and Kieran what?'

Fynn stuttered. 'Well, you know ... that kiss ...'

Bridget was stunned. This was why Fynn had behaved so oddly recently; he must have seen them. While it explained everything, it made her furious with herself and to hide it, she stood up and put her hands on her hips.

'Oh, for crying out loud, Fynn, my life is not just about you and Kieran, you know. I have a lot on my plate and I don't need this!'

She turned on her heel and slammed the café door behind her, making the teacups on the table rattle.

* * *

In the cottage kitchen, Molly and Betty were listening intently to Bridget's summing up of her day. Dreading Molly's caustic comments about what an idiot she had been, she was too overwhelmed by shame to confess that she'd kissed Kieran, so only mentioned that she'd bumped into Fynn, casually saying that it hadn't gone well. Betty jumped to her feet and grabbed a piece of paper and a pencil and sat down again.

'Right, let's concentrate on the police side of things,' she said. 'Let's write down everything that's making Bridget's neck hairs stand on end,' she began, and the girls systematically went through the changes in Helga followed by her strange desire to stay in prison, then onto Lena and finally, Karin.

Molly and Betty sat up straight, ready to cross-examine Bridget as if they were in a courtroom.

'Let's go over the facts,' Molly started, taking over the notebook. 'Where was Helga from in Germany?'

'Somewhere in the south I think, but I don't really know. She was picked up in London.'

'Just tell us everything that made you feel a bit uneasy,' Betty said. She, like Alister, was a great believer in instinct and having worked alongside Bridget for more than six months, she knew that her antennae were reliable.

Bridget thought back. It had started with Helga and her vehement defence of the Nazi regime. Somehow, it had a hollow ring to it and Bridget had started to wonder who Helga was trying to convince. *Was someone watching her, threatening her?* she wondered and was that person Lena? Then she thought of the drawing that Karin had done – that was a scene that kept replaying over and over in her mind. The trauma on the child's face had sent shockwaves through the policewoman's body. She knew of many children who had seen terrible things already in this war, and Karin looked tormented, but more than that, Bridget told the girls, completely conflicted somehow.

Betty was scribbling notes, writing down everything that Bridget said while Molly was sitting forward, listening intently.

'And then there's why on earth Helga fled Germany,' Bridget said. 'That doesn't make sense at all.'

Without any details of Helga's previous life in Germany, she was at a complete loss. It would be impossible to find out any more without insider information and the only people they had to ask were Helga herself and a little child.

Molly underlined the words *Previous life?* 'Let's move on,' she prompted. 'What about Lena?'

'Hmm, well, she's not working alone, I'm sure of that and I've a feeling she's got some hold on Helga but I've no idea what.'

'Didn't you feel there was a possibility Lena was getting some messages from Germany?' Betty put in.

'Yes,' Bridget said, 'but how? I mean, any letters they get are carefully scrutinised and, despite all our checks, we haven't managed to track down any missing radios or torches to signal to something out at sea. Oh, I don't know, I could be making that up, they just all looked so smug, as if they knew something they shouldn't and the news about all those poor people in Katyn wasn't even in the papers.'

Betty did a last scrawled note with a flourish and twisted it round to face Bridget.

'Go on then, make of this jumble what you will,' she said. Bridget glanced over at all the notes and as she put the paper back down on the table, gave a deep sigh.

'I have no idea,' she said, finally, 'but I have a strange feeling they are all connected.'

'Talking of connected, Bridget,' Molly broke in, 'what about Kieran and Fynn?'

At which point Bridget got down onto the floor and put her arms around Greeba, who was curled up, as usual, by her feet.

'I'm giving up men. I only need my dog,' she said and buried her face in the animal's fur coat.

The other two laughed.

Chapter Eighteen

It was June and a group of new internees had arrived. They were standing to one side at the roll call at the Golf Links Hotel, looking bewildered and confused, a mix of Jews and supporters of the fascist, Oswald Mosely. Standing slightly apart, were two women whose facial expressions caught Bridget's eye. They looked completely at ease, which was in sharp contrast with everyone else.

Once she'd finished checking the list, Bridget went over to them.

'Hello, are you settling in all right?'

The women turned to her with enthusiasm.

'Oh yes, we are so lucky to be here,' one of them answered. 'We are Jews, you see, and we are pleased to be here on this beautiful island.'

Bridget was taken aback. It was unusual for internees to be so excited by their new situation.

'What are your names?' she asked them.

'*Ich heisse Berta,* oh excuse me, I do not want to speak that language any more . . . and my sister, she is Ester,' one said.

'And where do you both come from, Berta?'

Both women spoke at once.

'Berliner,' Ester said.

'Tübingen,' said Berta, turning to glare at her sister.

'Ah yes, we come from Tübingen now,' Ester said quickly, glaring at her sister. 'We used to live in Berlin but that was a long time ago.'

'Good,' said Bridget. 'Well, I'm sure you'll find others from that area too. I'll come and see you in a couple of days to see how you're getting on. Where is your accommodation?'

Berta looked anything but pleased at the prospect of a visit from a Manx policewoman, but Ester said, 'Oh . . . *Ja* . . . that would be good. We are to stay at The Imperial Hotel, I think.'

Bridget smiled but was carefully studying the women's faces. She was not going to forget these two.

* * *

It was becoming a regular weekly occurrence for Mona Quayle to meet Erika Schneider at Collinson's Café and although her mother's English was greatly improving, Greta always came to help with translations. The café was full and Greta searched around for a table.

'There is room here.' Berta and Ester, two newcomers were sitting on their own, smiling effusively at everyone.

One of them pulled her chair out of the way so the little group could fit round the back.

'Hello,' she said with a broad smile, 'my name is Berta. We are only just arrived here.'

Greta smiled back and introduced herself.

'And this is my sister, Ester,' the woman said, and was about to say something else when Greta was distracted by the waitress standing waiting for their order. She sat down, not noticing that although Berta's back was to her table, she did not shuffle her chair out of hearing.

Mona had applied for a pass into the camp on the pretext of seeing her granddaughter, but it was really the German woman she wanted to see. They were finding their shared interest in herbs and remedies was giving them both a new lease of life, and it was one that Erika, in particular, embraced with enthusiasm and relief.

The cosy chats with the Manx woman took her mind off wondering about her three sons, two of whom, as Greta explained to Mona, were contactable through the Wehrmacht but nothing had been heard from her third son, Karl, since the Luftwaffe plane he was on had crashed over the south coast of England.

Erika was listening to Greta's translation with a pained expression. Whenever she thought of Karl, there were none of her usual reassuring warm feelings, just a terrifying void in her heart which made her wake at night in a cold sweat.

The two women found they had a great deal to teach each other, and Erika was touched that Mona had brought a pencil and pad to write down her advice. It made her feel more worthwhile than she had done in a long time. She discovered it was easy to confide in her new friend and soon confessed how it had been a struggle to keep the family farm going after her husband died from wounds that became infected after the Great War. With days that started at five o'clock in the morning and ended at bedtime, she told Mona, there had been no time to go into the abandoned cowshed where she kept her plants.

'I wanted to keep them for my Karl,' she said, the pride sounding in her voice. 'He is training to be a doctor and was so interested in it all . . . but now, I do not even know if he lives . . .'

Here, Erika paused and her eyes filled with tears, before she finally added that there wasn't a herb concoction in the world that would help her to know what had happened to her youngest son.

Seeing her mother was overcome, Greta spoke for her. 'We lived in a town called Tübingen, it is in the south and once my brothers left, she had no one to defend her or to work the farm and my mother became more and more isolated. The problem was, I had moved to England and the Gestapo started to ask questions about why her daughter had moved to the country of our enemy. It was then she began to see people who had been our friends cross the street to avoid her. You have to understand, everyone was suspicious and oh, so scared.'

Mona felt a chill in her heart. She reached over and put her hand over Erika's. Talking to this woman was making her realise what it must have been like to live under a regime when you were never sure whom you could trust.

There was a pause and then Erika spoke in broken English.

'It got so bad, Mona, I even hear of a man not far away in Kirchentellinsfurt. He had Jewish family in Poland and with no trial, nothing, they put . . . what you call, a rope on his neck . . . and they . . . they . . . from his own tree.' She could not speak the word.

'I am no longer safe. Because of Greta in England, they all start to fear me and no one speaks to me. It was only going to be a short moment before they know I am not a friend of Hitler.'

Erika turned to Greta; she couldn't tell her story well enough in English so spoke in rapid German, before allowing her daughter to translate. As the story unfolded, Greta took a deep breath, thinking it was no wonder it had taken so long for her mother to share her perilous journey. Listening carefully she translated how, with only a small bag, her mother had taken trains and walked at night until she came to the border with France near Strasbourg, where many people feel more French than German. There, she explained, there was a woman . . .

'Yes, yes, tell her it was my good French that saved me,' Erika interrupted.

Greta nodded and turned back to Mona. '*Meine Mutter* speaks fluent French and when this woman threatened her with a big spade, was able to explain that she was, in fact, escaping the Nazis.

'That night, the woman talked of how her own sons had been conscripted into the German forces as part of the "*malgré nous*"- which I think means against our will. Forbidden to speak her native French, this woman . . . she was delighted to talk in her own language to Mama without fear of being betrayed.'

'That night, we were just mothers,' Erika put in, 'just mothers of our sons. She saved me and she knew people. . . .' At this point, Erika hesitated: she was still wary of speaking openly. 'La Main Noire,' she whispered, 'the resistance people, they helped me and then, then, at last, I reach my Greta.'

With this, her eyes filled with tears and she reached her hand over to Greta's face, stroking it as if she still could not believe she was sitting next to her daughter, so many miles away from danger.

There was a silence as they all digested the words that had just been spoken. Mona had listened with quiet horror to the story of Erika's escape, feeling privileged to be the recipient of so much trust, and with a slow nod, she acknowledged how much it had taken Erika to finally tell her story.

Erika sat back, exhausted, and after a long moment of silence at the table said, 'It is a long time that I talk about these things.'

'But we are friends,' Mona said, surprised at her own words.

'Yes,' Erika agreed, 'and one day, when this war is over, maybe you will come to Germany to see my herbs.'

A woman who'd never travelled to the north of the Island, Mona chuckled at this, making Erika laugh too.

'What are you two plotting?' Bridget's voice came from behind them and both women jumped back, guiltily.

'Oh, my goodness,' Bridget went on, pulling a chair up to join them. 'You're as bad as each other. You're like little children who've been caught out doing something naughty.'

'What is . . . naughty?' Erika asked.

Mona touched the side of her nose with her forefinger and grinned, saying, 'Just you ignore my granddaughter, Erika. She has far too much to say.' But then three new customers came in and Mona's face took on a pained expression; she was experiencing what was becoming a familiar tightening in her chest every time she saw one of these defeated internees.

'What is it, Granny?' Bridget asked.

'I don't know, this feeling of mine gets worst every time I see women like them, I feel their anguish.' She clutched her chest, trying to blot out the constriction that instantly took hold of her insides. 'It's just something Erika has said

about a man near to her farm who was hanged in somewhere called Kirchen . . .?

'Yes, Kirchentellinsfurt,' Greta supplied.

'Yes, Kirchen . . . whatever, well, Breesha, they came
at night and they hanged him from his own tree – just
because he had Jewish blood in him. What the Jews, and
ordinary people in Germany, have been through . . . it's far
worse than we know.'

Erika nodded; she didn't understand everything Mona
had just said, but she did understand the sentiment. It
was a new experience being in close proximity to so many
Jews, and she was surprised how their stories, always
understated, suggested huge persecution. Slowly, German
women like her in the camp, were beginning to suspect a
systematic annihilation of Jewish people and it was leaving
them with a horror they hardly dared acknowledge.

Bridget noticed the fearful expression on Erika's face
and gently took her hand.

'It's all right, Frau Schneider, You're safe here. Hitler
won't get across the English Channel. Mr Churchill will
make sure of that. And don't listen to my grandmother.
She thinks she knows everything about the world, but
she's never been off the Island.'

'I don't need to,' her grandmother retorted, touching
first her head and then her heart. 'I see it all in here and
I feel it all in here, but you never know, maybe it's time I
explored a little more.'

Bridget leaned over with a grin and gave her a hug. 'Yes, Granny, one day you're going to travel north to Onchan, aren't you?'

The Island was only small compared to traipsing across London, Bridget thought, but to the Manx, any journey that involved travelling up and down any of its thirty miles always seemed like a voyage to another galaxy.

At that moment, the door opened and Lena came in, her head held back in that challenging way she had about her and Mona and Erika both bristled. They stood up to go, wanting to escape the tense atmosphere that suddenly pervaded the café.

'Come on, Breesha, you can make me a cup of tea in that police station of yours,' Mona said, looking over her shoulder at the German who had just come in. These Nazi women prompted a different feeling in her chest – this was one of anger.

'I will, Granny, just wait outside for me, I'll be there in a minute. Frau Schneider, I'll escort you back to your accommodation on the way if you like. It was good to see you and I really am very pleased that you're having these meetings with my grandmother. I know it does her a lot of good.'

'Me also,' Frau Schneider said, and the two elderly women went arm in arm out into the road outside.

Bridget put her arm on Greta's to waylay her and said, 'Greta, just one question before you go. Where is your farm?'

'In Tübingen,' she replied. 'It is in the south.'

Bridget felt a shiver of excitement. 'And where was this poor man from?'

'Kirchentellinsfurt, it is not far,' Greta told her.

Bridget thanked her and made her way straight over to Lena, who looked up with dislike.

'Lena, where is Helga from?'

Lena looked up, surprised. This police officer was so abrupt, her questions never gave her chance to think. 'Somewhere in the south, *ich denke,* perhaps near to Stuttgart,' she said before she could stop herself. She hated giving any information to this young woman.

With that, Bridget turned on her heels, too intent on finding an atlas to notice Berta turn around to give Lena a small satisfied nod.

Chapter Nineteen

'Mum? Are you in?' There was no reply, so Bridget made her way to the back of the house where the wash house was. An elegant villa, the house was brick built in typical 1930s style. Its construction had been overseen personally by her father, Patrick. A collector of antique books, who searched far and wide for that elusive first edition, his orderly young life had been thrown into confusion when he espied the bohemian Jenny Quayle in an art gallery in Nice. He was immediately entranced by the tall, willowy girl with the most beautiful, untamed dark hair he had ever seen, and he pursued her as if she were a rare copy of Byron's poetry. Eventually he tracked her down at her home in the Isle of Man and throwing all customary caution to the wind, promised to buy her a house opposite the sea if she would just become his bride.

Today was Monday and the washing was being done as normal. *Heaven help any German dictator who thought they could interrupt Nora's domestic timetable,* Bridget thought. Nora was the home help who'd been with the family for years and her efforts to bring some order to the chaotic Harrison household may have been valiant but generally, they were a waste of time. Making the most of the early summer sunshine, the sheets were draped over the line in the back garden and Nora emerged from the wash house, pink-cheeked from stirring the hot dolly tub with the huge wooden pincers. Behind her came Jenny Harrison, looking more as if she belonged in a Rossetti painting than a wash house, with her long hair escaping the ineffectual headscarf and a billowing blue dress, totally unsuited to doing the laundry. Bridget hugged them both. She adored her mother and had known Nora since she was a child so loved her like a member of the family.

'I'm just going up to my bedroom,' Bridget told her mother, not giving her a chance to get a word in and ran straight upstairs. Rummaging under the bed, she found the box with her schoolbooks in and triumphantly emerged clutching the atlas she'd had as a child. She found the page with a map of Germany on it and ran her finger down the page until she came to the town of Tübingen. Then she carefully checked all the place names around it.

'Yes!' she exclaimed. 'There – that's Stuttgart and it's not too far away but damn, there's nowhere called Kirchen-whatever – or at least this atlas doesn't show it.'

She ran onto the landing to bump into her mother who had followed her daughter upstairs.

'Are you staying for lunch? I think Nora cooked some fritters you could have.'

'No thanks, Mum, I just need to talk to Father. He went to southern Germany on his book tour, didn't he?'

Her mother nodded. 'I think so, let's go and ask him. It'll do him good to come out of that study for a minute, he's in there every day.'

Bridget ran down the stairs, clutching the atlas and banged open the study door. Her father looked up from his notes with an annoyed expression.

'It's lovely to see you, Bridget, but do you have to make so much noise?'

She went around the desk and gave him a peck on the cheek.

'It's good for you to have some noise, Dad, it's too quiet in this house.'

She looked towards her mother, who was beaming at having at least one of her children in the house, albeit for just a few moments.

'You're right, Bridget, he spends far too much time locked away in here. We used to go on walks on lovely days like this, didn't we, Patrick?'

'Yes, maybe later, dear,' he said looking down at his notes.

Bridget didn't hear him; she was too busy spreading the atlas out on his desk.

'When you went on your tour of southern Germany, did you go anywhere near here . . . Stuttgart? Do you know this place called. . . . Tübingen?' she demanded, moving her finger across the map.

He tutted at her taking over his space, but then gave in and scrutinised the places she was pointing to.

'Yes!' His face suddenly took on an animation Bridget hadn't seen for years. 'Oh, I met some wonderful people on that trip. They were so kind.'

'You didn't, by any chance, hear of somewhere near there called . . . umm, I think it was Kirchen . . . tellins . . . furt.'

'Yes, yes, I do,' he replied slowly. 'Well, I didn't go there but I do remember meeting a wonderful Jewish Rabbi who had travelled from there to meet me, so it wasn't far away . . .'

His voice faded and then he coughed.

'What about it, Father?'

'I think his name was Cohen; he was so knowledgeable about ancient books. I spent a wonderful afternoon with him, he was a lovely man, so kind and gentle.'

'Was?' Bridget queried.

'Oh, I don't know, Bridget, anything could have happened to him. He took me to see an incredible synagogue in the town of Tübingen, but I think the synagogue was destroyed, just before the war. But what's all this about?'

'Never you mind,' she answered mysteriously.

'Gracious, Bridget. What are you up to?'

'Nothing, well, that's to say, you know I can't tell you.'

She hugged the atlas – and that information – to herself and beamed. 'Thank you, Daddy!' And with those affectionate words, she kissed her mother and raced out of the door.

Her parents stared after her. They were used to their whirlwind daughter, but it was always as if some sunshine had left the room when she went. For a brief moment, Patrick grinned at his wife and she gave a delighted smile back which lit up her face, reminding him of the young woman he had married.

'I haven't seen her that animated since she got back here,' Jenny said with a satisfied grin.

'No, you're right,' Patrick nodded, 'she's been very down since she got back. But you know our Bridget, give her a mystery and she comes to life. Anyway, I must get on, Jenny. I have a great deal to do.'

His wife closed her mouth, and the door behind her, with a click that reminded her of how her husband had got into the habit of shutting her out just as easily, leaving her to echo around the empty house alone.

* * *

Bridget's mind was working very fast; there were several things about the afternoon that had set her skin tingling and she wondered if any of this information might help her find the key to the secrets that Helga was keeping. Wrapping her arms around herself, she walked briskly down the road.

She had seen some grim rumours in the newspapers of the sort of reprisals that were randomly enacted in Germany and she wondered whether there was just a chance, a small chance, that the man who was hanged in that town, Kirchentellinsfurt, could be the same man who haunted Karin's dreams.

Shivering with excitement, Bridget needed to get to roll call but on her way back, she went to check out the open-air swimming pool at the bottom of the hill, in the hope that Nancy was there, having her regular swim. Scanning the crowd, Bridget couldn't see Nancy at first, but then she spotted a figure in a red, spotted bathing suit powering up and down the pool, causing havoc amongst the children, who were trying to play in the shallow end. Bridget went up to the edge of the deep end of the pool and waited for Nancy to reach her to make her turn.

'Where did you come from?' her friend asked, breathlessly.

'Just on my rounds,' Bridget replied with a smile. 'I wondered whether you were free tonight. I need to clear my head. Do you want to come round?'

'No, let's have a proper natter without Molly looking daggers at me. Shall we risk outraging the locals by meeting at the Falcon's Nest? We can sit on the lounge side and fade into that terrible wallpaper,' Nancy called, as she set off on her next length.

Bridget called after her, 'See you at eight.'

A hand in mid-front crawl action gave a thumbs up, splashing water onto the woman's face doing breaststroke next to her.

Bridget licked her lips, tasting the cooling water. She would have loved a swim, and almost envied Nancy for a second, but then remembered the morning's activities and loosened her far-too-hot uniform to set off down the road. Bridget just loved this tantalising thought that she might be onto something; no swim could make up for it. In any case, she told herself, she preferred her exhilarating morning dips in the sea with Greeba, delightedly splashing next to her. Hugging her suspicions to herself, she spotted Ursula, sitting with Karin on a low wall. They both looked lost and quite forlorn, she noticed with a frown.

'Hello, you two,' she called over.

Ursula looked up and forced a smile.

'Hello, Officer Harrison.'

Bridget went and sat on the wall next to Karin, who was swinging her legs slowly backwards and forwards.

'How are you both?'

'OK,' the little girl replied, unconvincingly. Ursula said nothing, she hadn't slept all week since Ruth had told her their enquiries had yielded no information about her little brother and sister. And although the kindly Quaker

SHIRLEY MANN

woman had said no more, Ursula was gripped with panic that they had been killed in one of the subsequent bombing raids.

'Karin,' Bridget said, 'I just need to ask you something. Did you live near a place called Kirchentellinsfurt?'

The child froze and then nodded. Any excitement that the pieces of the jigsaw might have been slowly slotting into place were wiped out by the utterly miserable expression on Karin's face. So Bridget rushed on to give her some good news quickly.

'You know your mummy is going to court soon, let's hope it won't be too long before she's allowed home.'

'Mmm,' Karin said, looking down at her feet. 'She doesn't want me anymore,' she muttered, looking plaintively at the police officer next to her. 'If she loved me, she would have taken that bail thing to come back for a while.'

Bridget looked over the child's head towards Ursula, who simply shrugged.

'It seems neither of us are wanted,' Ursula said, her face sad and despondent.

'Oh, Ursula, that certainly isn't true. What makes you say that?'

The girl started to stutter, then in a flat voice, she blurted out, 'I think my brother and sister are dead.'

And with that chilling statement, Ursula took hold of Karin's little hand, gave a curt goodbye and the pair of

206

them dragged their feet off down the street. Bridget stared after them, wishing she could do more to help ease their pain. But then she remembered that time was racing on and she needed to get to roll call. She always felt like she was taking two steps forward and one back.

Chapter Twenty

It was a distracted Bridget who made her way to the Falcon's Nest that night. Waiting for Nancy at the doorway, she noticed how the June weather had changed with the tide and now gusts of wind were tugging at her hair. The temperature had dropped too.

Looking rather pleased with herself, Nancy greeted her friend. 'Well, I did think you looked mysterious earlier, Bridg, but now you just look glum. Are you OK?'

Bridget gave a nod. She didn't want to admit to Nancy, of all people, that she was feeling out of her depth. Her conversation with Ursula and Karin had unsettled her. A policewoman had to know how to unravel all these tangled strands and as things stood, Bridget was just feeling choked by them all.

Nancy was too eager to impart her own news to notice Bridget's reticence.

'Guess what? I've got a posting ... and, you'll never believe it, they've given in to my pleading and it's here – on the Island!' Nancy said with a giggle.

'Where? What?' Bridget exclaimed, pleased to think about anything but the problems within Rushen Internment Camp.

Nancy touched the side of her nose but her eyes twinkled.

'Maybe somewhere near Cregneash . . .'

Bridget knew that some secret work was going on in that cordoned-off area with the little thatched cottages but she had no idea what it was.

'What will you be doing?' she asked, without thinking.

'Oh, come on. As someone who isn't about to tell me why *you* were so pleased with yourself this afternoon, you know better than to ask me,' Nancy laughed, and took Bridget's arm to steer her into the pub. 'Let's go, we need to make the most of the last days of my freedom!'

'How's your father?' Bridget asked.

'Hmm, well, basically it's because of him that they're allowing me to stay but he's no better. I'm not sure he's ever going to improve, to be honest.'

'I'm so sorry, Nancy. Anyway, I'm delighted you're going to be sticking around. Let's get a drink to celebrate!'

* * *

The old men around the bar, left behind by conscription, parted like the Red Sea and tutted with disapproval, but Nancy strode through them confidently to order.

'It's like going back in time, coming back here,' Nancy turned to whisper to Bridget. 'This lot have no idea how many women go to pubs on their own in London.' Bridget looked around, feeling a little awkward without a male escort. She was beginning to regret her impulse, knowing her reputation would be discussed and condemned before she had taken her first sip.

'Hello,' a familiar voice said.

It was Fynn and he looked very unsure as to whether he was pleased to see them or not, but Bridget looked around with relief.

'Oh, it's good to see you, Fynn, I was beginning to feel like a fallen woman.' Her joking words hid the shudder that had reverberated through her body when she saw his tanned face and blue eyes. Kieran may have been like an old wound opening up, but Fynn unleashed an emotion she had yet to identify. She was constantly surprised at the strength of it.

'Well, I suppose I can at least provide you with a male escort,' he said with a frown. The bar, which had gone quiet when the girls walked in on their own, suddenly became noisy again with relief, and Bridget had to shout their orders for two 'gin and Its' into his ear. While the barman poured the gin and Italian vermouth into glasses, Fynn took a long gulp of his beer to steady the nerves that were rising in his throat. After the embarrassment of his outburst at the café, he'd suffered hours of torment, finally convincing himself that there were various possible explanations: firstly, that both Kieran and Bridget had had too much to drink and the kiss meant nothing, secondly, that Kieran had been his usual flirtatious self but that Bridget wasn't interested. The third option – that she still loved Kieran – was too painful to contemplate.

The trio went to sit at their usual table in the corner and Nancy, unaware of the tension between her companions, launched into a conversation.

'How's Kieran?' she asked him.

Oh, back to my beloved brother, Fynn thought, but then out loud, said, 'It looks like he might be sent to Cregneash.'

Nancy squealed with delight. 'Oh, I'm going to Cregneash too! I've got a posting there.'

Fynn's face brightened. He had seen how this girl had looked at his brother and, for a brief moment, he felt a glimmer of hope.

Nancy was talking about the places they'd gone to in London. Their lively chatter about landmark she'd only heard about on the wireless made him feel like a country boy who'd never travelled and he inwardly cursed his brother, fate and that terrible sense of duty that had dictated his future. Bridget noticed how quiet Fynn had become and turned the conversation around to some of his rescue missions on the lifeboat, prompting Fynn to tell her the most dangerous ones he had ever been involved in.

Bridget thought how typical it was of Fynn to immediately regale them with stories of others' heroism, but she felt a fierce pride, knowing how frequently he risked his life to save others. She was about to tell him so when the door flew open, letting in a sudden gust of wind and one of the lifeboatmen rushed in. He had on all his yellow water-proofs but they were smattered with rain. His eyes darted around the room but then he spotted Fynn.

'Oh, thank God I've found you!' he said, his breath coming in short bursts. 'We've got to go. Coastguard been on. Fishing boat on rocks.'

Fynn immediately put his drink down and ran to the door. At the last moment, he turned but his face gave nothing away. Bridget had no idea whether he regretted being interrupted or was grateful for the chance to escape.

The whole bar followed, their drinks abandoned and the girls joined them. A fishing boat in trouble was a dis-aster for the whole community and they needed to show their support for their brave lifeboatmen as well as the fishermen.

On their way to the jetty, they hugged their coats around them. The cold was more like February than June.

Fearful of the power of the wind, Bridget shouted into Nancy's ear, 'This is turning into a real storm.' She peered to try to spot Fynn, but all she could see was a blur of yel-low jackets, as the lifeboatmen made their way efficiently round the boat to get it into the heaving water at the end of the slipway. It was unusual for the wind to affect the inner sanctuary of the bay, but on this night, the weather had its own ideas. Every head was turned towards the lifeboat, willing it to succeed.

A crowd had gathered around them, alerted by the sound of the sirens from police cars and ambulances which had been called by the coastguard. It was well past curfew, so the onlookers were all locals, but further up the village, anxious faces of internees were pressed up against the windows of the hotels and boarding houses, craning their necks to see what was happening. For many of them, the sound of the clanging bells recalled disturbing memories and more than one of them had their hands clutched to their breasts.

At that moment, Molly ran up to them, followed by Betty.

'We heard the commotion! People are saying it's the Kelly family. Isn't one of them . . .' She stopped. She was only just getting to know all the locals.

'Yes,' Bridget said softly, 'one brother's a policeman at Peel but the rest of them . . . and their dad . . . are all fishermen.'

As she scanned the crowd, she saw a woman in a plaid scarf, clinging onto a younger girl next to her.

Bridget nodded towards her. 'There's Mrs Kelly and her daughter, Lilee. That poor woman, that's three of her men out there.'

Alister came up behind them.

'The coastguard spotted them near the cliffs round the corner under Bradda Head. I don't fancy their chances on a night like this.' It may have been early summer but the black clouds had darkened the sky and cold gusts were whistling around the bay.

The little crowd stood, transfixed, gazing into the turbulent water in front of them, all cursing the vagaries of island weather. Some were clutching their arms around themselves, others held themselves erect, like statues. Many of them reached an arm out to the person next to them, searching for warmth and comfort. The Island was never closer than when catastrophe struck and the people of Port Erin held together in solidarity, sending out their combined strength into the stormy air. The boat roared into life and sped off around the corner. Once the engine noise had faded, there was no sound except the wind and the thrashing of the waves.

The people in the crowd all leaned towards the edge of the bay, trying to be the first to see the reassuring shape of the lifeboat heading back but time dragged on and it became increasingly dark and cold. Each person was trying to dispel the thoughts of that tiny fishing boat being flung against the rock face and in weather like this, not only the men on the trawler would be at risk, but also the lifeboat crew trying to save them. The throng felt every minute of the next hour, checking their watches and stamping their feet to keep the circulation moving, but at the end of it, some were beginning to shake their heads. As the wind howled and the rain lashed down, anxious faces continued to stare into the distance, searching for a light, a sound, a shadow that might herald a successful rescue mission.

Bridget stood with Nancy, Molly and Betty outside the lifeboat station. They'd linked arms but they were all shivering.

* * *

Around the corner, out of sight from the jetty, the lifeboat was pitching and tossing in the waves that were crashing against its hull. A lone flare had alerted the coastguard and cursing the stubborn fishermen who refused to wear life jackets, Fynn focused his binoculars on the moving horizon.

Narrowing his eyes and peering all around, he eventually shouted, 'I see them, I see them!' and pointed towards the dark shape of a vessel that was wedged on its side on some rocks under the towering wall of Bradda Head. The boat had a gaping hole in its side and was taking in water fast. They would need to get close in, which was dangerous in a storm like this, and the coxswain was looking nervously at the sheer rock face that was not nearly far enough away.

Through his binoculars, Fynn could just about see two figures clinging to the wheelhouse, their hair plastered to their faces. They were waving their arms frantically at the approaching lifeboat.

He grabbed the megaphone and yelled, trying to make his voice heard over the tumult of the gale that was whistling around them.

'Hold on, hold on, we're coming!'

He saw the younger Kelly boy's white face turn towards the light of the lifeboat. He looked like a ghost already. His brother was clinging onto his arm, which was obviously hurt, but with his other hand he was frantically waving at the front of the boat. Fynn yelled to his shipmates, 'You get these two in, I'll look for their dad!' And with that, he leaned over the prow. It was almost impossible to see anything, but Fynn reached back to grab the flashlight and strafed the hull of the trawler and the inky waters beneath.

He was shaking his head, thinking that it was like looking for a needle in a heaving haystack, when he spotted a pale hand, hanging onto a line that had toppled with its owner, over the front of the boat.

'I've got him, I've got him – it's Ted, but we need to get closer!' Fynn yelled.

'We can get to the side of them for the two lads but we'd have to get at him from on-board,' the coxswain said with a shake of his head.

'Right,' said Fynn, with a grim expression, trying to assess how he was going get to the man clinging for his life just feet above the swirling waters. As he watched, the pale hand slipped and Ted Kelly's body slid down the hull and into the sea.

Fynn threw out a lifebuoy ring with a lifeline attached. He reached back, attached another line to himself and was then heard to say, 'Oh what the hell . . .' and a splash was heard. The coxswain, Rory Corkill was furious; this was not the protocol they had all practised over and over again. He yelled to one of the other crew and between them, they threw out another lifebuoy, while keeping the light trained on the two bodies floundering in the sea.

Fynn grabbed onto the hand that was intermittently appearing above the heaving waves and pulled it up so that the drowning man's head rose above the surface, spluttering and gasping for air. Fynn immediately put him onto his back to perform the life-saving technique he knew so well, but the wind was still whipping up the waters around him and Ted Kelly was panicking.

Fynn yelled into his ear, 'If you don't keep still, Ted, I'm going to drop you and then we'll never get to the Falcon for that last pint.'

The familiar voice seemed to resonate with the floundering figure and he stopped struggling, allowing Fynn to put the lifebuoy over his head and yank them both in on the lifeline so that the coxswain could drag him towards the lifeboat. He pushed Ted forward and felt the relief as strong arms reached down to haul the trawler captain aboard.

It was only then that Fynn felt the weight of his boots start to pull him down.

Putting the life ring around his own neck, Fynn hurriedly pushed off one boot then the other and started to edge his way forward, flailing his arms enough to get nearer to the lifeboat. He tried to clamber up but it was only with the help of three of the crew that he was able to get a foothold and drag himself onto the wet deck.

'I don't know whether to hug you or punch you,' Rory Corkill said. 'You know the rules, you never put yourself in danger to carry out a rescue.'

'I'll remember that next time,' Fynn said with a rueful smile.

'You certainly will . . . but in the meantime, you owe us a pair of boots,' the coxswain told him, as he handed him a hot drink from his flask.

Chapter Twenty-One

'I can see them!' Bridget shouted, jumping up and down. The imposing hull of the lifeboat was coming around the corner. She peered into the darkness to count the people on board and punched Molly on the arm in delight when she spotted Fynn standing next to three figures in blankets.

Once the boat came towards the slipway, a huge cheer went up from the people in the crowd, who parted to let the ambulance stretchers through, their joyous clapping resounding in the wind. The girls had to move out of the way but Bridget felt a fierce pride as Fynn helped the soaking fishermen leave the boat and she went over to him.

'You're wet through,' she said alarmed.

'Yes,' Rory Corkill called over. 'He decided to go for a swim, didn't you, Moore?'

Bridget stared at Fynn questioningly. This had obviously not been a normal rescue.

She looked so relieved to see him that Fynn wanted to immediately wrap his arms around her, but every time he came near this girl, all he could see was her head reaching up to kiss his brother. He stumbled backwards.

'Not now, Bridget. Not now.'

She stiffened and gulped, watching him walk away with the rest of the crew to get checked by the ambulance crew.

Betty came up to her and took her arm.

'Honestly, Bridg, what are we going to do with you two? I'd married Joe in the time it takes you two to have a sensible conversation.'

Bridget dropped her head in misery. How could she expect Fynn to understand how conflicted she was feeling, when she didn't understand it herself?

'Come on,' Betty said, 'you look exhausted, let's get home and get that kettle on.'

Even the cold kitchen at the cottage seemed like a warm refuge after the freezing tarmac near the Lifeboat Station. A jug of hot chocolate was produced by Molly and they all sat cradling their drinks, quietly reflecting on the night's events, until Nancy broke the silence by reaching over and offering them all one of Jenny Harrison's famous oat biscuits.

'Here you are, these will help.'

'I'm sorry, Nancy, you wanted tonight to be a celebration of your new job,' Bridget said, mindlessly biting on a biscuit.

Nancy waved her arm dismissively. 'Don't be ridiculous, I'm just so glad the Kelly family were rescued. That Fynn's a bit of a hero, isn't he?'

'We just never know how much, do we?' Molly put in. 'And you know what he's like, he's never going to tell us.'

Betty watched carefully as Bridget suddenly stopped munching, looking thoughtful.

'Are you OK, Bridg?'

'Yes, yes, I think I am.' She sighed deeply. 'I'm just so tired, I think I'll just take my drink and get to bed.'

And with that, she stood up.

As she reached the door, she turned.

'I've known Fynn since I was a little girl. No matter what our relationship is now, I'd never have forgiven myself if anything had happened to him, I just wouldn't.'

* * *

When she'd gone, the three girls looked at each other.

Nancy spoke first.

'I don't know what she's waiting for. She obviously loves him, why can't she just tell him?'

Molly looked thoughtful. She watched Bridget more than the others and knew she was hiding something.

'She's close to breaking point.' It was a frank statement but one they all agreed with. 'I think we need to find out what's going on.'

Betty nodded. 'She's worrying so much about Karin and Ursula, adding Fynn to her list isn't going to help.'

Nancy laughed. 'When did men ever help a situation?'

Molly gave a slight sneer. 'That's certainly true. They just complicate things.'

'So, what do we do?' Betty asked.

After a few moments, Nancy clapped her hands in glee.

'I know. What she needs is a holiday!'

Molly scoffed. 'We can't have holidays!'

'No, but surely you can have a forty-eight hour leave? My father's stable at the moment and my mum's been on at me to take a break before the posting starts. And, as for Bridget, well, she needs to get out into nature. You know what she's like, she's wedded to the wild. She needs to get away from that camp. Maybe we all do.'

The three girls put their heads together and plotted.

* * *

Bridget kept her thoughts about Fynn to herself and in any case, there was little time to dwell on them. Amidst the usual squabbles, petty crimes and welfare issues, there was something about the two new women that made Bridget's spine tingle. Every time she saw them, she felt they were being overly ingratiating to all the Jewish women, who surprisingly held back rather than welcoming them into their fold.

After watching the pair at roll call one night, Bridget discussed them with Molly and Betty.

'I've tried to talk to them but they're so pushy, they set my nerves on edge,' she said.

'And,' she said with a flourish, 'they couldn't seem to decide whether they came from Berlin or Tübingen.'

Betty interrupted. 'I've heard things were chaotic for all Jews after Kristallnacht. For the first time, they realised that the Nazis were out to kill as many of them as possible. I mean, that was in '38 so if they fled then, it's quite likely their records could be muddled.'

'Hmm, perhaps,' Bridget agreed, 'but there was something unsettling about them. I can't put my finger on it. No, actually,' she said suddenly, 'do you know what it was? They were behaving like excited tourists. People feel all sort of emotions when they arrive, but they don't usually behave like children on a seaside holiday.'

'OK, Bridg, leave it with us,' Betty said, 'we'll see what we can find out. You've got enough to deal with. We can check out their story. Anyway, we've got a forty-eight hour leave to organise.'

'Oh, thank you,' Bridget said, smiling warmly at them both, grateful for their support. She really was feeling exhausted and agreed the prospect of a night away might just be the tonic she needed.

'Oh, and we've asked both Fynn and Kieran,' Molly added casually.

Bridget pushed her hair off her forehead and sighed. *Was nothing ever straightforward,* she thought?

* * *

Damian O'Callaghan had heard nothing for a while from Lena but then, on his regular check, he spotted a piece of paper crammed in behind the stone in the church porch. A few of her words were hard to decipher as she had used German script for some letters, but once he worked out the plea he had been expecting for so long, his mouth sneered up into a satisfied smile.

We need your help. I must not be seen with you so we must be careful. I will meet you at three o'clock behind The Imperial.

Dressed in his overalls at five minutes to three that afternoon, Damian whistled as he made his way to the back door of the hotel, carrying his bag of tools.

As a handyman, Damian could wander in and out of hotels and boarding houses without attracting attention and, checking the kitchen staff were not on duty, he moved along the lead pipes, using his wrench to bang them with a knowledgeable air, until he heard a whisper from the back door. Edging backwards towards it, he saw Lena's face looking anxiously around the door frame.

'Hello, darlin',' he said cheerfully, ignoring her finger which she pressed against her lips and then, smiling broadly, he leaned in conspiratorially and whispered, 'So, you need us, do yer? Thought you might . . . but you haven't heard my price yet.'

'It's not about the money, we need to know you can be trusted,' Lena said through clenched lips. 'We have made the checks, but I need to hear it from you.'

'So, checks is it? Will this do yer?' His grin changed into a bitter sneer and he rolled up his sleeve to show a scar that stretched from wrist to elbow.

'I got this when I was five. I tried to stop the bastards stringing up me *da*. They sliced at me with a bayonet. That enough for yer, darlin'?'

'Just know that if you betray us, we will kill you,' Lena said darkly.

'To be sure,' he said with a sly grin, 'and if you betray us, I think you'll find we won't be keen on letting you live either.'

There was a moment's silence while the two of them sized each other up and then Lena nodded.

'So, *das ist gut*. We will work together. We will meet one week from now.'

* * *

Kieran didn't know whether to feel relieved or nervous at the news that he had finally been accepted to work on the new project at Cregneash, starting on Monday. The last month had been unbearably hard but when the Wing

Commander Pickering had looked him straight in the eye and asked, 'Can you control the drinking?' he'd been forced to admit that he was finding it harder than he thought. The warning that followed left him in no doubt that this was his last chance, so he was pleasantly surprised to find a message from Nancy in his pigeonhole inviting him to join the girls in a group camping trip that Saturday – a plan that fitted in perfectly with his new posting. Twiddling the piece of paper in his hand, he mused that being close to Bridget might help him to deal with the disturbing memory of her soft lips on his. Tortured with guilt that he had trampled on Fynn's feelings, he'd casually asked his sister about Bridget and had been surprised by Kathleen's ready admission that *everyone* knew about her childhood crush on Kieran. Everyone except himself, he thought. But now they were adults, and he hoped that seeing Bridget in the hut where they had all spent so much of their childhood, she might once again become nothing more than the little sister of his two best friends.

He went to use the camp telephone.

* * *

Bridget, Nancy and Betty were waiting at the bus stop the following Saturday morning, an excited Greeba at their feet, sensing an adventure. Nancy and Betty were carrying rucksacks with everything from blackout material for the windows to pans for making food hanging out of every corner of them. Betty gave him a wave.

'Over here!' she called and then, as he reached them, she said, 'Good, now all we need is Fynn and we can get off.'

'Is Fynn coming?' Kieran asked. 'I wasn't sure he'd be able to get time off the farm.' He felt a touch of irritation and realised he'd been hoping to spend time with Bridget alone, to sort out his feelings without his brother being around.

'When he heard you were coming, he talked to Kathleen and she said she could cope,' Bridget told him. No one but Kathleen knew how determined she was that Fynn should not be left out of this little gathering.

Bridget was nervous enough about this weekend. Firstly, she had too much on her mind to be taking time off and secondly, it seemed like a disaster waiting to happen. Any hopes that Sergeant Robinson would forbid it were soon dashed by a very resolute Molly, backed up by Alister, who insisted they could manage. So, with the proviso that they telephoned the station first thing Sunday morning to make sure there were no problems, the trip was sanctioned.

At that moment, a tractor appeared over the horizon.

'Trust Fynn to make an entrance,' said Kieran with a wry laugh.

But when his brother swung down from the leather seat, Fynn's face was anything but cheerful.

'Got a cow that's in trouble,' he said grumpily. 'Got to wait for the vet to come, I'll try and join you but I think I'll be lucky.'

Bridget answered quietly, 'We'll miss you, Fynn. We've brought some toasting forks. Maybe you could join us later?' Kieran looked suspiciously at her, completely bemused, wondering whether he had imagined that night at the dance.

'Hm,' snorted Fynn. 'Anyway, I just wanted to come and let you know,' and he swung back onto the tractor and drove off with more vigour than needed.

The little foursome got the bus to Dalby and then tramped over the fields, preceded by an impatient Greeba, until they came across the old stone barn where all the Harrisons and the Moore brothers had camped so many times in their youth. Niarbyl was as beautiful as ever, Bridget noticed, and in the distance, over the clear horizon, she could just see the Mountains of Mourne in Ireland. White Beach spread below them, where the children had watched for seals and basking sharks, and she remembered Fynn telling her that the rocks were four hundred and eighty million years old – a fact that had made her ten-year-old jaw drop.

The building had been a shepherd's shelter and over the winters, a man called William lived in it, making it a basic, but cosy, little hut.

'I'll get some wood for a fire,' Kieran told them, heading off towards a copse.

'I'll make it light-proof,' Bridget said, 'then we won't get into trouble for breaking the blackout but hopefully, if this sky doesn't cloud over, we can go to watch one of Niarbyl's amazing summer sunsets.' Walking through the creaking door, she found Nancy and Betty had already started to lay out their blankets on the wooden slabs that were on each side of the wall. She looked around in panic to realise the only space left was next to Kieran.

'I'll leave this area for Fynn in case he changes his mind and I'll curl up in this old armchair.' Bridget patted the chair and a haze of dust rose from it. She coughed and the other two girls started to laugh.

'We tried that and that's why we decided to bag these,' Betty said, patting her coat into a pillow shape on the plinth. Kieran came in, his arms full of twigs.

'So, we're all set for a fire when it gets chilly!' he said, triumphantly, and laid them at the side of the fireplace while he used one of the twigs to scoop out the ashes that had been there for years. Betty and Nancy were giggling in the corner as they tried to get a primus stove going. They'd hardly been able to struggle off the bus with what seemed like enough equipment for a whole battalion but when they were able to make a very creditable supper of potatoes, beans and bread, Bridget was glad they had ignored her objections to the large pile of supplies.

After an early supper, they all went onto the hills overlooking the beach, Greeba romping ahead. They stood in awe as the July sun slowly sank in the west, sending the sky above them a dark shade of burning red. Kieran shuddered; it reminded him too much of the flames around his cockpit on the day in 1940 when his aircraft had plunged into the sea. He turned to go back to the hut and, eventually, dragging their eyes away from the incredible burnished sky, the rest followed, excited about toasting their bread on the fire. Once the dog was snoring contentedly at their feet, Nancy commented on how normal it all seemed; it made each one of them think of a time before the war, when young people like them could take a holiday and leave all their cares behind them.

Bridget caught Kieran's eye and they both smiled. The scene took them back to the numerous visits they had made here as children. She felt her stomach turn over; he was as good-looking as he had been when they were ten. Her heart sank. Was she never going to be cured of this man?

Chapter Twenty-Two

It was a pensive little group that sat gazing into the fire, each of them thinking about the lives they could have had without the war, but as they pretended to read a book or flick through a magazine, the temperature dropped and Bridget shivered.

'You cold, Bridget?' Kieran asked.

She wrapped her arms around herself and shrugged.

'A little maybe.'

Kieran immediately jumped up and volunteered to go outside for more wood. He told himself it was because he needed to get as far away as possible from the appealing aroma of cider, but the reality was he was unnerved by the proximity of Bridget. Gathering sticks, he wondered what the hell was going on. He'd thought Fynn was very keen on Bridget, but with the recent coolness between them, he knew something had gone badly wrong. Surely Fynn couldn't know anything about the kiss at the dance . . . could he?

'No,' he said out loud to himself. 'Now, get back in there and remember Bridget Harrison is just like a cousin to you.'

Walking back in, Kieran gave a satisfied smile to the girls in the room, confident he'd sorted the situation for good.

Betty was in charge of topping up the pan on the fire with cider and was making the most of the opportunity to refill her own cup. She was in the middle of a large glug when there was a sound outside and Fynn came in, brushing the makeshift blackout curtain to one side. Betty took a large gulp of her drink and giggled. 'Hello Fynn, Bridget's cold and I was just about to suggest she and Kieran should cuddle up to keep warm.'

'Oh, sorry,' Fynn said, his voice sharp, 'have I interrupted something?'

Bridget immediately got to her feet and, almost tripping over an enthusiastic Greeba, ran over to welcome Fynn, unable to believe he'd chosen that moment to join them. She glared at Betty.

'No, of course not, Betty's just joking. Oh Fynn, it's lovely to see you. I'm so glad you made it.'

Kieran looked up, relieved that he'd put aside any amorous thoughts about Bridget. His brother was the man for her, not a washed-up pilot with a damaged hand who had needed alcohol to be brave.

'Sorted the cow out, did you, Fynn? Everything all right?'

Fynn nodded curtly and Nancy handed him a tin mug of hot cider.

'Here, have this,' she said. 'It will warm you up.'

'Seems this room's warm enough,' Fynn replied.

Bridget started to prattle on about how Betty and Nancy had brought enough stuff for a week, to mask her agonisingly muddled feelings at the prospect of both brothers in the same room.

'Put some more sticks on, Kieran,' Nancy said, pulling her arms around herself. Once the flames took hold of the new wood, Kieran settled down on the chair next to the fire, while Fynn hovered in the middle of the room.

'Oh, do sit down, Fynn,' Kieran told his brother. 'You'd make a cat nervous.'

Fynn skirted around Bridget to sit on the other side of the fire next to Nancy.

Kieran's shoulders relaxed and he remembered the times he had been in this hut as a young boy, making fires with his best friends and his elder brother. He gave a deep sigh, thinking how the war had changed all of them.

His gaze rested on Bridget and he watched as the firelight caught the dark flecks in her eyes. She tossed back her hair and feeling an uncomfortable tightening of his groin, he shifted in his seat. Glancing over towards Fynn, he noticed he was chatting in an animated fashion to Nancy. A thought occurred to Kieran that if his brother really didn't want Bridget . . . then maybe . . .

Kieran jumped to his feet; he really needed to banish such thoughts.

'Shall we play a card game?' he said, moving swiftly across to his pack to unearth a deck of cards. On the other side of the fireplace, Nancy was watching him with interest. She had a plan of her own when it came to Kieran Moore and the prospect of being at Cregneash with him was an opportunity she was not going to waste.

Betty, however, was basking in the warm glow of three drinks and was just having a good time, rather than being an anxious wife of a soldier, thousands of miles away in Africa. She felt a moment of guilt as she thought of her husband facing the enemy in the desert and quickly took another gulp of cider.

The game of snap instigated a more light-hearted atmosphere and finally, amidst the battling over who was cheating, even Fynn relaxed.

* * *

The night was not exactly a comfortable one for Bridget, Fynn and Kieran; the three of them tossed and turned, their thoughts jumbled and confusing, but Betty and Nancy slept like logs. Hearing the sounds of the birds, Nancy jumped up to tend to the dying embers of the fire for morning tea while Betty, nursing a thick head, offered to take Greeba and walk to the telephone to ring Sergeant Robinson.

The hut went quiet again until Bridget stretched in the armchair and wiped the sleep out of her eye. She looked over to Fynn who was intermittently snoring on the floor, his eyes crumpled into a frown, and then she glimpsed Kieran with his tousled hair flopped onto his coat that he was using as a pillow.

'They're like the Babes in the Wood, aren't they?' Nancy whispered.

Bridget, who was actually thinking they looked more like Cain and Abel, gave a weak nod.

The door opened and Betty came back, making the two men stir. Kieran yawned and Fynn jumped to his feet, embarrassed to be the last to wake.

'Sorry,' he mumbled. 'It's just I'm normally up for milking . . .'

Bridget smiled at him. His face looked like a little boy who had been caught with his hand in the biscuit tin.

'You're on holiday, Fynn,' she told him. 'It's allowed.' And she handed him a mug of tea.

At that moment, the drone of planes was heard above them. Nancy raced to the door, her heart thumping but then called back, 'It's all right, they're ours.'

Betty stamped her feet. 'Can't we just forget this damned war for two minutes?'

Fynn went over and put a friendly arm around her shoulder, giving her a reassuring smile.

'Yes, we can, Betty.' And he looked around at them all. 'Come on, everyone. Let's go for a walk. It's a lovely day and I've only got a few hours before I need to get back.

SHIRLEY MANN

I know a beautiful spot near here where we can have our sandwiches. It's an eighth century chapel and it's just along the coastal path'

Betty's frown lifted and Bridget gave Fynn a grateful smile.

* * *

It was on the hills above Niarbyl that Bridget took her first clear breath for weeks. She looked down at the grass beneath her feet and smiled. It was this connection with the earth that she'd missed so much when her shoes had pounded the pavements of London. Too busy looking down at the ground with satisfaction, she failed to notice Fynn had stopped in front of her to look at the view and she bumped into him.

'Oh, I'm sorry,' she said and then, seeing him turn around to face her, she grabbed the opportunity to continue. 'Fynn, I wish we could be friends again.'

He cocked his head on one side, considering her suggestion and so before he could reply, she blurted out, 'I miss you, you see. I miss our talks, our dates.' She was on the point of saying *your arms around me* when Kieran came up behind them and Fynn's face fell.

Bridget was so angry with both of them: Fynn for making assumptions about her and Kieran for being a shadow she couldn't dispel from her life. But, she reluctantly

236

acknowledged, she was more cross with herself. Shaking the grass off her shoes, she stomped off over the field.

Betty ran to follow her.

'Are you OK, Bridget?'

'No, I'm not,' she replied 'Sometimes I just wish men would disappear off the face of the earth.'

Betty's face crumpled into a frown. 'No, Bridg, believe me, when they do, you miss them like hell.'

Bridget felt ashamed of her selfishness and linked her arm with Betty's.

'Of course, I'm sorry, Betty. I was just being self-absorbed and self-indulgent. That was not a nice thing to say.'

'What wasn't?' Kieran piped up, and then not waiting for a reply, he added, 'Isn't it time for those sandwiches we brought with us? I'm starving.'

Betty raised her eyes to heaven. The only thing that really mattered to men, she whispered to Bridget with a chuckle, was food.

* * *

It was as they sat around on some rocks overlooking the sea that Bridget weighed up the two men sitting ten paces apart in front of her. If she had any sort of conscience, she would pick one, once and for all; if there was any sort of justice in the world, she would have no doubts and if the gods cared at all, they would not be brothers. It then occurred to her that her dilemma was a waste of time as neither of them seemed very interested in *her*.

The sun shone on her face and she munched her Marmite sandwich despondently. Her personal problems seemed so insignificant when she compared them to the dramas that had been unfolding down at Rushen. First there was Helga who was a complete enigma and then there was a niggling feeling that there were undercurrents in the camp she couldn't quite put her finger on. Remembering her father's words that if you can't solve the big problems, then start with a little one, she suddenly sat up. There was one person she could maybe give some hope to.

'I'm going to see if I can find Ursula Apler's brother and sister,' she announced to Betty, hugging her knees in.

'Good idea,' Betty muttered mid-sandwich. 'And what else are you single-handedly going to do, Bridget Harrison?'

'I think she's going to win the war, all by herself,' Nancy called from the rock behind them.

They both started to laugh and reluctantly, Bridget joined in. Somehow, because this was her island, she felt it was her responsibility to make the internees' lives better.

'Come on,' Betty suddenly said, jumping up. 'Let's race back to the hut, we need to get back before curfew so we can do roll call. Molly'll be tearing her hair out trying to please the sarge all on her own.'

Nancy stayed put. She was hoping to hang back until Kieran was ready to walk down but Fynn had taken the challenge of a race seriously and was already grabbing his brother's arm to pull him to his feet.

'OK, Kier, on your marks, get set, GO . . .!' he shouted and took off at quite a pace down the hill, pursued by Kieran who was throwing back his head in laughter.

Betty came up behind Bridget. 'It's really lovely to see the two boys not squabbling, isn't it?'

Bridget looked at the two men and had to agree. It had been so long since they had behaved like the close brothers they had once been; it was a welcome sight. She sighed to think that she could be the cause of a rift between them and ran to catch them up.

Chapter Twenty-Three

Meeting up with an internee from Rushen Camp was a complicated arrangement and Damian O'Callaghan was beginning to wonder whether the price he had quoted was enough to make it worthwhile to help these Nazis, even one as attractive as Lena Braun. He approached St Catherine's church porch and felt, once again, with his fingers behind the stone in the wall for a message. But it was, as it had been on every previous occasion in the last few weeks, empty. Then he heard a low cough from behind him and turned round to see the blonde curls of Lena.

''Bout time you turned up, me darlin'. I was beginning to think you'd gone off me. But we all know you can't resist these smilin' eyes of mine.'

Lena frowned at him. She didn't have time for his flirting.

'We have help that has arrived,' she told him bluntly. 'They are here to organise an escape. We need to get some of us out to Ireland and then from there, back to the fight. We can no longer sit here while our country needs us.'

'Absolutely, *acushla*, whatever you say,' Damian said with a grin. 'But ye know, once you set foot on the Emerald Isle, you'll never want to leave it.'

'Herr O'Callaghan,' she said sternly. 'This is not a game. This is dangerous work. I'm not sure you are the man to do it.' And with that she tossed her head back and started to walk away. He moved sharply in front of her. His eyes, that normally twinkled, had turned as grey as the sea on a wet day and with a vice-like grip he took hold of her shoulders and twisted her round, so that he had his forearm under her chin. As the pressure tightened, she struggled to breathe. Lena knew that just one sharp yank of that sinewy arm would end her life and, gasping for breath, she heard his whispered threat.

'Don't ever, *ever*, underestimate an O'Callaghan or you'll find this pretty little neck will snap like a twig.' She felt his fingers expertly pressing until she squealed in pain, then he twirled her around and smiled again.

'Y'see, we *can* be friends. Just let's be sure who's in charge here and, believe me, for sure, it isn't your Hitler or you and your friends, young lady.'

Lena was shaken and felt a chill creep up her body. She had seen the Gestapo at work with their brutality, but this was different. Damian O'Callaghan's cheerful persona masked someone who was more ruthless than she could ever have guessed. To a straight-thinking German, such duplicity was beyond her comprehension and with a jolt, she realised she had completely under-estimated this man.

'I'm sorry,' she murmured, feigning a cowed expression. 'I just want to make sure this all happens without . . .' She searched for the word.

'Mishap is what you mean,' he said coolly. 'No, missy, you'd better understand . . . we don't allow *mishaps*.'

He went on. 'After all, I'd hate to see that lovely little body of yours join the "mishaps" we've already had to send to the graveyards. No, to be sure, you're far too pretty for that. So, Lena Braun, what is it you want from me?'

Lena hesitated. This man already knew enough to get her imprisoned by the Manx authorities or, she thought with a chill, something even worse, so she spoke quickly.

'We need transport. A boat, maybe.'

'All right, missy,' O'Callaghan said, the twinkle returning to his eyes. 'I think we can arrange that. I'll let you know how much.'

'And there's something else,' Lena said, after a pause. This man's ability to travel the Island unchallenged had given her an idea. 'I need some notes delivering to Douglas. To the gaol there. Can you do that?'

He shrugged and mentally added more costs to his bill.

'OK, anything else?'

'No, not at the moment,' Lena replied, as evenly as she could. But, in her head, she was wondering whether she was making a pact with the devil.

'So, everythin's grand then,' he said slyly. 'The IRA and the Nazis make a formidable team, don't you think, darlin'?'

* * *

By the time the girls got back to the camp, the internees were pacing up and down, waiting to get the tedious necessity of roll call over and done with.

Bridget saw Ursula's pale face at the back of the crowd and felt the familiar concern tightening in her stomach. Then she spotted the reassuring figure of Ruth.

'Have you got a minute?' she asked and took her over to one side.

'I think we need to keep a close eye on Ursula, she looks completely defeated.'

'Yes, of course,' the Quaker woman replied. 'She was showing such interest … and I have to say, a real aptitude for the craft group; her crocheting is wonderful – but now … oh, I don't know, Bridget, it's as if she's given up.'

Bridget leaned forward and gave her a hug.

'I know, so any help you can give would be wonderful.'

Ruth looked closely at the young policewoman's face. 'Bridget, you can't keep taking all these worries on your head. There is help, you know.' And she glanced up to the skies.

Bridget couldn't help but smile. This woman's faith might have power but right now, it was her practical skills she needed.

'Have you been able to unearth any new information about Ursula's siblings?' she asked.

Ruth mulled over the inquiries she'd already made but then shook her head.

'No, I've tried everything, but, you know they were all hiding from the authorities. There are no records of them because they weren't registered with anyone. There was another raid, just after Ursula was arrested, I just hope they weren't . . . oh, I don't know, let's hope they've been taken in by the Red Cross but so far, I haven't been able to track them down.'

'OK, thanks, Ruth,' Bridget said and slowly walked away.

* * *

'Sarge,' Bridget said before she had even taken her hat off, 'can I go to Liverpool?'

Sergeant Robinson looked up from the pile of paperwork on her desk that never seemed to get any smaller.

'Sorry, Bridget, what did you say?'

Under the piercing stern gaze, Bridget faltered.

'I . . . um . . . was just wondering whether I could go over to Liverpool.'

'Certainly not.'

The sergeant went back to her papers and waved her hand in dismissal.

Bridget opened her mouth to say something but then clamped it shut and marched noisily out of the room.

She went straight to Alister, willing as always to listen.

'I need to go to Liverpool,' she told him, propping her elbows up on the front desk of the police station.

'Uh huh . . .' Alister said.

Bridget stamped her feet like the determined little girl he'd once known.

'I need to find out about Ursula's family. The information we've got is hopeless, there's no documentation and unless I go in person, no one's going to tell me anything.'

She looked at the large man in front of her.

'Well?'

'Well, what, young Bridget?' the older man said with a smile. 'What do you expect me to do? You know how dangerous the Irish Sea is and she,' he said, jerking his head in the direction of the sergeant's office, 'will never let you go. It's too risky.'

Bridget's face crumpled. She hated being foiled in her plans.

'I do know,' she wailed, 'but there must be something I can do. I can't just sit here and watch Ursula disintegrate in front of me and take Karin down with her.'

Alister thought for a minute and then his face cleared and he smiled.

'Why don't you go and make a nice cup of tea,' he said, 'that'll make you feel better.'

Once she'd gone, he turned to his address book.

* * *

Nancy put her kitbag down while she fumbled for the piece of paper she needed to show the two guards by the front fence at Cregneash. She'd been told to guard the document with her life and had tucked it away in the handbag she'd clasped like a baby all the way up the hill, but now she was struggling to find it. They waited impatiently, frowning at the new WAAF. The bland entrance had no signs but there was a large, white disc above them that gave a clue of the exciting plane-detection technology that was being developed there. Nancy nervously took everything out of her WAAF bag, unearthing a key to her parents' house, a shopping list, a pencil and there, tucked in the handkerchief, she found the piece of paper.

She handed it over with a sigh of relief.

'You need to keep better track of that,' one of the guards said. He gave her a stern look. 'You'll not get in without it.'

'Sorry,' she muttered, thinking they weren't nearly as friendly as the elderly commissionaire at Broadcasting House, who had cheerily wished her 'good morning' when she passed through the turnstile there. She didn't dare ask them which way she should go, so stood looking from left to right at the long row of Nissan huts facing her.

'Nancy!' a voice called to her from the side of one of them. It was Kieran. She automatically saluted his superior rank.

'Oh, I'm so pleased to see a friendly face!' she told him, and made her way over, giving a slightly triumphant glance at the dour guards but they had already moved on to the next person in the queue.

'I heard you were coming this morning, so I thought I'd come and greet you,' Kieran said. 'Come on, I'll show you round.'

'Don't I have to report somewhere?'

'Yes, but I've talked to your superior and I've said I'll take you over there.'

Nancy followed him gratefully as he strode off, noting all the salutes he received as they walked. She felt she was in the presence of a god and scuttled to catch him up. Most of the people here were RAF and she was glad she blended in with her familiar uniform. The need for absolute trustworthiness had been drilled into everyone who passed through those gates and, shivering with excitement, Nancy had been only too willing to comply with all the restrictions that would be put on her to be part of the groundbreaking work that was going on here . . . whatever that was.

Kieran pointed out the NAAFI, the washrooms with their metal sinks and skirted past the low buildings that had been hurriedly erected to house the growing number of people who were being drafted in to work at Cregneash. They were hidden under earth and then topped with camouflaged netting with guide ropes held in place by large concrete rings.

Eventually, he took her to an office with the words 'Admin' on the door.

'Here's where I leave you, but I'm sure we'll bump into each other again. The watches are round the clock so we'll probably pass each other at midnight or something.' He grinned. Kieran was loving being part of something so important and he was finding the experimental work with radar absorbing. Experienced pilots like him had been brought in once it had been realised that the new RDF system needed more than technology to identify enemy aircraft; it needed human interpretation and with that knowledge, instinct and skill in place, the success rate against enemy aircraft was rising significantly. His experience of flying, along with his training work at Jurby, made him an ideal candidate and he was finally beginning to feel he had some value again.

Kieran glanced back at the tall girl with shining, brown curls. Since the trip to Niarbyl, he'd been plagued with dreams about Bridget Harrison and felt he needed a distraction. It crossed his mind that if Nancy Gorry was going to be a regular sight around the station, she might provide him with a diversion. He made his way across to the transmitter bunker to report for duty with a spring in his step.

Chapter Twenty-Four

Nancy followed the stern warrant officer, trying not to clench her fists. The explanations she'd been given about the work being done here had made her raise her eyebrows. She'd had no idea that Britain was so advanced in its use of aircraft detection, and she was ridiculously nervous. Her work at the BBC had been seen as essential for communication but now she was in the Women's Royal Auxiliary Airforce, and this was different. As soon as she had seen the heavily camouflaged buildings and experienced the high level of security, she'd worked herself up into a panic. Her actions would now involve people in airplanes who could die if she sent the wrong information.

'You'll work at this desk,' the warrant officer was saying, pointing at a front desk in a room full of girls with headphones and notepads and screens in front of them. They hardly looked up to notice the new girl joining their ranks, but were frantically talking into their microphones and scribbling notes that were regularly collected by a young lad in RAF uniform scurrying between the rows and holding a metal basket. When he got to the front, he raced to the door and disappeared down the corridor.

Nancy went to sit down but the woman was speaking again so she rapidly got back up onto her feet. 'You will work eight hours on and eight hours off, there will be no such thing as day and night and your leave time will be very limited. If you are due to work, you will find a bed in the huts, use the NAAFI for food and if you're not, you will be taken with five other girls off your watch by taxi from here down into Port St Mary, where you will bunk with the WAAFs at Moorlands Hotel. You may visit your family and will have some leave but obviously, now you have signed the Official Secrets Act,' and here she glared threateningly at Nancy, 'you will say *nothing* about your work here.'

At that, one of the girls on the front row glanced up and grinned at Nancy; she had obviously heard all this before.

Nancy finally sat down in front of a machine she was told was a goneo. The woman in charge explained that it was Nancy's job to find out the angles of the planes that were coming in and pass that information to the plotters, who would then push their long sticks across maps to pinpoint the changing locations of the enemy.

To begin with, she was so nervous, she kept missing the crucial pieces of information that would pinpoint the enemy. But then she made herself calm down and took herself back to the huge room at Olympia in Blackpool, where they had played music, loud chatter and inserted squeals and squelches to put off the young trainees trying to make sense of what was coming out of their headphones.

After two hours, a break was called and Nancy, with relief, took off her headphones. She realised how tense her whole body had been and she stretched. The girl next to her leaned across.

'Hello, I'm Frances, but everyone calls me Frankie. Who are you?'

'Nancy.'

'Welcome to Cregneash. It's hard work but you'll love it. The only thing is, I hope you aren't expecting a life outside of here. We don't get much!'

Nancy wondered how she was going to get to see her father and give her mother support. She also had a small pang about the fun nights with Bridget and the girls but then shrugged and concentrated on the room around her. Several girls were looking over towards her with interest. She smiled warmly at them all.

Frankie got up and beckoned for Nancy to follow her. 'I'll show you where the kitchen is. We're allowed to get a cuppa and go to the bog if we're quick. Come on.'

The day flew by with only a short break for a quick bowl of macaroni cheese for midday dinner. A familiar smell of Spam fritters was emanating from the kitchen at one end of the NAAFI and Frankie nudged her.

'You'll never guess what's on the menu tonight,' she laughed. 'Well, it is Thursday so no surprise there. Fish pie tomorrow to keep the Catholics happy. Same every week so you'll soon get the hang of it.'

Nancy was thinking back to her time in London when Spam fritters would have been so very welcome and didn't want to admit that they, and fish pie, sounded just great to her. She felt she was going to enjoy it here and gave Frankie a huge grin.

When they finished their watch, several of the girls walked back to the Nissan huts where their bunks were. They had made Nancy feel so welcome, she felt a part of the group already, especially when Frankie linked arms to steer her around the buildings.

'Hey, Nancy,' Kieran's voice called from behind them. The little group stopped in their tracks and stared at the good-looking Squadron leader. They all saluted and stepped back, leaving Nancy alone in the middle of the pathway. She suddenly felt embarrassed, worrying that his recognition of her might suggest she wanted to put herself above the other girls so she mumbled something in response.

Kieran had no idea he was causing a mild sensation. 'I'm off at eight, shall we meet in the NAAFI?' he asked her.

Nancy looked around at Frankie, who was torn between astonishment and awe.

'I'm not sure,' she said hesitantly. 'What were you planning to do, Frankie?'

'Oh, well, we've got Domestic Night in the hut. You know, mending, polishing, all that fun stuff you won't be able to get out of,' she said sympathetically.

'In that case,' Nancy said, with a tinge of regret in her voice, 'sorry, Kieran, another time.'

'Of course, goodnight ladies,' and, with a smart click of his heels, he turned away from the farewell salutes and left behind a stunned silence, broken finally by a girl called Doris, with blonde, rolled hair.

'How the *hell* do you know the dreamboat of Cregneash?'

They all stood expectantly.

Nancy shuffled her feet and mumbled something, but Frankie took hold of her by the shoulders and looked sternly into her face.

'Come on, we're waiting . . .'

Nancy giggled nervously.

'I . . . my friend . . . he . . . camping trip . . . um . . . you know.'

By now, the whole group had surrounded her and she was being spun around to face one then the other.

'You went camping with him?!' one called Patty said, her mouth dropping open.

'Did you see him get undressed for bed?'

'Did you SHARE a bed with him?' Doris put in as Patty pretended to swoon.

Nancy realised she was in danger of rising to the ranks of heroine just by knowing Squadron Leader Kieran

Moore, and rushed to burst her new friends' bubble before it got out of hand.

'There are lots in line before me. Believe me, I'm nothing to him.'

Frankie looked disappointed.

'Oh well, girls, we may still be in with a chance then! Let's kidnap this girl and torture her for as much information about him as possible. Are you ticklish?' she asked threateningly.

Nancy started to laugh and began to run towards their barracks, the girls all pursuing her purposefully. When they fell into the hut, they all collapsed in a heap on top of her in giggles. Nancy squirmed and wriggled, her laugh ringing out above the cacophony of noise. When she finally emerged, her curls squashed around her head, she looked around gratefully. She loved the camaraderie of the WAAF and wondered, not for the first time, why it had taken her so long to join up.

* * *

Helga's clothes were beginning to look as if they were hanging off a clothesline, rather than the body of what had once been a large woman, and Bridget was concerned. Calling to update her on the forthcoming hearing, she asked, 'What's the matter, Helga? You can tell me.'

Helga's face crumpled and her body deflated like a pierced balloon.

'*Ich kann nicht, ich kann nicht,*' she sobbed.

Bridget reached across and put her hand on Helga's thin, gnarled knuckles that were clenching the dirty skirt she was wearing.

'Yes, you can. You have to, Helga. I'm being called as a character witness in a few days. I need to be able to help you.'

Helga simply shook her head, but as they sat in silence, Bridget noticed a piece of paper tucked under the pillow. On the corner of it was a drawing of a tree with something hanging beneath it, but this one was not drawn by a child.

Helga saw where Bridget was looking and turned round to grasp it, but Bridget was too quick for her.

'I need to look at this,' she said with as much official-dom as she could muster. The sternness of her voice made Helga drop back onto the concrete plinth. It was also as if she had no more fight left in her. Bridget stood up to put some distance between the piece of paper in her hand and the prisoner.

The words were in German which caused Bridget to stall but she looked closely at the drawing. The image of a figure hanging from a tree sent a chill up Bridget's spine. A woman's body was dangling from one of the branches. She knew the woman was supposed to be Helga but on the woman's chest, next to her drooping head, there was a huge yellow J. It was too blatant to be anything but a threat to the prisoner in front of her and Bridget looked at her in shock. Surely this ardent Nazi couldn't be a Jew?

She gently went and sat next to Helga and showed her the drawing. Helga's eyes were wide with fear.

'Are you a Jew, Helga?'

'*Nein, aber, ja. Nein, mein Großfater . . .* he . . .'

'Your grandfather was a Jew?' Bridget whispered. She could not believe what she was hearing.

'Ja, I am a dirty Jew,' Helga said, her voice hardening.

'There is no such thing as a dirty Jew, Helga,' Bridget said, her sympathy waning.

'But the führer . . . he say . . .'

'I don't care what the führer says,' Bridget said angrily. 'Now listen to me, Helga, this prejudice is what started this war. We . . . the Jews . . . we're all just people, *just people*, for God's sake.'

Helga looked suspiciously at her. These words were heretical, and ones she had not dared whisper into her intransigent mind since she had fled Germany in the middle of the night, clutching Karin in one hand and a small suitcase in another.

Helga looked keenly at Bridget. How could she confess her terrible secret? How could she admit she belonged to that race? But then, she looked at the note in the policewoman's hands. Someone already knew.

'I'm waiting, Helga. You have to tell me what's going on here. If I don't know the truth, I can't help you – or Karin.'

But Helga just shook her head. The terror of being discovered was so great, she felt the tendrils of the

Jewish-hating swastika reaching across first the English Channel, then the Irish Sea to strangle the life out of her and she clasped at her throat defensively.

Bridget only had a few days to get anything out of this woman. She wracked her brains as to how she was going to do it but was at a loss. Standing up, she started to pace the little cell, then it came to her. Bluffing was going to be her weapon.

'Helga, you know what? I don't need you to tell me. Lena's already said enough, hasn't she?' She pointed at the piece of paper in her hand and watched closely. Helga's face went pale. Bridget tried to keep her own face impassive, but a huge thrill passed through her. Her hunch had been right.

She persevered.

'Somehow, she has been getting these notes to you. So, she knows the truth about you.' It wasn't a question. 'How long do you think it will be before everyone knows. Karin's alone in that camp. Do you think the Nazis won't take it out on a child?'

Bridget was flailing around like a boat in a storm now, but she was gratified to see Helga bite her lip while she battled with her innermost thoughts.

After an agonising silence of several minutes, Helga started to speak, falteringly at first and then the words came out in a torrent.

'I have more . . .' And with that, she fumbled under her pillow to produce a pile of notes that had fluttered their way through the barred window above them during the last few weeks.

'They are so ... *schrecklich* ... you know, they are *schaurig, böse* ... *evil*.'

Bridget didn't understand the words on the pages she was handed over, but flicking through the black scrawled letters with their threatening drawings, she understood the terror these pieces of paper instilled in Helga. They were similar to ones that had been pushed under some of the Jewish women's doors.

She sat down again next to the shivering figure on the plinth.

'You are in the Isle of Man, not Germany, Helga. There are laws against this sort of thing. We do not allow it. You are not under Hitler's power now.'

This assertion caused Helga to pause. Surrounded by so many Germans, hearing her own language in the streets, it had not really sunk in that she was no longer subject to Nazi control.

Bridget went on.

'I can help you, but you have to tell me the truth, Helga. I need to know the whole story, then I can tell the hearing that you've been blackmailed and that it made you act irrationally. I can say that everything you've done has been to protect Karin. This will help you, Helga.'

Helga didn't understand everything Bridget was saying but the reassuring tone helped to stop the shivering. She sat back and closed her eyes. She was so tired of acting a part and was exhausted by the anger.

Bit by bit, her eyes closed and leaning back on the cold cell wall, she told Bridget her story. After a while, Helga looked up to see the effect of her words, expecting condemnation, but Bridget's hand was shaking as her pencil flew across the pages. When Helga reached the part about the soldier threatening to rape little Karin, Bridget held her hand out like someone grasping for help. Helga grabbed it fiercely and their eyes met in a moment of complete empathy. Bridget had heard about the treachery and cruelty that was happening all over Europe, but this story was more chilling than she could bear.

As Helga's voice finally tailed off, Bridget slowly got to her feet. She reached out and hugged the woman in front of her.

'I will do whatever I can to help you – and Karin. This nightmare has to stop.'

The warmth of the hug brought tears to Helga's eyes and as she watched Bridget quietly close the door behind her, Helga felt a huge weight had been lifted from her shoulders. It was so good to take off the mask she had been hiding behind. The time in gaol had given her too much time to think, but for the first time, she dared to think that this strange island's justice system might give her a chance to start again. She had no idea where her parents were. She suspected her flight had made it even more difficult for them to hide her mother's heritage and she was engulfed in guilt. Finally, she understood why they had been prepared to betray anyone and everyone to protect their own. But the more she heard about what was happening to Jews, the more she feared for her mother and father's safety too.

She just hoped they would understand why she had had to get Karin out of Germany.

Chapter Twenty-Five

Kieran found himself regularly peering around the tarmac between the huts and realised he was looking for Nancy. He still couldn't get the appealing image of Bridget standing on tiptoe to kiss him out of his head but then he would see his brother's face and it all seemed so wrong. Nancy was also a beautiful young woman – but without the complications. Obsessed for so long with his deformed hand, he'd almost forgotten what it was to be tied up in knots by women. Without alcohol to dull his reasoning, he was finally facing the possibility that he'd buried Kieran Moore along with all his fellow airman after the Battle of Britain. A victim of survivor's guilt and obsessed with his deformed hand, Kieran knew he had been hiding away from the world, until he'd been shaken out of his self-absorption by the gentle kiss of his childhood friend. He felt a huge gratitude to Bridget but couldn't shake the feeling that she was not the right woman for him.

A pragmatic young pilot, he decided he would leave it to fate.

One evening, as he was coming out of the operations room, it seemed possible that fate had a plan of its own.

'Evening, Sir,' Nancy's cheery voice greeted him from the other side of the tarmac. Giving the obligatory salute, she didn't let him know that she constantly searched around every corner looking for him. Unaware of Bridget's torment, she was hoping that a secret operation camp at the southern tip of the Isle of Man might offer her the chance she was waiting for.

He turned, delighted, towards her and returned her salute.

'Hello, Nancy, how nice to see you! Have you just finished or are you just starting?'

'Finished,' she said, taking his arm purposefully. 'So, a drink, perhaps?'

Kieran took a sharp intake of breath. It was all too easy to say yes.

'I can't,' he said finally.

'Can't drink or can't join me?' Nancy asked suspiciously, a shiver edging up her spine.

Kieran turned to face her and took hold of her shoulders. This was so hard but if he didn't say something now, he never would.

'I can't drink,' he said, flatly. 'I was drinking too much, Nancy, I can't control it if I start.'

He waited, feeling the tension in his neck. This could ruin everything. Nancy's face crumpled and he watched her stumble. He reached out his arm to steady her.

'Are you OK?'

'Yes, well, maybe, well, actually no,' Nancy replied, taking a sharp breath. She glanced around to check that no one was listening

'Can we go somewhere?' she asked.

'Yes, of course, let's go up towards Meayll,' he said, puzzled.

The three-thousand-year-old archaeological site was on the top of the hill above the camp and they wandered up the track but neither of them noticed the beautiful July sky above them, full of stars that twinkled innocently in defiance of both the chaos in the world below and the tension in the young couple who were standing nervously next to Meayll Circle.

Kieran waited patiently.

'I can't deal with people who have a drinking problem,' she said, making his heart sink.

She looked sideways at the horror on his face.

'I'm sorry, Kieran, it's just that I. . . .'

Kieran was regretting his honesty that might have jeopardised any relationship with this lovely woman.

Nancy started to pace around him. After a few moments, she stopped.

'This boyfriend, you see, he . . . he hit me.'

And with that she stopped and faced him, waiting to see the disgust on his face. But there was nothing but concern.

'*He hit you?*'

He could not believe it. How could anyone use violence against a young woman, any woman, like this?

She dropped down onto a rock and put her head in her hands. Her shoulders started to shake but Nancy went on, muttering towards her shoes:

'He seemed so normal, so nice. In fact . . . he was a well-known newsreader at the BBC . . . but when he drank, which was often, he would turn into this . . . this monster.'

She looked up at Kieran, not sure how much to tell him.

'There was one night, when he'd had a lot of whisky, he pushed me against the wall. It was done with such force, I ended up in hospital. I swore then I would never have anything to do with a man who didn't know when to stop drinking.'

Kieran didn't know what to say. Suddenly engulfed by a huge guilt for being someone who was of the same sex as her attacker, he was aware too, that he was someone who had allowed himself to be controlled by drink. A terrifying thought went through his head: in a drunken stupor, *could he ever have become violent*? He shook himself. He'd never been a man prone to anger, but it left him with a niggling doubt and that made bile rise in his throat. He knew the power of drink and it had frightened him, but it had never, not for one moment, occurred to him that he would lose control.

Nancy coughed and stood up. She wasn't sure what reaction she had expected from Kieran, but she had expected something. This silence seemed to resound up to the dark skies above them.

She brushed down her skirt and turned to go back down the track, but Kieran touched her arm to stop her.

'I'm so sorry,' he said. 'I feel so dreadful. I had no idea.'

And he turned her towards him, taking her face in his hands. He looked deep into her brown eyes.

'I promise you that I have never, would never, *could* never attack any woman. I am so sorry you were subjected to that and I will do anything I can to restore your faith in men.'

Nancy examined his expression thoroughly. There was an honesty there, but she still felt that distrust of men that she had suffered since those days in London. She shook her head.

'I'm sorry, Kieran. I do believe you, but I told you, I cannot, ever again, deal with a man who drinks too much.'

And with that, she walked slowly back down the hill.

Kieran stretched his arms out towards her but then they flopped uselessly to his side.

* * *

The rest of the week was agony for Kieran; it was as if the bar in the mess was beckoning him every time he passed it. He could cope when he was rushed off his feet, dealing with a relentless workload, but this week had been plagued by summer mists and there was little happening in the skies around Britain. That gave him far too much time to constantly conjure up Nancy's devastated expression and he felt his hand twitching, longing for the oblivion offered by beer. The officers he worked with were all grateful for the rest and willingly headed towards the mess at the end of their duty watches, while Kieran used every excuse he could think of not to join them. Eventually, they confronted him, fed up with the spurious excuses he kept coming up with.

'What's up with you, old chap?' Walter challenged him, as he tried to scuttle past them.

'Yes, spill the beans, tell us what this is all about,' Mitch joined in. 'You trying to avoid us? You never come for a drink.'

Kieran looked from one to the other. An RAF man was judged by his ability to hold his drink and he suspected he would become a pariah if he told them the truth. He decided he would prefer to be thought of as a snob than a bore.

He made his voice sound as superior as he could.

'No, I don't drink in mess bars. I find they get full of people who become loud and out of control.'

Mitch and Walter reeled back as if stung. They'd always found Kieran to be a likeable man and his words shocked them.

'Right,' Walter said, distaste spreading across his face. 'Now we know, OK, Mitch, let's go and meet some *real* friends,' he said meaningfully, and they strode off, their heads leaning in to discuss the shocking conversation. Kieran felt utterly miserable and very lonely. He'd also never needed a drink more.

* * *

The summer mist was a blessing to Nancy and, wanting to avoid bumping into Kieran, she used the weather as a chance to ask for some leave to go home to be with her parents. She was furious that it had taken her so long to dare to believe she might be able to love again, only to have that hope dashed into tiny pieces, and was torn between wanting to enfold Kieran Moore in her arms and a desire to push him off the nearest cliff.

She hadn't spoken to anyone about her problems but after a particularly difficult day at home with a truculent father who wouldn't accept the limitations of his ailing body and a mother who was fretting about her niece working in a hospital in the besieged island of Malta, Nancy called to see Bridget.

* * *

'I need to talk to you,' she said, as they made their way into 'The Snug' but when they opened the door, Molly was there, deep in some paperwork.

'Oh, hello,' Molly said unenthusiastically, and went back to her documents.

'I'll get us a cup of tea,' Bridget was saying, but she too looked distracted. Nancy felt her spirits sink. She really needed a conversation with her friend, but Molly was there between them, like a barrier.

The chat between Nancy and Bridget was perfunctory and once she had finished her tea, Nancy stood up to go, only pausing by the front door when she heard Bridget say, 'What was it you wanted to talk to me about, Nanxy?'

Nancy shook her head. 'It doesn't matter.' But then it all spilled out. 'I don't know what to do about Kieran.'

Bridget jerked back, as if stung.

'*Kieran*?'

'Yes, I just . . . he . . . oh, Bridg, I can't stop thinking about him but he . . .' She so wanted to confide in her friend but she had never told Bridget about her experiences in London, and didn't know whether anyone knew about Kieran's drinking. Her voice tailed off. She'd prepared this speech on her way to the cottage but there were too many secrets.

Bridget put her arm around Nancy.

'If you feel like that . . . and . . . if . . . he does too . . .' she stumbled over her words, 'then I wish you luck.'

Bridget closed the door behind her friend and slowly sank to the floor.

Molly heard the noise and came into the corridor to find her friend sitting with her head in her hands.

She ran over to her and knelt down next to her.

'Oh Bridget, what on earth's the matter?'

A forlorn face looked up at her, making Molly's heart ache.

'I kissed Kieran,' Bridget said, 'and now I think Nancy's fallen for him.'

'Ah,' was all Molly could think of to say.

'I can't tell Nancy but it was at the dance at Jurby. I'd had too much to drink and, oh, Molly, I've loved him all my life and I don't know how to stop.'

Molly stroked her arm. She needed time to think.

'Do you still love him?' she asked, after a pause.

'I don't think so, I think I love Fynn. I mean . . . when he went out on that rescue, I was terrified something would happen to him, but Kieran, he's my fantasy . . . the one I've had since I was little. Oh, why do they have to be brothers and why, oh why, did Kieran have to come back?'

Molly took a moment to gather her thoughts.

'I think Kieran had to come back. After all, you had to face him one day. Does Fynn know?'

'He saw us kiss,' was the despondent reply.

Molly couldn't help it; she found her mouth turning upwards into a grin at the look on Bridget's face.

'You really know how to complicate things, don't you Bridget Harrison?' And getting to her feet, she reached out her hand to pull her friend up.

'Come on, I think it's time to make some peppermint creams. Blow the sugar rations, this is an emergency.'

Chapter Twenty-Six

The morning of the hearing in the Court of General Gaol Delivery was a bright July day, but even the warm rays of sunshine could not stop Bridget from shivering.

As the police van drew up she ran towards it to greet Helga, who almost fell into Bridget's arms, her handcuffs clanking against Bridget's metal buttons.

'It's all right, Helga, I'm here,' Bridget whispered and the nails digging into her arm told her how much that meant to the prisoner.

She gently led the German prisoner to the court, followed by two policemen. Helga looked around nervously as she was taken from Bridget by a couple of men in black gowns, one of whom went in front of her whilst the other went behind. Another police officer gave a brief nod to acknowledge Bridget and went to stand behind Helga in the dock.

It was a large room with wooden benches, full of important-looking men in stiff collars and horsehair wigs with a carved chair high up at the front. The men had black gowns draped from their shoulders and were all shuffling papers, peering intently at the typing on them, making final mental notes. As Helga was led to a compartment in front of the raised bench at the front, she looked at the large crowd in the public gallery behind and felt herself going dizzy. She was about to expose the fact that her life had been a lie to the entire world.

A deep voice from the doorway called out, 'All rise,' and everyone in the room stood up respectfully, as the judge, known as the Deemster, came in from a doorway behind the raised bench. The policeman pushed Helga roughly to her feet and she looked fearfully at the man who would decide her fate.

They all sat down to hear the indictment and Helga's whispered, 'Guilty.' That is, apart from the prosecuting advocate, Geoffrey Lewin, who stood up straight, confident that this case would be over within half an hour. His opening words sent a chill to everyone in that courtroom and all Helga could see out of the corner of her eye were people nodding in agreement.

'Your Honour, you see before you a woman who sums up everything that this terrible war represents – anger, bitterness, intolerance and violence.'

Confident he had a sympathetic audience, Mr Lewin then went on sneeringly to sum up the day Ursula had been threatened with a knife, prompting Helga to shrink behind the wooden rail in front of her. She almost felt the manacles on her wrists tightening with every word he uttered.

Ending his statement with a matter-of-fact assertion; that this prisoner deserved the condemnation of every right-minded person who was against the tyranny that was terrorising much of Europe, Helga heard the courtroom murmur in agreement – that she merited nothing less than being thrown into a gaol and the key being thrown away. If it weren't for Karin, she thought, she would never have subjected herself to this. But then the memory of that little girl's gentle face caused her to suddenly heave with a tortured sob and she wondered how would Karin ever forgive her ... for committing this crime, for abandoning her in this strange land and for lying to her?

The Deemster's face was a study of non-committal impartiality, but then his eyes fell on Helga and for a brief second, she saw a contempt that made her blood run cold. Then her defence advocate stood up. Paul Curren was a lawyer in his early sixties, with grey hair peeping out from the wig he was wearing. He had lost weight since the war started, no longer the willing recipient of endless sherries and sandwiches at legal functions, but his stature had not diminished. He knew he was the best advocate on the Island, and he was about to make sure that reputation soared to new heights. Alerted by Bridget, he had visited Helga on several occasions, probing her story until every tiny detail was exposed. He'd then questioned Bridget, Ursula, Ruth and even little Karin. Helga was not sure what he was about to say, but she felt a glimmer of hope when he gave a reassuring little nod towards her.

'Your Honour, I agree with everything the prosecution has alleged.'

There was a communal gasp in the room and even the Deemster looked surprised.

'But,' he went on, after a dramatic pause, 'I submit that that Nazi who was wielding a knife outside Christian's Cottage is not the woman who sits in the dock before you.' He paused for effect.

'She, Your Honour, is the granddaughter of a Jew and by that association, an enemy of *everything* the Nazi regime represents.'

There was absolute silence that echoed around the walls of the courtroom, and in one corner of the public gallery was Damian O'Callaghan, told by Lena to attend. Now he knew why she'd wanted those notes delivered. This woman was a prime candidate for blackmailing – but this revelation in open court might take that power away. He sat forward and listened intently. The local newspaper reporters held their pencils above their spiral notebooks in disbelief.

Mr Curren held his audience in the palm of his hand and was making the most of every moment.

'I propose to explain to you how she adopted the shroud of a vehement Nazi, as a device to deceive the Gestapo who were prowling the streets of her town, looking for people, just like Helga Fischer, to make a gruesome example of.'

Seeing the perplexed faces all around him, Mr Curren gave a satisfied tiny smile and went on. 'Mrs Fischer was brought up by parents, who, terrified that their family background would condemn them, concealed their Jewish heritage and adopted a fierce shield of defence by claiming to be ardent supporters of Hitler.'

By now, all that could be heard were the scratchings of the frantic pencils of the local press flying across the pages of their notebooks. Mr Curren was enjoying every minute of this unusual case.

'I want to tell you about a night in 1940 when news of a particularly brutal attack on the Jewish ghettos in Poland was reported on German wireless. On that same night, all this woman knew was that she had a telegram in her hand, telling her that her husband, a man con-scripted into the German army to quell those Jews, had been killed. At the same time, the neighbour of Helga Fischer's family became distraught, worrying about his relatives in Warsaw and he drank himself into a state of agitation. In a moment of confrontation, when Helga Fischer's mother tried to maintain her Nazi façade and loudly proclaimed the neighbour as the son of a Jew, he revealed the terrible secret that Helga's parents had kept hidden for so many years, shouting it out to the whole street.'

The Deemster leaned forward as Mr Curren lowered his voice, in a bid to increase the tension.

'I have to tell you, Your Honour, it was that night that the prisoner's parents made a decision in a desperate attempt to save their own family. They denounced their neighbour to the Gestapo to prove their loyalty to Hitler.'

Helga lowered her head. She was shaking.

'Later that night,' the advocate went on, 'Helga Fischer watched as her neighbour was strung up on the fruit tree outside the two houses by men in black leather coats and balaclavas. In a bedroom at the front of the house, hiding behind a curtain, was a little girl, an innocent bystander to the deceit and brutality of adults. Your Honour, that child is the daughter of the prisoner; what she saw that night haunts her to this very day.

'I put it to you, Your Honour, that this woman did what any mother would do – she packed her bag and, dragging her little girl's hand, she fled, desperate to hide any evidence of either her own Jewish grandfather or any connection with that dreadful murder. At that moment, she decided to live a lie.'

The advocate, holding onto the lapels of his gown, looked carefully around the courtroom, his eyes finally resting on the Deemster, who was staring at Helga as if she were a stranger who had only just walked in the room.

Mr Curren had to stop his mouth forming a slow smile.

Encouraged by the change of atmosphere, he then went on to appeal to the one thing the Manx people might value more highly than judgment and prejudice. Their pride.

'And now, Your Honour, I come to this Island, a place known for its tolerance, pity and compassion. Hosting so many aliens started out as a necessity inflicted on them by the British Government, but has since become a matter of Island honour, and I suggest there are few Manx households in Rushen Camp who have not reconsidered many of their original bigotry. Instead of a terrifying enemy, they have found some of these internees are simply people who have suffered; some at the hands of the enemy, some at the hands of their own neighbours "across" as they call the mainland. These women have been separated from their families, their homes and in many cases, the safety of the country they had hoped would provide them with a future. The reason these camps have finally become such a success is because the wonderful Manx people have looked beyond the labels and the religious practices to discover the mother, daughter, sister or grandmother behind.'

He glanced around the room to see people sitting a little straighter in their seats and he knew he had struck exactly the right note.

'Unfortunately,' he went on, 'that tolerance has not stretched to all our guests here. They are some who have brought with them their pernicious teachings, their evil beliefs and their dangerous modus operandi. I want you all to look at the woman in the dock in front of you and see, not a perpetrator but a victim.'

He glared around the room, daring anyone to disagree with him, and Helga shrank in her seat, exactly as he had intended. She suddenly looked very vulnerable and very pathetic.

'I call to the stand, WPC Bridget Harrison.'

* * *

Bridget took the oath and then in a calm, controlled voice, she explained how she had gradually found out how Helga was acting a part to protect her daughter. Before she could finish her statement, she was challenged by the prosecution, who accused her of being a naive young policewoman without experience of dealing with people who practised deception. At this, Bridget bristled and looked the prosecutor firmly in the eye.

'I can assure you, Mr Lewin, I am a professional police officer who has worked in the more criminally active parts of London, and I am anything but naïve. I think my career file will testify to that.' In a voice that resonated with authority, Bridget outlined one case after another where she had dealt with the gang underworld of the capital, exposing the rackets they were running to exploit the bereaved and the homeless, preying on the victims of heavy bombing and destruction.

There was more than one person in the public gallery whose eyebrows raised with new respect at the young police officer standing erect below them and the Deemster, who had a daughter in the Air Transport Auxiliary, flying many different types of aircraft to waiting RAF stations all over Britain, smiled in recognition of the unsuspected strength and ability of this new breed of young women.

As rehearsed with the advocate, Bridget went on to explain how her line of inquiry had led to suspicions that Helga was being blackmailed and finally, to Helga's tortured admission. With an ongoing investigation as to how threatening messages came to be pushed through the barred windows of the gaol in Douglas, she was unable to name any perpetrators, but she said enough to suggest there had been a conspiracy to threaten Karin that would have terrified any mother. At this, Damian O'Callaghan glanced warily around him. But every eye was focused on the scene in front of them.

When she retold the story about little Karin drawing the picture of a man hanging from a tree, there was a gasp of horror and many a woman in the public gallery dived into their handbags for a handkerchief.

The plan had been at this stage for the defence to call Ruth to the witness box, but Mr Curren took a risk by not calling her, deciding not to waste the suspense of the moment.

He dismissed Bridget and said in a voice tremulous with drama, 'You have heard from Mr Lewin how this woman fooled everyone with her persona of a typically angry Nazi, but you will also hear something I suspect you do not expect to hear – a defence of her actions from her victim. Your Honour, I call Ursula Apler.'

Chapter Twenty-Seven

Ursula shuffled down the aisle, her head bowed and her hands clenched. All the way down she was saying over and over to herself, 'I am doing this for Karin, I am doing this for Karin.'

Mr Curren came out from behind his bench to take her arm and squeezing it gently, he whispered, 'You're doing wonderfully. Just answer my questions as we discussed and it will be fine.'

Once she had been sworn in, Ursula took a deep breath and quickly looked around her. She rapidly passed over Helga's stunned face to search for Bridget, letting out a relieved sigh when she spotted her. Trying to dispel the memories of her own timidity as the victim crouched in terror at Helga's feet, Ursula took strength from the reassuring nod from Bridget, and stood up a little straighter, knowing that if she could walk into that courtroom to defend a woman who had threatened her with a knife, then there was hope for all of them.

Mr Curren began by reiterating the dramatic events of that day outside Christian's Cottage. Ursula felt her knees wobbling but she made herself glance over at Helga. The face that greeted her was one of such guilty anguish that Ursula reluctantly smiled reassuringly at the woman whose terrible personal story had just evoked tears in the courtroom. Helga jerked back in astonishment; she was not expecting such kindness from a Jew.

'Miss Apler?' Mr Curren was asking.

'I am sorry,' Ursula said, realising she had missed a question.

'I was asking you whether, after all you have been through, you have any ill feelings towards the defendant.'

'No, none,' Ursula answered clearly and loudly.

There was a communal intake of breath in the public gallery and even the Deemster looked in surprise over his glasses.

'And may I ask why not?' Mr Curren said.

'Because,' and here Ursula looked directly at the imposing judge at the front of the room, 'this war has made all of us into people we are not. I was very frightened, yes, when Helga attacked me, but I know now why she needed to do it. She had to attack me to show the Nazi supporters that she hated people of the Jewish faith. It was the only way to make sure her daughter would be safe.'

As Ursula became more animated, her German accent intensified and she lifted her head high.

'*Es stimmt,* I did steal her soap but you understand, I arrived here with nothing and for one moment, just one moment, I wanted to be clean.'

'But did you deserve to be threatened with a knife?' Mr Curren asked, pre-empting the prosecutor who was about to stand up and object.

'*Nein,*' Ursula said, shaking her head. 'It *maked* me angry, but I was just a child when my mother took me to England. She was killed in a bomb and I have no idea where my sister and brother are. I have no one so when I talk to Karin, Helga's daughter, I just . . . I just want to protect her.'

She looked up appealingly at the austere man at the front of the court and tears filled her eyes. In the dock, Helga leaned forward, her hands grasping the wooden bench beneath her.

'You see, she is so small and she does not understand what is happening,' Ursula was saying. 'She saw terrible things at her house and then she is dragged across Europe, facing so many dangers. I know what that is like, I cannot let her suffer any more and . . .' her shoulders suddenly drooped, 'for me, I have no anger left.'

Mr Curren broke in. 'What do you believe will happen to Karin if her mother goes to prison?'

Ursula spoke the next words quietly but their impact was thunderous.

'She will die.'

Helga gasped and clutched her hand to her chest. For a second, Ursula's eyes met hers and their enmity was erased by the mutual love of a little girl.

After a long pause, Ursula looked up and spoke directly to the man in the large chair towering over them all. There was a chilled silence in the courtroom. Even *she* was surprised at the strength of her voice when she uttered the next words.

'I have been attacked by this woman but I can forgive her. I think I, too, would have done this thing if I had a beautiful little daughter like Karin..'

She looked back at the public gallery and challenged each of them with fierce eyes.

'We are at war, my people are being killed. I am here today because I must try to make one thing right. It is important, very important. You have to understand . . . it is all I can do.'

With that, Ursula almost fell back against the wood at the back of the witness box. She was emotionally drained and her strength was failing her.

'You may sit down, Miss Apler,' Mr Curren said in a kind voice, 'unless the prosecution has any questions?'

Geoffrey Lewin stood up. He opened his mouth to speak but then shook his head and sat down again. It was as if the young woman before them had delved into each person's soul to find a remaining vestige of humanity.

'Do you wish to call the defendant?' the Deemster asked Mr Curren.

This was a question that had been going round and round in the defence advocate's head for days. He made a decision. He hoped it was the right one.

'No, Your Honour, you have the reports and her English is not good. I fear it would lead to misunderstandings. I also think there is little left to say after Miss Apler's evidence. I'm sure you will agree.'

The Deemster stood up and the whole courtroom rose to their feet.

'I will retire to consider my judgement,' he said curtly, and sweeping his gown around him, left the room.

* * *

'All rise,' the usher was calling. The door leading to the judge's chambers finally opened to herald the arrival of the man who would deliver the verdict that would change Helga's life forever.

He had considered the reports of the welfare, read Ruth's testimonial and re-read Bridget's and Ursula's statements. The law demanded retribution, but the testimony had been compelling. This prisoner had been a victim of both her own family history and of the fierce hatred of the extremists who were being harboured at Rushen Camp. He had a responsibility to despatch justice, while demonstrating the fair-minded attitudes of the Isle of Man. But he was angry that the prejudices and hatred that were pervading Europe had found its way into his beloved island.

He coughed and banged his gavel.

'This is a very unusual case, and one that perhaps sums up the wartime complexities of dealing with what would normally be an obvious condemnation of an act that is unforgiveable in our law-abiding society.'

He consulted his notes.

'I am bound to give a custodial sentence, but I want to pay tribute to Policewoman Bridget Harrison – her determination to unearth the truth behind this case has impacted my decision.'

Bridget flushed and looked down at her hands. She felt embarrassed and looked quickly at Ruth, who had been such a help in this case, and was relieved to see her generous, beaming smile.

The Deemster continued.

'But the person who deserves the gratitude of this court, and especially of the defendant, is Miss Apler. I think we were all humbled to hear her remind us of our responsibility as human beings, and to realise that there is so often another story to be told. Bearing all that in mind, while not forgetting my own responsibilities as a member of the judiciary, I am prepared to be lenient in this case to protect an innocent child.'

His next words echoed around the walls of the totally silent courtroom.

'I have considered all the background and, bearing in mind the admission of guilt by the defendant, I sentence this woman to six months in prison.'

Helga gasped.

'But,' he went on, 'as she has already been held for a considerable length of time, I will say to the defendant, your sentence has been served and you are free to go.'

With that, the Deemster stood up, and everyone scrambled to their feet in response to the hurried call by the usher.

Damian O'Callaghan had heard enough and made his way out to report back to Lena. She would not be pleased that all her efforts to blackmail Helga Fischer had been in vain, and now they would need to find another way to ensure her co-operation.

Helga staggered and reached out her hand to grab the wooden ledge in front of her. She uttered a yelp and Bridget rushed forward to grab her before she fell.

* * *

By the time Bridget got back to the police station, there was a reception committee waiting for her.

Alister led the clapping.

'Well done, young Bridget, you did an amazing job!'

Molly and Betty stepped forward and flung their arms around her, but Sergeant Robinson stood in the background, a frown on her face.

'Yes, yes, you did very well but I want to see you in my office, now.'

Bridget's smile faded and with a grimace to the others, she followed her superior into the next room.

'I need an explanation,' the sergeant said, sitting down and folding her arms. 'Why didn't you tell me the full story about Helga's Jewish background as it was unfolding?'

Bridget squirmed.

'I'd been asked by Mr Curren not to reveal the full facts so that he could surprise the court,' she said simply, but that explanation did nothing to improve the mood of Maureen Robinson.

'I am your superior, not Mr Curren,' the sergeant told the young policewoman curtly.

'I know and I'm really sorry, Sarge, but I was only trying to do my best for Karin and that seemed the only way to deal with it.'

'Well, it's a shame because your work has been very promising, but I cannot have a subordinate who does not follow the rules. You may have jeopardised your career with this approach.'

Bridget's heart sank, feeling all her good work had been for nothing.

'If you want to redeem yourself,' the sergeant went on, 'I suggest you get some evidence that Lena is behind the blackmailing – and keep an eye on Helga. I'm not sure where her loyalties lie now her story has been exposed.'

And with that, the sergeant waved her hand in dismissal and turned back to her paperwork.

Bridget crept out of the door, feeling wretched, to be greeted by Molly and Betty who immediately took her by the arm and propelled her out of the main door. They turned on her as soon as they reached the open air.

'We don't care what that witch says, we think you're a heroine!' Betty said. Molly nodded.

'Yes, we do, so let's get home and see whether we can unearth that bottle of sherry I think may be at the back of the cupboard. You deserve a celebration.'

They linked arms and started to make their way along towards their cottage but then the sirens sounded.

'Darn it,' Betty said, pulling both of them into the sand-bag hideout near the beach.

*　*　*

At Cregneash, there were service people scurrying in all directions, responding to the alarm. It was rare for a raid to target the Island but there was always the anxiety that the top-secret work going on there had been discovered.

Kieran was running towards a solid concrete bunker, covered with netting. He felt remarkably calm, he noticed with satisfaction. It was as if the fearless pilot was beginning to re-emerge and there was nobody more delighted than he was. In front of him, he spotted the brown curls of Nancy and called ahead to her over everyone's heads.

'Nancy, Nancy, wait for me.' Nancy turned and hesitated for a brief second to wait for him, giving a weak salute. She knew her heart was thumping, she just wasn't sure whether it was the aircraft or Kieran Moore that was causing it.

'Do you know if they're ours or not?' she asked shakily. Neither of them had time to answer as the planes appeared on the horizon, making them both look up to check the insignia. At the sight of the chilling black cross, he shook his head and gently pushed her down the steps to safety, shuffling along to make way for the large crowd of RAF personnel who had followed them.

There was silence while the whole group held their breath. Even if the planes did not intend to bomb the Island, there was always a chance that one of them would off-load a bomb to make their return home quicker. It would be a desperate irony if one rogue incendiary fell on the very installation that was giving Britain the radar advantage it desperately needed.

Nancy shivered and Kieran willingly wrapped his arms around her. For a second she froze, but then there was the noise of a plane right overhead and she sank back, grateful for any protection his strong arms could give her. The noise above seemed to go on for forever and every person in that bunker could picture the terrifying shapes of the aircraft above, blotting out the sky. Nancy was feeling the familiar shaking that afflicted her in an air raid, ever since her own street in London was bombed, and she pulled in closer to Kieran. No one made a sound, almost as if they believed the pilots above might hear them, and many a white face was pointed up to the ceiling above, wondering whether it would suddenly be cracked open by a weapon of horrifying power. Kieran nuzzled into Nancy's hair, smelling the Eau de Cologne the WAAF women used when they couldn't get shampoo. He was surprised how it made him dizzy. After the noise of the aircraft faded into the distance, the 'All Clear' sounded and immediately, the chattering below rose to a crescendo. Nancy was about to pull back in embarrassment when Kieran tightened his embrace.

'Don't rush,' he whispered into her ear. 'I'm loving being your knight in shining armour,' and he laughed. Nancy gave a rueful smile and retorted, 'I'm not sure even a DFC could save me from a five-hundred-pound bomb.'

'Oh, you'd be surprised,' Kieran chuckled.

The crowd in front of them started to disperse and slowly, Nancy extricated herself from his arms but then shuddered.

Kieran looked concerned. 'Are you all right?'

'Sort of, I'm always like that in a raid, it just reminds me . . .'

He didn't need to be told. There wasn't one person by this stage in the war who could hear the drone of a plane above without experiencing a flashback to a dramatic event that still haunted them. After nearly four years of war, there was no one on the British Isles or in much of Europe, for that matter, who did not have memories of a harbinger of doom heading towards them.

'I understand, Nancy,' he told her, blotting out his own recollections of tangled wreckage and blazing trails in the sky.

She was leaning down, straightening her skirt to regain her composure and he reached his hands down to gently lift her head. Looking straight into her eyes, he said, 'I'm sorry I let my drinking get out of control, Nancy. I had too many memories and I tried to use alcohol to squash them.' And with this he stretched his damaged hand out in front of him. 'And I couldn't cope with this . . .'

She looked at the twisted fingers and nodded.

'I understand, really, I do, but I can't take the risk. I'm sorry, Kieran.' And with that, she turned on her heel and went slowly up the steps back into the evening air. He swore quietly.

Chapter Twenty-Eight

Molly and Betty peered over the sandbags to check the empty skies as the 'all clear' sounded. Next to them, two women sprang to their feet and with a relieved titter, brushed themselves down. The Manx were always slightly embarrassed about their initial panic when a raid passed harmlessly over their heads, but Bridget, whose memories of London were all too vivid, had no such qualms; she knew that the fact that the Island managed to carry on a life beneath the bombers' wings, unseen in its darkness, was pure luck, not design.

'Northern Ireland's in for it tonight,' she said, having noted the direction of the planes. 'Poor Belfast, all those shipyards are too tempting for the Jerries to ignore.'

In silence, the girls clambered over the sandbags to make their way home but then Fynn's voice came from behind them.

'Are you girls OK?'

'Yes, fine, nothing that a good iron won't solve,' Betty laughed, straightening her rucked-up skirt.

'You go ahead,' Bridget whispered to them both and waited for Fynn.

'Were you at the Lifeboat Station?'

He nodded. 'Just left it and was heading for home.'

'Did you get to a shelter?' Bridget asked.

'Not exactly,' he said, smiling. 'There wasn't enough time. I hid down by the harbour wall. Forgot the tide was in.

To prove it, he shook his wet trouser legs and she laughed but then looked serious.

'You know, Fynn, I can't help but feel guilty every time the planes ignore us and take their payload to someone else. It's just not fair.' She stamped in frustration.

'No, it'd be much better if they'd bomb us as well,' he said with a wry grin.

Bridget glanced up at him. He always managed to put her dramatic tendencies back in proportion somehow and she felt lighter as a result. Too intent on looking inwards and agonising over every single detail, his common sense was a welcome, calming balm in her life.

'Oh OK, OK, I know,' she said, pouting like a thwarted child. 'It's just that . . .'

'Just what, Bridget? Just that you're here and not in the middle of London?' he said, with a trace of bitterness.

'Well yes, in a way. I've finally been feeling I was doing something really useful there. The Island is, oh I don't know, it's always too safe.'

'Hmm,' Fynn said, in that placid tone he had, 'unless you happen to be a young Jewish girl being threatened with a knife, or a child having nightmares about a lynching, or what about some blackmailing? None of that of any interest to you WPC Harrison?'

She gave him a gentle nudge and a rueful grin.

'All right, I give in. It's just that I need to be good at something, you know? I spent my whole childhood following you boys around like a spare part, then I moved to London and Nancy was, oh, I don't know, living such a glamorous life, I could never compete. I just, for once, wanted to feel that I was making a difference. I mean, you do it all the time, risking your life to save people.'

Fynn immediately looked embarrassed; he hated anyone thinking he was a hero.

Betty's voice came from down the jetty.

'Bridget, are you coming?'

She was about to say something else but instead reached up and gave Fynn a peck on the cheek.

'You're so good for me, Fynn,' and turned to join the others.

'Yes,' he murmured towards her receding back, 'but I'm not sure you're good for me.'

*　*　*

Karin was standing outside The Balmoral Hotel, clinging onto Ursula's skirt in the morning sun. She peeked around at the familiar figure of her mother who was kneeling in front of her, arms outstretched, with tears on her face, but Karin wasn't sure and pulled tighter on the skirt. Ursula turned around to take her gently by the shoulders and explain in German that her mother was now going to take care of her, but the little girl shrank back even further. She was never sure whether her mother was going to be cross or not, convinced she had chosen to stay in gaol all those months to avoid being with her.

Helga stood up, looking desperately at Bridget who was standing in the background.

'It'll take time, Helga,' she said, 'she's been through so much that she doesn't understand.'

Helga shook her head. This was not the homecoming she'd envisaged so many times in that cell. She'd become a prostitute and exposed her terrible secret for one reason and one reason only – to safeguard Karin.

Ruth came out of the front door, her practicality a welcome interruption to the tension.

'Hello, Bridget, well, I think the first thing we need to do is get some dinner for Karin and her mum, don't you? It's kippers today, you like those don't you, Karin?'

Karin nodded very slowly. It seemed all these women had expectations of her, but she had no idea what they were. First there was Ursula, whose warm arms had wrapped themselves around her every night when those bad thoughts came, then there was the policewoman, Bridget, who wasn't scary, despite that uniform and also there was Ruth, who looked a bit like her own grandmother, her *oma* in Kirchentellinsfurt.

The little girl was completely confused. That man Hitler had changed everyone and everything and the angry mother who had brought her to this island bore very little resemblance to the woman who had played tea shops with her at their home in Germany.

Helga held out her hand, but Karin skirted around it and took Ruth's hand instead, not noticing the crushed expression on her mother's face.

Bridget put her arm around Helga.

'Just be patient.' And she led them all into the hotel.

Helga and Karin had been moved to The Balmoral, away from the house with all the Nazis in, but as they entered the dining room, a silence descended on the room. Helga's chin raised in defiance, and she went towards a table in the corner, ignoring the bowed heads and the whispering all around her.

The hotel was a mix of conscientious objectors, fascists and, to Helga's horror, Jews. Bridget noticed the sudden revulsion that crossed Helga's face and knew there were many years of hatred to quell before this woman accepted the fact that she was one of them. For the first time, she realised what Sergeant Robinson had meant when she had told Bridget to keep an eye on Helga. There was so much conflict going on in

Helga's head, it made her vulnerable to influence from all directions.

The whispering got louder and Ursula leaned in to translate.

'They're saying she is still a Nazi and loyal to Hitler and that she deserved to rot in prison.'

Catching Ursula's words, Karin shivered. The word, Hitler, always made her think that everything that had happened was her fault, because she'd prayed to *Gott* every night to make that man disappear.

Berta and Ester came over to the table. Bridget looked up with interest; she hadn't made her mind up about these two.

'*Wilkommen zurüch,*' Berta said with a fixed smile.

'Please speak English,' Bridget said.

'Of course, I am so sorry, it is very good to speak the language of the people who will one day win this war, no? I wanted to say hello to this lovely little girl.'

'Hmm,' said Bridget. The effusiveness made her squirm for some reason and the way Berta looked at Karin made her bristle.

Ester smiled too.

'Your story is very . . . interesting. I would like to hear how you escaped.'

Helga looked extremely uncomfortable and was certainly not ready to become this pair's best friend.

'I think Helga has enough to deal with at the moment,' Bridget said flatly.

SHIRLEY MANN

'Of course, of course. Goodbye, little one. I am sure we will meet again . . . but *viellicht, Frau Fischer,* we can talk again.'

'Perhaps,' Helga said, looking nervously around the room to the other women, who were listening to every word that was being said.

Before Bridget went off duty, she cornered Ruth in the lobby of the hotel.

'What do you think, Ruth?'

'This isn't going to be easy,' the Quaker woman replied. 'No one on either side seems to want to trust Helga.'

'No, well, to be honest, would you?' Bridget asked her, checking to make sure no one could overhear. 'She was terrifying as a Nazi and then, hey presto, she's one of the good guys. The Nazis will hate her for deceiving them and the Jews will be very wary of her in case this is a front too.

'All except Berta and Ester, they were strangely willing to welcome her back into the fold. Even Ursula has kept her distance, and it was all due to her that Helga got off.'

'Well, I'm off to check on Ursula,' Ruth said, 'she's going to find that bed horrendously empty tonight.'

'Good idea,' Bridget agreed, glancing through to see Karin sitting cross-legged on the floor, fiddling with her dolly's string hair.

* * *

300

Now that Damian O'Callaghan was freed from his role of reluctant courier to a gaol in Douglas, he headed straight down to Peel Harbour to meet his Irish friend, Captain Michael Ryan, a man who made shadowy trips across the Irish Sea in his boat, avoiding all authorities and concocting dubious paperwork for his cargos. Since Britain had imposed a tax on cattle from the south of Ireland, he had been smuggling cows over to the north and then illegally transporting them to the Isle of Man or on to Liverpool.

Damian calculated that six Nazi escapees could easily be hidden in the empty hold on his journey back to Ireland.

All Irish boats sailed unarmed and usually alone, identifying themselves as neutrals with an Irish tricolour and the word EIRE in large letters on their sides and decks. Their bright lights that were supposed to protect them instead often drew fire from both sides, so Captain Ryan had become an expert at sliding along coastlines unseen during the early hours of the morning, and as a consequence, was a rather popular man with organisations that did not want to be traced. Throughout August, the two comrades spent long, alcohol-fuelled nights in The Creek Inn working out the details of their latest plan.

Lena, however, was trying to think about her own plan. There were three very important Nazis at Peveril Camp at Peel who were working on their tunnel to get to the outside of the wire, and the arrangements at Rushen for herself and her two superiors had to be just as thorough. To achieve that, they needed information from someone the police trusted, and Helga was the perfect candidate. All she had to do now was work out a way to revive her blackmailing.

Chapter Twenty-Nine

On a warm afternoon in October, Helga took Karin down to the beach. Her initial euphoria of being released from prison had been replaced with a recognition of the fact that neither of them belonged anywhere. During the flight from Germany, she'd had no time to process any rational thoughts; she just knew she had to get Karin away from the danger that had thrown everything she had ever believed into uncertainty. Once on the Isle of Man, she'd taken on that familiar shroud of being a Nazi to avoid detection and it had felt very natural. Now, it was as if she had been stripped of all her clothes and was standing naked, ready to be ridiculed.

She gave her daughter an old tin can and the child started to listlessly fill it and empty it of sand. She looked so lost and dejected and it made Helga's heart sink. Unable to make headway in her relationship with her daughter, she'd hoped a simple pleasure like playing on the beach would be a moment to be savoured but there was no hope or joy in the child's face. A dark shadow suddenly blotted out the sun from behind. It was Lena; she had been searching for them for weeks to try to get a moment alone. In their own language, she began to speak.

'She doesn't look very happy, does she? It's so hard when you're a mother whose past catches up with her, don't you think? It must be so confusing for the child; she looks as if she would willingly go with someone who showed her some kindness.'

Her next words confirmed Helga's suspicions that Lena had been the author of those terrible notes.

'I, of course, knew you were lying. Now you've condemned yourself with your own words and everyone knows your disgusting little secret.'

There was a pause as the air around Helga seemed to turn to ice. The memory of the notes that fluttered from the gaol window came back to her.

'I've heard these waters can be treacherous beyond this bay. Karin's such a beautiful little girl, isn't she? And so tiny, you could almost pop her under your coat and no one would know. Just remember that, Helga, when we need you.'

And then she was gone.

The sun disappeared behind the clouds but Helga was already shivering, and abruptly took hold of Karin's hand to drag her back towards The Imperial. She was shaking and needed time to recover, so she fiercely warned Karin not to move as she went to slowly take her coat off.

Karin hovered by the lounge door but then she spotted a child playing in the corner. Like her, she was about six years of age and was happily filling in a scrapbook, getting glue everywhere, watched by her indulgent mother. The child looked up and smiled in welcome.

Karin went warily over.

In English, with just a trace of a Jewish accent, the little girl spoke. 'Hello, I'm Rebecca. Do you want to help me?'

Karin looked sceptical. She had spent so much time in the company of adults, avoiding all other children, but, when the girl patted the chair next to her, she went to sit down.

'What are you doing?' she asked her.

'I'm making a scrapbook. It's so I remember who I am.' She carefully cut out a picture from a tattered magazine; it was of a pair of candles.

'What is it?' Karin asked.

The girl reverently touched the picture.

'It is the Sabbath candle. They are lit as the sun goes down on Fridays and they stay there until we see the three stars on Saturdays.

Proud of her knowledge, she went on, 'We do it to remember how the world was made in six days and then God, he rests.'

She leaned forward to confide in a respectful voice. 'My mother says it's important We don't forget.' Suddenly looking sad, she added, 'We left Germany because we weren't allowed to remember any more. My papa, he is here too, in a camp somewhere here but my grandparents . . .' She started to cry and Karin put her arm around her. She had no idea what was going on but she felt the pain this child was suffering and had an uneasy feeling this story had something to do with her friend, the man from next door. At that moment, her own mother came back. When she spotted the two children bent over a magazine of Jewish images, she stormed across the room.

'Get away from her,' she hissed in German to Karin.

'*Es tut mir leid, Mama*,' Karin said, jumping up guiltily. She looked longingly at the child who was the first person of her own age she had found the confidence to talk to in months, but Helga hurried forward and snatched her hand, tugging her away. Karin looked confused and upset and glanced back sorrowfully at the child.

'She was just telling me about the lovely candles they light,' she said, tripping over her feet in an effort to keep up.

Helga didn't speak until they got around the corner by the entrance, and then she turned around furiously to kneel down and face Karin.

In rapid German, she said, 'You never, do you hear me, *never* speak to strangers again and . . . especially not Jews. We are not Jews. *We are not Jews.*'

She started to shake. She'd spent so much time in gaol imagining her life when she got out, how she and Karin would live quietly until the war was over and then go back and find her parents, but Lena had brutally made her realise she would never be free of her past and now that past was putting her beloved child in danger.

Karin didn't know what to do. She wanted to reach out and be hugged by her mother, but her mother was that angry person again and the child's bottom lip quivered.

At that moment, Ruth was coming into the entrance of the hotel. She saw the crouched figure of Helga and the quivering one of little Karin and hurried forward to take Helga by the shoulders. She pulled her to her feet, saying gently, 'What is it, Helga, what's happened?'

Helga's eyes were wild with distress and she simply grabbed Karin's arm and fled towards the stairs, leaving Ruth to stare after her, puzzled.

* * *

Helga spent every day of the next few weeks nervously peering around corners, avoiding everyone, and never wanting to let Karin out of her sight. Finally Ruth insisted that it was time Karin joined the other children at the school at Dandy Hill and she reluctantly had to agree. One day, when walking briskly to pick her up, Helga turned a corner to find Berta standing by the side of the road. With a sickly smile, she stepped in front of Helga and spoke in rapid German.

'Hello, how are you? It's been such a difficult time for you, hasn't it? Are you all right?'

Helga was so taken by surprise at the sudden kindness, she found herself welling up with tears.

'No,' she said, pathetically. Berta and her sister were the only ones who had spoken to her in weeks and she desperately needed a friend.

'I don't know who I am any longer.'

Berta took hold of her elbow firmly.

'I know, I know. It's hard when everything you believe is taken from you. But there comes a time, Helga, when you have to decide which side you're on.'

Her mouth was still smiling but her grip tightened.

'You know, I can help you.'

Helga started to feel uneasy.

'How?' she said tentatively.

'You want to belong, don't you, Helga?'

She nodded slowly.

Ever since the court case, she had been floundering, unable to accept her Jewish heritage but no longer sure that fascism provided the answers either, but none of that mattered as long as Karin was safe.

'Yes,' Helga whispered.

'Well then,' Berta said brightly. 'Let's see how we can help each other,' and she leaned in confidingly. 'You know, Lena doesn't understand what it's like when people think you're a Jew, does she, but you and I, we know, don't we?'

A suspicion started to worm its way into Helga's mind.

'But . . . I thought you were a J—'

'Never mind what I am, what matters now is what *you* are. Oh, my dear Helga, I *can* protect you and your daughter from people like Lena, but that protection comes at a price. You've proved you're good at keeping secrets but, if you want Karin to be safe, then I strongly advise you to keep this little conversation between you and me. Have you got that?' Berta's fingernails pressed hard into Helga's forearm.

Again, Helga nodded, but every sinew in her body had tensed. If this woman was not a Jew, then what was she? She looked carefully at the face that was inches from her own and recognised, with distress, the same terrifying menace she had seen in Lena.

'What must I do?' she asked.

The corners of Berta's mouth tilted up slightly.

'We need you to report back to us. You must tell Ester or I *everything* you hear.'

Helga hung her head. She had no idea how she was going to do that.

'You are trusted by the policewomen in the camp. We want you to make sure that they believe you are a reformed character.'

As she turned to go, Berta added, 'Remember, Helga, not a word . . . or . . .' The words hung in the air as she walked away.

* * *

Throughout that winter, Berta or Ester seemed to be waiting around every corner, seizing the opportunity to pull Helga to one side, demanding information. Helga tried to find unimportant details she could pacify them with, such as which policewoman was doing roll call or who was taking the internees over to Port St Mary, but their frustrations with her were growing and her arm was sore with the bruises their increasingly tight grips inflicted on her. They were more interested in the dates and lists of repatriations right through to the spring, information about which internees were being watched, and details of the policewomen's rotas and they made sure Helga knew her little snippets of information were not enough.

Then there was another problem for Helga: every time Bridget would pop in to see them, her concern and open affection for Karin was so genuine, it left Helga with a crushing feeling of betrayal.

On one of her visits, Bridget spotted Karin sitting on her own in a tattered armchair, staring into space. The lounge was full as residents were not allowed to use their bedrooms during the day, but Karin was sitting upright, like an animal waiting to be attacked. Bridget made her way towards her, a worried expression on her face.

'Hello, Karin, how are you?'

Karin shrugged. The nightmares were back; her mother had become angry again and, after so long of being scared to talk to anyone, she wasn't allowed to be friends with the only other child in the hotel. Also, she missed Ursula.

'Where's your mother?' Karin motioned to the other side of the room with her finger. Bridget gave the little girl an affectionate pat on her head and went over.

As soon as she approached Helga, Bridget knew there was something wrong. Her chair was turned away from everyone else in the room and she was facing the wall. Sensing Bridget behind her, she jerked to her feet and her eyes looked terrified.

'It's all right, Helga, I'm just here to check on Karin.'

Then she looked closer.

'What's the matter, Helga?'

There was no reply, but Helga was frantically searching to see if anyone was listening.

Bridget went back to get Karin, took Helga's arm and steered them both out of the room. She'd had enough of this.

When they all got outside The Imperial, Bridget moved them around the corner on the other side of the road from the hotel.

She turned Helga to face her.

'You can either tell me here and now or we can go to the station, Helga. Which is it to be?'

Helga's shoulders seemed to shrink into herself. She was completely torn. How could she keep Karin safe if she told this policewoman what had happened to her over the last few weeks?

'OK, the station it is,' said Bridget, seeing her hesitation.

'*Nein, nein.*' Helga pulled her arm out of the way and jumped backwards.

Karin suddenly cried.

'I . . . want to go home, I want to go home but . . .' And here her face crumpled and big tear drops fell from her eyes. 'I don't know where my home is anymore.'

Both women knelt down next to the shaking figure in front of them, and Bridget looked over Karin's head towards Helga.

'This can't go on, we can help you . . . help you both, but you have to let us.'

The German grabbed her chest and started to pant, she could not breathe.

Bridget recognised the signs of a panic attack and looked around for help. She saw two young boys on their way to the beach.

'Boys, run quickly to the police station and get help,' she called, and when they hesitated, she yelled, 'now!' Then she thought again. 'No, only one of you go, the other one, go to the shop and get me a brown paper bag, quickly.'

The two boys sped off and Bridget tried to get Helga to breathe steadily. Karin was standing, her hands hanging at her side. She'd gone very pale, worrying that she had caused this.

Bridget looked around again. Helga was lying on the ground, clutching her chest and gulping air and there was no one else in sight.

Apart, she realised, from Berta who had appeared from around the corner.

'Berta,' she called, 'Berta, come and help me.'

Helga squealed in terror and Bridget looked down at her. The fear in her face was like reading a book. The policewoman just had to decipher the words on the page.

Berta came running over and leaned over the figure on the ground. Bridget watched her face very carefully. Berta's expression was signalling a warning that Helga could not miss.

Berta looked up with a concerned expression and said innocently, 'What can I do?'

All suspicions had to wait, they needed to get Helga to her feet.

'Help me get her up.'

Berta put her hand under Helga's shoulder and helped her up, slyly giving her a firm pinch with her fingers.

One of the boys was running towards them, a paper bag in his hand. He handed it over and Bridget immediately told Helga to breathe into the bag, slowly and steadily. Bit by bit, her breathing slowed and the colour came back into her face, which was more than could be said for Karin's that was whiter than the clouds above.

In the distance came the sound of the police car, its bell ringing. By the time it had reached the front, Bridget was delighted to see the reassuring large figure of Alister in the driving seat. He jumped out and, as if she were a feather, picked Helga up and put her gently into the back seat.

'I will take the child,' Berta said, 'do not worry.'

Helga lurched forward as if she was about to fall out of the car and Bridget took the hint. That little girl was not going out of her sight.

'No, it's all right, Berta, thank you for your help but we'll take it from here.'

Berta looked thwarted and her mouth twisted into a narrow line, but she backed off and the car set off up the hill.

Chapter Thirty

Molly, Bridget and Betty were all sitting on hard-backed chairs in Sergeant Robinson's office, watching her concentration as she fingered some notes in front of her.

'Your reports are very comprehensive, but Helga's refusal to talk is extremely concerning. She seems to be caught in the middle of whatever is happening here but is terrified of saying anything,' she said, looking at the three of them.

'So where are Helga and Karin now?'

Bridget spoke first. 'I've finally had them transferred again, this time to The Haven Boarding House at Port St Mary. I don't know what to do with them; I just keep moving them. The only internees there are Italians and they don't speak a word of English so they should be safer. I've told them to stay close to the hotel.'

'Did Helga give you any explanation?' the sergeant asked.

'No, none, but I'm sure it's something to do with Berta and Ester. I just don't understand what.'

'Hmm,' the sergeant said, 'I don't want to alert them by getting them in for questioning just yet, we just need to keep an eye on them.'

'It's Karin we're all worried about,' Betty put in. 'The little mite's hanging on by a thread.'

There was silence, they all knew this was a child who desperately needed to leave all her fears behind and learn how to play again.

'I think Ursula can help,' Molly said, 'she's the only one Karin trusts.'

'Yes,' Bridget agreed, 'I know Karin misses her. But she needs other children too.'

'Hmm,' the sergeant said, 'I think Alister may have come up with solution to that. Wait a minute.'

And she popped her head out of the doorway.

'Alister, have you got a moment?'

The three girls looked surprised. It was rare that these two sergeants even acknowledged each other, let alone had a civil conversation.

Alister came into the room, looking like a child who had won a large jar of sweets.

'Do you want to tell them what you've been up to, Sergeant?' Maureen Robinson said, sitting back at her desk with an air of disapproval that was belied by a twinkle in her eyes.

They all looked up expectantly.

'I've found them,' Alister said, with a broad grin, 'Judith and Daniel Apler . . . Ursula's brother and sister.'

There was a loud gasp from all of the girls and then Bridget ran to put her arms around Alister excitedly.

'Oh Alister, oh,' was all she could say, and it took Molly to ask the question Bridget's muffled voice could not.

'How?'

There was nothing Alister Cubbon liked better than a long tale and he leaned back against the wall, ready to enjoy every minute of his triumph.

'I've got a friend in the Welfare Office over there, Alf Harris. Lovely man, his wife runs a nice little haberdashery shop in Allerton . . .'

A cough from Maureen made him stand up straight again.

'Ah yes, well I got in touch with him and between us, we managed to track down the woman who'd taken the children that day. It seems she was from the Liverpool Seaman's organisation and thought their dad had been killed on a boat so she took them to their orphanage at Frankby – it's on the Wirral, you know.'

'Sergeant Cubbon,' Maureen said in a warning voice.

'I'm getting to it, I'm getting to it,' he said, glancing over at her with irritation. It had taken a long time for him to put the enquiries in place and he wanted to make sure that Robinson woman knew how clever he'd been.

'Anyway, he's managed to sort out the paperwork and is putting them on a ferry next week. They'll be here Saturday.'

He raised his chin and spread his arms, like a performer waiting for applause.

Molly and Betty joined Bridget in her hug of his large frame. Bridget was crying; she knew what this would mean to Ursula.

Sergeant Robinson stood up in an effort to regain some decorum and said officiously, 'Right, Molly, you get Ursula to wait outside Helga's new boarding house next Saturday at two. Bridget, if you pick the children up from the boat you should get here by then and . . .' here she paused, 'Betty, make sure Helga and Karin are there too.'

Betty looked puzzled but Bridget clapped her hands in delight.

'Of course,' she said, 'Ursula's sister – Judith isn't it? She's not too much older than Karin. They can be friends. Oh, that little girl needs a friend.'

And with that, she ran around the wooden desk to clasp her superior in a warm hug.

For a brief second, Maureen Robinson's eyes softened but then she brushed Bridget off and stood up.

'Very well, very well. That's enough. Now, girls, it's nearly time for roll call, so quick, quick, let's get a move on. And I want reports on everything Berta and Ester do, so back to it, all of you.'

She ushered them out but as Alister turned to go, she stopped him.

'Thank you.'

Alister Cubbon was sometimes surprised by life's twists and turns but this one moment of gratitude from his erstwhile enemy took his breath away.

* * *

Ursula was sitting, swinging her legs on the wall outside a boarding house in Port St Mary, with Molly standing impatiently by her side. She'd been told to be there for two o'clock but had no idea why. The days were seeming interminable but every time a new list of women to be repatriated was read out, she felt a quiver of panic. Although desperate to get back to Liverpool to search for her brother and sister, her future was as dark as the memory of the railway arches in Bentinck Street and she did not dare think what fate had in store for her. Helga and Karin were by The Haven's front window, waiting anxiously too. Helga was nervous as to why Betty had insisted they should be there and none of it made sense but to be honest, Helga thought, since she had been released from prison, nothing on the Island had made sense to her.

She peered into the distance to see Bridget approaching with two children, who were skipping along and laughing.

They both had an ice cream wafer in their hands, despite the cold January day.

Ursula stood up and stared; she grabbed the wall behind her and felt her knees buckle.

At that moment, the older child, a little girl with new, pink ribbons in her pigtails spotted a familiar figure and stopped in her tracks. Then, flinging her ice cream to the floor, she started to run along the pavement, her speed quickening as she got nearer to the girl next to the wall. The little boy watched her, puzzled, then he shrugged and carried on licking his delicious ice cream, hanging onto Bridget's hand.

'Judith, Judith, *bist du es wirklich*? Is it really you?' Ursula said in a quiet voice, worried that by speaking out loud, the vision running towards her might disappear.

Judith Apler ran full pelt to be gathered into her sister's arms. Their hair entangled and they clung to each other, their shoulders heaving with sobs.

Her cheeks drenched in tears, Ursula tore her eyes away from her beloved sister to search the pavement behind. Seeing the little boy, she stepped forward, making sure she still hung onto Judith 's hand.

'It can't be Daniel, *can it*? Oh, I don't believe it. You're so grown up.'

Daniel squinted suspiciously, he didn't know this girl but then Judith turned to him and taking his little puzzled face in her hands said haltingly, 'This, Daniel, is Ursula . . . Ursula, our sister.'

Daniel looked warily at the figure in front of him. Every night that he could remember, Judith had told him about their sister who would one day come and find them but, in his imagination, she was taller, with golden hair that shone around her head, not this ordinary person dressed in an old, faded dress and tattered coat. An expression of disappointment crossed his face and he went back to concentrate on his ice cream.

Ursula knelt down next to him, and, trying to keep the emotion that was overwhelming her out of her voice, began to speak.

'Hello, Daniel, you won't remember me but I'm your big sister, Ursula. I can't tell you how much I've missed you. *Oh, mein lieber Junge.*'

Daniel frowned; he'd been told not to speak that language.

Judith spoke from behind, her voice older than her years.

'We don't speak German anymore.'

Ursula nodded, she didn't care which language she spoke, she just couldn't believe her brother and sister were here with her on the Isle of Man.

She turned questioningly to Bridget who simply shrugged and smiled.

'It's my colleague, Sergeant Cubbon, you have to thank. I'll explain it all later but now there's someone else I want Judith to meet, if she's ready.'

At this particular moment, Ursula would have followed Bridget to the end of the earth for bringing about this miracle so, with the first beaming smile Bridget had ever seen on her face, said, 'We have all the time in the world to be together; what is it you want us to do?'

'Come with me, all of you,' Bridget said, leading the way up the steps to the entrance porch of the boarding house where Helga and Karin were waiting, their curiosity aroused by the scene they had just witnessed.

'Judith, this is Karin, she's about your age and could do with a friend.'

Judith was feeling full of love for the whole world so ran forward to give Karin a hug.

Karin wanted to stiffen and pull back but when she felt the warm, welcoming arms around her, she couldn't help but respond.

'Hello, Karin,' Judith said, and with the straightfor-wardness of an eight-year-old, added, 'So, we're going to be friends, are we? Well, that's really nice. I don't know anyone here, except . . .' she said, looking shyly at Ursula, 'my sister.'

She looked around at everyone and gave a dazzling smile.

'I'm going to like it here.'

Daniel finished off his ice cream with a satisfied grin and wiped his mouth with the back of his hand. He was going to like it here too.

Chapter Thirty-One

Between their normal duties and keeping surveillance on Berta and Ester, it was rare that the girls had the chance to enjoy a night out, but in early February it was Betty's birthday so Molly decided they needed a celebration.

'Pass me the sugar water, I can't get my hair to stay in the same place.'

'Who's pinched my shoelace? I need it to get this hair to roll back in place.'

'I stink of Eau de Cologne. Oh, for the day when we can get proper shampoo so I won't have to rub this darned stuff in my poor scalp. It's red raw.'

'You look gorgeous, Bridget,' Molly said and then felt embarrassed. She could have bitten her tongue off. 'You, too, Betty.'

'We all do. Douglas'll be lucky to have us,' Bridget said cheerfully. Despite endless efforts to find out more about Berta and Ester, the trail had gone cold but, in the meantime, she'd received something that almost approached praise from Sergeant Robinson. Helga had looked calmer than she had done in months, Ursula was like a different girl and best of all, Karin was inseparable from her new friend. She felt she deserved a night off.

By the time they got to the dance at the Villa Marina in Douglas, all their eyes were shining with anticipation. The first people they saw were Kieran and Nancy surrounded by a crowd of people the girls didn't know. Bridget went over and tapped Nancy on the shoulder, trying not to look at Kieran who looked ridiculously handsome in his RAF uniform.

'Hello, you, long time no see.'

Nancy turned round to joyfully give her friend a hug.

'Bridg . . . it's been so long, I've missed you. What a shame Fynn's too busy to join us. Kieran asked him but he's just too busy.'

Before Bridget could answer, Kieran butted in.

'Hello, Bridget, it's good to see you.' He looked genu-inely delighted and Bridget felt a little glow of pleasure. It made her squirm inside. Somehow, every time this man looked at her, it made her want to readjust her pigtails. He reduced her to a besotted schoolgirl.

He suddenly grabbed her hand. 'But, come on, dance with me, I love this one.'

The band was playing 'Paper Doll' by the Mills Brothers and its gentle tones led the couple around the floor. Kieran chatted on happily about how he was really enjoying his 'new work' without telling her anything about it. As they negotiated a tricky bit of footwork, he glanced sideways at Bridget and breathed a sigh of relief. Yes, she was just Bridget, his friends' sister. Exceptionally pretty, yes, but he could admire her like a fond brother or cousin. Glancing beyond her, he saw Nancy and a shiver went through him. He knew that it was just such a feeling he had been searching for. He simply needed to convince Nancy Gorry he could be trusted.

'You seem much better, Kieran,' Bridget said, noticing how the tense expression on his face had lifted.

He looked down with genuine affection. 'Do you know what? I am, Bridg, I really am. I think I've beaten the drink and people are beginning to respect me again. Yes, I'm doing all right.'

Bridget was listening to his words but she couldn't help but notice how his eyes kept searching for Nancy.

'Getting on well with Nancy, are you?' she asked bluntly.

Kieran looked up in mock surprise.

'Who?' And then he started to laugh. 'Hmm, you know me too well, don't you?'

Bridget had an answer to that, but she kept it to herself. Yes, of course she knew him well, she had scrutinised his every move, every word, every expression since she was six.

'Can we go and get some fresh air, Bridget, I need to talk to you?' Kieran said, pulling her towards the door. She had no option but to follow him, but she was not sure she wanted to hear what he was about to say.

*　*　*

Kieran turned to face Bridget next to a low wall and she sat down slowly next to him, shivering in the winter air but avoiding touching his warm touch. She thought of the years she had spent idolising Kieran Moore and a feeling of impending loss started to creep up her body.

Kieran offered her a cigarette and lit one for himself.

'You're one of my oldest friends,' he said, not noticing the way she winced. 'I think we need to talk about that kiss. I don't think we can ignore it, can we?'

He put his finger under her chin and raised her eyes to meet his.

Bridget was silent for a very brief moment before she blurted out, 'I've loved you since I was six, Kieran. I think part of me still does and always will.'

She paused and then her shoulders dropped. Perhaps it was time to let go. Her thoughts clarifying for the first time in years, she went on, 'But, do you know what, Kieran? I think you're an ideal I've built up. I suspect that's not really you.'

Kieran shook his head regretfully.

'I'm anything but an ideal,' he told her, 'I'm actually a bit of a wreck. You'd be so much better off with Fynn . . .'

Here he waited, watching with satisfaction as she blushed.

'You know he's the man you need, Bridg, he's everything I ever wanted to be, and he really loves you.'

She looked up in surprise.

'I don't think he does. Well, if he ever did, he certainly doesn't now,' and her face fell, suddenly overwhelmed by the thought of Fynn not caring for her.

'Anyway,' Kieran was saying, feeling that he had satisfactorily put a ghost to rest, 'if we're the friends I hope we are, I need your help. I think I've fallen, I mean *really fallen* for Nancy, but . . .'

Bridget felt a spark of irritation. She wanted time to adjust to the thoughts that were going through her head but this was all moving too fast for her. Her stomach lurched as she recognised the pain she'd suffered so many times before. It reminded her of the end of a film where the wrong man walks slowly into the distance. It was just how she should deal with the blank screen left behind.

'But what?' she forced herself to say.

Kieran's head drooped and it was all she could do not to gather him into her arms; adoring this man was a habit, an addiction almost. It wasn't going to be so easy to pass him on to her friend.

'You're the only one I can tell; but, Bridg, it's the drink. Did you know about her boyfriend?'

Bridget was taken aback. It was such a sudden change of subject. She made herself concentrate.

Kieran paused; he didn't want to betray any of Nancy's secrets but Bridget was biting her lip in thought. She slowly nodded, alarmed at how everything suddenly fell into place: Nancy's abrupt need to escape London, even the decision to join the WAAF. It brought back an encounter she'd had one night with Nancy when they bumped into a friend of hers in Piccadilly. He was a newsreader at the BBC, Bridget remembered, but when Nancy had said they needed to go, already late to meet friends, he'd grabbed her arm roughly. The intensity of his glare had alerted the trainee policewoman but Nancy simply brushed Bridget's concerns aside. A few nights later, Bridget spotted some bruises on the side of Nancy's face only to be told she had bumped into a doorway.

'Not exactly,' Bridget told Kieran, 'but, yes, now you mention it, I did meet him once and, to be honest, I didn't like him. There was something about him.'

Kieran searched for the strength to say the words that had been haunting him. 'What if I become like that after drinking too much? Sometimes, Bridg, I had no idea what I was doing, I could be like that man.'

Bridget sat up straight. This was the friend of her brothers, and he needed her help. It was almost a relief to think of him in those terms. She considered carefully before replying, remembering the large number of drunks in London, desperate to consume anything from cheap cider to meths to blot out reality and she knew the power of drink.

There was a long pause.

'From what I've seen, Kieran, the men who behave like that have aggression in them, it's not something that just appears out of nowhere. I've known you nearly all my life, and I can honestly say I've never seen you lose your temper, even when Aedan broke your bicycle. No, I don't think that would ever be you. And anyway, you're not drinking now, are you?'

'No,' he replied hesitantly, 'but it's always there, like a magnet. Every time I go near a bar, every time someone offers me a drink. I'm not sure I'm strong enough to avoid it for the rest of my life.'

Bridget had no answer except to say, 'You have to believe in yourself, Kieran. You're stronger than you know and if you feel what I think you feel for Nancy, then you will never let her, or yourself, down.'

Kieran looked unconvinced but he gave Bridget a grateful smile and stood up to go back inside. He had felt incredibly relieved that Bridget was just, well, Bridget, the friend he'd known all his life. It felt right, he thought with a satisfied sigh. He put his arm around her shoulders and gave her a brotherly squeeze. Bridget realised then that one night so many months ago might end up being the only time she would feel the soft lips of the boy she'd loved all her life.

The music playing was Frank Sinatra's new song, 'You'll never know' and its words resonated with more than one of the little group in that hall that night.

For Bridget, the years of adoring Kieran Moore from afar were as etched into her being as the marks from years of dancing feet on the wooden floor below her. She hoped she'd taken the first steps to break free of them.

Nancy was watching warily as the pair made their way back across the dance floor, unsure whether she was more worried about Kieran telling Bridget how she had spurned him or the fact that the pair of them had been out for a cosy chat. She shook her head, wishing she could unjumble her thoughts.

Someone else whose thoughts were in a muddle was Molly. She was in a turmoil, her emotions swirling around like a maelstrom. By the time they all got off the bus, she told the other two she had a headache and was going for a walk. Huddling her coat around her, she walked at a fast pace along the promenade. As she neared the beach, she heard a voice behind her. It was Sergeant Robinson.

'Molly, Is that you?'

Molly turned around to see the sergeant walking briskly towards her.

'Just getting a bit of fresh air, I do find it hard to sleep sometimes, don't you?'

Molly nodded and walked towards her superior, realising she didn't even know where the sergeant lived.

'Is your place near here?'

'Yes, just around the corner. I often walk at night, it helps me clear my head.'

'I wish it would clear mine,' Molly muttered.

The sergeant looked sideways at the girl next to her. She'd been watching the way Molly looked at Bridget and recognised that agonising ache that was undoubtedly hitting her in the stomach.

'Are you all right, Molly?'

It was dark, Molly had had two gins and her mouth opened before she remembered who she was talking to.

'No, Sarge, I'm not. But I can't talk about it. I just think I'm going insane.'

Maureen Robinson felt a pang of sympathy for this girl. She reminded her of herself at a younger age.

She spoke carefully. 'You're not going insane, Molly. I can assure you of that. But the rest of the world might think you are. The 1940s may not be ready for what you're feeling.'

Molly had no idea what emotions were erupting inside her but hearing those words gave her a moment's hope that someone might know what she was going through.

The moon came out from the cloud above and Molly looked into her superior's face to find not just understanding but an empathy that sent a shock wave through her.

Were there more people who felt like her? she wondered, *women and men who walked around looking perfectly normal but who suffered like she was suffering?*

She suddenly felt overwhelmed with embarrassment, muttered a hurried goodbye and ran towards the girls' cottage. Maureen Robinson looked with pity at the retreating figure. When she got back to her room, she went over to the walnut sideboard with an array of photographs of her nieces and nephews and reached to the back where there was one of a woman astride a horse. Maureen ran her finger slowly over the woman's features and then closed her eyes to remember the touch of that skin. She pulled the photo towards her and hugged it towards her.

'Oh Molly,' she said. 'My poor, poor girl.'

Chapter Thirty-Two

Lena was making her way along the street towards St Catherine's Church, thinking about the tensions that were beginning to erupt in some of the 'brown' houses between those who were determined to follow Hitler to the end and those who were sensing a change in fortunes in the war. Lena, however, had no time for such debates but her quarry hadn't been seen in weeks and she was worried that despite threats, Helga had confided in those damned policewomen. Her associates, thwarted in their attempts to find out repatriation dates so they could organise the daring escape on a night when the police would be busy, had turned on her. The plans for the escape from the men's camp at Peel and for Lena and the two spies at Rushen Camp were almost in place but they needed dates and they needed them fast. Feeling like a schoolgirl who had been called into the head teacher's office, she hurried towards the church, failing to notice Ursula coming from the other direction. The sight of the passionate Nazi made Ursula stiffen but Lena had already disappeared into the church.

Hearing a low whistle, Ursula's eyes narrowed. Bridget had mentioned that she didn't trust Lena and the young Jewish girl was determined to help the policewoman in any way she could.

Ducking down, she dropped back around the corner to avoid being seen and craned her neck to watch.

Lena came out after a few moments, looking annoyed, and then hurriedly disappeared up the street away from the beach.

Ursula was about to emerge from her hiding space around the corner when she saw two more women come out of the church porch.

She recognised them as the two Jewish women, Berta and Ester, and was puzzled, knowing how much all the Nazis avoided anyone of the Jewish faith.

I need to find Bridget, she thought.

* * *

Bridget was in the kitchen at the police station, making her third pot of tea of the day for Sergeant Robinson when Alister called from the front desk.

'A young lady to see you, Bridget.'

Bridget emerged, a cup and saucer in hand and beamed with delight when she saw Ursula.

'Just wait a moment, while I take this in and I'll be with you,' she said, knocking on Sergeant Robinson's door.

'Did I miss the tea round?' Alister said plaintively. Bridget came back out to the front desk and gave him a pat on the arm.

'Oh Alister, you did, I'm sorry but the water's hot, do you think you'll manage to put a few leaves in to make your own?'

'Hmm, I don't get the preferential treatment that one does,' Alister said, jerking his head towards Sergeant Robinson's room.

'No, but I love you more,' Bridget whispered with a grin and turning towards Ursula, said, 'What can I do for you?'

Ursula suddenly looked shy; she wasn't used to being in the spotlight.

Bridget signalled for Ursula to follow her into the interview room and shut the door behind them both.

'Now, what is it?'

Ursula faltered. She really had no evidence, she just suspected something was wrong.

'It's just that I saw Lena,' she said.

Bridget sat up straight and wondered whether she needed to get out her notebook. She decided not, this young girl just wanted her to listen.

'Yes?'

'I saw her coming out of St Catherine's church.'

'And . . .?' Bridget persevered.

'Then I saw those two Jewish women, Berta and Ester, they came out behind her.'

The hairs on the back of Bridget's neck stood up. This could be the evidence they'd been looking for.

'What happened next?'

Ursula looked crestfallen.

'No, only that, but I thought you needed to know.'

Bridget leaned across and covered the girl's hand in her own.

'Yes, I absolutely did, Ursula, you've done a wonderful job. Now, you leave it to me but please, don't say anything to anyone outside about this. We have some work to do.'

She stood up and opened the door so that Ursula could pass her.

'Thank you so much,' she said, 'just be careful and don't let Berta and Ester know you suspect something. It could be dangerous for you.'

At this, Ursula looked frightened. She was beginning to wish she hadn't said anything.

*　*　*

The rest of Bridget's day was spent ploughing through internee files. She needed to find a connection between Lena and the two Jewish women, but the records were bland and very short. She called Sergeant Robinson in to recount Ursula's strange tale and to make sure she hadn't missed anything, but the sergeant was equally puzzled.

'It's this blasted war,' the sergeant said, irritated. 'No papers are as they should be, we have no idea who many of these women are, and there's no means of getting real detail about their backgrounds. Look at Helga, we had no idea what she'd been through.'

She and Bridget were frowning over the documents when Betty came in, looking for the duty rota.

'Are these Ester and Berta's ID cards?' she asked, peering over their shoulders.

'Hmm, looks as if the name Sara's been added as an afterthought,' she said, casually. And with that, she carried on across the room towards the filing cabinet.

Every Jewish woman in the camp had Sara written next to their names to identify them for their religion – a practice condemned by the girls as branding.

Maureen Robinson and Bridget peered carefully at the documents.

'She's right!' Maureen Robinson said. 'Look, there's hardly any room but the name's squeezed in on both.'

'Do you think they've been tampered with?' Bridget asked. And with that, she called over to Betty who was rifling through the filing cabinet.

'Let's have a look at some of the other Jewish women's cards.'

Betty abandoned her own search to flick through the cardboard files, then she came over and fanned out a pile of papers in front of them all.

The three women examined each of the other identity papers carefully and compared them with Berta and Ester's.

'I think you might be right, Betty,' Sergeant Robinson said, a slow smile spread over her face.

'Well done, Officer, this is really interesting,' she added with an excited expression. 'But in the meantime, I want you all to take turns to watch these two and see if they give us any clues as to what the hell is going on.'

She loved a good detective trail but Bridget was looking more concerned. Now she had Berta and Ester, in addition to Lena, to worry about. And it made her shiver to think about the implications for them all if these Jewish women were not who they said they were.

*   *   *

The instructions Lena had been given when she first arrived at the camp had simply been to intimidate and disrupt, so that her fellow internees knew they were still being watched. But once her two new superiors arrived, the atmosphere changed completely and meetings at the church had left Lena with no doubt that she would be expected to implement whatever action might be necessary. And that might include the murder of a small child.

Lena Braun had killed before. Her commitment to the Nazi cause was total but she had never threatened harm to a child and had gone to St Catherine's Church on this occasion with trepidation, but this time, the emphasis was on the escape plan. To restore her credibility, Lena had asserted that she was perfectly capable of organising the escape and had arrangements already in hand.

Ester had looked doubtful but by the time Lena had given them an update on her liaisons with Damian O'Callaghan, Berta had nodded and agreed she should continue, but added a warning.

'If this goes wrong, Lena, it is not only your neck that is on the line but also your family in Germany. Just remember that. Now, if your plan is to work, we need someone to get us a radio. Helga Fischer is the obvious choice, isn't she?'

Lena shivered at the name. She didn't want to admit she had no idea where Helga was hiding and was running through possible vulnerable internees in her head, until she looked up and smiled. She knew exactly where to find an internee who would fit the bill.

* * *

There was an uproar at The Balmoral. The chatter was all about how someone had broken into the kitchen and stolen a radio that had been hidden in one of the cupboards. Bridget made her way through the large crowd that had gathered in the street outside to try to restore calm. The excitement had broken the monotony of living behind the wire and all the internees – and locals – were buzzing with anticipation as to what drama would unfold next.

The doors opened and Sergeant Robinson emerged with Ursula Apler in handcuffs. Bridget gasped.

Several women in the crowd nudged each other as they saw the young Jewish girl being led up the street towards the police station and then after a moment's silence, a commotion broke out.

'I can't believe it, why would she need a radio?'

'I bet she wanted it to contact the enemy.'

'I've never trusted her, ever since she defended that Nazi woman.'

Bridget turned to glower at the woman who had made that last remark, but she was as puzzled as they were. Her first job, however, was to disperse the crowd.

'Please return to the dining room or wherever you are supposed to be this morning,' she said and waved her arms to encourage them all back in the hotel, trying to ignore the mutterings.

Having ushered them all back in, she hurried back to the police station.

'What's going on, Alister?' she asked.

'Search me. She's in there . . .' He jerked his head towards the interview room.

'Do you think I can go in?'

'Well, Molly's already gone in, so I suppose so.'

Bridget tentatively knocked and then went into the room. Ursula was sitting upright opposite the sergeant, tears glistening in her eyes. Molly was standing with her arms crossed, leaning against the back wall. Ursula looked up pleadingly at Bridget.

'Miss Apler is about to tell me why she tried to steal a radio,' the sergeant was saying. But Ursula just dropped her head and fiddled with her fingers in her lap.

'Sarge, could I have a minute, outside?' Bridget asked.

'Yes, stay with the prisoner, Molly, I'll be back in a minute.'

Outside in the corridor, Sergeant Robinson waited patiently while Bridget gathered her thoughts.

'I know this girl, Sarge, She wouldn't hurt a fly and she certainly isn't a thief, let alone a spy. I think there's more to this than meets the eye.'

'I agree with you,' Sergeant Robinson said, 'but we need to get to the bottom of it before the bigwigs turn up. You know what they're like about anything to do with security. Once they get here, we'll lose Ursula to them and we won't have a chance.'

'I . . . I wonder . . . could I have some time alone with her?' Bridget asked.

The sergeant thought for a moment and then nodded.

'OK, but make it quick. I think you've got about quarter of an hour.'

Once Molly and the sergeant had left the room, Bridget pulled her chair up to Ursula's and took hold of her hands.

'Look at me, Ursula. I *want* to help you but you *have* to help me. We've got very little time before the Commandant and the Chief Inspector from Douglas arrive and if we don't have an explanation for them, they'll take you off to a gaol up there.'

Ursula looked so terrified, Bridget wanted to put her arms around her and give her a hug, but this was a prisoner and any breach of professionalism could come back to haunt her in a courtroom. Bridget decided to go through her list of questions.

'So, did you take the radio?'

Ursula's reply was so quiet, Bridget had to lean in to hear her.

'I was made to . . .'

Bridget waited.

The girl in front of her looked absolutely terrified. She had obviously been threatened.

A whisper came out of Ursula . . . 'It was Karin . . .'

Bridget looked incredulous.

'Karin?'

'No not Karin, but for Karin.'

This made more sense and Bridget squeezed the girl's hands to encourage her.

'So, was it Lena who made you do it?'

Ursula shook her head which gave Bridget the opening she had been looking for.

'Someone else?'

There was a slight nod.

'Who then?' Ursula looked with a panicked expression around the room, as if the perpetrators could walk in at any moment.

This was it, the evidence she had been craving, Bridget thought with a quiver.

'Was it Berta? Ester? It was, wasn't it, Ursula?'

Without a denial, Bridget persevered. 'But why, Ursula?'

The young girl was about to speak when the door banged open and two large men walked in.

'Thank you, WPC . . . Harrison, is it?' the Chief Inspector said. 'We'll take over now.'

Bridget had no choice but to leave the room and the Commandant closed the door firmly behind her.

She was livid and was about to express her indignation in no uncertain terms, when the sergeant signalled to her to move into the back kitchen where the men could not hear them.

As soon as they got in there, Bridget let out a furious tirade of how she suspected Berta and Ester were somehow involved and that just as Ursula was just about to tell her everything, those two men had come in and ruined it.

Molly came in and got out three cups.

'I think a cup of tea's in order,' she said evenly, taking in Bridget's bright-red face. She wanted to put her arm around Bridget to soothe her but didn't trust herself.

Sergeant Robinson leaned back on the cupboards and waited.

Once the tea had been poured, Bridget had calmed down a little, but she was not giving up yet.

'Can I go and find Berta and Ester. Surely we can at least bring them in for questioning?' she asked her superior, who nodded. Putting down her cup and saucer, Bridget continued. 'Can I . . . and can Molly come with me, Sarge?'

Molly looked so touched to have been asked that the sergeant could not resist indulging a moment's hope on the young woman's face.

'Yes, of course, but be careful. Something's going on and we don't want them to think we suspect them of this . . . not yet. They've covered their tracks so far, but even so, I really do think those two might be dangerous.'

Chapter Thirty-Three

Bridget and Molly scoured the Balmoral Hotel for Berta and Ester but couldn't find them anywhere. They began asking the internees in the dining room, who were bored as usual, and delighted to have a diversion. The few hundred left in the camp were becoming increasingly restless, so any gossip or rumours gave the internees a focus that they had no intention of wasting. The policewomen were barraged with questions about Ursula that neither of them wanted to answer, so, having firmly established that no one had seen their suspects, the two girls made their way quickly to the entrance. Molly closed the door on the excited chatter that their visit had prompted and turned to Bridget.

'Phew, that was hard going.'

'Yes, they're all bored out of their minds and obsessed with getting away from here. I feel sorry for them, it must be dreadful to have so little to do.'

Bridget turned towards the street, thinking.

'I know,' she said, 'let's try St Catherine's Church. Ursula saw them hanging around there, so let's try it. They might be using it as a place where they can meet without being overheard.'

They made their way around the corner and then slowed their pace as they approached the porch. Putting a finger on her lips, Bridget tiptoed into the entrance and they both put their heads to one side to listen.

Straining their ears, they heard low murmurings.

Molly signalled to Bridget to get nearer to the door and they both crept forward.

The voices were indistinct, but Bridget was sure they were speaking German.

At that moment, the door creaked open and a hand tentatively pushed the door.

Bridget signalled to Molly to cover the back door and moved forward. She grabbed the handle and was about to push the door fully open when an arm pushed Bridget out of the way, making her fall back against a loose brick in the wall. She was knocked to the floor and unable to see the two figures who stepped over her to run off down the road.

Bridget struggled to her feet but went dizzy and fell back down again. Putting her hand up to her head to feel for any bumps, her palm came away covered in blood. She felt she was about to faint.

In the distance, Molly was shouting at the two retreating figures, but just as she was about to run after them, she spotted Bridget with blood streaming down her face.

Changing direction to run back, she took the crumpled body of the injured policewoman in her arms.

Molly looked after the two characters running away but decided they would have to wait; after all, they were behind barbed wire on an island, there was nowhere they could hide. Bridget, however, needed her and she felt a huge surge of comfort that she could be the one to help.

'Bridget, Bridget, can you hear me?' she asked, cradling the bleeding girl in her arms.

There was a slight murmur.

Molly took out her whistle and blew it as hard as she could. Bridget didn't even react to the piercing sound. Molly began to be seriously concerned, the blood was flowing everywhere, through Bridget's hair, down her face and onto her uniform and her eyes were closing.

'Please, please, Bridget, don't go unconscious on me. I'll get some help, I promise.'

Molly blew her whistle again but everywhere was chillingly quiet. She wondered whether she could lay Bridget on the ground for a moment while she went out to look for help but when she loosened her arms, Bridget squirmed and tightened her grip.

Molly shouted and then blew her whistle again.

A woman's face appeared, she was pushing a pram and in it, a small infant was beginning to cry.

'Oh my God,' she gasped. 'What's happened?'

By now the baby was loudly crying. The woman didn't wait for a reply, the need for help was obvious.

'I think the lifeboat's just come in, I'll get them. It's just the babba's in need of 'er milk, I 'ave to go.'

Molly nodded and mouthed a thank you as the woman's face withdrew. She breathed a sigh of relief.

'Someone's coming, Bridget, someone's coming.'

Just along the road, Fynn was returning from a false alarm with his crew and saw the handyman, Damian O'Callaghan, in front of him heading towards the church. But when the woman with the baby came out of the porch screaming in panic, the handyman suddenly veered off towards the beach, unwilling to become involved in a drama at the very place he used for clandestine meetings.

Fynn had no time to worry about an unhelpful Irishman but instead ran towards the woman who begged him to get an ambulance. He cupped his hands around his mouth and yelled to his crew in the distance.

'Stretcher, now!'

Molly heard the call and said gently to the worryingly still figure in her lap, 'They're coming, Bridg, they're coming,' and she leaned down and gently kissed her forehead.

'It'll be all right, my love, oh my poor darling.'

She heard a noise and looked up to see Fynn standing over her. She panicked he may have heard her love-stricken words but Fynn's expression was one of professionalism as he took in the blood, the collapsed figure of Bridget and Molly's worried face.

'What happened?' Fynn asked.

'She fell, no, she was pushed against this wall. She must have struck her head.'

He nodded and very gently manoeuvred Bridget's hair at the back of her head to one side to glimpse a deep cut that was oozing fresh blood all the time.

He reached forward and gently prised Bridget out of Molly's arms. She felt her heart was being taken with it.

He lifted her up as if she were as light as a feather and turned to where his friends had appeared with a stretcher.

Molly felt guilty. *Where's all your training gone?* she asked herself. The first aid course and the practicalities of dealing with an incident like this had gone completely out of her mind, her only thought had been to cradle the ailing Bridget, rather than do anything useful.

'Thank you, Fynn,' she said, shakily getting to her feet.

He put his hand on her shoulder. 'It's all right, Molly, you've had a shock. Just take it easy, we'll take it from here.'

He turned to the others. 'Let's get her on this stretcher.' 'You've rung the ambulance, haven't you, Albert?'

Albert nodded. 'It won't be long. Here, here's a clean pad.'

Fynn took it and gently applied pressure to the wound; he was watching closely for changes in her breathing but was reassured to find it was steady. As he peered at her, she opened her eyes.

'It's all right, Bridget, I'm here, you'll be OK, we've called for an ambulance. How are you feeling?'

There was a pause, then Bridget opened her eyes and whispered, 'It hurts, Fynn, but, oh, I'm so glad it's you. You'll look after me, won't you?'

It was at that moment that Fynn Moore felt his heart constrict and he knew he was going to do everything in his power to fight for this woman.

'Damn that brother of mine,' he thought to himself, 'he's not having her.'

'Yes, always,' he told her simply. Molly's shoulders drooped.

* * *

Ursula was shaking but she wasn't sure whether it was fear or cold. The little cell was bare except for a wooden bed with a stained mattress on it and a bucket in one corner. A rough blanket was folded at one end of the bed. Above her was a barred window and she could only just see the sky if she stood on tiptoe.

In danger of collapsing into tears, she pulled her shoulders back and fiercely told herself that she had been through so much since she had arrived on the Island and surely the note she had left with Karin for Bridget would exonerate her from all this. She just hoped Bridget had found it.

The door opened to reveal the Chief Inspector's large frame almost blocking the doorway.

'Follow me,' he ordered and turned on his heels to march down the corridor. Ursula went behind, trying to slink along the wall to make herself invisible.

He took her to an interview room and closed the door behind them.

'Now, do you want to tell me what happened? Or,' he said, threateningly, 'do you want to save it for the court?'

Ursula shivered at the word 'court.' It brought back too many memories but she could not tell him what had really happened and how Berta and Ester had given her no choice – it was steal the radio or Karin would suffer.

Ursula looked at the man but said nothing. Over and over, she tried to think whether she'd done anything that could put Karin in jeopardy but no, she thought with relief, she'd done as she'd been told and had prised the padlock open to find the radio hidden behind the crockery at the back of the cupboard. She'd then taken the radio to the back wall where Berta was waiting to take it from her but as she crept back into the kitchen, the cook had come in and caught her, screwdriver and padlock in hand.

Ursula decided to put her trust in Bridget coming to rescue her, so clasped her hands together in her lap and stared down at them.

'You do realise how serious this is, don't you, Miss Apler? You know the penalties for internees who steal? And for those who break into Manx property? Let alone for someone who steals a radio?'

'I want to see Bridget,' Ursula said plaintively but the Chief Inspector ignored her. Paul Morris had been brought over from Manchester to deal with serious crimes at these camps; he prided himself on his interrogation techniques and did not need a whippersnapper of a young police-woman to get involved.

He proceeded to go over the facts, which were that the cupboard had been found prised open and the radio gone. This prisoner had been discovered coming out of the kitchen, but the radio was nowhere to be seen. His line of questioning took him down several avenues, but every one of them was met by a stony silence. Finally, his patience snapped.

'Very well, if you won't tell me what happened, perhaps a few nights in a cold cell will jog your memory.' He stood up and led her back to her isolation.

* * *

Bridget was lying in a hospital bed with a bandage wrapped around her head, struggling to remember what had happened, but it was all a bit hazy. She just remembered Fynn's arms around her, placing her gently on the stretcher and felt a warm glow.

Drifting in and out of sleep, she vaguely heard voices coming into the ward. She thought one was Sergeant Robinson and another was her father, but she couldn't concentrate and closed her eyes again.

It was twenty-four hours before she could sit up and eat a little of the porridge that was brought to her bedside, allowing her to focus on the events that had resulted in her being injured. She remembered going to the hotel and then she tried to think what had happened next.

Exhausted with the effort, she put the spoon down and lay back on the pillow. When she opened her eyes again, Molly was sitting at her bedside, holding her hand.

'Oh Molly, it's good to see you,' she said. 'I've been trying to remember what happened but it's all a bit fuzzy.'

Molly leaned forward to bring Bridget up to date but a nurse, who was straightening the bed next to Bridget, coughed loudly and gave Molly a warning look.

'Now, no talk about work, you two,' she said. 'This patient just needs to get better, not be fretting.'

And moving to plump up Bridget's pillows, the nurse added, 'A few days in bed, some good food and then you'll be all ready to go home, won't you?'

Molly looked chastened and sat back again. 'They're sending you to your parents' for a few days, I think.'

Bridget groaned. She wasn't sure she needed her mother's ineffectual fussing. She'd have preferred to have gone to her grandmother's.

'Visiting time's up,' the nurse said briskly, checking the watch on the top of her apron.

Molly stood up and reluctantly let Bridget's hand fall onto the folded-back sheet.

'Betty wants to come and see you, 'but I think she'll have to wait until you get to your parents' house,' she said, looking questioningly at the nurse, who nodded.

Molly left the ward, looking back with concern at the wan face of Bridget, but then the nurse caught her up to tell her, 'I know she's pale but she's strong and she's making a good recovery. It won't be long before she'll be jitterbugging again.'

Molly gave a weak smile, unwilling to show how worried she had been.

* * *

The station was buzzing by the time Molly got back from the hospital. Sergeant Robinson had brought Berta and Ester in for questioning and put them in separate interview rooms. Alister was on the front desk at usual. His face was flushed with indignation.

'What's going on, Alister?' Molly asked.

'I have no idea,' he said. 'You know the dragon keeps me out of the loop on anything to do with the women internees. So much for a truce between us. I've just been told to get on with minding the desk.'

'Oh, she's not that bad,' Molly said, thinking of the female sergeant's kindness to her.

'Hah!' Alister said, his mouth forming a very childish pout. 'Anyway, how's young Bridget?'

Molly grinned. 'No trouble at all – yet – but she will be when she starts to feel better.'

Alister chuckled.

'Yes, once she realises she's missing out on all the fun here, she'll have a lot to say.'

One of the interview room doors opened and Berta emerged, an innocent, bewildered look on her face. At the same time, Ester emerged from a separate room, followed by Betty who simply shrugged her shoulders at the sergeant's inquisitive glance.

Sergeant Robinson spoke to both women. 'You can go for now, but we will be keeping an eye on you and we may call you in again for more questioning.'

Berta made her way to the door but turned as she got there.

'We don't understand. We are Jews. We have done nothing,' she said innocently and, taking Ester's arm, she steered her out onto the street. But once they were out of sight, they both sneered with satisfaction.

Chapter Thirty-Four

Kathleen was shifting bales of hay while Fynn was on the other side of the barn mucking out. It suited his mood to pick up the stinking cow dung and throw it roughly onto a wheelbarrow. After an hour of them working in silence together, Fynn put his fork down and turned to her.

'I need to talk to you.'

Kathleen sat on the bale she was about to move and waited. She thought her brother was about to talk about Bridget but his next words took her by surprise.

'Do you know Damian O'Callaghan?'

'The handyman?' she queried.

'Yes,' Fynn replied 'Well, it's just he was near the church when Bridget was attacked but didn't help and then I was talking to some of the lads from Peel . . . apparently, he's been seen huddled in a corner of the Creek Inn with a seaman they all recognised but no one seemed to be able to remember his name.

'The lads seemed to think there were some rumours about this seaman cattle smuggling,' he continued. 'Maybe

I'll ask a few farmers around here, see if they know any-thing.'

'You won't get any sense out of them,' Kathleen said, helping him to usher some cows out into the field. 'If they are taking illegal cattle, they're not going to tell anyone.' Then she thought for a moment.

'He's Irish, O' Callaghan, isn't he?' she asked him.

'Yes, why?'

'Oh, it's just there was a rumour that the IRA might be active here, that's all.'

Fynn looked thoughtfully at his sister.

'Bridget's in no fit state to deal with any of this, but I might just see what I can find out.'

He turned back to his wheelbarrow, but Kathleen hadn't finished with him yet.

'So, how's the romance going with Bridget, then?'

'It isn't,' was the gruff reply.

'Right, so you still haven't told her how you feel then? Good, that's my Fynn. He'll go and risk his life, face untold dangers and rescue people from storms but he's too scared to tell a girl he loves her.'

Fynn looked up in shock. Kath was known for being straightforward, but she had never challenged him quite so bluntly.

Kath flung another bale onto her shoulder. 'Right, if you're not going to have her, I think that Molly girl will.'

'What? What *on earth* are you talking about?'

'Don't you see the way she looks at Bridget?'

Fynn gasped. So obsessed with her infatuation for his brother, no other option had ever occurred to him. He thought back to the times he had seen Bridget and Molly together. They had certainly seemed close.

'No, surely not. You don't think . . . Is it possible that Bridget . . .?'

'Nope, don't think so,' Kath replied, throwing the hay down noisily.

Fynn stopped, his fork in the air. Could this be the real reason why she had spurned him? He groaned.

'Oh, stop worrying, you ninny,' Kath said, playfully pushing him on the arm. 'I don't think Molly is her type.'

Fynn was too busy thinking it was time he dealt with at least one of his fears to hear her mutter, 'At least, I hope not.'

* * *

Fynn stood on the beach near Port St Mary. He was pacing up and down nervously. The next half hour would decide his future.

In the distance, he spotted the familiar figure of his brother.

They two men shook hands like strangers.

'I haven't got long, Fynn. What's this about?' Kieran asked without any preamble. 'Mum and dad all right?'

'Yes, yes, they're fine.'

Fynn took in the smart RAF uniform with the insignia in front of him. He hoped he wasn't about to lose both his brother and the girl he loved, but it was now or never, he decided.

'Do you love Bridget?'

Kieran looked taken aback.

'No,' he said, 'no, I don't. Don't get me wrong, she's a lovely girl but she's *your girl*, isn't she?'

Fynn scuffed his boots against the rocks.

'To be honest, Kier, I just don't know. She's loved you for years, I don't know if I can ever compete. I mean look at you . . .' he waved his arm expansively.

Kieran gave a bitter laugh.

'You've got to be kidding, Fynn. I'm a mess.' He held up his damaged hand. 'You only have to look at this, it makes me a sorry excuse for a hero, don't you think? And . . .' Here he stopped for a moment. 'I think you know I drink too much. I hope I'm winning that battle but, oh Fynn, it's so hard.'

At that moment, Kieran looked like the little boy Fynn had spent so many years trying to protect. He gathered him in his arms and gave him a warm hug and for a moment, the two brothers clung together.

Kieran was the first to speak.

'Anyway, I actually think I've found the girl for me,' he said, looking sheepish. 'It's Nancy. I've just got to convince her she can trust me.' Haltingly, he told his brother about Nancy's experiences with the newsreader in London.

Once he'd finished, Fynn took hold of Kieran by his shoulders and looked straight at him, his piercing blue eyes offering the strength and surety that Kieran had looked for all his life.

'You can do it, but you can't ever touch another drink . . . that's ever, do you hear me? And if Nancy's the girl I think she is, she'll help you to overcome that particular fear. The hand, that's a whole other matter, but it doesn't have to be. You're still you; that brave pilot that saved lives. There are men alive today who would have died if it hadn't been for you. No, Kieran, no injury can ever take that from you. And there's an awful lot left of your body that's still intact, not to mention that ugly face of yours!'

Kieran smiled ruefully. 'I've missed you, big brother.'

* * *

Karin was in the corner of the lounge of the Port St Mary guest house. She took out a piece of paper that she'd hidden in her storybook and looked again at it. Her reading was improving but Ursula's hand writing was causing her some difficulty. Karin concentrated, trying to remember what Ursula had said when she gave her the note.

'If anything happens to me or anyone threatens you, then you must take this straight away to Bridget.'

Karin's forehead creased into a frown. Ursula had vanished and she hadn't seen Bridget for a few days. The other two policewomen were around, though, so maybe she should give them the note, she thought.

Her mother was talking to Ruth at the other end of the room but looked upset. Karin wondered what had happened.

'I'm sorry, Helga, but I had to tell you,' Ruth was saying. 'I've been trying to track down your parents for months and I know how dreadful this information is for you.'

She put a comforting hand on the German woman's shoulder and then turned back towards the door.

Helga sat down quickly on a chair next to her, feeling faint. The news that her flight had led to questions by the Gestapo and the eventual arrest of her parents made her feel sick. She'd only tried to protect Karin but by disappearing, she'd implicated her parents and it had only been a matter of time before her mother's Jewish background had been unearthed. Her father had been charged as an accessory to harbouring a Jew and he too had been arrested. The last information Ruth had been able to glean was that they had both been transported to a camp and no one had heard anything since. Helga, of all people, knew the significance of those camps. She now, in all probability, had no home, no parents and nowhere to belong.

Karin came over to her and put her little arms around her.

'What is it, Mama? Why are you sad?'

Helga shook herself and, putting on a false smile, spoke in English now that her daughter refused to speak German. She needed to change the subject.

'What are you doing, my little one? Is it your work for the school?'

'No, Mama . . . er, well, yes maybe.'

Helga was feeling on edge and frustration crossed her face, making Karin tense up. She was never sure what mood her mother was going to be in, but Helga stretched her hand out and stroked her daughter's hair to calm herself before saying, more gently, 'Perhaps, I help you?' It was just going to be her and Karin now, she thought.

For a brief moment, Karin wondered whether to confide in her mother about the note but then decided she dare not, it was too risky. She might be angry.

She pointed to a word in her storybook. 'I don't understand this.'

Helga looked at the word; it meant nothing to her and the fact that her daughter's English was better than hers left her with a feeling of inadequacy.

Karin noticed the expression of shame in her mother's face and suddenly felt sorry for her.

'Why don't you sit with me, Mama, and we'll read the story together. I can help you with your English. And then perhaps we might be allowed to join the walk to the sweet shop, the one in Port Erin. They have the best penny tray I've ever seen.'

Helga thought for a moment. She'd been warned not to venture out from the guest house but Karin looked so appealingly at her that she couldn't resist.

'I would like that . . . so much, Karin.'

And for the next hour, the two heads were bowed together as the child taught the mother. But later that afternoon, on their way to the sweet shop in Port Erin, Helga had cause to regret her rash promise to Karin.

* * *

Lena was deep in thought on her walk towards St Catherine's Church. It was February 1944 and the allies were increasing their bombing raids on German cities. The secret Nazi network headquarters at the Peveril camp in Peel were making increasing, more desperate demands and for the first time, she was beginning to wonder whether the Germany she believed in so fervently was actually losing its grip in this war.

Casting her eyes around her, she checked the street to make sure no one was watching and veered into the porch of the church. There, she removed the loose brick that had caused Bridget's head injury and felt behind it for the note she had been expecting.

Quickly putting it in her pocket, she checked the road again, before edging back out of the porch to hurry off down the street.

It was only when she reached the far end of the promenade that she read the message that her contacts had left for her. It was written on thin paper and the words were so faint, they were hard to read but their demands were unequivocal.

It is vital we know the exact date for the next repatriations.

Lena let out a sigh and put the paper in her mouth, chewing slowly to try get enough saliva in her tongue to help her swallow. The tunnel in Peel was almost ready and the boat was prepared, her superiors just needed to be absolutely certain that a day of chaotic repatriations would be enough to keep the authorities out of their way.

Lena felt the paper slowly edging its way down her throat while assessing the situation. She could not be seen anywhere near the police station where the list of dates was kept, and neither could her colleagues. They were all being watched. She felt frustrated. Helga Fischer was a perfect choice; trusted by the policewoman and desperate not to be seen to be a friend of the Nazis. The only problem was, she seemed to have disappeared from the camp.

There was a noise to her left and Lena looked up to see Helga and Karin walking hand in hand towards her. Feeling her prayers had been answered, she gave a cheery wave to the child.

Helga stopped suddenly but then started to veer off the pavement, putting her head down to hurry past as quickly as possible but Karin dragged her towards the smiling woman. Helga was furious she had given in to Karin's mithering after all Bridget's warnings about being seen out and about.

'Hello,' Karin said, in her usual friendly manner, 'Mama and I are going to the beach to look for shells before we go to the sweet shop.'

Helga looked sharply at Lena. She wanted nothing to do with her, but Lena seized her opportunity; she was not going to waste this chance.

'I come also,' she said, moving to walk next to them.

Helga took a sharp intake of breath. *What was this woman up to now,* she thought?

Lena started talking in German about the way the camp was gradually emptying and how she longed to leave too. She was about to innocently bring up the subject of the repatriations when Karin interrupted. 'We don't speak German now, Mama is learning English. We are going to live in England forever.'

Lena's smile froze on her lips. This was exactly the sort of thing the 'new order' was worried about, the next generation being brainwashed to forget the Fatherland.

Helga stopped and turned to Karin.

'I think it is now too cold to go to the beach. We will go back.'

Karin protested but her mother took her firmly by the hand and started to walk away. Lena moved around so she was in front of them both to hiss in German, 'Do you remember our little chat with you? About how you need to remember who you are and where your loyalties are these days?'

Helga didn't speak, refusing to meet the woman's threatening eyes.

'I need the list of the dates for repatriations,' Lena went on. 'As soon as it comes out on the first of March, get it and put it in the porch of the church over there. I don't care how you do it, but, believe me, it will be so much better . . . for you both . . . if you do.' She reached down and ruffled Karin's hair, speaking in a friendly voice that belied the chilling intent behind the words. 'One day, very soon, *kleines Mädchen*, we go to the sea together.'

And then she turned away to leave Helga to grab Karin's hand protectively and pull her close to her.

The little girl looked quizzically at her mother. They had spent such a lovely afternoon together, reading and then walking, but again, her mother's lips had tightened into a line and Karin shivered, feeling a familiar dread come over her and her little fingers touched the letter from Ursula in her pocket.

'I need to go to see the police ladies,' she said slowly.

'What for?'

'Just . . . I just do, Mama. Please,' she said, looking fearfully up at her mother's face.

Helga felt sick. All she wanted to do was to get Karin away from all these threats and dangers. Perhaps her daughter was right; it was time to get some help.

Chapter Thirty-Five

Bridget was feeling so much better but that meant that boredom had set in. The constant ticking of the grandfather clock in her parents' house seemed to magnify the slow passing of time. She was mulling over everything that had happened since Helga's attack on Ursula and was making notes, drawing lines between them to try to establish connections, but it ended up being a muddle of scribbles and she threw it on the table in frustration. She'd reached forward to take another of her mother's delicious oaty biscuits just as her father came in. He was carrying her child's atlas.

'Put this back in your room, will you, Bridget? There isn't room for it in my study.'

Bridget grinned. Her father's study was notorious for its ramshackle piles of books which her mother was not allowed to dust or tidy.

Seeing the atlas made her jump up as a thought occurred to her but then she went dizzy so had to sit down again quickly. Her head still hurt.

'Daddy, do you remember you told me about a synagogue in that town in southern Germany?'

Her father looked surprised. He was used to his daughter's butterfly mind but this was a complete change of tack.

'Yes,' he said slowly, with no idea what was coming next.

'Well, tell me about it.'

Her father gave a wry smile but gave in and went on to describe a tall building with two long, arched windows that were surrounded by an elaborately decorated and beautiful frontage.

'The Jews were forbidden from gathering outside by the wooden fence,' he told her. 'It was a beautiful building and the rabbi, he was so proud of it, but . . .' Her father shook his head. 'I think that's all gone now and maybe Rabbi Cohen too, if the terrible rumours are to be believed.'

'Anything else you can tell me about the Jews in that area?'

'Well, it was such a hot day when I met Rabbi Cohen and all the youngsters at the synagogue were complaining that they weren't allowed in the swimming pool anymore either.'

Bridget sat back in the chair and then started scribbling furiously on her paper. She finally had a plan; she just needed to get back to work.

* * *

The next day, she arrived at the police station to be greeted by Ruth who was just on her way in.

'Ah, Bridget, good to see you back. What's been happening, have you any idea? No, of course you haven't, you're only just back.'

She seemed in a fluster so Bridget shepherded her inside.

'You sit there, Ruth, Alister'll sort you out with a cuppa, won't you, Alister?' and she went to knock at Sergeant Robinson's door. Alister shrugged and turned to make his way to the kitchen, muttering about the good old days when there were no women to boss him around in his own police station.

The sergeant was perched on the edge of her desk, swinging her legs while she pondered the two people sitting in front of her. One was Helga and the other was Karin. Hovering behind them were Molly and Betty, who were looking intrigued.

Karin jumped up and ran to Bridget, wrapping her arms around her waist.

'I thought you were dead, I thought you were dead,' she sobbed. 'And Ursula, I think she's dead too and it's all my fault.'

Bridget looked flummoxed but knelt down next to the child, holding her by the shoulders.

'What do you mean, Karin, I'm here, I'm fine. I just had a little bump on my head. And Ursula ...' with this she looked around at the sergeant who nodded reassuringly, before telling the child, 'Ursula's fine, she's just talking to some men in Douglas.'

Bridget turned to Helga, who looked paler than usual.

'What's going on, Helga?'

'I do not know, she say we must come to see you.'

Karin brought out a tattered piece of paper from her coat pocket.

'This is for you, well, I think it is, as you are alive.' She looked from one to the other, terrified as if she might have done something wrong.

Her mother leaned across and took her hand.

'Just tell them, like you told me, *meine Liebling*.'

'You need to read this. It is from Ursula,' Karin said, looking frightened. Her mother gathered the little girl into her arms while Bridget read Ursula's words.

> *Bridget, you must know I am going to steal a radio from the kitchen at the hotel. I do not want to, but I must – otherwise, Lena and her friends will hurt Karin. I cannot risk that but I want you to know I am only doing this to protect Karin. I don't want to be a bad person so please understand why I am doing this. I dare not say more but I am not a thief.*
> *Ursula*

Bridget quickly passed the note over to the sergeant who pursed her lips, before saying to Karin, a little brusquely, 'Why didn't you bring this earlier?' But then saw the little girl's face crumple and so she softened her voice. 'It's all right, Karin, you did well to bring this now.'

Bridget stroked Karin's hair. 'You're a very clever girl and you've done very well. I'm proud of you.'

Sergeant Robinson went towards the door and motioned to Molly and Betty to follow her.

'You two have got other work to do and I've some telephone calls to make,' she said.

Bridget was left alone with Helga and her daughter.

'What made you come here?' she asked.

Helga became nervous. Lena's threats were still at the forefront of her mind.

Bridget felt exasperated.

'You have to tell me, Helga. It's time all this ended.'

The German woman glanced down at her hands. Since she had heard about her parents being taken to a camp, she had no choice but to believe they were dead. She had no one else in the whole world except Karin. *Could this all end?* she wondered. *Could she ever be free of all this intrigue? Would she ever know which side she was on?*

Karin made the decision for her.

'There are bad women here, they make Mama cross and worried. She thinks they will hurt me.'

'What's been happening, Helga?' Bridget asked. 'Who's been threatening you, what did they tell you to do?'

'I cannot,' Helga spluttered, 'they will hurt . . .' and she stopped, glancing at Karin.

Karin suddenly looked fierce.

'They will not hurt me, Mama, I can fight them,' and she held up her fists like a boxer.

The two older women couldn't help but smile but then Bridget became serious again.

'I need to deal with this, Helga but our first priority is to get you to somewhere safe you really can't be reached. This situation is getting too dangerous. Just stay here a moment, will you, please?'

She went out to the front desk and, after a long discussion with Sergeant Robinson who was preparing her arguments to persuade the Chief Inspector in Douglas to release Ursula, she picked up the telephone and dialled a familiar number.

By the time she had come back into the room, Helga had made a decision.

'They want me to get a list of when the repatriations are happening,' she mumbled.

'Why?'

'I do not know but I am to put the list in the church, at the entrance. There is a loose stone.'

Bridget rubbed her head; she knew that stone only too well, she thought.

'And when are you to do this?' she asked.

'By five o'clock on the first day of March,' was the reply.

* * *

Bridget felt a little bubble of excitement inside her as she made her way to Colley's Café; there was huge pressure on her and she was running out of time. The police had already concocted a bogus list of dates to drop off at the church and, after endless negotiation and paperwork, Helga and Karin were well out of the way at her parents' house in Castletown.

As she had hoped, Berta and Ester were there, huddled by the window. They weren't talking but seemed to be covertly listening to the unguarded conversation between three German women behind them that Bridget recognised as conscientious objectors. Dealing with these two was way overdue, she thought. She just had to hope the planned trap would work.

There was an empty chair at the table, so Bridget sat down, to the surprise of Berta and Ester. She started off the conversation by talking about how cold it was that February and how she longed for those lovely summer days when they could all go swimming. She then casually mentioned how one of the other women had talked about the lovely swimming pool in Tübingen.

'Do you know it?' Bridget asked innocently. Berta replied warily that it was a lovely pool and they'd gone there frequently. Bridget made a mental tick in her brain, remembering Jews were not allowed to use it. She went on. 'Someone was also telling me about the synagogue in Kirkenstellinsfurt near there. You probably went there too, didn't you?'

This time it was Ester who nodded when the translation was made.

'*Ja*,' she said, suspiciously, but Bridget was in full flow. She moved onto the next piece of information her father had given her about how Jews were not allowed to congregate outside the synagogue.

'They said the brick wall at the front was where all of you used to gather before the service, is that right?'

Ester gave Berta a warning look but her friend was too anxious to agree with everything Bridget said.

'Ah yes, we Jews like to talk with each other.'

Bridget was really beginning to enjoy herself now. She'd always known these little snippets of information would come in useful.

She had one more card to play.

'Oh, I meant to ask you; did you go to the cinema in Port Erin when it was used for Rosh Hashanah?' she asked, bringing the sword of Damocles finally down on the women's necks.

Ester gave a vague reply, giving nothing away. She was beginning to be nervous about all these questions.

'I thought you'd like it,' Bridget said casually. 'They even managed to get a cow's horn for the shofar.'

'Mmm,' Ester agreed.

'Was that cow's horn OK?' Bridget asked innocently.

'*Oh . . . ja*, the cow's horn, it is good,' Berta said, now starting to twitch in her seat.

'It was a shame there wasn't a ram's horn available,' Bridget went on, noticing Ester's discomfort growing. 'I've heard it really should be a ram.'

Bridget's intuition had been right. These women had never been in a synagogue and knew nothing about the customs of the Rosh Hashanah ceremony. They were not Jews at all.

Chapter Thirty-Six

Fynn walked into the police station at Port Erin, looking very ill at ease, but Bridget emerged from the room at the back to greet him with an enormous smile. If Alister hadn't been there, she wondered whether she would have stepped forward to hug him but as it was, they both shifted their feet in embarrassment. Alister looked on with amusement.

'I'm sorry to interrupt you, but can I have a word, Bridget? In private. It's about work,' Fynn said hurriedly, seeing Alister raise his eyebrows.

'Of course,' Bridget said, feeling oddly disappointed, and ushered him into one of the interview rooms. She stood waiting, trying not to let her heart thump.

Fynn launched straight in. 'Do you know any of the policemen at Peveril Camp? It's just they're from London and I thought you might have met them there . . .' he tailed off, feeling rather foolish.

'Um, yes, actually I do. Well, to be exact, Molly does, Walter Carter, why?'

Fynn looked to check the door was shut and whispered, 'Did you hear about the attempted escape there?'

'Yes, of course, it was in all the papers. They dug a tunnel to the outside of the wire. Why?'

'I think they may need to know there might be another escape planned.' Fynn said in that matter-of-fact way he had.

She gasped.

Fynn quickly told her everything he had found out and Bridget got out her notebook so she didn't miss anything. After a couple of minutes, she went to find Sergeant Robinson. This was far bigger than anything she'd suspected and completely distracted her from any thoughts about her and Fynn's relationship.

It was after a great number of probing questions that Fynn finally emerged, feeling more worthwhile than he had done since he'd thrown his application form for the navy in the bin.

Sergeant Robinson ran after him.

'Mr Moore?'

He stopped and she took his arm to take him back into her office.

'I'm sorry, but I've just had a word with the authorities and we may need you to do more,' she said. 'I think a lifeboat may be less conspicuous than a military vessel so please listen closely to what I'm about to say.'

* * *

It was at the end of March and the camp was busy with repatriations. About a hundred women queued, clutching their sparse belongings. Some looked excited and others looked apprehensive. A ferry to their homes either on the mainland they had learned to call 'across' or to Germany was a thrilling prospect for those who had somewhere – and someone – to go back to, but for many the Island had become their home and they were loath to leave. Molly and Betty rushed around with clipboards, checking every detail and searching every piece of luggage, while helping Ruth to fill out the paperwork. They wanted to get the women onto the buses to Douglas as soon as possible.

Sergeant Robinson and Bridget were ensconced in the police station with three plain-clothed military men who were going through every detail of the operation to come. It had been four weeks since Bridget and Maureen had watched Damian O'Callaghan sneak into the church porch to pick up the bogus lists and dates that had been left for him. The note he left in reply told the authorities everything they needed to know and the men in trenchcoats were reluctantly impressed with the way the subterfuge had all been dealt with.

Sergeant Robinson outlined the plan for the next part of the plan and try as they might to find fault with it, the men in trench coats eventually shrugged and approved it. The sergeant was in her element as they referred to her for information and details about roads and the layout of the camp. Bridget stood quietly by but every sinew in her body was pulled tight. She had never experienced anything like this in London and she couldn't help but smile at the memory of how angry she had been at being sent to 'babysit' the internees.

'So, you're sure the suspects will be there tonight ready to be picked up, are you?' an older man with a moustache said.

'Yessir,' Sergeant Robinson replied, pulling up to attention. 'The last note from O'Callaghan made it clear.'

One of the other men was looking in awe at the women in front of him. 'You know this is dangerous, don't you?'

Sergeant Robinson jerked her head up and looked down her nose at the man.

'Of course, we're trained policewomen, we know what we're doing.'

'Good, because we've no manpower to help you, we're all needed in Peel now. So, good luck to you.'

And he picked up the trilby from the desk in front of him and clicked his heels, before twirling to go out through the door.

Bridget smiled inwardly; no one would be fooled by that trench coat; this was a military man through and through.

* * *

A few hours later, after curfew, the four policewomen positioned themselves around the corner from St Catherine's Church. They all strained their ears listening for the engine that would herald the arrival of the pick-up vehicle.

At nine o'clock, Damian O'Callaghan's old work van with its handyman logo came into view. It was travelling slowly and without lights but this time it wasn't to comply with blackout rules; it was simply to make sure he wasn't seen.

From the other direction came the sound of muffled footsteps and three figures made their way along the dark shadows. As soon as the vehicle came to a halt, its engine still running, Alister ran from one direction and the four policewomen came up behind the figures.

Alister flung open the van door and grabbed hold of the arm of the man sitting in the driving seat. Damian O'Callaghan looked with surprise at the fifty-year-old and sneered but he had reckoned without Alister's secret training sessions and within a couple of seconds, the experienced IRA man found himself face down on the street with his arms behind him being encased in steel handcuffs. Alister muttered a caution through gritted teeth; he really didn't care about this man's rights.

On the other side of the road, Bridget, Molly and Betty were grabbing hold of one figure each and wrestled them to the floor. Berta and Ester gasped with surprise as they were firmly sat upon but Lena wriggled out of Bridget's hold and made a run for it.

Bridget scrambled to her feet and set off in pursuit. She was not going to let this woman go.

Judging the distance, she flung herself at the fleeing body, just managing to grab hold of her collar and they both fell with a thump to the ground. At that moment, Lena's hand came up and Bridget saw the cold steel of a knife pointing towards her face.

'Oh, no you don't.' Sergeant Robinson's voice came from behind and she threw herself between Bridget and Lena, her arm raised to flick away the weapon. As it clattered to the floor, Bridget managed to get to her feet to see her fearsome superior spreadeagled across Lena Braun's body, her lisle stocking tops and suspenders on show to the world. Not thinking, she immediately leaned down and covered them with the sergeant's skirt and then collected herself.

'Sorry, Sarge, I just didn't think you'd want that in the report.'

Maureen grimaced from her prone position and mumbled into Lena's back.

'Quite right too, but maybe you could just help me get this prisoner secured and ready to be arrested properly.'

Between them, they manhandled Lena to her feet and she stood facing them both but then spat into Bridget's face.

'You, you *Schlampe!*' she yelled and in a torrent of German cursed Bridget to hell.

'That won't do you any good now,' Sergeant Robinson said, 'but, yes, it's due to this very fine police officer that you will now spend many years in a British jail.' She handcuffed the woman and with Bridget's help, she got her over to the police van that was waiting around the corner. Bridget wanted to heave a sigh of relief but her mind immediately went to a man on a lifeboat heading around the west coast of the Island towards Peel.

* * *

The lifeboat was crowded and Fynn's reduced crew were having to step over crouched figures to carry out their normal jobs. But there was no complaining. They all knew this was a crucial mission and its success depended on the absolute precision of its execution.

Amidst the tension and nerves that were palpable, Fynn was at the helm, trying not to grin. This excitement was what he'd been missing and for once, he felt he was playing an important part in something bigger than worrying about feed stocks.

The authorities had not been able to pinpoint where the boat would pick up its cargo of Nazis so the lifeboat had been deputised to innocently patrol the seas around the west coast. They wanted to make sure all 'passengers' were on board before they intervened to ensure maximum evidence. Fynn was pleased it was a choppy night; it gave credence to the presence of the lifeboat and he hoped, would give them an edge when it came to sudden manoeuvres. The waves were lashing against the hull and some of the crouched figures on the deck were groaning and clasping their stomachs.

The boat had been up and down the coast about three times when it came within sight of Peel Harbour. The coxswain, who was on the bow with a pair of binoculars, finally signalled that he had spotted their quarry, moving silently around St Patrick's Isle. Immediately, the men who were on the deck lay down flat, ignoring the wet and the cold. They each had handguns they were clasping tightly and hidden under a tarpaulin next to Fynn was a Bren light machine gun.

Fynn went over the extensive briefing in his head. The crew were only there to sail the boat, they were not to engage with the enemy in any way and in the event of any fighting, were to keep out of the way as much as possible. He knew there would be three naval vessels that would emerge from Peel Harbour as soon as Captain Ryan's boat was spotted but for this first encounter, the lifeboat was on its own.

Peering out from the helm, Fynn saw a large fishing trawler moving towards open water, its dark shadows barely visible under the moonless sky. He thought the escapees were lucky that the day of the repatriations fitted in with the waning of the moon. Picturing the escaped internees packed into cattle pens, he felt a moment's pity for them, but then he thought about men like his brother who were fighting so hard to keep the British shores safe from tyranny. His resolve hardened and his hands gripped the wooden wheel tighter.

At that moment, the trawler started to pick up speed; it must have spotted the lifeboat, Fynn thought. It was possible that when three internees did not arrive from Rushen Camp, the captain had suspected a problem and was already on high alert. The plan was to ask the trawler for help to pick up a stranded fishing boat whose mast had broken, and knowing the rule of the sea was that ships never ignored a plea for help, he waited while the signal was sent with his pulse racing. If it came back as a negative response, that would be enough to enable the lifeboat to interfere.

After a long pause, the message came back saying they were unable to help as they had livestock on board and did not have time to divert their course.

On the orders of the military commanding officer, Fynn thrust the lifeboat into top speed and raced across the waves, thumping its hull up and down on the water that suddenly seemed like an unyielding wall. They had been told to cut off the trawler's path while the naval boats approached from the shore side.

When they got within hailing distance, he could see the naval vessels approaching from the other direction. This boat was trapped and that would be when it would be at its most dangerous.

A flash of light and the sound of machine-gun fire strafed the air in answer to the question and Fynn and the rest of the crew automatically ducked. Hanging onto the wheel from his crouched position, Fynn was sailing blind; he couldn't see where he was going and for the first time, he realised what his brother had faced every day with the RAF. But he shook his head to quickly dispel the thought – now was not the time to do anything but give his full concentration to the task in hand. Two men next to him raced to uncover the Bren gun, all pretence abandoned and started firing back. Now the naval boats were manoeuvring around to attack the boat from both sides but they were under orders not to sink it. They needed the captain and the internees alive to interrogate them and break this Nazi network once and for all.

Now the night was being shattered by a volley of fire from the naval boats and from the lifeboat's machine gun calculated to hit the water on all sides of the trawler, but still it was trying to make a run for it. The trawler veered around to starboard, almost skimming the hull of the lifeboat that had slowed to allow the gunners to pinpoint their targets. Fynn glanced up from his haunches and saw a man he thought was probably Captain Ryan, frantically giving orders to his crew but they looked terrified. They were used to cattle smuggling but this cargo of internees was unleashing a hell they did not want to face. One of them reached for the stop lever and the boat slowed. The crew seemed to be hovering, not quite sure what to do and one, in particular, was shouting back at the captain.

All of a sudden, Fynn saw Ryan take out his handgun and shoot the man in the forehead, causing him to drop like a stone. Ryan swirled around to swing his arm with the finger on the trigger and sweep the semi-circle of men who were standing dumbstruck, threatening the next person who would question his orders.

The naval officer next to Fynn took aim and fired but the shot hit the trawler's wooden wheelhouse. In a fury, Ryan turned towards the lifeboat and pointed his gun. In that split second, Fynn lurched to grab the naval officer's legs and in a rugby tackle his sports master would have been proud of, he pulled him out of the way of a hail of bullets that were being unleashed by Ryan.

The other man on the lifeboat's Bren gun took aim and let loose several rounds of ammunition. Ryan collapsed onto the deck.

Seeing their captain lying still, blood seeping through his sou'wester, the rest of the crew raised their arms in submission. Searchlights were switched on and they all blinked in the sudden glare. By now, the lifeboat had thrown over a line to be hurriedly put in position and the figures who had lain so quietly on the lifeboat's deck raced across, their handguns raised.

Fynn and his crew stood quietly. They had done their job; now it was up to the professionals.

Chapter Thirty-Seven

Molly, Betty and Bridget were sitting on chairs in their kitchen. They were all warming their hands around their cups of hot chocolate, in need of some comfort to soothe the adrenalin that had been flooding into their bloodstreams.

Bridget spoke first, voicing what they were all thinking.

'I just hope Fynn and his friends are OK.'

They were all quiet for a moment, knowing that although their ordeal was over, the lifeboat men's was just beginning. Molly glanced at her watch. It was one o'clock in the morning; about the time the trap was going to be sprung out in the cold, windy Irish Sea. She changed the subject and said with pride in her voice, 'It's all down to you, you know, Bridg, without you, we'd never have had the evidence. But how did you know they were spies?'

Bridget leaned forward to speak.

'Well, once we knew the radios were being used to listen to coded messages during the "Germany Calling" propaganda broadcasts, we knew they were using repatriated internees to take Nazi propaganda across on the ferry with them to form a welcoming committee for Hitler's troops when they invaded.

'Ah,' Betty said, 'that's why we had to search all their bags.'

'Yes, and they'd planted Berta and Ester here as spies to put that plan into operation, knowing no one would ever suspect Jews.'

'Yes, but how did you know Berta and Ester weren't Jews?' Molly asked.

Bridget put her finger to the side of her nose and winked. 'I have to thank my father for that. Once I knew he'd been to that area, I asked him a pile of questions. To be honest, I'd no idea whether the information he gave me would ever be of any use, but I just thought the more I knew the better. He told me things that only a real Jew would know about their local area.

'And do you know anything about the Rosh Hashanah ceremony?' she went on. 'No? Well, neither did they.'

'Do you think we've really made a difference over here on this little island?' Betty asked, slowly. She could not believe their actions could help stop a network so insidious from infiltrating Britain.

'Yes, I think perhaps we have,' Bridget conceded, getting to her feet. 'I just hope Fynn is able to do his bit . . . but safely,' she said with a shiver. 'But for now, as there is no chance of sleep, I'm going to take Greeba out.'

The dog scrambled to her feet – she had almost given up on a night's walk.

The air, as always, cleared Bridget's head gazing out at the dark sea. The bay in front of her may have been calm but with the wind tussling her hair, she knew it would be a different story around the headland and she pressed her hands to her chest as if to relieve the tension that was gripping her. She tried to tune her heartbeat to the gentle rhythm that had dominated this bay for millions of years. It normally gave her a comfort that no matter what the human race was doing, nature continued regardless. But tonight, there was no solace.

Bridget had arrived back on her home island a young girl, angry at having all her plans thwarted. Now she wondered whether she had perhaps had a small part in changing the history of the war and she had . . . here she stopped . . . she was about to say, found a man to love. It hit her like the cold wind and she let out a little sigh. She leaned down to fondle Greeba's ears who, as usual, was sitting waiting to absorb any confidences she cared to utter.

'I think I've finally grown up,' she told her dog. 'You see, Greeba, it seems that after all, I am completely and utterly head over heels in love with Fynn Moore.'

Standing up again, she wondered how she could have missed the signs for so long. His gentle teasing, the way he listened, really listened to her, and how he was like Bradda

Head she could see in the distance – a rock of strength that was solid under her feet.

Breaking into a trot, Bridget ran along the path, her arms spread behind her and her head tossed back.

'I'm in love!' she shouted to the wind. 'I'm really, *really in love* with the most wonderful man ever ...' And then she ground to a halt and clasped her arms around her as every hair on her head stood on end. 'Oh my God,' she whispered, ' I hope he's safe. I couldn't bear anything to happen to him – especially now, before I've even told him.'

As if sensing her deep thoughts, Greeba came up and nuzzled her. Bridget put her arms around the dog's neck and pulled her close, but then the dog decided to have a good shake and Bridget got covered in sand.

'Oh, you horrible animal,' she smiled. 'Get away from me.'

Greeba dashed off to get a stick which she promptly laid down next to Bridget and chewed.

'Oh, Greeb, if only life was as simple for us,' she said to the animal, who only glanced with one eye at her mistress; she didn't care about Nazi spies or dramatic sea rescues; she was too intent on destroying the stick before anyone took it off her.

It was a thoughtful Bridget who started to make her way back to the cottage, thinking of all the time she had wasted; first with trying to impress Nancy and then her superiors and finally, of all those months of keeping Fynn hanging on a string.

'I just want the chance to tell him,' she said out loud, coming along the pathway to the cottage.

'Tell him what?' a familiar voice asked from the shadows.

Bridget jumped and then flew into Fynn Moore's arms.

'Oh, you're alive, you're alive!' And she started to sob.

Fynn wrapped her into his embrace and, unable to speak, just let the warmth of her body seep into his freezing torso. He had been on his way to her cottage, straight from the lifeboat station, desperate to know that Bridget's plan had worked and that she was safe. The relief overwhelmed him and he almost felt weak.

He raised her head from his chest to wipe her tear-stained cheeks.

'And you, Bridget, are you OK? Did it all work?'

She nodded and gulped at the same time.

'Oh Fynn, it did and now here you are, all alive and everything,' and she buried her face in his wet jumper again.

He turned them both towards the cottage and with his arm around her they went in to find both Molly and Betty still up. A hot chocolate in his hands, they swapped stories about the evening's events, Fynn leaving out any mention of his own heroism.

It was only when dawn was breaking that the girls finally said goodnight to Fynn and Bridget took him to the front door.

She clung to him and he willingly responded but then drew back.

'Tell him what, Bridget?'

She looked puzzled for a moment but then smiled, and taking his face gently in her hands, she looked up at him.

'Tell him that I love him with every fibre of my being.'

Fynn took a deep breath. Ever since the age of twelve, he had dreamed of this moment and he was not going to rush it.

'And I love you, my beloved Bridget. I always have and I always will.'

Chapter Thirty-Eight

By spring 1944, there was an air of excitement as the arrangements increased in preparation for the closure of the internment camps, but Bridget was distracted, unable to find the time to meet Fynn, who was equally being overwhelmed with work with the demands for higher yields on the farm.

'Honestly,' she told Betty, 'here I am, finally admitting I'm totally besotted with the man, and I can hardly remember what he looks like.'

Betty chose not to mention that after four years she had to constantly check the small black-and-white photograph in her purse to check her Joe's face and tried to put on a sympathetic expression.

Any social life had been put on hold while the policewomen dealt with the plans to send a large number of internees back as part of the Gothenburg Exchange of prisoners. It was a complex arrangement with neutral Sweden and involved some returning to their lives in Britain and the rest being returned to Germany. When the latest list was due to be announced, a large crowd of women crowded into the large Golf Links hotel, jostling to get as near as possible to Betty, who was holding the sheets of paper that would decide their fates. Molly and Bridget stood behind her, waiting to deal with any arguments or even fights that might erupt when names were – or were not – read out.

Betty started at the letter 'A' and worked her way through, trying to ignore the uproar every time a new name was announced. Ursula was standing to one side, her brother and sister at her side. With the surname Apler, if her name was going to be called, it would be at the start of the announcement. Her eyes closed as if she couldn't bear to watch Betty's mouth move and held her breath.

After several names, Betty announced 'Ursula Apler,' and Ursula clasped her hand to her mouth. She wasn't sure how she felt; certainly not the elation others around her were feeling; all she could think was that she had no home to go back to in England and she certainly didn't want to be sent back to Germany.

She hadn't dared think about how she was going to manage when she went back to Liverpool. There was nothing there for them and, although there'd been so little spare money here, they'd all been comfortable in their little room and had been fed regularly.

Bridget was standing behind them; these repatriations were taking every bit of emotional strength out of her as she battled with endless paperwork, displaced internees and women unsure of what future they faced once they left these safe shores. But when she spotted Ursula putting a protective arm around Daniel and Judith, she knew she would have to conjure up one more miracle.

On the other side of the room, Erika Schneider and Greta were also wrapping their arms around each other in delight that their names were on the list..

'At last, *Gott sei Dank,* perhaps I will hear news of my boys, my Karl,' Erika was saying, but her daughter was not listening. She was too busy composing a letter in her head to her beloved Albert and imagining the delicious smells of the bakery that she had missed so much.

In Castletown, Helga was cocooned in Mr Harrison's study, frowning to concentrate on a first edition of a Grimms' *Fairy Tales* while Bridget's father watched on, like a teacher watching a favourite pupil. Now he was beginning to see beyond the bleached blonde hair, he was thoroughly enjoying helping this German woman and once he discovered that her father had been a bookseller, he encouraged her love of old books, finding a knowledge and insight he hadn't been expecting. At the sound of the telephone in the hallway, he jumped up. Patrick was proud of his Bakelite telephone; it was the only one on the whole road but when he returned to the room, he looked troubled.

'That was Sergeant Robinson on the phone. They can't send you home, Helga, they're worried for your safety. There are people there who would wish you harm.'

Helga shrugged. She had no great wish to return to a country where she did not belong and where there might be more people like Lena, Berta and Ester. News had filtered through that O'Callaghan and the three German prisoners had been sent to a court across in Manchester and were awaiting trial and Helga was quite happy to have a sea between them and her.

'May I see that book by Thomas Mann again,' she asked politely, saying her English words carefully. 'It is a beautiful book.' She didn't mention how she had originally been terrified of even looking at a book by someone as anti-Nazi as Mann but once she'd started to read his words, she'd become entranced with his language, realising his story of sickness echoed the sickness that had pervaded Europe. It had been a moment of recognition of how indoctrinated she'd been and the weekly sessions with the man from the government were helping her to see things very differently indeed.

Patrick happily reached up to the top shelf to lovingly finger the German edition of *Der Zauberberg*. He'd been lucky to find it as a student before there was any suggestion of censorship in Germany but he was particularly fond of 'The Magic Mountain' story. He knew most editions had since been burned.

Sitting down next to her, he was surprised to find he was relieved that she, and that bright little button, Karin, were not being sent back yet, but at that moment the door opened and Bridget came in. She looked exhausted but was followed by a smiling Karin, hanging onto the hand of her heroine.

'Look who's here, look who's here,' the little girl said, jumping up and down.

'Hello, Bridget,' her father said, rising to greet his daughter. But when he saw how pale she was, he gently led her to an armchair. Helga too stood up, never sure what news this policewoman would bring.

'Hello,' Bridget said, thumping down onto the leather seat. 'Oh, it's good to get a break, it's been unbelievably busy.'

Karin jumped up and down in front of her, making her laugh.

'Are you going to stay and have tea with us?' Then she realised how presumptuous she had been and looked at her mother in embarrassment.

'You are right, *meine Liebling*, we should not expect anything from these kind people.' She looked towards Mr Harrison apologetically. 'Please do not be cross with Karin, it is just you make us so welcome here, it is like home.'

Patrick leaned across and patted Helga's hand.

'No need to apologise, my dear. In fact, if you wait there . . .' And he left the room.

Bridget shrugged her shoulders; she never had any idea what was going on in this house so she sat back for a moment, taking her first rest of the day. Karin ran over to go and sit next to her mother, who gave her such a warm smile that Karin clutched her hands to her face. 'Oh Mama,' she cried, 'you really are my mama, the one . . . oh you . . . I . . . oh, it's just so lovely to see you happy.'

Helga pulled her daughter up onto her knee. She had so much time to make up with this little one and buried her head in the curls in front of her, smelling them with delight. Her head smelt of carbolic soap but to Helga, it was filled with a perfume that she had almost forgotten.

The door opened to reveal Bridget's parents; her mother was looking flushed and excited.

'We have something to ask you, Helga, and of, course, Bridget and the authorities will have to approve as well, but would you and Karin like to stay – until the war's over at least? Patrick thinks Helga could help him with his cataloguing and Karin, well, we just don't want to lose her.'

Karin leapt down from her mother's knee and ran to clasp Mrs Harrison around the waist, her shoulders started to heave and Jenny leaned down, concerned.

'You don't have to, if you don't want to,' she told the little girl hurriedly.

'Want to? Want to? Oh, *Frau* Harrison, you've made me the happiest I've ever been in my whole, whole life!'

Karin waved her arms around the room. 'This house, it makes me happy, it makes . . .' and here she stopped for a moment, glancing shyly at her mother, 'Mama happy too. If we could stay, it would . . . well, it would make me very, very, very happy indeed.'

Bridget was too stunned to speak. Were the two people smiling indulgently really her parents who had been pursuing their separate interests for years, living almost separate lives? She wondered what had happened to prompt such a change. But then seeing them both look down affectionately at Karin's dark golden head, she knew.

* * *

Ruth didn't waste any time before talking to Bridget about Ursula.

'I just don't know what to suggest,' she said. 'I mean Ursula has no one; she was living under an archway. I can't bear the thought of her going back to that.'

Bridget agreed, but with hundreds of internees still to deal with, had no idea how to help. She patted Ruth on the arm. 'I don't know what we can do but we'll all put our thinking caps on. Leave it with me.'

As she said those words, she winced. A mere policewoman couldn't solve all these women's problems. The sergeant was getting tetchy with them all as the pressure mounted to get the Gothenburg contingent ready. Molly was dispirited and at every available moment, disappeared off on her motorbike on some spurious 'official' errand while Betty was distracted by letters from her husband telling her they were making their way up Italy. Reports of yet more fierce fighting at Monte Cassino in the newspapers were giving her nightmares and none of the three young policewomen were getting much sleep in their little room at the top of the house.

Bridget went to lie down on her bed under the eaves in the girls' cottage, just to try and catch forty winks before her next shift began. She lifted up the beautiful, crocheted blanket she'd bought from Ursula to cuddle under it. All of a sudden, it came to her, and she leapt out of bed to run to the station to use the telephone.

* * *

Two days later she went to find Ursula, who was, as usual, sitting on the wall where she watched the tide go in and out. The little ones were squabbling over a bit of wood that Daniel wanted as a train and Judith wanted as a doll. Ursula had a crocheting needle in her hands and was working on a yellow and blue blanket.

'Hello, you three,' she said, seeing their faces light up as she approached and sat down next to them.

'Any idea what you're going to do when you get off the ferry in Liverpool, Ursula?'

Ursula shook her head. She'd just been discussing that with Ruth and was despairing of ever finding a solution.

'How would you like to work in a haberdashery shop in Liverpool?'

The German girl looked blankly at her. She had no idea what a haberdashery shop was.

'It's a shop where they sell things for sewing, crocheting and knitting,' Bridget explained.

It took a moment for her to process the words but then Ursula dropped her blanket and grasped Bridget's hand.

'A shop?' she queried. 'A shop where they sell things? For sewing?'

'Yes,' Bridget laughed. 'Sergeant Cubbon's friend's wife has a haberdashery shop in Liverpool and she needs help. There's a little flat above the shop and you could all live there. It's only small but . . .'

She didn't get any further. Ursula jumped to her feet and grabbed her, twirling her around. She was so full of joy it brought tears to Bridget's eyes.

There are times in a policewoman's life, she thought, when there is the chance to really make a difference to someone's life. This was one of them.

* * *

Erika was looking around with a concerned frown. Everyone was ready to leave and the street in front of her was empty, beyond the line of internees waiting impatiently at Port Erin bus station. She was on the point of giving up when she saw a figure hurrying down the road, clutching a wicker basket.

'Mona, Mona,' she shouted. '*Ich bin hier drüben.*'

Mona Quayle ran towards her friend as fast as her bony knees would allow and clasped her firmly in her arms.

'I thought I'd missed you. That stupid guard took ages to let me through.'

'We have to leave in just one moment,' Erika told her. 'You have my address in England? I will write to you and I will try to write the English. I don't know if I still have a farm but, oh, my friend, if I ever get back to my home, it would be so good to see you there.'

Mona, who had never been off the Island in her entire life looked sceptical but something in her knew; she really wanted to see this German woman again before she died.

Digging into her basket, she brought out a paper bag. 'I've got you some herbs and things that might help you get through the next months,' she told Erika. 'They are special to the Island and I think they'll help.'

She held out her arms and Erika walked into them. They both knew how much they'd helped each other over the last few years and it brought tears to Greta's eyes as she watched the two friends cling to each other.

Mona looked deep into Erika's eyes. 'You will find your Karl, I know you will, and one day you will all be there to see him become a doctor.' She leaned forward and whispered. 'I saw it in the smoke, Erika. It will happen.'

Erika patted her hand gratefully. She believed every word Mona told her, knowing her 'sight' was legendary.

Mona suddenly threw back her head and laughed. 'So, my German friend, who'd have thought I could learn to love someone from that country? It seems I've found out how to travel in my mind further than the shores of this island and as Bridget will tell you, that's quite something for me. It's a strange world out there but if there are more people like you, who knows, perhaps I might go and investigate it sometime.'

Erika hadn't understood all of Mona's words so Greta translated for her. Finally understanding, Erika grinned and told her daughter, 'I am not sure the world is ready for Mona Quayle but, oh, I would love to be there when it meets her.'

Mona listened to Greta's translation of her mother's words and then gave a girlish giggle that belied the grey hair and the wrinkled skin, before watching her friend get on the bus. On her way back to the checkpoint, Mona changed her mind and turned towards the police station where she glared suspiciously at Alister whose back was to the counter. He looked every inch the formidable policeman with his large frame and uniform but when he turned around, she scrutinised him more closely.

'Hmm,' she said, looking him up and down. 'That uniform's just a front, isn't it? I can see beyond it, you know. You're not fooling me with all those shiny buttons, you're struggling, aren't you? Had enough now.' It was a statement, not a question.

Alister was taken aback; he was not used to such personal scrutiny from a stranger but then the door opened from the back kitchen and Bridget walked in.

'Oh, hello, Granny. What are you doing here?'

Alister looked the woman up and down with interest, noting her shawl tucked into her skirt and the wicker basket on her arm. So, this was the famous Mona Quayle, was it? He'd often thought about visiting her and asking her advice about his arthritis but had always worried someone would see him going into her house. His professional reputation could be damaged by being spotted going to see a 'fairy doctor' but now she was here, he thought.

He was about to speak when she plonked a small bag of herbs on the desk.

'Try these, they should help,' she said to him, leaving him speechless. And then she turned to her granddaughter.

'Is there somewhere we can talk?'

Bridget showed Mona into the interview room but immediately turned on her grandmother and said, 'I'm working, Granny, you can't just waltz in here and expect a chat.'

'Hah, well, as you haven't been to see me in ages, I'm sure you can take five minutes, this is important.' She fixed Bridget with a piercing stare.

'Do you like men, Bridget?'

Used to challenging questions by her grandmother, this one took Bridget completely by surprise.

'*What*?'

'I think the word is pardon,' Mona replied, as if talking to a five-year-old.

'All right, pardon, then.'

'I asked a simple question, it deserves a simple answer,' her grandmother said, sitting down and crossing her arms.

Bridget looked flummoxed but stuttered. 'Yes, of course I do.' She hadn't told her family about her and Fynn, hugging the secret to herself until the war decided to allow them some time together.

'Well, that's one thing out of the way,' her granny went on. 'So, why haven't you decided on one then? It seems you had two of them at your beck and call but I think we both know which one you should be with.'

She turned as she opened a little paper bag she had in her basket. 'Right, half of those are for you and the other half are for him. Make sure you both take them on a full moon, they'll work much better.' And then, with a flourish, she swept out of the room.

Bridget smiled to herself and put the herbs in the bin. She didn't need them and gave a delicious chuckle that, for once, she might just be able to surprise that grandmother of hers.

Chapter Thirty-Nine

It was in June 1944 that the Isle of Man joined with the rest of the country to celebrate the landings of the Allies in Normandy. For the first time in five years, there was a feeling of optimism that the end of the war might finally be in sight. The next huge repatriation of internees was planned for the autumn and the girls had had little time to themselves, but Molly had organised a celebratory drink not only to toast the invasion of Europe but also Bridget's twenty-third birthday.

'Well, at least we can all get together to celebrate VE day,' she said, smiling. Bridget's face immediately lit up.

'Yes, Fynn has actually said he can join us, which is a miracle, considering the demands the War Ags are putting on farmers.' After years of food convoys being attacked, Britain was under increasing pressure by the Agricultural Executive to feed the nation and farmers like the Moore family were at their wits end of how to make every spare inch of land yield a crop. Fynn hadn't seen the world outside the farm for months and that included Bridget.

That night, before they'd even settled into their seats at the Falcon's Nest, Kieran coughed and stood up to make an announcement.

'Nancy and I are getting married,' he said with a grin.

There was a moment's stunned silence before everyone clamoured around the couple. Bridget made sure she was the first to rush to give them both a hug and Fynn couldn't conceal his delight; this finally closed the door on any lingering concerns he might have had.

Molly looked sharply at Bridget, wondering whether this announcement was really a suitable birthday present for her friend, but Bridget was smiling with genuine pleasure and when Fynn caught her eye with a quizzical look, she gave him such a beaming grin that any awkwardness evaporated.

'We have to celebrate!' Betty said, heading for the bar, 'and no excuses this time, Kieran, you have to have a proper drink.'

She was oblivious of the tension that suddenly developed at the table behind her and cheerfully called the barman over to put in a full order.

When she presented Kieran with his pint, he felt his fingers twitching towards it. Everyone always expected men to drink. Every celebration, every disappointment in his life, had always involved him reaching for a pint, it was almost impossible to resist. He looked at the head on the golden-brown liquid and licked his lips.

Nancy was fingering her new diamond engagement ring and the colour drained from her face. It had taken her a long time to trust Kieran but looking at the scene in front of her, she saw a lifetime of feeling this sickness in her stomach every time they went out together for a social evening.

Kieran was about to reach out to take the pint glass when Fynn picked it up instead.

Very gently, he said, 'I think that one's mine, mate.'

His brother dragged his eyes from the pint and it was as if a veil lifted from his eyes. He could do this; the moment had passed.

Kieran put his hand out and put it on his brother's shoulder to give him a light squeeze. Fynn had been sending for information from a new organisation called Alcoholics Anonymous in America and together they'd poured over the reports and the advice. The knowledge that he was not the only person to be afflicted with this had helped Kieran enormously, but he knew it was a battle he was going to have to face every day of his life.

'Yes, you're right, Fynn, thanks. I'll just have a lemonade. Sorry, Betty, but I don't drink; I have a problem with alcohol. There, Nancy, I've said it.'

Nancy reached in her handbag for her handkerchief; she was more relieved than she could have believed possible. She looked gratefully towards Fynn, but he had already gone to the bar to get Kieran's soft drink.

Bridget suddenly felt a huge surge of pride and when Fynn sat back down again, she pressed his hand with hers, wondering why she had fought this for so long.

As the Falcon closed that evening, Kieran and Nancy headed back to Cregneash and the girls walked in front, determinedly leaving Fynn and Bridget to walk alone.

His arm draped around her, she reached her hand across his chest to feel the warmth of his palm on her shoulder and dropped her head against him.

Stopping, he turned to her and looked searchingly at her.

'Any regrets, Bridg?'

'None, Fynn, none at all,' she said and reached up to press her lips against his. He pushed her back into the shadows and held her tight, all the passions he had stored up for so long, unleashed.

She leaned into him and felt a heat burning through her whole body. She'd felt some sexual attraction to men before but nothing like this. It was like coming home but also like the most exciting experience of her life at the same time.

Moaning gently, they moved against each other, and it took every sinew of Fynn's body to draw away and pull her back into the light.

He was panting slightly as he began to speak. 'No, Bridget, you … we … deserve better than this.' And with that, he got down on one knee and delved into his pocket.

He'd been carrying this little velvet box around for months, fingering it for reassurance every time a moment's nagging doubt assailed him. He held it out in front of him and looked pleadingly at her.

She jumped up and down on the spot like the little girl he had once known and clasped her hands to her mouth.

'Oh, Fynn, oh Fynn!' she said excitedly.

'Is that a yes?' he asked breathlessly.

'Of course it's a yes!' she squealed and jumped to wrap her arms and her legs around him, but the straight policewoman's skirt would not yield and she almost fell onto the floor, laughing.

He reached down to pull her up, grinning. 'Well, that was a sight of your suspenders I wasn't expecting.'

'Well, I hope they're more glam than Sergeant Robinson's,' she told him, chuckling.

'I don't think I'm going to ask about that, Mrs Moore' he said with a sheepish smile, and he placed the ring very firmly on the third finger of her left hand.

She took a deep breath and touched it reverently with her other hand. It was beautiful.

'It was my grandmother's,' he told her softly. 'She always told me it would one day fit on your finger.'

'That's odd,' Bridget said, 'my grandmother always knew we should be together too. Think of all that time we've wasted.'

'Not any more,' Fynn said, grabbing her hand and starting to run towards the cottage. 'Come on, I suspect there are two bridesmaids we need to talk to.'

The two of them raced along the front, their laughter filling the air.

Epilogue

May 6th 1945

The three policewomen were a little tipsy, crowded round their kitchen table. They, like the rest of the Island, were all off duty and they'd already ploughed their way through two ciders each when Betty jumped up.

'We've got to go, Churchill's broadcast's on the wireless at three and we need to meet the others first.'

Betty's cheeks were especially pink, she'd received a letter from Joe and was already planning their life back in Hackney.

The camp was almost empty and the landladies were beginning to spruce up their guest houses to welcome holidaymakers once again, while the islanders tried to get used to the fact that they might finally be able to reclaim their homes. The girls had been forced to mediate in disputes over damaged furniture and stolen cutlery, supplies of which depleted with every departing consignment of internees. They complained they were more like prefects in school squabbles rather than policewomen but, every time they had a spare moment, it was the future, not the present, that preoccupied them all.

Bridget polished her buttons for the celebrations and gave a deep sigh of contentment. Freed of her childhood obsession with Kieran, she was unable to believe she'd taken so long to allow Fynn into her heart and that realisation left her feeling quite giddy. For the first time, she had started to share her dreams and ideas with someone and was working out a plan that would allow her to stay on the Island as a member of its own police force. It made her smile that, after all her resentment, she was about to make a life for herself there.

Her grandmother, somewhat smugly, Bridget thought, had summed it up when she said, 'I told you not to try and battle against fate, my Breesha. If you let it, it's got more idea than you of what's good for you.' And with that, she'd gone into her old chest to search out a hat that might be suitable for the forthcoming wedding.

Betty was another one daydreaming about what life had in store. She had no doubt her future entailed a glowing picture of domestic bliss with Joe, and ignoring the possibility that he might be sent out to the fight the ongoing war in the Far East, she was spending every evening cutting out recipes from women's magazines and using up all their rations to try out new dishes.

'What are you going to do, Molly, once it's finally all over?' she asked, making her way down the hallway to get her hat off the stand.

Molly shrugged. She was resigned to a future alone.

'I'll probably go back to Limehouse. My sister's written to say she needs help with the boat or maybe I'll go for a promotion; I think I'd make a good sergeant,' she said and turned to walk off down the path.

Bridget and Betty looked sorrowfully after her. It seemed the spark had gone out of Molly and neither of them knew how to bring it back.

There was bunting everywhere to celebrate Victory in Europe day, a bonfire was going to be lit on Port Erin beach and for the first time, the Manx were allowing themselves the belief that this day might herald the end of the dreadful war in the east and that peace all over the world might follow.

Betty, Molly and Bridget linked arms to snake their way along Shore Road, joining others who were doing the Conga. Even the sun was shining.

By the time they arrived at the beach, the crowd had grown and someone was handing out jugs of beer from a table with chequered cloth on it. It took the girls a moment to realise it was Alister and Sergeant Robinson, working happily side by side. Bridget looked to find the tall figure of Fynn and grinned when she spotted him, the same happiness she'd been feeling for months now, bubbling up inside her. Kieran was there too, arm in arm with Nancy and Bridget realised she felt absolutely nothing but delight at their relationship. It was like being released from a yoke that she had carried all her life.

'Hello, you,' Fynn said, leaning down to kiss her.

She took his face in her hands and gave him a proper kiss, to his surprise, feeling that now familiar thrill surging through her body.

'What brought that on?'

'Nothing, just today and the wonderfulness of it all,' she told him happily.

Fynn caught her looking over towards Kieran and had a moment's qualm.

'You all right, Bridget?'

She looked him in the eyes and said wholeheartedly, her eyes brimming with tears, 'Oh, I am, Fynn. I really am.'

From behind him, Fynn heard Molly's voice. He looked around and noted the bleak expression on the blonde policewoman's face as she determinedly talked to Alister. Fynn gave Bridget a wink and turned away to disappear into the throng.

He returned two minutes later with his sister, Kathleen.

'Molly, have you met my sister, Kath?' he asked.

Just across from the little group was Sergeant Robinson and Alister. Alister was too intent on contentedly supping his pint but Maureen Robinson gave a little smile.

Acknowledgements

I know it's my name that's on these books but I do wish there was a way for me to give full acknowledgement to the army of people who help me, so I hope this will go some way to express my deep appreciation of them all.

First and foremost, I have to thank my husband, Kevin and my daughters, Sarah and Jayne. I know this is often said, but I really could not have done this one without them. One of my school reports once said: 'If there's an easy and a hard way to do something, this child will find the hard way' and I certainly lived up to that assessment with *Bridget's War*, and would not have got through if it hadn't been for them. Their encouragement, critical appraisals and ideas have kept me going when my own confidence failed.

This fact that this book is based on the Isle of Man meant I needed the help of so many people on the Island. The idea came to me when I was staying with our lovely friend, Jane Prescott and her personal interest in the book, her knowledge and her inspiration has been beyond anything I might have expected or hoped for. I've also had the invaluable help of Dean Johnson whose knowledge of the police processes meant I could develop Bridget's role with accuracy.

It was inevitable that my research would, by this stage, necessarily have to manage without first-hand reports which is why hearing direct from Charles Faragher about his mother, Millicent's life as a policewoman in Rushen Camp Internment Camp provided me with the authenticity I was desperate for. Bridget came to life as soon as I watched a video he sent me of his mother which was invaluable and helped me understand the everyday tasks the policewomen would perform.

On the first day that the Island opened its borders after Covid, thanks to arrangements put in place by John Quirk of the Rushen Heritage Trust, I was on a plane over to meet his colleagues, Doreen Moule and Alison Graham. They helped to write the book, *Friend or Foe* which has been my 'bible' throughout the writing process. Their knowledge, interest and support are typical of people on the Island and I am incredibly grateful to them.

Learning about what happened at the top-secret radar project at Cregneash was crucial to Nancy's story and Lyn Dunachie provided a wonderful link between me and her mother, Betty Blanchard who worked there. To be able to discover what she did and even what a goneo was, again helped me to focus in on that detail that I love to use in my books.

Anna Billings was a very useful scout, checking out roads and churches for me with her husband, Steve, and her knowledge of the Isle of Man was another useful resource for me.

I spent quite some time at the Manx Heritage Museum and had the unstinting help of the team there, especially Sarah Christian and Wendy Thirkettle and a trip to Jurby Church yielded not only a couple of tasty cakes but also help about the RAF Station up there from Sandra Kerrison.

In addition, I would like to express my thanks to Michael Kneale of the Manx Aviation and Heritage Museum, Paula Howell for her help about King William College and Sue Karran who helped me during my initial research; Peter Walton, my go-to RAF source and Michael and Fenella Bazin. Manx Nostalgia Facebook group were incredibly helpful on many an occasion and I found Culture Vannin's online resources invaluable. Hildegard Wiesehofer is kind enough to look over my German and any mistakes are mine not hers . And as always, I have to mention the wider 'Unit', the rest of my family, especially my sister, Hilary, for their unfailing belief in me.

In addition to *Friend or Foe*, I had the help of a long list of reference books that included: *Living With The Wire* by Yvonne M Cresswell; *Island of Barbed Wire* by Connery Chappell and *Involuntary Guests* by Alan Franklin.

As always, there is a huge professional team behind these books and without Kate Barker, my agent, Clare

Johnson-Creek and Salma Bagum and all the team at Bonnier Books and its imprint, Zaffre, I would never get them to this stage. I'm also grateful to Caroline Kirkpatrick for her insightful line edits and to Kati Nicholl for the eagle-eyed proof-reading.

Finally, I have to acknowledge Greeba, who was Jane Prescott's dog, sadly no longer with us. Her lolloping welcome every time we visited inspired her namesake in this book and I was delighted to be able to include a dog at last.

I've really enjoyed learning more about the history of the Isle of Man and all these resources and people have helped me deepen my appreciation for an Island I've loved for so many years and I hope, made *Bridget's War* into an authentic reflection of the amazing work that the Island did to welcome all those 'alien' women.

Hello dear reader;

Hello, what a personal journey this book has been! Thank you so much for sharing it with me. The Isle of Man has a very special place in my heart because my parents lived there for the last eight years of my father's life and they are both buried there at Malew near Castletown where they lived. It was while I was visiting a friend over there on one of my subsequent visits that we went to the Manx Heritage Museum and I picked up a book about the internment camps during WW2. To discover that there was one of these camps in the south of the Island for three thousand women and that they mixed German Nazis, Jews, conscientious objectors, fascists etc all together behind a cordon of barbed wire presented an idea for a novel to me that I found hard to resist.

But, lovely reader, let me tell you that such a 'lightbulb' moment was only the precursor to endless days and nights of angst. The problem was that I know the Island to a certain degree but I have never lived there and I was terrified of getting something wrong. As you may know if you've read my other books, my journalistic background makes me panic if I don't have a safety blanket of facts and because of the passing of time, it was inevitable that this book would not have the surety of a first-hand account. I am so very grateful to all the people I have mentioned in the Acknowledgements. I'm sure I must have irritated them with my constant barrage of questions but, as always with the Manx, they were unstintingly generous with their time and seemed to appreciate it when someone takes the time and trouble to find out the minutiae that makes the Isle of Man such an individual place.

For me, it is a magical island and amidst its natural beauty and charm, there is a special quality that makes it unique.

This book was a little different from my others in that Bridget is a policewoman and that meant I needed a bit of a detective story. I am extremely grateful that the original publication date was postponed because that enabled me to go back and check the details over and over again but I have to say, I am in awe of writers of detective novels who scatter the breadcrumb clues without any of the torment that I suffered - or maybe they just hide it better.

As always, I loved creating the characters and took great delight in developing Mona in particular. I hope she represents the way the Island weaves its spell

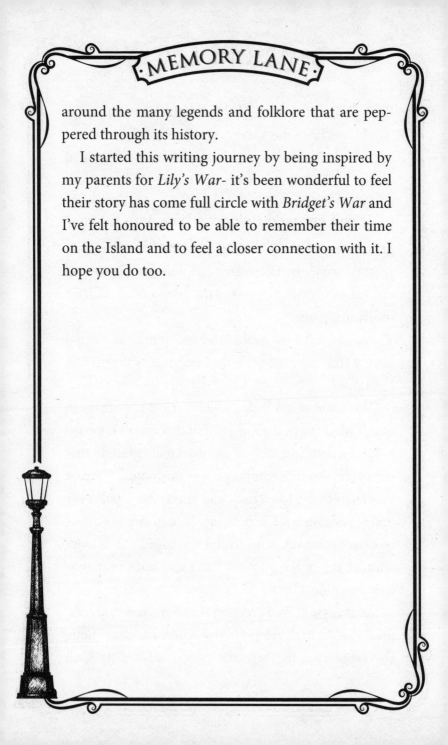

·MEMORY LANE·

around the many legends and folklore that are peppered through its history.

I started this writing journey by being inspired by my parents for *Lily's War*- it's been wonderful to feel their story has come full circle with *Bridget's War* and I've felt honoured to be able to remember their time on the Island and to feel a closer connection with it. I hope you do too.

If you enjoyed *Bridget's War*, you'll love these other titles by Shirley Mann . . .

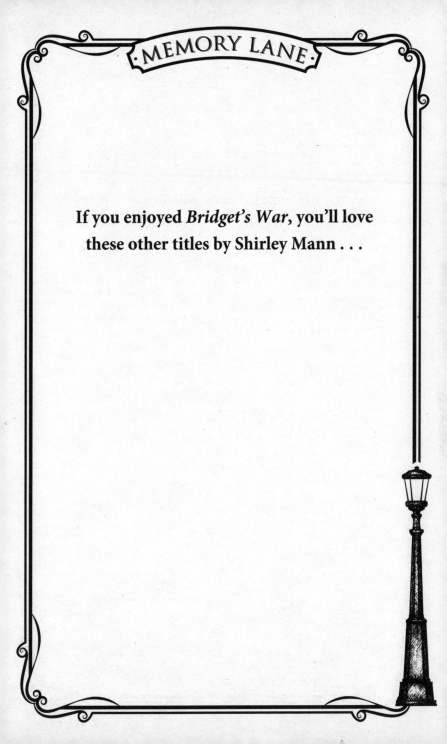

Bobby's War

It's World War II and Bobby Hollis has joined the Air Transport Auxiliary in a team known as the 'glamour girls' – amazing women who pilot aircraft all around the country.

Bobby always wanted to escape life on the family farm and the ATA seemed like the perfect opportunity for her. But there's always something standing in her way. Like a demanding father, who wants to marry her off to a rich man. And the family secrets that threaten to engulf everything.

As Bobby navigates her way through life, and love, she has to learn that controlling a huge, four-engined bomber might just be easier than controlling her own life . . .

Available now.

Hannah's War

It's 1942 and at nineteen years old Hannah Compton has the world at her feet. But with World War II raging, the country is in turmoil, and Hannah decides to do her bit for the War effort. Hannah's beloved grandfather taught her to grow vegetables in his market garden and inspires her to become one of over 200,000 women joining the Land Army.

As Hannah gets used to the punishing farm work and makes some friends, she starts to settle in. But she simply can't get used to living side by side with the German prisoners of war. Then a young German doctor steps in to save Hannah's life and everything she thought she knew is brought into question.

Available now.

Lily's War

World War II is in full swing and Lily Mullins is determined to do her bit for the war effort. Her friends and sweetheart have all joined up and Lily's sure there must be a role for her that goes further than knitting socks for the troops!

When she decides to volunteer for the Women's Auxiliary Air Force, Lily soon discovers that she has a talent as a wireless operator. Helped along the way by a special gang of girls, she finds strengths she didn't know she had and realises that the safety of the country might just be in her hands . . .

Meanwhile, Danny is determined to marry Lily, but his letters home become more and more distant. Will a long separation mean the end of their love story?

Available now.

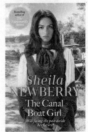